RATS' ALLEY

William Garner

RATS' ALLEY

A Methuen Paperback

A Methuen Paperback

RATS' ALLEY

British Library Cataloguing in Publication Data

Garner, William, *1920–*
Rats' alley.
I. Title
823'.914[F]   PR6057.A675

ISBN 0–413–56680–3

First published in Great Britain 1984
by William Heinemann Ltd
This edition published 1985
and reprinted 1987
by Methuen London Ltd
11 New Fetter Lane, London EC4P 4EE
Copyright © William Garner 1984
Printed and bound in Great Britain
by Cox & Wyman Ltd, Reading

Extract from *The Waste Land* on p. vi by T S Eliot
reproduced by kind permission of Faber & Faber Ltd

This one for Lesley

"I think we are in rats' alley where
the dead men lost their bones."
                    T. S. Eliot
                    The Waste Land

ONE

Air Force One sat on the Gatwick runway like a termite queen aswarm with workers. As the smaller of London's two major airports, Gatwick had been chosen for the departure because it made security tighter. The American grip was absolute. The entire airport might have been built solely for the occasion, in the style of the American imperial presidency, later to be given to the British because it was less trouble than taking it away.

Steve Archer, in charge of British security, was close to churlishness. The sun shone. The green hills beyond the farthest boundary of the airport basked as beguilingly as in any English Tourist Board publicity picture, yet the only thought in his mind was that if he never had to work with American presidential security again, it would be far too soon. Chief Superintendent Placket of Special Branch, chaste in his best suit, was equally sour.

"Can't say I'm sorry to see him go, sir."

Archer smiled without pleasure, lighting another cigarette with the slick skill of the heavy smoker. Minor county in background, Londoner by choice rather than birth, he was never less than formally dressed on duty, yet managed to give the impression of the country landowner come to town.

"Haven't been able to call your life your own? You're not the only one." They were in a temporary structure of scaffolding and prefabricated panels that had been set alongside the control tower. Since the man operating the elaborate communications system only feet away, together with six others crowding its

1

small space, was a US Secret Service agent, they kept their voices down.

Even young Sibley, normally bright and eager, had developed a look, part stubborn, part sullen, that testified to the pressure they had all been under during the four-day state visit. "One President, one President's wife, hundreds of bloody odds and sods."

Archer turned on him with quiet ferocity, his dark good looks tough and bony in the absence of the usual lazy charm. "Well, you can belt up for a start, my lad. People in your situation take what comes and like it." Mr Morpurgo, Sibley thought resentfully, had been more considerate in his day, but Mr Morpurgo had gone, out on his ear and that was that.

Placket took the heat off. "Here they come, sir."

People were emerging from the terminal building, immediately below. The operative at the console said, "Okay, Kingpin, we have action. Our state is go and stable." He flipped keys. "Unity to all crews. The Eagle is go."

Archer raised a sardonic eyebrow at Placket. The agent spoke again. "Say again, please. Did you say plasma?" Below them, the initial dribble of luminaries clotted along the red carpet that slashed the concrete apron in the direction of Air Force One. Very few of the security guard dogs, Archer noted irritably, were his own. Almost at once, the President and First Lady, HRH, the Prime Minister and Foreign Secretary appeared with a fresh wake of staff, agents and hangers-on.

The President turned to look up at the spectator gallery. The smile gleamed. He raised his arms, rotating both hands at the wrists as if unscrewing faucets. His wife, too, waved, but more formally, favour rather than friendliness.

"Waving at their own people," Placket muttered. "Two security men to every spectator up there."

The console operator was looking toward Archer. "Pardon me, sir. Would you speak with Mr Church? Number 5, sir, right there."

"Steve?" Church, as head of the US Secret Service, was in charge of all security. "Listen, we have a minor glitch. I'd appreciate your help."

Archer made himself sound pleasant. "You've got it."

"We have a power failure on the blood box. We need the replacement." One of us, Archer thought with a new spasm of irritation, doesn't speak the language. I didn't know it was me.

Church resolved the problem. "The plasma refrigerator on the big white bird. No problem in itself, just a fuse and they're fixing it right now, but the plasma's been out of its temperature bracket, maybe only a short time, maybe not, we don't know. We have to draw the back-up, okay?"

That damn plasma flask! Throughout his visit, the President had been followed by an emergency supply of his blood group. On every state occasion – the night at Windsor Castle, for example – it was solemnly pushed to a waiting power point by an agent with a contraption like a dumbwaiter; the Yanks referred to it as the buggy. The blood, euphemistically, was referred to as plasma.

He understood now. There was always a back-up blood supply in case the emergency arrangements had an emergency. All the same, it was not the job of British Security Directorate to push dumbwaiters around.

"Tom Hennessey's on his way to the airport medical centre, but I have almost all my people deployed for embarkation," Church was saying. "I can't pull anyone out to ride shotgun on the buggy. Can you provide a couple of guys?"

Within moments, Sibley was on his way down to casualty unit. Placket, taking over a spare network phone, steered two men from the VIP departure lounge. Others checked that the route was clear to the tarmac.

Archer decided he might as well go down to the apron for the climax of four days that had played havoc with the past three months. Just his bad luck; barely settled in after Morpurgo's ignominious departure, barely adjusted to the disruption caused in his personal and family life by Morpurgo's damnable affair with Helga; and now this.

In his dark, immaculate suit with its antique inch of breast-pocket handkerchief, his discreetly striped tie, his brushed-back and brilliantined hair, Doug Church looked more like the dean of some Bible Belt evangelical college than the commander of the President's Praetorian Guard. With him was a man Archer had seen several times during the visit, but never met. Sharp-faced, thin-lipped, he had the deeply-trenched cheeks of the driven man.

Church waved an introduction. "Ralph Priestley, Steve Archer. Steve's head of counterintelligence in the British MI5, running the British security back-up this past few days. Steve, Ralph is kind of quartermaster on the President's trips, responsible for logistics."

They shook hands. Priestley managed a busy nod. "Glad·to know you, Steve. You people have done a fine job." The standard American small change for services rendered, Archer thought acidly. He was sick of it, sick, too, of being "you people".

Church patted him on the shoulder, an educated gorilla in a Brooks Brothers suit. "Thanks for the assist, old buddy. Here comes the blood buggy now."

It was steered by Tom Hennessey. In Buckingham Palace, on the night of the first banquet, Hennessey had made a joke. "Think one of your traditional prowlers'll get through to the President's room tonight? Make sure she's blonde, well stacked and free from herpes, okay?" Archer had smiled and seethed; British security had a low rating in Washington these days.

Hennessey had another joke ready. "They tell me this is the box you use for the Royals, Steve, that right?"

Archer forced another smile. "If that's what they tell you."

The President was taking his final leave. Except for the last outriders, like Church, everyone travelling in the big white Boeing would be aboard now. Ground crew gathered discreetly under the plane's tail, waiting to wheel away the steps.

Some distance away, the back-up flight waited to taxi forward once Air Force One was cleared for take-off. Two of the three cargo planes that had brought the customary paraphernalia, including the armoured limousines for the Secret Service and the Executive Protection Service, had already left. The third, known to the British as the Hoover, would suck up the remnants after the main departure.

Hennessey and the buggy continued toward the rear boarding hatch of Air Force One. Priestley intercepted. "The container. Nothing else."

Hennessey laughed. "What are you trying to do, Ralph? Set up a diplomatic incident? If this gismo is good enough for the

4

Queen of England, it has to be good enough for Air Force One, right?" The jibe, Archer felt, was directed as much against him as Priestley.

"Anyway," Hennessey was saying, "only going as far as the steps. Ain't no whichway I could wheel it up."

The ulcer lines on Priestley's face tautened. "You know the regulations. Anything that isn't on the manifest doesn't go. I don't make the rules. I'm just here to see they're carried out."

"Okay, Ralphie, okay, so I'll just carry the box up, okay? You want to push that buggy back where it came from?"

"Facetiousness" – Priestley had no sense of humour – "can kill. While I'm around, things go by the book."

Church was suddenly testy. "Ralph has his job to do, Tom. Get that goddam plasma aboard. The President's going up." Hennessey, still grinning, took the flask from its insulated box and mounted the steps to the rear hatch. The President's wife, already at the top of the boarding steps, turned for a last wave.

"Well, thank you, Doug." Priestley was still aggrieved. "Okay, so even if the buggy were the Queen's buggy and the box the Queen's box, I still have to say, 'Sorry, ma'am.'"

He turned to Archer. "Just on three hundred people with the President this trip. That's not counting the press, not my responsibility, praise be. The rest is. Air Force One. The back-up. Three freighters. Two choppers and two in reserve, all with their crews and service units. Fifty Secret Service Agents. Forty Executive Protection Agents. Two doctors, four medical personnel, okay? Two photographers – what am I saying? – three, the President has his wife along. Five technicians to process the prints" – It was a litany of grievance – "six stewards to handle in-flight service, two more for the galleys. Plus thirty-two members of White House staff, right down to the stenographers."

"And the guy who carries the President's doomsday bag." Church tried to be conciliatory.

"That's right! Well, okay, all you have to do is figure out the amount of baggage. Not even counting equipment and spares. You'll see why it has to be according to the book, Mr Archer. What comes out, goes back, less consumables, plus gifts, purchases, replenishments, and are *they* checked out!"

The President, breaking away at last, took the crimson steps two at a time, stopping at the top, nicely poised next to the Presidential seal as the photographers blitzed away. Once again he raised his hands and spun valves like a submariner with the klaxons sounding for a crash dive.

"Tom was only kidding, Ralph." Church patted Priestley perfunctorily. "That buggy came out with us, so did the box. They go aboard the back-up."

Priestley held out a cold hand to Archer. "I know it. You think I don't know what came out? But nobody cuts corners while I'm calling the shots. Mr Archer, nice meeting you, and thanks for everything."

Church, too, shook hands, then he and Priestley went up the rear steps while the President, vivid in electronic lightning, gave his valves a final spin, his teeth a final airing, and backed into the shadowy interior of Air Force One.

When it and the back-up plane had dwindled westward at the tip of long grey plumes of smoke, Archer felt something drain out of him. He walked slowly back to the terminal building, had a final word with his deputy, Eric Pottern, and with Chief Super Placket, distributed approbation among various other members of Security Directorate and Special Branch, then went down to his car. He would drive the twelve miles to Dorking, treat himself to a couple of drinks and a lazy lunch before continuing to London.

As he was getting out of his car in the hotel carpark, the great bareback sweep of Box Hill green and glowing in the late morning sun, the Hoover cargo plane, loading completed, took off. Hearing distant thunder as he headed for the bar, Archer checked his watch, then put in a call to Pottern.

"Gone?"

"Just."

"Thank Christ!"

"Amen."

"Go and get yourself a drink. You've earned it."

"Think I will. First thing I feel able to do without asking permission. We don't rate any more, Mr Archer, poor white trash."

"Times can change, Eric. We'll have to see what we can do to give them a nudge."

"Any idea when you'll move up, sir?"

"Not precisely, so no talking, but pretty soon. See you in my office, nine sharp, general review, all right? Then we'll try to get back to normal."

His office, once Johnny Morpurgo's, but now his, time he got used to the idea.

"Normal! Can't wait for that, Mr Archer. There's the Paddy, for a start."

"Irish terrorists, American Secret Servicemen," Archer said scandalously, "much of a muchness once you've stripped off the wrappings." He would have denied any accusation of anti-Americanism.

*   *   *

Sylvie Morpurgo had had a bad night, during which she and a decision she had been assiduously avoiding had finally met head-on. Now she must introduce it to Johnny.

And so she had changed her mind three times over what to wear. It was amusing but brought her close to tears; brisk, efficient, professional Sylvie Markham, top photographer, name her own fee, a nervous procrastinator.

With final decision she checked herself in the glass, went down. On the way, as always, she met her past; not so much her taste as the way in which it had changed. Johnny had almost always left house and furnishings to her, endlessly entoiled in unsocial working hours. A home, like life, was an endlessly extending patchwork of compromise. Who could clear a house from basement to attic and start all over again? Who could do likewise with a marriage? There, sometimes, one came to the end of compromise.

Morpurgo, breakfasting over a scamper through the papers, said good morning, their formal signal that nothing had changed, for better or worse, since yesterday. He took her in, a striking – some said beautiful – woman in her mid-forties, dressed for work in a trouser suit of dark blue linen with an emerald green shirt, a gold pendant watch and chain at her throat. She had hair the colour of ripe oats, a skin that tanned only lightly but glowed with its own vitality.

Morpurgo made the inventory every day. They had had

7

separate bedrooms since her return after his wretched affair with Helga Archer. It was part of his probation, except that probation, dependent upon good behaviour, was for a fixed term. His, seemingly, had no limit.

She, in her turn, saw him with the skilled eyes of someone who, through the lens, specialised in people and their habitats. A tall man, dark of hair, eyes and, occasionally, mood; with a doggedness that could turn stubborn, being based on opinions and prejudices firmly held. One of his firm opinions, that he made allowances for his prejudices, was debatable.

He watched her light the cigarette she always took with her coffee, automatically noting the neat, self-confident competence of her movements. Competent was an adjective specially coined for Sylvie. From the viewpoint of a smeared and shopworn security man, newly supernumerary, it was part of an enviable flawlessness which he, by abuse, had done his best to mar.

She watched him covertly, wondering how to begin. He was such a vulnerable target, plucked from power at the height of his career for what, leaving aside her own feelings, would have been little more than a peccadillo in someone less sensitively placed. But then, the question of whether or no a sin has been committed is seldom as important as by whom. A man close to the top of his country's internal security service, no matter how great his ability, threw more than his judgement into doubt in having an affair with his deputy's wife. Toppled by those who, perennially mistrusting, had been glad to see him go, lucky only in finding a desk with the Secret Intelligence Service, he must now, not yet fifty yet past his prime, begin all over again.

He spoke first. "How long will you be away?"

"Two weeks, three. It's hard to say."

"All in Spain."

"All in Spain. I showed you, remember." Now, she urged herself; say it now.

"Yes." He poured himself more coffee, then again pre-empted. "Sylvie, I know I've no right to ask, but . . . how much longer can this go on?"

"What?" She knew what. What she didn't know, not yet, was the answer.

8

"All these months." The face of a man, nothing very special about it, who, professionally, had learned to hide all emotion.

"I've been thinking a lot about it, Johnny."

There, she had embarked, but with an adverse wind, the cold wind of conscience. Johnny's kind of work had forced her to develop a talent into a career; carried her, to her surprise, close to the top. Faced with neglect in his turn, he had eventually fallen into temptation, trapped by a neurotic woman. Sylvie had assuaged personal guilt by coming back to him after the initial storm, but she was still making him pay. Now she was ready with a solution.

"You know this year's our silver wedding?" He said it awkwardly.

So that was where his mind had been. "Fancy your knowing."

"I can count."

"I'm just surprised you did." They had been so very young. His mother had raised heaven and earth to stop them. She, a girl's gift of early maturity, had handled her own parents like tame rabbits. She found herself smiling. "Did you have anything in mind?"

"Does it mean anything any more?"

If not now, then possibly never. "Johnny, do you have to stay there? Across the river?" Her Majesty's Secret Intelligence Service is not fashionably housed.

"Where on earth would I go?" He was surprised.

"There are other jobs. Millions of people have them."

"But someone has to have mine. And I happen to be good at it."

"You *were* good at it." She knew she was cruel. "But that job's gone. The job you've got now, well, Secret Service! So secret you don't know what the job is."

"Inter-service liaison's important." Untrue. Minor, very.

"Be honest, Johnny. Do you really prefer trotting back and forth between Lambeth, Gower Street and Grosvenor Square to the sort of thing you used to do? To looking after an American president, for instance?"

"Thank God I wasn't!" Sylvie had picked the wrong example. "Taking orders from people like Doug Church? Not even a real Secret Service, just a fancy name for a bodyguard. Do you know" – Something to change the tone of a conversation that was heading in the wrong direction – "those goons even tried to get Steve – Steve Archer, of all people! – to persuade the Palace staff to accept food-tasters at the banquets?"

She, too, was anxious to change course, but not in that direction. "Is it better to work for a wolf in lamb's clothing?"

She meant Lawrence Epworth, his new boss. Epworth, now effectively head of SIS, had saved him from unemployment after his disgrace and the Sattin spy business. She had a respect, he knew, for Epworth, but it was tempered with caution, since it would be too much – wouldn't it? – to say she was afraid of him.

"Is this anything to do with my question, Sylvie? Or have you forgotten my question?"

"How long is this going on was your question."

"Then why Epworth? You hardly know him."

"Oh, I know him." It was from Epworth, engaged in his own private mole-hunting during the Sattin affair, that Sylvie had learned about Johnny and Helga.

"You think you know him. Nobody knows him. That's the main thing to know about him."

"But you'll stay with him?"

"Do you see any alternative? Any serious alternative?"

She had him, sitting duck. "Yes. Would you consider coming in with me?"

When he had got over the new surprise, he grudgingly admired her tact. Come in with her. Summon taxis, carry bags. He shook his head.

"Not factotum, Johnny. Planning, arranging, business manager, all on a proper footing."

"Your business, not mine."

"Make it yours."

He had lost the initiative. "It wouldn't work, Sylvie." He saw her glance at her pendant watch. She had bought it herself. He could hardly have afforded it. He had no idea what she earned, had taken care not to show interest. But she had an agent, an accountant, a part-time secretary. She also had her own premises, just off Baker Street, that included a small but elegant flat. He had nearly lost her to that flat.

She checked her bag, unhappily aware that she must leave. "I'd like us to be happy again. Please believe that."

"Why can't we be, starting tomorrow? Starting today?"

"The past's in the way, can't you see that? It would be so much easier if you'd cut yourself off."

"Or if you cut yourself off from yours." He had not meant that to slip out, yet the jealousy, the resentment, lingered. If Sylvie hadn't discovered an ability and turned it into minor genius, none of this would have happened.

"There's no going back. We have to start from where we are." She prepared to leave.

He saw now that she had thought it through. To be her manager would free them both from painful associations, few of them lost in his moving south of the river. It could, he supposed, even be a real job. And it would bring them closer, much closer.

Or would it? Sylvie moved around constantly, abroad as well as at home. In a short time she would be off to Spain. Wasn't it, after all, simply a way of tying him down while she retained her professional freedom?

The thought was unworthy. He made a disguised act of contrition. "You couldn't" – An attempt at a joke – "afford me."

"Don't be too sure." She, too, spoke lightly, but with underlying seriousness.

In due course she would have money from her parents, would, not to put too fine a point on it, be filthy rich. She was probably on her way to being filthy rich now. Certainly the Baker Street place was no garret. He would not take her money. He had bedded and then married her when he had only just stopped being a poor student, not much better off as a research worker for the TUC. He had thought, in his callowness, that he was winning her for the real world. Now, with a talent very much of the real world, she had been readopted by a class he deeply mistrusted if not despised.

"As for qualifications" – Sylvie, too, was trying to talk herself out of a tactical error – "the only thing that counts is common sense. You could do it standing on your head." She smiled again. "Just the way Epworth has you."

"I don't know what you mean."

"I don't think he really knows what to do with you. He's

11

keeping you upside down like a tortoise, so you can't run away.
Come in with me and you'd soon find your feet."

"Share the same job? We don't even share the same bedroom."

She was instantly serious. "Don't think I wasn't hurt, Johnny.
It hurt like bloody hell. We have to learn all over again." She
planted a quick, cool kiss on his cheek. "Just think it over."

He held her. "I'm what I do, Sylvie. If I do what you do, what
would that make me?"

"In that case, watch out for Epworth. Sooner or later you'll find
yourself doing what he does, whatever that is. What will that
make you? I wonder."

She slipped gently free. "I might as well give you the rest. I'd
like us to move, too."

The other thrust of a two-pronged attack; leave his job to work
for Sylvie, leave his home for a house better suited to Sylvie's
needs.

"Move?"

"Yes. Leave this." She gestured. "We've grown out of it,
Johnny."

They had lived, most of their married lives, in a tall, thin town
house in an unfashionable part of Kensington, in a street that led
nowhere and was always choked with parked cars. He had been
proud, all those years ago, to be able to raise a mortgage, to buy
his own property. Sylvie's parents had been prepared to put up
the money. He had refused. Sylvie had understood. Now she
proposed to demolish the entire foundations of his existence.

"I'm happy enough here. Was, anyway, could be again. It's us
that matter, not the house."

"You could be just as happy somewhere else, Johnny. It's us
that matter, not the house." That was the real Sylvie, capturing
the heart of his argument to show him it was only a mirror image.
She made to go. "If we moved, I'd sell the other place." She
meant the flat.

No more separate lives, that was the offer then. But it would
not be so, because she would still be living a separate life, to
which he would only be an adjunct. He was hazily aware of
inconsistency.

"It's far enough to go to see mum as it is." That was pathetic!
His mother lived her widow's life in Wandsworth, far over the

river, there was no easy way to visit her. As always, thinking of his mother he felt guilt. He must go again, soon.

Sylvie collected her expensive crocodile-skin case. "Remember that CIA man? Not Warren Claas. Weber. The thin one, the one I liked."

"Pierre Weber. Yes." He had had cause.

"He said half people's troubles are because they only accept facts that match their prejudices, only most of their facts are prejudices too. You ought to go and see your mother again, Johnny. She's not as well as she might be."

He waited until she was at the street door. "They're two separate things, Sylvie, our jobs and our lives. Let's not make the mistake of getting them mixed up again."

She nodded. "That's the sort of thing Pierre Weber meant." She waved him a sad little kiss. "Think it over. Don't hurry. It's too important."

Looking after the President! he thought, getting ready to leave himself. I can't even look after Sylvie. I can't even look after myself.

*   *   *

When Morpurgo left Security Directorate and Curzon Street, Steve Archer had waited until the following Friday before changing offices, even then only going up long enough to arrange his personal possessions before leaving to weekend with friends in Norfolk. The following Monday, looking down, as often before when he was Johnny's 2 i/c, on to Curzon Street and the sliding roof of the Mirabelle, it was as if the room had always been his. Everyone else seemed to feel the same way, and in no time at all it was as if John Morpurgo had never been.

True, he was only across the river in Lambeth. True, that very queer fish, Lawrence Epworth, had given him some sort of job that brought him, once a week, to the modest early Victorian house in Gower Street, as Pegley's poodle. There, according to Eric Pottern, who sometimes represented Security Directorate at the weekly coordination meetings, he was inconspicuous at the foot of the long table in the high-ceilinged first-floor room that had been an elegant enough salon a century and a half earlier.

There, seemingly, he sat mumchance while Lassalle from CIA's

13

London station, Quincey from Curzon Street, Pegley himself and a floating population of special interest people went over such of their respective organisations' activities as impinged upon others' territories, exclusive of matters they hadn't the slightest intention of discussing. Archer saw no reason to disbelieve Eric Pottern's view that Morpurgo was no longer of any significance in the London intelligence community.

He knew it gave Eric, who had never hit it off with Morpurgo, more than a little satisfaction. So far as Archer himself was concerned, a man who had seduced the wife of a loyal deputy, brought about her mental collapse, split a family and wrecked a marriage, not to mention making himself a security risk, was worth nothing, not even a good gloat.

Not that he could fault Johnny's professionalism, the way he had held a very mixed team together, nor the honesty with which he had stuck to his half-witted political principles in a tightly knit fraternity where, broad church or not, lefties were very much in a minority.

Anyway, Archer had always believed that Morpurgo was in the wrong job, totally unfitted for the task of protecting the British way of life from its enemies at home and abroad. It took people with another sort of honesty to do the job, people who accepted that the world was made up of two kinds of people, leaders and led, and saw no reason to hide or be apologetic about the fact that they were leaders, were – that supposedly dirty word – the elite.

The commies, the way Steve Archer saw it, had reached exactly the same conclusion, with the result that they had the rawest, most nakedly self-interested elite in the world. That they could be matched by any bunch of wet lefties, half of them advantaged class traitors anyway, was too ridiculous for words.

The old adage had proved itself yet again; blood will out. Johnny Morpurgo had been betrayed by his own genes. It had been as inevitable, one realised, as the outcome of all those infinitely boring Greek tragedies one had been obliged to construe in one's schooldays. Those who failed to honour the gods, or sought to escape their appointed fate, were inexorably brought down; something like that; Greek had never been among one's strong subjects.

The Director-General knew it, even though Morpurgo had been his protégé. It was why he had put Steve Archer in charge of the arrangements for the American state visit. The D-G knew the value of social background, savoir faire. Johnny, for all his natural ability, would have gone down like a lead balloon at the Palace, malleable where he should have been polite but firm, jagged and obstinate when what was required was diplomacy.

Now all that remained of that infinitely tiresome visit was to reply to numerous letters, mostly from the White House, that might have and probably had been churned out by the same word processor, so closely did they resemble each other in style and content. He was glad of the interruption when Eric Pottern came in, carrying a lengthy print-out on yellow high-security paper.

"Just in. Thought you'd find it interesting." Pottern had not been promoted for looks or charm. He was the epitome, or so Archer believed, of hard-working conventionality, Curzon Street style, a faded monochrome snapshot of a man with a secret, almost sly sense of humour that tended to cater to his chief's own taste in the amusing.

Archer read and then re-read the print-out. "Good Lord!"

"Interesting, I thought." Pottern kept his feelings in boxes.

Archer checked the classification. "Any distribution yet?"

"Thought you'd like to see it first. It won't mean much to the Director-General."

"Accidental explosion. Master Doug Church must have loved that one."

"Wonder what on earth they were carrying that could cause an emergency landing?"

"A bunch of goons like that? Anything from hand grenades to cruise missiles, shouldn't wonder." Archer was still savouring the news that those who had so frequently and maddeningly called him and his "you people" had apparently dropped a resounding clanger. "How did Watchett get hold of this one? Nothing in general traffic, let alone the media."

"Diverted to some military field in Maryland," Pottern said blandly. "Shutters down, Secret Service repair crew flown across from Beltsville."

"You didn't answer my question."

"Careless talk." Pottern pretended to look disapproving. "Theirs. Well, one of them, anyway." He developed a slow smile. "Watchett holds his bourbon better than most Yanks."

Archer's was a methodical and linear mind. "I can see why they wouldn't want talk. Wouldn't look good, the President's Praetorians blowing themselves up." He too was smiling.

"They were carrying an arsenal as well as all those armoured Cadillacs. I'd love to know what it was that went off." Pottern was wistful.

"Bound to be an enquiry. Secret, of course, but secret enquiries in the States have a useful habit of leaking. Thank God this is only a reasonably free country."

Pottern wasted no time searching for irony that experience had taught him would not be found.

Archer chuckled. "That chap Priestley will be sniffing around, see if someone sneaked in an illicit case of champagne."

Pottern frowned, then his face cleared. "Oh, the bloke who made a fuss about the dumbwaiter."

"The very one. Nearly a stand-up fight, Priestley, Church and that buffoon, Hennessey." His recollection stung, Archer mimicked an American accent. "I wanna tell you, you people have done a great job."

He reflected happily. "I mean, Eric, if you could have witnessed that perfectly ridiculous scene, three grown men arguing over a bottle of blood, whether it should be allowed to go in the plane or not."

Pottern nodded. "You told me. The blood wagon."

"The bloody blood wagon. Nearly a stand-up fight, I tell you. I mean, it might just as well have been a bloody bomb."

About to laugh once more, he checked. "It was the back-up plane they had to divert? The one we called the Hoover?"

Pottern nodded, his eyes, a sort of mould-green, politely attentive. He cleared his throat, a dry, apologetic sound. "Sounds silly, I know, but we could ferret about a bit."

TWO

"You did say forty *trillion* dollars?" Mark Folger, archetypal banker, emotional as polished pink granite, was smiling politely as Dobrovsky showed him into Cochran's Manhattan office suite. Brewster Cochran's sense of humour was notoriously uncertain.

Cochran's great paw, all bone and muscle, enveloped Folger's hand. Under extreme pressure, a wince all but popped out on Folger's face. "Forty trillion, man. That's forty thousand thousand million, four and thirteen zeros. Brought you running, huh?" Folger's hand was still under geological compression.

"Running?" Folger slid his released hand protectively into a pocket of his dark blue, London-built suit. "44th at 5th is solid, I baled out and walked."

Cochran guffawed. "You *walked?* When was the last time you trod a sidewalk? Okay, sit down. I'll have Dob come back and polish the soles of your shoes." He planted Folger in the outsize sofa like a steam hammer driving a pile. Dobrovsky materialised, lizard-swift and noiseless.

"Two whisky sours."

"Before noon?" Folger's protest was too late. Cochran's factotum and ex-roughneck in more ways than one was gone.

"Enjoy it, Markus." Nobody else called Mark Folger Markus. "First time you broke a rule since you smoked at junior academy, right?" In his rumpled suit, the knot of his tie already awry, the white of his shirt startling against his flushed, meaty face, he had less the appearance of an oil magnate than what one financial journalist had called the Chicago look, hog butcher to the world.

17

Dobrovsky was back with the drinks. Folger accepted reluctantly. "All right, Brewster, you've had your joke. Now let's hear how Promethean Oil is going to make that kind of money. I doubt there's so much oil left in the world except maybe in the Antarctic."

"Still brought you running, though." Standing over Folger, Cochran was rising and sinking on the balls of his feet like a hot air balloon ready for lift-off.

"You're a client. Promeco isn't the smallest company on our books. Soon would be, mind, if I charged for home visits."

"Hey!" Cochran feigned amusement. "You made a funny. People like you should only make funnies when the client dies and leaves everything to your head office computer. Okay, so you think I'm making funnies too? Stay right where you are. I'm going to show you where all that oil is going to come from."

He buttoned. Dobrovsky slithered in. "Shoot, Dob." Taking a noisy gulp of his drink, ice rattling against strong white incisors, Cochran crash-landed on the sofa.

Automatic blinds slowly squeezed out the view of midtown Manhattan, the glass and concrete of more ambitious structures than Promeco's headquarters disdaining them across the Avenue of the Americas. Folger tried another joke. "How big will the new Promeco building be, Brewster? Two hundred storeys, or are you planning something really tall?"

Cochran jeered. "So Esso I'm not. Not yet."

"Exxon," Folger corrected automatically. "Haven't been Esso in the US this ten years and more."

"Listen, Markus, Brew Cochran's been in oil long enough to have worked with folk who knew Exxon as Standard Oil. And okay, so I don't have some fancy sky tower. No fountains and Persian carpets. No control room full of video screens hooked up to God." Lights dimmed and went out. "Stick around, Markus, it's all going to happen."

A screen lit up. Countdown figures flickered, then they were cruising like flies over a dunghill landscape, hills verging on the mountainous cicatriced with the tight, contour-hugging whorls made by earth-moving equipment. The invisible aircraft made a gentle course correction. A tall metal structure reared, around it a

18

huddle of temporary buildings, a scatter of storage tanks gleaming silver under a high sun.

His vigour jouncing Folger through the sofa, Cochran jabbed a finger. "Colony site. Closed spring of '82, put two thousand men on the highway."

Revelation came to Folger, accompanied by disbelief and annoyance. Easy, he warned himself. Since anything a wild man like Cochran got himself into was potentially destabilising, he had to know more.

"Colony! Are you crazy, Brewster? Oil from shale is a dead duck! Colony cost four hundred million dollars, all of it lost. Don't tell me that's what . . ."

Cochran took no notice. Colorado, plastered luminously across the far wall, tilted under a starboard course correction. "Five hundred million barrels of crude locked up in the rock on that one site."

Folger called on his patience and diplomacy. "But it won't make real money, ever, not what Big Oil calls money. Not what *you* call money, damn it!"

Cochran finished his drink with a quick jerk of his big, close-cropped head, hair a million silver needles. "Think ol' Brew lost his marbles, right?"

Watch out when he goes Okie, Folger warned himself. Any time now he's going to start calling himself lil ol' Brew, blackstrap accent resurrected to syrup opposition and sugar-coat the mean streak.

"No." Promethean Oil, twenty-fourth largest independent in the United States, last posted annual sales six and a quarter billion dollars, was part-owned and wholly run less by a man than an elemental force with criminal tendencies, but no fool. "I think I must have lost mine. I should have stayed in that traffic snarl and died peacefully of old age."

Their surrogate plane banked for a second run over the Colony site. Folger searched for the right words to stem a human landslide. "Listen, while I tell you what you already know. Exxon figured it would take two or three billion dollars to develop a process that would cook the oil out of that rock. What happened? Six billion, Brewster, on a pilot project, and the price of crude dropping worldwide like an express elevator.

"We aren't basically afraid of that kind of money, you know that. But when Exxon, biggest people in oil, biggest company in the world, says a project isn't economically viable, we don't wait for the proof, we believe. We believe. Didn't you just tell me Promeco wasn't Exxon?"

Cochran was still hypnotised by the picture on the screen. "Five hundred million barrels. A month's supply for the whole US and not one goddam Arab in sight. But that's peanuts. That's not what it's about." He made a possessive sweep of the hand. "That whole area, the Piceance Basin, know how much oil? One point two trillion, that's how much. *Trillion*, Markus! More than one thousand billion barrels of good oil. Enough to run this whole country for the next two centuries and all on dry land, good American soil. Not one solitary tanker between here and the Gulf, imagine! Between here and Venezuela, Nigeria" – His voice took on a cold tincture of venom – "Libya, any crackpot, trigger-happy, gouging foreign country in the whole fucking world!"

There was no need of that final crudity to remind Folger of Brewster Cochran's feelings about Libya. "Brew, let's try to get this thing in proportion. That oil is inseparable from the shale by any economically viable process. Exxon pulled out because it's too tough to crack, and if Exxon says it's too tough, it's too tough, period. No bank is going to ante up one single dollar."

"Can it, Markus!" Cochran's voice carried a million volts. "Just go on looking." A small town had come on screen, a new town, many of its buildings clearly unfinished. "Parachute, little town, that aimed to grow big till Exxon chickened out. Now the few that's left sit in the Old Bank Saloon and O'Leary's Pub, crying into their Coors over what might have been. Coming up now, over to starboard there, that's Battlement Mesa. See all the unfinished construction? Schools, supermarket, shopping mall, even a leisure centre."

He drove an elbow into Folger's fleshy ribs. "Ain't worth a piggy bank right now" – Here he goes, Folger warned himself; lil ol' Brew – "but all that could surely change if lil ol' Brew decides not to leave those two towns to lie paws up. I mean" – In came the elbow again – "if Chase Manhattan or Morgan Guaranty, say, decided to buy into the action."

Folger's self-control wilted. "What action, for God's sake?" Battlement Mesa flickered, blacked out. Lights came on.

"Intermission." Cochran took off from the sofa like the launch of the space shuttle. Folger felt stifled. His volcanic client seemed to be depleting the big room of its oxygen.

"Morgan? Chase? They aren't going to put one dime into any more schemes for oil from shale. Hell, Brewster, I remember Paul Getty saying many a time that oil from shale had had a rosy future for the past fifty years."

Cochran hoisted himself up on the front of his big desk, facing Folger. There was a bowl of oranges on the desk. Folger wondered distractedly whether this madman had gone vegetarian or macro, crazy enough for anything. Cochran's feet thumped carelessly against polished mahogany. His right hand engulfed an orange. "Markus, my good friend, how would Empire State and Union like to be in at the beginning of a technological revolution?"

"Technology Promeco has and Exxon doesn't?" Folger was unable to disguise his scepticism.

"You got it!" The orange rotated mesmerically in Cochran's fingers. "Let me put it another way. How would you like to be there when I bring those billions of barrels of shale oil out of the ground easier" – His hand slowly closed – "than this?" Golden juice gushed suddenly through his fingers to spatter the pale carpet. Dobrovsky appeared miraculously with damp cloth and snowy towel.

"No mining." Cochran allowed his hand to be cleansed. "No cooking. No billion-ton spoil heaps to bring the conservationists running like the world was on fire." Dobrovsky slipped away bearing crushed orange.

Cochran slid from his perch, belly more muscle than flab for all it bulged hugely above the waistband. Folger could believe all those stories of his dubious past. Cochran loomed dauntingly over the banker, friend of presidents, of half of Washington, preventing him from rising.

"How would you, biggest financial hotshot in the oil business, like to be the guy who grubstaked Brew Cochran to bring up the biggest undeveloped reserves since Socal and Texaco got their feet under the table with the Saudis?"

He captured Folger's hand, hauled him effortlessly up. "C'm'on. Let's you and me lunch at the University Club while Brewster Cochran lets you in on a fortune."

*   *   *

Barzelian and his Director met in the silence room. Windowless, door like an airlock, bunker walls, World War Three could have been proclaimed on bullhorns and no one outside the wiser.

The Director, Central Intelligence, was a zealot and a pro's pro, sweating it out through the '60s and '70s in various dumps and hellholes, no political base or royal favour to promote him over the heads of ticket punchers and career-plotters.

His accession had come when Congress balked at a presidential nomination just too blatantly unworthy for any amount of patronage and arm-twisting to get through on the nod. He had had good experience of the world's back alleys, less of Washington, but quickly discovered that Washington was where a good many of the back alleys began and ended. A New Englander, Vermont granite with a cultivated topsoil, he fooled quite a few people until they tripped over hidden rock.

Barzelian was a freak, a genealogical joke. "Watch out for me. I'm a Missourian Armenian, an Armenian Missourian, mean as a mule, crafty as a carpet dealer. I'll believe nothing you tell me, make you believe everything I say, cheat you out of your birthright and sell you the Grand Canyon as prime real estate." It was part of his power that everyone laughed and secretly believed him. His chocolate-coated guile and DCI's chill-souled fundamentalism made them as jointly lethal as trapdoor and noose.

There was nothing in the room but a table and some steel and plastic chairs. DCI sat upright as a Georgetown dowager. Barzelian overflowed his seat like a jellyfish on a spade.

"The President wants to see us at three this p.m. Doug Church will be there. So will Dick Goss." Richard Goss was the President's National Security Adviser.

Barzelian, who treated his doctor's perennial lectures on weight control as a form of entertainment, broke the rhythm of his placid huff and puff. "They know it was a hit. The bang-bang boys have

22

zeroed in on the blood buggy. That's as far as it's gone with Church. All these days, the President is thinking, and those guys have come up with nothing."

"So he's calling in the brains."

"We know who did it." Even in this room, Barzelian spoke softly.

"We certainly do." DCI was grim.

"But we are not about to say so."

"You," DCI said, "are as twisty as used string."

"Double helix, twists within twists. Anyway, don't knock used string. Sometimes you lose belt and suspenders both."

"Doug Church is sore as hell over the accident story. Direct reflection on the competence of the Secret Service."

"Doug Church!" Barzelian left the rest of the comment to the curl of his fleshy lips. "You wonder why the President's holding the get-together, right?"

"The President loving us the way he does, you bet!"

"Schaffer was up to town this morning."

"Schaffer?" DCI was surprised. Head of the National Security Agency at Fort Meade, General Schaffer's affection for Washington was comparable with Jehovah's for the Cities of the Plain. "In person?"

"According to Pierre Weber."

"Pierre know why?"

"Uh-uh."

"Do you?"

Barzelian pondered, a labyrinthine process. "Heard the CIA was in back of an assassination attempt on the President?"

"You better not be right, you and your goddam Armenian sense of humour." DCI had very little.

"That was Missouri pessimism. Anyway, mitigating circumstances, we didn't succeed. The President's around to prove it."

DCI looked with instinctive unease at the thick walls. "You expect that Sun Belt sonofabitch to be grateful?"

"Why not? We could just as easily have succeeded." Barzelian and his chair parted company with the slow majesty of a sunrise. "We try again, right? Something different."

"Whatever it takes, if it takes it."

Barzelian operated the door controls. "About this afternoon. I have the feeling we are about to be given a clue that will put us on to ourselves. Beautiful!"

"Bar." DCI unfolded, rangy, polar cap hairstyle, an old rooster with quick-freeze eyes. "What if we have to track us down?"

Barzelian rolled his eyes, drawing one plump forefinger across the invisible line between his bottom chin and his shoulders.

*   *   *

Mark Folger pushed back his chair from the remains of the University Club's cold buffet. "I can't believe it."

"Ever know ol' Brew tell you a lie?"

Ol' Brew, Folger knew, would bury a knife between his shoulder-blades if enough depended on it. "No, but . . ."

"Still think ol' Brew has popped his cork?"

"Cut it out, will you? Anyway, I'm no scientist."

Cochran chuckled meatily. "Me neither. Don't need to be. Buy 'em, dime a dozen. Listen, I put close on two million bucks of my own money into this one. Hell, even my board doesn't know, leave alone stockholders. You think I'm about to pick up and run this late on? No sir! Ol' Brew knows a winning hand when he sees one." He shot Folger a hard look. "Well, what do you say?"

Folger shook his head, wrestling with too many ideas, too much doubt. "Exxon, all that knowhow, why didn't *they* come up with it?"

"Always has to be a first guy, right? Whole bunch of people with the same general idea, just one who's a standout. That's my boy."

"A Britisher? Doesn't American technology rate any more?"

"Sure it does. Costs more, too. Plus I get a better tax deal over there, and I tapped some pretty smart research. This boy Golding did the preliminary work on a post-graduate grant at Queen Mary College, London, and he still has the key to the door. Exxon didn't slip up, just weren't looking in the right direction."

Folger had come to poke careful fun at a figure of forty trillion dollars – *trillion*, for Heaven's sake! Now at least some of it was beginning to stack up before him like gaming chips on a lucky run. That kind of shock to a delicate world economy could be as much a threat as the bomb.

"Brewster, check that I've got it straight. Instead of gigantic

24

excavations, massive furnaces, billions of tons of spoil, you simply add this – what did you call it? culture? – to the shale beds, and it goes to work."

"Don't say 'simply'. Easy, not simple."

"All right. Anyway, the shale may look like rock but to these bugs it's a sponge. They set to work releasing the oil and from then on you pump it up just as you would from a traditional field, is that correct?"

"Bet your ass it's correct, give or take a few details. Once that stuff takes, it just goes on working, nothing to add, like they say in the fast food recipes. It's – hey! Remember *Fantasia*, that Disney film? How Mickey got a hold of the magician's spell book when he was out of town, had the broom start fetching in water? Got all the water he needed, took an axe to that broom to stop it bringing in more?"

Cochran, who, as well as his whisky sour, had drunk wine and a couple of feral pre-lunch martinis, was half over the table, eyes bright as silver dollars, but he still kept his voice down.

"Well sir, he cuts that lil ol' broom in half but each half turns into a new broom and goes on fetching water. He whacks away with that axe like Lizzy Borden, but each time there's just another bunch of brooms hauling water until that whole place is knee-deep, okay?"

He lowered his voice to a hoarse whisper. "Only we aren't talking about water, Markus. We're talking about oil, millions of barrels, billions of barrels, good rich crude that would fetch near on twenty dollars a barrel even in bad times, and times ain't going to stay bad for always."

One of his big hands had reached to grab Folger's wrist. Folger's whole forearm was doing a little dance to Cochran's compulsive rhythm. "Thirty-five. Forty. Maybe forty-five by the '90s, isn't an expert, won't say that's the way it's going to be."

The grip on Folger's wrist tightened. "Know how much it's going to cost to get that oil up after tax write-offs on investment?"

Mesmerised, wanting and yet unable to disbelieve, Folger shook his head.

"Maybe a dollar a barrel, maybe I'm being pessimistic. Okay, mister banker, do your sums."

Folger found himself swallowing. If it were even one tenth true!

Cochran pressed his advantage. "And what works on shale is going to work on all those billions of tons of tar sand up in Canada. Brazil, Thailand, other places, they have shale too. I have options. Trillions, mister! Tens of trillions of dollars! More, over a period, than the gross national product. More than the national debt."

Even dismissing the fantasy figures, it was still dynamite. Folger thought of the global economic impact with the US pulling out of the international oil market, maybe even competing with the traditional exporters, and went cold. "What sort of estimates do you have for initial costs? Quite a sum, or you wouldn't be talking to me."

"More than I can put up on my own or you're damn right I wouldn't be!"

"So how much? Assuming I believe all this."

"You believe, Markus, or you wouldn't be asking." Cochran drew slowly on his cigar, eyes narrowed against the smoke, or against Folger, or both. "A ballpark number, okay?"

"Couldn't be anything else, not so early."

"A billion and a half over five years, mostly in the first three. After that, if everything goes right, we'll be getting rich faster than anyone since the Saudis hit the jackpot, whole thing self-financing. We won't be bringing up oil, Markus. We'll be bringing up dreams. Promeco is going to fly so high, Wall Street'll need the space shuttle to keep up."

He shook Folger's wrist, gently but powerfully, Shylock foreclosing on one pound of prime meat. "So what do you say?"

"It couldn't be my decision alone." Damn right! He was going to have to talk behind those closed doors in Washington.

"But yours would be the one that counted."

"I'd have to have figures. In confidence."

"You'll get them."

"A complete technical presentation."

"That too."

"But first" — Folger hesitated, the significance, the sheer threat unbalancing him — "I'd want to see for myself."

Cochran's face split in a wide, white, wolfish grin. "Thought you'd never ask! My plane, we don't want talk. Let's have our secretaries settle dates." He released Folger's hand, held up his own to signal for the check.

                    *   *   *

The President was at his great oak desk, Doug Church standing uneasily by. Richard Goss, National Security Adviser, sat at one end of one of the two sofas, the low occasional table between them pyrotechnic with flowers; red carnations, snapdragons and an assortment of what DCI, no horticulturalist, classified as daisies. The black leather folder of the President's daily security report still lay on his desk.

"Mr President." DCI nodded a greeting at the other two men.

"Mel, Bar, how've you been?" The President's voice had small warmth for men not of his choosing, a service too independent for his liking. After the Soviets, DCI rated him the greatest threat.

The President stood. "Let's sit over here, gentlemen."

He took one of the two wing-back chairs by the screened fireplace for himself, waved DCI to the other. Barzelian and Church took the sofa facing Goss's, the occasional table's silent demonstration of flower power between them. Faint through the windows came the first grumble of thunder. The Washington Monument stood against a sky filled with purple broccoli.

The President, a man on the make who had made it and found that the job was always bigger than the man who filled it, fluttered his fingers once on the arms of his chair, blue eyes, suntan and a face that was strangely dead at close quarters. "We're here to talk security." His fingers ran through another stationary arpeggio. "Man takes on the presidency, he accepts the risk of being killed, goes with the job."

Got to give him that, DCI thought reluctantly, he does accept it, and still sleeps nights.

Church stirred. The President saw. "I know. The Secret Service has a list of names. All the folks who're potential president killers."

Church nodded. "Twenty-seven thousand plus." Detecting an unwise note of pride, Barzelian made a plump, wry *moue*, unseen.

27

"Sure, you have a list." The President focused on Church. "I know that."

"And we know where every single one of them is, all the time."

"Sure you do." The President's Houston drawl was saw-toothed. "And not one person involved in any assassination attempt in the past twenty years ever showed up on that list."

Church studied his shiny toecaps, blood rising in his cheeks.

"And tell me this. Was any name on that list at Gatwick airport a while back? If so, how'd he get through? If not, why not?

"The risk goes with the job," the President repeated. "Which does not mean that this president is going to take it lying down. Where we have information, we act on it. Where we don't – " His glacial gaze switched to DCI – "we go seek it."

Outside, the sky had become a morbid puce. The President stood to put on lights. He remained on his feet, waving them down almost impatiently as they all made to rise.

"Dick?" He turned toward Dick Goss, who had maintained a cat-like stillness.

Richard Goss was self-effacing, softly-spoken, legal background governing careful speech. His yellow scratchpad went everywhere with him. He had it now. He even glanced at it, though it was virgin.

"General Schaffer came up from Fort Meade this morning. Wanted to hand something over in person."

DCI kept his eyes away from Barzelian, whose breath scraped the silence as delicately as a surgeon's blade. The President stood quite motionless, as if he were no more than a spectator.

"What he brought" – Goss jerked his bald head toward the President's desk – "is right there in the security briefing file." He gave DCI a squinting smile. "You'll get your copy, Mel."

No copy for Church, Barzelian noted. Bye-bye, Doug old man.

Goss gave a prim little cough. "You know all about the facility we share with the British at Cheltenham, England."

They all knew about it. The belated rooting out of a British employee and Moscow spy in '82, though only after devastating harm had been done, had been another nail in the coffin of Anglo-American security cooperation.

Goss twitched his lips. "Not another leak. You could say the opposite, you'll see why. In with the big stuff, Soviet armed forces movements, military traffic, that kind of thing, the British monitor all radio and landline traffic to and from foreign embassies in the UK."

"That's one hell of a lot of material." The President came to sit with them once more. "Most of it third-grade peanuts." His eyes jerked to and fro among them incessantly.

"Trouble is," Goss said, "that kind of stuff is only a drop in the bucket when it gets in with NSA's main source material."

"Takes time." The President resented it. "All that gee-whizz technology and it still takes time."

"Analysis," Goss explained. "Computer analysis, key subjects, key words, source and target, that kind of stuff. Outside of Warsaw Pact countries, embassy traffic is pretty low-grade."

DCI, Brer Rabbit, sat tight and said nothing. He never knew how Barzelian got half of his information.

"Queries take time too," Goss said. "And if there's something you'd rather not draw attention to, you have another problem."

DCI nodded. "Go back with an AP1 and it's like nudging the British in the ribs."

"What the NSA computers spotted was this. Just after the bomb exploded in the cargo plane, one London embassy – well, you can hardly call it an embassy – had a traffic surge, near on ten times normal. Dropped back for roughly the period it would have taken that freighter to complete its journey if it hadn't been limping, peaked again around touchdown time, then back to normal. Time search showed a similar peak the previous day."

Doug Church looked blank. "A little embassy," Barzelian repeated. "Not really an embassy at all. It has to be Libya."

"That's right." The President was harsh.

Doug Church, catching up, shook his head. "Won't stand up."

The President looked. "How's that again?"

"Not one damn thing that ties in, Mr President."

"Glad to hear you've turned up one damn thing, Doug. I was beginning to wonder. Now remind me" – The President turned his fire on DCI – "how many times Langley has already screwed up on Libya."

Oh well, DCI told himself, nothing comes free. He began the recital. "We raised the coup of '80, Mr President. They managed

29

to put it down. We fixed a hit on Gaddafi in June, same year. The guy missed."

"Got him in the shoulder." Barzelian's professional pride was hurt.

"When you're planning a hit" – The President was in no mood for quibbles – "the shoulder's a miss."

"February '82," DCI continued doggedly, "second attempt nicked Gaddafi in the jaw. Second coup, November '82, Gaddafi got wind, invited himself to Peking, stayed over until his security people had tidied up."

Barzelian made a rescue bid, loving the whole thing. "It's a tough one, Mr President. Those people run the country tighter than the Cosmos Club, right here in Washington. You don't get in unless you're someone. You're no one unless they say so."

"Or unless" – The President was scathing – "you're a visiting terrorist." He rose again, marching toward the tall windows. No one attempted to stand. A bolt of forked lightning streaked the blue-black sky like a running crack. Back to them, he rested his hands on the small table that held pictures of his wife and family, shiny-bright in their shiny-bright frames. Thunder rattled.

He spoke without turning. "I did not become president of this country to see its security, or mine, kicked around by half-assed fanatics who think they have the right to do as they please because God gave them some oil wells. I am not prepared to forget what happened back there at Gatwick."

The sermon continued, delivered to the Rose Garden promenade. "Hit squads sent to kill a US president in '81. Tanks and planes ready to make trouble over half of North Africa. Arms to commie revolutionaries in Central America. Goon teams touring the Middle East and Europe to rub out any of their nationals that step out of line. And now this." His voice rose. "I am sick and tired of seeing this country of ours having to ride punches instead of hitting back, just because we're big and they're small." They all thought of Grenada.

He turned. "There's a story I hear, Mr Director. One of those goddam ex-US Army mercenaries they have out there in Tripoli is really a CIA deep cover man. True or false?"

"False, Mr President, worse luck."

"Okay." The President headed for his desk. "Dick, I don't have to tell you or Mel what I want."

"No, Mr President." Goss's gaze, tiptoeing over Doug Church, tried to creep up on Barzelian and say boo. "How was Gatwick security breached, by whom?"

"For starters." There was no mistaking the President's meaning.

No one had ever caught Barzelian napping long enough to say boo. "Just bear one thing in mind, Dick. We can't use the Brits." He too let his gaze walk over Church, but took no trouble to remove its boots. "Doug here wouldn't want them to know we were caught with our pants down."

Church reddened. "Now just a minute!"

". . . and we can't," Barzelian finished imperturbably, "go gum-shoeing around with our little notepads and ballpoints without putting them wise."

"Damn right!" The President snapped up the proffered bait. "We have them by the balls on security these days, and that's the way it's going to stay."

"Not," Barzelian finished carefully, "that the Brits might not have goofed anyway."

Church was into the trap almost before Barzelian had finished. "The British were our boys on that job. They breathed when we said breathe, you don't catch me trusting them."

"So." Barzelian blinked amiably, heavy jowls wobbling as he nodded. "I guess we'll have to look someplace else. I'm sure Doug here won't object if we ask his men a few questions."

"What's keeping you?" The President produced his coldest smile. "Dick, stay on a minute, will you?"

DCI, Barzelian and Church went down the red-carpeted corridor in silence. It seemed twice as long as usual. When Church turned off, Barzelian chuckled. "I guess we fixed his wagon."

In the Oval Office, the President had begun again. "That business of those crazy guys over there in Libya trying to get their hands on nuclear missile technology."

"We never stop watching, Mr President. The Pakistanis said no. The Indians won't listen. The Chinese gave them the oriental

31

bum's rush. They've been all over the world offering big money, but they've found no takers."

The President glowered, then launched into a speech. "Dick, listen to me. The days when we could send in the Marines to teach some two-bit country its manners have gone for good, looks like, but I want that goddam chunk of desert hurt. Full powers, whatever a president of these United States can swing without going public, you've got it.

"Track down the guys who tried that hit, dust them off, no question. But that's not enough. I want something to remind that punk country it used to be nothing but sand."

"We'll take a good look, Mr President." Goss stood.

"You do that. Unofficial sanctions of some kind, maybe? Put the arm on our friends and those who owe us. Find the jugular. Push 'em back a ways toward dates and camels."

He watched Goss walk to the door.

"Dick."

"Mr President?"

"Church is out."

"Yes, Mr President."

"And Dick."

"Mr President."

"Not too many goddam camels."

THREE

Among many Government properties in London, some famous, some as secret as the Queen's investment portfolio, are two in the sleazy South Bank borough of Lambeth. Conveniently reached from Lambeth North Underground station for those without the price of a taxi, they have sufficient in common to make their differences an exercise in irony.

Barely a stone's throw from each other, both are tower blocks of talented ugliness. Both have grandiloquent names; Hercules House, Century House. Both are concerned with the processing of information, both havens for a considerable quantity of civil servants ranging from clerks to a brace of Directors-General.

There resemblance ends. Hercules House, brashly blazoned, is the headquarters of the Central Office of Information, Government's mouthpiece. Century House, with a foyer as bleak as the entrance to a functionary's hell, is anonymous, marked only by a Mobil filling station where some of its senior denizens have accounts at the tax-payer's expense. It is also one of Government's ears. A London cabby, asked for Century House, may well say, "Secret Service? Right you are, guv."

Morpurgo, returning from lunch, did not take a taxi. He was only crossing a couple of roads from the Hercules Tavern, little patronised by his SIS colleagues, where he had a beer and a sandwich in customary solitude.

He suspected, by now, that he would always be an outsider. To begin with, he had been recruited in the aftermath of an SIS palace revolution engineered by Epworth, himself something of an outsider, though now, in spite of a new Director-General, effective head of SIS. The previous Director-General's head had been one of those that rolled.

Another *décapité* had been Humphrey Fish, Eastern European and Soviet coordinator, who had subsequently gassed himself to death in the double garage of his expensive Georgian-style house in Esher. Morpurgo's acquisition of Fish's office, though positively not his job, had not increased his popularity in his new, looking-glass world.

But then, Morpurgo had come to Century House from Curzon Street, known to supercilious Centurions as the Home and Colonial, after a downmarket grocery chain founded in the heyday of empire. Its population of ex-service officers, sometime policemen and heterogeneous civil servants has never endeared itself to the elite and dilettante Centurions with their *Times* crossword puzzle minds and Foreign Office connections.

It also remains unforgiven, decades on, for the rough going-over it was authorised to give SIS in the wake of the Philby circus.

Further to Morpurgo's disadvantage was the fact that Steve Archer, formerly SIS, still had many friends south of the river. They found the business of Helga Archer unpardonable on the triple grounds of security, the old boy net, and being found out. But then – and this was what weighed against Morpurgo most of all – what could you expect from a known 'lefty', grammar school boy and one-time trade unionist who openly voted Labour?

All in all, very little going for him, but, like it or not, he was stuck with it. Any further career change, not counting Sylvie's personal offer, would certainly see him fare worse than a beadroll of socially acceptable moles.

He showed his pass in the bare lobby, again at the sector barrier on the fourteenth of the twenty above-ground floors. Everyone knew that the constant checks were part of the con-tinuing effort to persuade the Americans that SIS still had a part to play in the world outside Northern Ireland. Warren Claas, in the privacy of the American embassy, said that they checked on who went to the bathroom inside Century House, but probably let the window cleaners go up and down outside with zoom lens Exactas, tape recorders and expanding suitcases.

Mrs Pringle said, "Mr Epworth asked for you, Mr Morpurgo, just after you went out."

He found Epworth contemplating his panoramic view of unlovely South London, his attention concentrated, apparently, on a passenger train and eight toy blue coaches that finicked slowly along the viaduct toward the Elephant and Castle, Herne Hill and the clerical recruitment camps of Croydon.

"You're a musical chap. What do you – mmmm – know about the music of the Crusades?"

Morpurgo made his usual effort. "I'm only a bloody part-time piano player, you know that." The real purpose of Epworth's frequent questions, even without his enigmatic mmmms and the non sequiturs that never were, was something for soothsayers.

"Mmmm." Epworth watched the train shuttle its way south.

Going to give me nothing, Morpurgo realised. "Crumhorn? Shawm? Rebec?" Epworth's passions, if you could use such a word of such a man, were all arcane, ranging from unblended and very dry sherries bought in small parcels from single vineyards, to musica antiqua. Epworth himself played shawm, crumhorn and sometimes, as he put it, doubled on bombard.

Backlighted by the long window, his meagre, baby-fine hair, receded to the crown of his round skull, was almost invisible. Fingers intertwined at the level of a hollow chest, tall, stooped figure as gangling as an adolescent boy's, though he must be fiftyish, central casting would have had him down for curates and junior classics masters.

He leaned toward Morpurgo confidentially. "First Crusade, 1095. The Fourth ended in 1204."

"Ah." It was sometimes difficult to treat Epworth with respect, most unwise not to.

"No crumhorn." Epworth seated himself at his desk, a modest object considering his supernal if ill-defined standing in SIS. Status rules, operating here as elsewhere in the Civil Service, prescribed his entitlement, right down to the number and nature of the pictures on his modular plastic walls, but on his sudden accession – Morpurgo, newly purchased, had had a ringside seat – he had conjured up unsanctified miracles. His pictures, for example, unimpressively framed, architectural rather than artistic, were landscapes by Amaryllis Epworth, devoted to

Lawrence, four children and the Surrey Federation of Women's Institutes. Morpurgo knew her only through her photograph on Epworth's desk.

Epworth's official designation was Chief Operations Co-ordinator, responsible for the controlling of the six operational departments. It was a title of his own devising, planned, in Morpurgo's view, less to inform than conceal. But then, so was Lawrence Epworth.

"Bladder pipe." He said it with an almost surgical earnestness. "And the – mmmm – douçaine, not that anyone's exactly sure what *that* was. The shawm, like the nakers, was a Saracen military instrument."

He produced his soft, disarming giggle, beguiling to the unwary.

From time to time, Morpurgo attempted to take on his new master at his own deep game; mixed strategies, minimax, the random injection of inconsequentialities. "Sylvie wants to move."

As usual, he lost. "I know. Or rather – " Epworth made a tiny gesture of refutation – "shall we say? anticipated. Listen."

In the amateur but highly skilled early music group of which he was a member, his role was woodwind, but he could give a decent account of himself in a chorus; male soprano.

He sang:

> *Au tens plain de felonnie,*
> *D'envie et de traïson,*
> *De tort et de mesprison,*
> *Sanz bien et sanz cortoisie,*
> *Et que entre nos baron*
> *Faisons tout le siecle empirier*
> *Que je vol esconmenïer*
> *Ceus qui plus offrent reson,*
> *Lors veuil dire une chanson.*

The tune, ancient, mournful, was, though Morpurgo understood nothing of the words, strangely moving.

"Thibaud de Champagne, Fourth Crusade. Free translation." – Epworth shuffled files identified only by cypher clusters, without really examining them – "In these times of wickedness,

36

injustice, falseness, when decency's gone – mmmm – out of the window, those of us in positions of power make things worse, especially when the wisest are given the push, which is why I sing this song." He blinked anxiously at Morpurgo.

"Who's been given the push? And how could you have guessed about Sylvie?" The second question was foolish, like trying to grill the Delphic Oracle. For all his etiolated personality, Epworth had a genius for extracting information where none was on offer.

"Sylvie? Isn't it obvious? She goes up and up. She must have somewhere to come down to, somewhere that's comfortable and convenient. That place of yours in Holland Park, not even Holland Park, really, let's say – mmmm – Shepherd's Bush *bis* . . ."

"Damn it, I didn't think you were a snob."

"No. Please." Epworth looked stricken, it was all an act. "You don't really think that? The Knight of the Long Knives, that's who."

"Sir Hugh?" Morpurgo was staggered. "Given the push?"

"Alas!"

"But . . . for God's sake, why?" Hugh Wyndham, Director-General of Morpurgo's old firm in Curzon Street, was one of the intelligence community's institutions, two more years to go before retirement.

"Cheltenham, mainly. That's not what you'll hear, but they've just given him long enough to make it decent. *Pour encourager les autres.* Oh, a touch of politics, of course, sharp tongue and all that." It was how the Knight had earned his nickname.

"Kicked out? Just like that?"

"Inveigled, that's the word they prefer, into early retirement. The call" – Epworth's feminine hands outlined blue remembered hills – "of the Sussex wilds. Of course, Whitehall needed a head for the platter. And for Washington."

"It's official?" All that crap about the Crusades; typical Epworth!

"So far as these things ever are. End of next month. He'll take leave first."

"Who'll get his slot? Do you know?"

Epworth went Cheshire Cat, a smile in two dimensions. "Steve Archer."

For Morpurgo it was like walking into a plate-glass door.

Epworth folded his fingers upon each other. "Mmmm, thought you ought to know. Before you found out." He wore a baby's abstract frown.

Morpurgo found something to say. "I suppose you ought to be pleased when your former deputy makes it to the top."

Epworth waggled his fingers, checking for broken bones.

"Especially since there was a time when you were screwing his wife." Waste of time, nothing shocked Epworth, but the bitterness was hard to bear, even now. Morpurgo deserved his blame, but Steve, years older than Helga anyway – German refugee, any port in a storm – had been judge, jury and hangman's tout.

At the mention of Morpurgo's moral dereliction, Epworth splayed his fingers like wings above his bony knuckles.

"Well, he always thought he ought to have my job." Morpurgo couldn't leave it alone. "Felt his class had a natural right to give orders to mine." Epworth's silence was provocative. "Steve's not a forgiving man. That's why Helga tried to kill herself."

No response.

"Why *did* you hire me? for Christ's sake."

Epworth's mild grey eyes stopped blinking. "The one man I could be sure of, no previous involvement in plot and counterplot. I'm new in the job too, you know." His soft giggle. "We might have a rainy day. You're – mmmm – my umbrella."

Morpurgo was less umbrella than punctured teddy bear, stuffing spilling out.

"You've not seen Archer lately?" Epworth was studying him with open interest.

"Not since I left. Goes out of his way not to be at Gower Street for the liaison meetings. Of course" – The dire change of circumstances was not yet fully plumbed – "he may do the opposite now."

In due course, next Honours, it would be knighthood; Sir Stephen Archer. Warren Claas, who, as a Philistine Mid-Westerner, had small time for the instantly fossilising rituals of the British upper stratae, would be privately pungent.

"I gather he's barely finished – mmmm – tidying up after the state visit."

"I should have thought all that was well out of the way by now."

Epworth's eyes filmed. "Mmmm. Incidentally, I hear the top man in the American Secret Service is being eased out, just like the Knight."

Always remember, they said on the training courses, and he himself often repeated it, always remember, when someone says, "Oh, by the way" or "Incidentally", to listen twice as hard. "When you meet Death," old Fawcett used to put it with relish, "on a stroll, you'll know your time's up when he casually says, 'Oh, by the way . . .'".

But Morpurgo, to whom American presidents and state visits, like royalty itself, were part of a system he was sworn to defend but found it hard to enthuse over, failed to respond. "Not surprised. I gather they ruffled a few feathers, food tasters, guns in the Palace, that sort of thing."

Epworth became vague again. "Yes, well, none of our business, thank goodness. I'm thinking of taking you off liaison, anyway. Pegley will do well enough handling it on his own, Eton, Trinity, Archer rather cares for that sort of thing, doesn't he?"

"You mean I'm out of a job."

"Mmmm, not exactly, just thinking about it." This time Epworth got as far as opening one of his files. "Don't turn Sylvie down in a hurry. Good thing to up sticks once in a while, gets rid of accumulated rubbish."

Morpurgo, still picking his way through bits of fallen sky, missed the multiple possibilities of meaning.

* * *

"Not just a different ball game," Mark Folger said. "A whole new league." He was still hoping he might be taking it too seriously. Brewster Cochran's talk – not often, but often enough – outran his achievement.

They jounced over a railway crossing. Mingled with the green balm of the British countryside, he could smell warm creosote from the wooden ties. "So already you're broadening your experience." Cochran was a wolf at feeding time.

They turned down a short residential road, turned again and were in a miniature industrial estate; agricultural supplies, extruded plastics, concrete garden furniture, beyond which a

39

brick structure with a glass and metal extension flew the Promeco house flag; Prometheus with a flaming torch, an eagle hovering menacingly.

A plate glass door swung open. A man, youngish, baby-faced and curly-haired, appeared, squinting against the bright light. He wore a crumpled off-the-peg suit, ballpoints ranged like medals on his breast.

"Goldy!" Cochran enveloped his hand in a ten-fingered vice and Folger winced in sympathy. "Mark, meet Charlie Golding. He heads up this project. Goldy, this is Mark Folger, biggest non-oil man in the oil business, come to see whether you're worth a wooden nickel."

Folger, bulldozed inside by Cochran's palm, saw that Golding was a man with a literal mind, Cochran's joke making him look anxious. "Coffee's ready, Mr Cochran, if you'll come up to the office."

"Oil now, coffee later." Cochran was driving them all toward the glass annexe. "And call me Brew, how many times do I have to say it? Know what's wrong with this country, Markus? Too goddam much respect."

They passed through a door: RESTRICTED AREA. POSITIVELY NO ADMITTANCE WITHOUT AUTHORITY. Golding saw Folger take in the wording. "It's okay, Mr Folger, only a P1 area, but we keep strict security." Anxiety as a way of life, Folger decided. Above them, fascines of brightly-coloured pipe-run reminded him of the Centre Pompidou in Paris.

Cochran burst through another door like Bionic Man, revealing a kind of indoor chemical plant, the Beaubourg atmosphere even more pronounced. Pipes in rainbow array sliced high space in Mondrian progressions, vines festooned with the metallic fruit of valves. There was a warm, lactic smell, a subliminal throbbing through the soles of the feet.

"This" – Cochran slapped the surface of a steel vessel labelled C1 FERMENTER, then embraced the scene like a Texas rancher indicating dawn-to-dusk acres – " is where we grow the work force."

Golding seemed willing to let him make the running. Awed? Folger wondered, in the presence of such power as he and Cochran represented. There were only two other inhabitants of

40

this high-tech jungle, a man and a girl, white-coated, quietly occupied. Folger began to be uneasily impressed.

Golding cleared his throat, a prominent Adam's apple jerking. "I have a small display over here."

Not much of a display; a card table with two glass phials holding beigey fluid, two glass dishes containing a kind of jelly on which something grew in small, nearly perfect circles.

"Make with the spiel, Goldy." Cochran was impatience barely contained.

Golding picked up the two small bottles. "These are the inocula."

"Bugs." Cochran was genially contemptuous. "We tamed a bunch of bugs."

"The count in the shale" – Golding hesitated, waiting to see if his master would interrupt again – "was nearly a hundred, amazing, really."

"The Colony site, Markus. We stole a bunch of bugs from Exxon, think they'll sue? Near on one hundred different kinds, can you believe it?" He gave Golding a rough hug, part prompt, part encouragement. "Go ahead, Goldy, what's keeping you?"

The Adam's apple bobbed once more. "*Escherichia coli.* And a bacillus related to *caldolyticus.* We screened all the micro . . . – uh – all the bugs we found in the shale. These seemed the best bet."

"That shale!" Cochran shook his steel-thatched head. "Just goddam lousy with bugs. Go on, son, don't let me stop you."

"Is Mr Folger . . ." Golding turned to Folger. "Do you know anything about genetic engineering, sir?"

Folger blinked, slow to absorb the revelation. "Brew, are you telling me all this is some kind of genetic engineering?"

"Damn right! What did you think, Markus, we just found ourselves some cute lil ol' bug would turn shale into oil for the asking?"

Folger felt unease, irritation, relief. "Do I have to tell you the heat's off in Wall Street on that burner, Brewster? Genentech-style instant fortunes, that's so much cold coffee. The money market's as leary of recombinant DNA as a gang of ecology freaks."

Cochran gripped his shoulder, crushing anacondas to death. "Got to trust me, Markus. Ol' Brew's blowing no smoke up anyone's ass, he's in oil, always was, always will be."

Elbowing Golding aside with friendly violence, he grabbed the two phials. "One of these bugs we just baby along, right? No tricks, no rejigging, just the way Ma Nature made it. But the other – the hell with fancy names, Goldy! – we really gave that baby the treatment."

He poked one of the Petri dishes. "This bug here's the one. Well sir, snip out a piece of that ol' bug here, stick in a piece there, pickin' and patchin' the way my maw used to make over an old coat. And we finish up with a completely new bug, see? One that can chew up a hunk of shale and spit out high quality crude, kind of stuff is going to make the cat crackers purr clean around the world. Just one snag, Markus my friend, but it near as all getout put paid to the entire project."

"Aerobic." As if he himself had had no part in this biochemical wizardry, Golding was barely audible. Folger, who had been wondering about the relationship between Cochran and this low-key, unimpressive man, guessed rightly that the technical problems were his be-all and end-all. He himself was beginning to feel increasingly anxious. A major new source of cheap crude, in the hands of a man like Brewster Cochran, determined to undercut every other producer, could juggernaut the world into permanent recession.

"Aerobic, hell! Needs oxygen, that's what. Air breather." Cochran jiggled one of the two phials. "Imagine that. We build something that turns rock into gold, black gold, the way an old nag turns grass into horse shit, but only in the laboratory. Down there in the bedrock" – He stamped the ground like Rumpelstiltskin in a rage – "it needs the one thing there ain't. It needs air." His eyes glittered mockingly at Folger.

"But if that's the case" – Folger had no intention of missing anything of this potentially awesome development – "you're back to the Exxon position, excavating millions of tons to get thousands of barrels. I'm no engineer, but . . . ."

Cochran, brandishing the other phial, punched his arm with brutal exuberance. "Two! Two cultures, how does that grab you, my fine Wall Street friend? One bug helps the other let loose the

42

most sensational, terrific, earthshaking goddam gusher since Lucas hit Spindletop!"

He touched the two phials together. "Pow! Who-o-o-sh! Billions of barrels! Trillions of dollars, didn't believe me, did you, Markus? Ain't science a wonderful thing? Turns rock into money!"

Golding's was an apologetic murmur after Cochran's ebullience. "We inject them together, Mr Folger. The aerogen releases oxygen from the rock. The anaerobe uses the oxygen to set free the oil."

Cochran approached his flushed face very close to Folger's. "Patentable, Markus. Not just the process. The goddam bug."

"Patent? A *bug*?"

"Damn right! US Supreme Court decision, Chakrabarty and General Electric versus the US Patent Office, 1980."

"The first patent granted on a manmade microorganism." Once again Golding's was the still small voice of fact. "Theirs was genetically engineered to break down oil spills."

"But ours" – Cochran's manner was charged with savage hubris – "will bring down monopolies, maybe countries, even."

"All that?" Folger made himself sound calm, unimpressed, but though he was not remotely given to flights of fancy, his surroundings, Cochran's exultant certainty, above all, Golding's quiet assurance, were beginning to fill his head with apocalyptic visions of catastrophe. "From this?"

"From this, Markus." Cochran paced a swift route through the trombone forest. "This process here churns out the oxygen-maker, straightforward addition of nutrients, right temperature and pressure, nothing so special I can't recite it like a kid on his two-times. And this" – He force-marched another route – "ends up right here as the oil-maker. After that they both go a little ways on, get themselves freeze-dried, then go into storage until we're ready to crack Big Oil like a walnut." His deliberately hayseed idiom was camouflage for a vulpine satisfaction.

"And the oil?" I have to see everything, Folger instructed himself. The transistor changed the world. This could wreck it.

"Show'm, Goldy."

They went into another area, more pipes, fewer vessels, some of the pipe-runs leading out of the building. The smell, too, had changed, less mysterious, suggestive of tar, house gas, above all of crude oil. Golding took a beaker, held it beneath a stopcock, eased the valve. Something flowed, semi-viscous, dark as the buried stratae from which it had been released. Its smell, unmistakable, identified it instantly as the lifeblood of industrial civilisation.

Folger experienced a potent *frisson*. He knew how Lucas must have felt at Spindletop, Twitchell in Saudi Arabia, but they had only been at the beginning. He could be witnessing the beginning of the end. Only Golding was unmoved, a man for whom the transformation of dirt into oil, far from presaging a devastation of the global economy, was no more than a predictably successful exercise in technology.

Cochran was staring at Folger with a ferocious calculation. "Trillions, Markus, that's the bottom line, for a paltry billion and a half up front. How's that for an offer you can't refuse?"

Golding, diffident, said, "If you gentlemen would care for a cup of coffee?"

In Golding's poky office, prefabricated airlessness, Folger struggled back to reality. "I'll need a sample of that crude, Brewster. I shall want an independent analysis." He forced himself to smile. "Hell, how do I know you two aren't setting me up for the world's biggest sting?"

"I'm air-freighting you fifty gallons, Markus. Run any tests you like, just keep quiet about the source, okay? And I have something for you to keep on your desk, kind of a historical souvenir, first run of crude from the biggest goddam gusher in the world."

He snapped his fingers. Golding produced a glass jar.

Folger gingerly removed the stopper to sniff, once more, the rank smell of success. His face changed. So, a moment later, did Cochran's. He grabbed the jar, took his coffee cup from its saucer, poured. The contents of the jar came reluctantly; thick, glutinous dribbles and rushes, a viscous chemical sludge. A mephitic odour spread through the room.

Golding, showing no emotion, said, "The main storage tank." He picked up a telephone, spoke matter-of-factly. They all waited. Sunlight, streaming into the room, drew out more of the noxious odour.

Golding, at last, said, "Yes," listened again, replaced the phone. "The main storage tank's full of that stuff. And Number 2 tank's beginning to turn."

They listened to him talking expertly, imperturbably, about bacterial plugging, chitins and gelatines, degradation and super-viscosity. Cochran, recovering heroically, took over. "A glitch, Markus. Just a glitch, too much of a hurry, my goddam im-patience. These things happen, early moon rockets blew up on the pad, right? This whole thing will be fixed before you know it, right, Goldy?"

Mark Folger, making all the appropriate noises, studied Golding surreptitiously and felt his initial relief begin to fade. It would be fixed all right, this was merely a temporary remission. He would have to talk to Dick Goss just as soon as he could get to Washington. This, in his expert judgement, was something for the personal attention of the National Security Adviser.

*   *   *

The Situation Room is in the West Wing basement of the White House. It was christened by President John F. Kennedy, who made use of it in going eyeball to eyeball with Kruschev over Cuba while the missile silos yawned. The domain of suc-cessive National Security Advisors, it is a charmless chamber, ceiling low, walls dark and cluttered, its strange atmosphere functional as a cash-and-carry warehouse.

Collaged with maps, satellite pictures, teletype and computer printouts, guarded by duty Marines and in-house Secret Servicemen, it is self-contained, from the National Security Adviser's office down to the secretarial bathrooms.

Dick Goss enjoyed his workaday confines, alive with the high-speech chatter of teleprinters and the comings and goings of visitors from State, Defense, the security services and various smaller organisations with unrevealing names and arcane res-ponsibilities. Promptly at nine every morning he went to the Oval Office to give the President and his senior staff their daily security briefing. For the remainder of most days, current threats to peace and security were discussed, assessed and given their priorities.

Today's first meeting was with Barzelian and Pierre Weber.

Weber had allowed himself to be driven over the state border from Langley with Barzelian. He had once been stopped on the Washington Beltway by a traffic cop and charged with driving in excess of the legal limit. He had vowed never again to sit behind a wheel in the District of Columbia unless guaranteed the one hundred per cent certain opportunity of running the sonofabitch down.

Foxy-haired, thin-faced, with the mournful eyes of a beagle, his occasional smiles burst on a sad world like the end of a solar eclipse. He would not willingly have run over a mouse, but was capable of stamping a rat to death.

Dick Goss opened with his standard question. "Well, what do we have?" Barzelian indicated Weber.

Weber managed to look as if his worst fears had just been realised. If his worst fears had just been realised they would all already be radioactive charcoal. "C4."

Goss frowned. "C4?"

"Plastic sheet explosive. Substituted for thermal insulation in the blood box. A very fancy variable time-frame detonator, the kind that's supposed to be under export embargo. Air Force One would have been around eight hundred miles out over the ocean when it blew. It would have taken out the main fore-and-aft control linkage, chance of survival negligible. Lucky it was in a less vulnerable place on the freighter."

"All right." Goss made a neat note on his yellow legal pad. "That's how. What matters is who." The tone mild, the point aggressive. Barzelian was playing himself at noughts and crosses.

Weber nodded. "Seems there was another VIP visit at Gatwick, day before the President left. Sons of the desert. Big stuff." He could look as inscrutable as an entire Chinese Triad.

"Libyans."

"Charter flight. Some construction industry exhibition in London. Normal security in the terminal building. Normal traffic pattern, which is dense."

Goss raised his thin eyebrows. "Normal security? That place was swarming with security the day before the President left. They don't leave everything to the last minute."

"Security on the planes, sure, heavy. Not so much in the buildings, beyond checking all systems go for the next day,

46

everything available that had to be available. Including the standby plasma."

"The Libyans" – Barzelian broke his breathy silence – "must have staged a diversion. Switched the plasma, fixed that fuse." His face was unreadable. He had just beaten himself at noughts and crosses by cheating.

Goss was stonily unamused. "You're trying to tell me some Arab got aboard Air Force One and fixed that fuse so it would blow? With Church's men, not to mention the British and Warren Claas's special group, as thick on the ground as locusts? Church says no outsider gets aboard that plane. I believe him."

"Not everyone," Weber said, "was Church's man. They have groundcrew to service the birds."

"Our groundcrews. Hand-picked. All American." Goss pressed, prosecuting counsel his favourite role. "A Libyan? Posing as groundstaff? That's strictly off the wall."

"Who said anything about Libyans, Dick?" Barzelian had switched to doodling, something humanoid but geometric, an Aztec godling.

Goss checked his notes carefully. "I thought you did. You or Pierre."

Weber wagged his head apologetically. "Let me straighten things out. There was this Libyan flight the previous day. The airport was running according to routine, scheduled flights, charters, commercials and private traffic. Our ships, under guard, were over toward the northern perimeter, you've got the sketch Church's people produced. The Libyan flight was nowhere in that direction, but there was a time when the terminal was awash with its passengers. Now, we can't ask the right questions without the British getting the wrong message, so we don't know exactly how it was done, but . . ."

He stopped. Goss was holding up his silver Cross pencil, a glistening wand in the concealed lighting. "I quote." He was referring to the file of statements from Church and his agents. "'Beautiful! They can prove nothing, but they're going to claim that a bunch of jigaboos got aboard Air Force One and nobody noticed. Boy, that's quite a number!' Unquote."

Goss gave no attribution, but Weber and Barzelian had no difficulty in identifying Doug Church's bruising style.

"What I was going to say" – Weber's melancholy patience was undisturbed – "was that we can prove what happened over where our planes were parked. And we don't disagree with Doug Church. The only people who went on and off Air Force One were Americans, not" – He let the word slip out like the reaction to a bad taste – "jigaboos. I mean they all had appropriate IDs."

For the first time, Goss's reaction was sharp. "Are you suggesting . . ."

". . . that one of Church's people sold out?" Barzelian rumbled, finishing for him. "No, Dick, we're not."

"But we have to tell you," Weber said with emphasized reluctance, "there was a time when there was one too many."

Goss promoted himself from counsel to judge. "Doug Church specifically states that that's impossible." He quoted, referring to the file again. "'What do you think? It's on the record. We check them from way back.'"

Barzelian stirred like the shifting of mountains, his swarthy, drooping face a perfect match for that unrevealing, horse-trader's voice. "But the fuse went. And the container blew up." His blackberry eyes conveyed the compassion of a cryogenic extortioner. "Will Doug tell us they just sat around waiting? Just sat about saying, 'Uh – hey, wouldn't it be great if the fuse on the icebox they keep the President's blood in blew out and we could plant this other box full of plastic explosive we just happen to have here?'"

The combination of tone and childishly elaborate humour was devastating.

Mouth pursed equivocally, Goss went back again to Church's statement. "'What I'm telling you'" – Even Goss's dry, nasal tone could not disguise Church's bruised dignity – "'is that I personally will vouch for every man on my strength and every man on that groundcrew, and I guess the same goes for Claas. If someone got aboard Air Force One, it must have been Superman.'" Goss peered at them over his glasses.

"Maybe." Weber was increasingly lugubrious. "Or American, which is pretty near the same, right?"

Goss's head came up, coldly disbelieving. "An American citizen?"

"American as violence. And apple pie."

"Bar? You're going to have a hard time convincing me."

Barzelian studied his doodle with exaggerated concentration, his chins a pink ruff collar. Goss watched him with growing disquiet. "One of Church's people?"

"No." Weber was a good man shocked by the iniquity of the human animal. "One of ours." He handed over a photograph. "Name of Hank Timothy."

Goss, staring at the photograph, pushed his glasses back up his nose, laid down his pencil, stared afresh. "Bar, the President asked Mel if it was true you had a deep cover man out there in Tripoli. Any connection?"

"The answer – you were there – was no. It's no again. This guy is not a deep cover man, though he still likes to spread the idea around. This man is ex-CIA. And a traitor."

Weber said, "Planned the hit, fixed the fuse, we still don't know how. But we showed the picture around. Four of Church's guys saw him."

Barzelian paused in his artwork. "Security adviser, arms buyer, hit squad trainer for Gaddafi's Jamahiriya."

"Ex-CIA. And a traitor." Goss was pink, taut and shiny with disgust. "An American prepared to kill his own president?"

"If," Weber said, "the price is right."

Goss sucked air tightly through his nose. "The President is going to want this man trashed. The President won't care how it's done, only when, and the when will have to be soon, or the rumpus – and believe me, it will be some rumpus! – will be heard clear out to Langley."

Neither of the others said anything. The President's hostility to Langley was something they lived with from day to day.

Dick Goss raised his voice, crisp as an autumn cold-snap. "I'm for the law. Grew up believing it comes above everything. But this guy goes, one piece or a million, if not today, tomorrow. I'm speaking for the President. He'll call Langley and speak to Mel. Unlimited powers."

"Unlimited powers." Weber was still on the course Barzelian had plotted, and the wind was steadying. "Unlimited powers," he repeated, and glanced toward Barzelian.

Goss was impatient now. "The President's word. Whatever it

takes, that's what he said. Find the guy. Fix him. And fix the Libyans, only this time so that it sticks."

"John Kennedy" – Weber was speaking lines practically written by Barzelian – "before they got him, said all a man needed to kill a president was a willingness to trade his life. He said no amount of protection was enough."

"Make your point," Goss said quietly, "since that had better not be it."

"Hank Timothy isn't willing to make that kind of trade. He'd trade my life. Yours. Not his. We can't go into Libya. He's going to be hard to tempt out." Now they were nearing the end of a roundabout journey.

"He was at Gatwick, right?"

"Oh, he moves around. He moves around the way rats move around, fast, quiet, and mostly in the dark."

"What tempts him?"

Presidents, Weber said, but not aloud. Aloud, he said, "He has the usual set-up in Switzerland."

"Banks there?"

"Gold. Or what trades for gold." Barzelian's elaborately sketched Aztec god, nearly finished, had become a devourer of men.

Goss removed his glasses, squeezed the bridge of his sharp nose. "We have this deal with the Swiss now. Proof of criminal record or intent and we get reasonable access to information. We could find out when and where he goes. Better yet, we could have them call him in."

For a lawyer, Weber thought, Goss was showing some aptitude for conspiracy.

Barzelian bared his multiplicity of small, neat teeth. "Dick, you check out that agreement, you'll find we have to make out a case. I don't see the President going for the idea of telling the Swiss government an ex-CIA man damn near succeeded in taking him out."

That was Weber's cue. "Hank kept up with some of Langley's out-country stringers after he was shown the door. We set most of them straight, but we use one or two to help us keep tabs on Hank."

"It didn't," Goss said thinly, "help too much this time."

50

Weber accepted the rebuke. "Hank made his play and lost out. It's dollars to a thin dime he'd like to know why. And, even more, whether we've figured out where the play started. He'd like to think he has us looking in left field while right field is wide open."

It did the trick. "You're telling me" – Goss was appalled – "he might try again?" He slammed the table. "This guy has to be fixed, and fast."

Weber had inched his way almost, but not quite, home. "We have a contact, smooth operator, who's about due for a meet with Hank. We slip him the occasional small parcel of product, trash-can stuff, that makes Hank think he has the key to Langley's Libyan files."

"Then what are we waiting for?" Goss was suddenly a man in a hurry.

Barzelian looked up finally. "We squelch him? With the President's okay?"

Goss jibbed at the word, not the deed. "The President gave this thing to me. I'm giving it to you. It had better work." Aware that he had stepped beyond the rule of law, he tried to restore a balance. "Rumpus, that was the word I used. Okay, so we have an operation. Why don't I tell the President it's Operation Rumpus?"

Barzelian, nodding ponderously, obliterated his Aztec god.

FOUR

Steve Archer and his red Jaguar arrived, as always, with a flourish, but a keen observer – wasn't Security Directorate full of them? – might have detected the beginnings of restraint. Did he brake more gently, trail slightly less dust than usual? And could it be said – the keen observer should have decided that it could – that his emergence was a trifle portentous, a hint of things to come?

A knighthood, per se, was nothing very much, given his background. What did matter was the certainty, now, of a place in the inner circle. Very shortly he would be a man in a position to know, or find out, and by no means theoretically, almost everything about almost everybody, good, bad or merely – Archer's own ultimate catch-all – criminally misguided.

He came up the weathered steps to the terrace, lit another cigarette, turned to view the small but delightful valley with a distinctly proprietorial air, a man who, given a few years, would be complacent in power. Security Directorate's country training and interrogation centre, universally if coyly known as The Other Place, victim of government parsimony but Palladian for all that, was peculiarly well-matched to Steve Archer's life style.

Eric Pottern gave his master a moment or two in which to enjoy his impending accession, then came respectfully out.

"Eric. Afternoon to you. You have developments, is that right? Paddy been on the blarney?"

"Yours is the biggest development, sir. And the best."

"Good of you to say so."

"When's the big day, sir?" Pottern had resolved to say sir just a little more often, now that it was almost official. He had taken Morpurgo's place; question – who would have to take Archer's?

"End of next month. The Knight's clearing his desk, taking accumulated leave from the weekend. We shan't see him again, not officially."

"Two little worries out of the way, then."

Archer cocked a sardonic eyebrow.

"Poking around at Gatwick without proper authority, for one."

"Yes, let's have that first. Sorry I wasn't around when you first came looking for me. Whitehall calls the tune now." Archer led the way to a terrace seat.

"Safer down here, in a way. Anyway, turns out there was quite a to-do at Gatwick the day before."

"Before what?" Archer watched a dove strut across the worn stone flags. Was this the only government establishment with doves on the strength, or did they have them at Chequers? Soon he would be in a position to find out.

"The day before we waved farewell to the big white bird. Normal traffic, you'll remember. Yank planes over on the north side, well out of the way."

"More security than groundcrew." Archer shuddered. "I remember! What sort of to-do?"

"Libyan charter flight. Passenger had a heart attack, not too serious as it turned out, he took off with the flight."

"That's the funny thing?"

"Half of it. An Arab woman, nationality unknown, might have been on the charter, might not. Diabetic, lost an insulin shot, lot of panic, so Sibley says."

"Sibley saw all this? Why didn't he say anything?"

"He didn't see it. He was there, though, running errands for the Yanks. The point is, general pandemonium in the medical centre for a good twenty minutes, so they told Sibley."

"Ah, Sibley's been back." Archer tapped another cigarette on his monogrammed gold case. He was the only man Pottern knew who still carried cigarettes in a case, monogrammed gold or not. "Go on, damn you."

"There was a period, hard to be sure how long without pressing too hard, when the medical centre wasn't manned. Everyone elsewhere, plus one of the nurses held up on a shift change."

Archer debouched a long stream of smoke. "You interest me."

"It seems some CIA man . . ." Pottern paused maliciously. "Fancy a cup of tea, sir? There's always some brewing in the day office."

"Like me to screw your bloody neck? What CIA man?"

"Yes, well, that's the point. No one direct from Langley was accredited to 'Eagle'. Only Claas's little bunch out of Grosvenor Square."

"You checked with Claas?" Archer was sharp. "No." Pottern's small smile had reassured him. "Don't think we'd want that, would we?"

"I rather thought not. Is it okay if I go on?"

"Far from okay if you don't, saucy bugger. A CIA man."

"Showed up from nowhere. Sorted things out in the medical centre. Quiet but firm, what the heck is going on here? Who are all these people? Still there when the duty doc got back."

"Show his ID?"

"Bush. The second." Pottern smirked. "Timothy Bush the second."

"Not accredited."

"Not on any list we were given."

"What did he want?"

"Nobody seems quite sure, just behaved as if he owned the place. Sibley's done some nice ferreting, very discreet."

"Sibley's a good lad. And friend Bush was around while the medical centre was unattended, minding shop?"

"Looks like it."

"Let's have some of that dreadful tea."

When Pottern returned with two standard-issue cups, blue-rimmed, tea the colour of old brown boots, Archer had done his thinking. "Hardly have expected us to get on to him, could he? Sheer luck, that business with the blood buggy. But you hadn't finished, had you? Anybody see him out on the apron?"

Pottern pulled a face. "This is where it got tricky, ask too many questions, start too many questions. Yes, Cox reckons he was out there at one stage. Remember we sent Cox to tell that Secret Service guy with the twitch, the one Chief Super Placket called Dracula, he was wanted on the phone? Well, Cox fancies he saw Bush out near the Yank planes."

"So he could have got to Air Force One? And blown that fuse."

"Reckon so. Reckon he did. Then vanished."

"But we don't know where." Archer scowled regretfully.

"On the charter flight. With the heart attack and the diabetic woman." Pottern was holding things back and enjoying it. "Incidentally, if that device had gone aboard Air Force One, it would have taken out half the hydraulics."

Archer had just realised something. "Hold on! Cox reckons he was out there? How does Cox know it was this particular merchant?"

Pottern's pleasure was sly. "From the ID."

"*What* bloody ID? Don't tell me he went out of his way to show it to Cox."

"Couldn't have Sibley nosing around too obviously, could I, sir? So Chief Super Capstick shoves a couple of blokes on to it from his Gatwick strength. Always making enquiries, that lot, immigration offences, undesirable aliens, fits in nicely, you might say. Start at the medical centre, people who actually saw him, then passport control, baggage check, so on and so forth. Doing it all the time. Anyway" – Pottern was a man hugging an inner pleasure – "enough to put together a description."

"Identikit." Archer was enlightened.

"No need." Pottern checked a smirk. "Picture."

"A photograph? Where the devil from?"

Pottern picked up their cups. "Come and see the other revelation. It's worth the wait."

Archer looked at his deputy with mingled humour and irritation. "Don't push your luck, chum. I've been known to turn nasty. Is this to do with the comrade? Damned if I see how. How is the comrade, anyway?"

The comrade, confusingly, was not a comrade, not in any sense. Steve Archer referred to everyone on the wrong side of his own unwritten but clearly conceived law as comrade. Espionage, subversion and, as in this case, terrorism; so far as he was concerned they were all manifestations of a diffuse but universal left-wing conspiracy.

The comrade was, in fact, Irish. In Archer's book this made him comrade Paddy, all Irishmen below a certain social level being Paddies. It could be muddling, especially to comrades and

Paddies, leading the unwise to regard Steve Archer as the archetypal British upper-class idiot. Unwise because, within the limits of what Morpurgo called his blinkers or, more precisely, his class blinkers, Archer was nobody's fool. Of course, Morpurgo, too, had his class blinkers. Archer had often, jokingly, called him comrade to his face; also, less jokingly, behind his back.

"Paddy," Pottern said as his chief stood up, "is in a delicate condition."

"Rough, is he?" The Paddy, scooped up in a Special Branch trawl, had been a quartermaster for the Irish National Liberation Army, the extremist breakaway wing of the extremist Provisional IRA.

"Looks, yes. Manners, not any more."

"I trust" – Mock severity – "they've been observing the rules."

"Oh dear me, yes." Pottern looked provocatively at Archer. "Ought you to come close to this any more? The boss should have clean hands. Able to stand up in front of retired judges, committees of enquiry, MPs like Joe Padley, assure them we're all kind at heart."

"Joe Padley" – Like all Curzon Street and Century House people, Archer detested the anti-Establishment, anti-authoritarian, Tribune Group Member of Parliament – "wouldn't believe me if I swore I hadn't eaten any babies since Christmas. Anyway, pretty soon, nothing but the occasional visit of inspection, okay?"

They went into the house through the elegant portico and Pottern rang for admission to the security wing, closed circuit television peering coldly. The release operated. They passed through.

Oates was waiting for them by the little day-staff office where, as always, a kettle was on the boil. He took his cigarette from its perch below his luxurious Stalin moustache. "Afternoon, Mr Archer."

Oates was Senior Medical Attendant, one of Security Directorate's chillier euphemisms, a large man with an air of gruff gentleness at variance with his job. Medical attendants were vulgarly known as dentists, but Oates gave the impression of a man who would only be cruel to be kind.

"Bit dicky today, sir." He fell in a respectful pace behind.

"Chats shook him up a bit, didn't sleep too well, neither." He unlocked another door. The place was a run-down Palladian mansion that, in a new age of enlightenment, had broken out in a rash of wooden huts collectively known as Soapbox City. Like most temporary arrangements by government departments, they had acquired a high degree of permanence.

Number 1 was a case in point, one of a cluster built during the Second World War, when the place had been a nest of mild-mannered scientists dedicated to saving civilisation by developing engines of horror. Oates knocked on the first door down. They waited amid a smell of pine resin, floor wax and antique dust. Someone unlocked and opened the door. It was Chief Superintendent Placket. He came out, closed it behind him.

"Day to you, Chief Superintendent." Archer nodded cheerfully, "I didn't know we had the pleasure."

"Afternoon, sir." Placket had the eyes and face of a man who had heard it all and believed none of it. "Is it in order to offer congratulations yet, sir?"

"A little premature, but thank you. How's the patient?"

"Singing a treat, sir. All we hoped and a little bit more." They went in.

The room was small, hot and crowded. The man in the chair at the centre was older than most of the Paddies they got, foxy-haired rather than black Irish. He had been a smiler, Archer guessed, the soft, sly wit that had made fools of the English over the centuries.

Steve Archer could tell people with sincerity that he liked the Irish, damn it! He also had strong feelings about the sufferings of political prisoners in communist countries, trial without jury, detention without trial, poor bastards, but would tell you it was different in Northern Ireland, only criminals; anyway, fight fire with fire. Their native genius, while admitted, didn't interest him. He was more concerned with settling the hash of anyone whose idea of a blow for freedom was to detonate, often among the innocent, ten or twenty pounds of explosive enriched with six-inch nails.

Behind the Paddy were two more chairs, one of them occupied by the implacable Inspector Garret, relentless for truth and promotion. Young Sibley, strained and a little anxious – Do him

57

good, Archer thought, lad's got to learn the rough side – leaned against the window, nothing outside but blank brick, while Sergeant Vaisey, spare-time martial arts enthusiast and devoted father of two, loomed over the focus of attention.

The Paddy had no marks on him, just the semi-obliteration of gross fatigue and psychological harrassment. Rules were rules, no overt violence. Overt, in the Branch's book, meant anything that showed for more than an hour or so. Placket, a master of the game, had, Archer knew, a highly effective act with a soldering iron up the anus; only switched on long enough to get warm, the story went, the mere hint being wonderfully sufficient.

Placket gestured. Vaisey, putting his bearded, normally friendly face very close, said, "Tell again about the picture, Patrick."

There was a long silence. Vaisey looked at Placket. Placket nodded. Vaisey and Garret closed in. Sibley shifted uneasily.

Before anything could happen, the man, his voice harsh, exhausted, said, "Didn't I tell you now? I know nothing more, they don't explain. You work to a cut-off and that's the whole truth of it."

"Don't know what, Patrick?"

"Names. Mother of God, names!"

"Only one name, Patrick. The one in the picture, tell it again."

The silence grew. The man's mouth suddenly gaped.

"Cut that out!" Archer's voice was calm but firm.

Placket took over, macho toughness in a grey Daks suit. "You're going down, Patrick. For a long, long time." His voice pressed, bully in velvet. "Have they told you what happens? Very moral, your average English villain, patriotic too, strong feelings about scum who blow up kids, horses, old ladies. Rough justice, Patrick, very rough when you're down for twenty years. Do yourself a favour, he's not one of yours."

Astonishingly, the man laughed, weak and breathless, but still a laugh. "Will you listen to this one, now? Well, he's not one of ours, isn't that the truth? He's for himself, that one, money, not causes. Yank bastard!"

"He? Who's he, Patrick?"

"Timothy, haven't I said it ten times already?" Pottern saw Archer stiffen.

"Timothy. Timothy what?"

"Timothy nothing. Hank. Hank Timothy, devil take him."

Back in the corridor, Archer hazarded a guess. "Well, Eric, you don't waste time. The – what did you call it? – microchip moron has its uses after all, yes?"

"I take it all back about that computer. I've wanted to put a name to that face ever since we snatched the shots."

"You're a smart chap, Eric. Let's see if I can keep up with you." In high good humour, Archer slid an arm through Pottern's, leading him back to the terrace.

"You – Sibley, anyway, credit where credit's due – managed to put together a fair description of the gent who claimed to be CIA. Then . . . let's see. Passport control, right? Yes, you got some sort of general ID from Sibley and Cox, put it to the duty immigration control officers, must have seen this chap, yes? Yes, minds like rat-traps. So you whipped them up to Horseferry Road, sat them down in front of that visual display unit, produced George Ridout and his light pen. George does some of his lightning sketches on the visual display screen. Sooner or later your blokes say, "That's him! Dead to rights!" George presses all the buttons, the electronic oracle comes up with a classification. George goes to the files and out pops – what? A dossier?"

"This, sir." Pottern wheeled his master into the little office used by Vickers, the establishment medical officer, when he was not in the bar.

The shot, as Pottern had indicated, was a snatch, taken unaware with a telephoto lens. As so often is the case, the subject appeared to be looking straight at the camera.

Fiftyish, good-looking in a fleshy sort of way. Women, Archer could see, might find him attractive, an air of know-it-all sophistication, but the main impression was hard-nosed confidence bordering on arrogance.

"*That* one!"

"That one. Gaddafi's Yank. Knew we'd get an ID some day." Pottern, entitled to triumph, showed none.

"You say Yank, Eric. They deny it. A copy of this print went to Langley through Claas. According to Claas, Langley circulated it high and low, got nowhere."

"Yank all the same." Pottern said it with certainty. "And

Paddy's just confirmed it. Remember where we got that picture, sir?"

"Vienna. Rathausplatz, outside the Sluka cafe. The Paddies were shopping for high velocity rifles." Archer laughed. "You weren't supposed to be there. All hell if you'd been caught out by the Centurions."

"He had an American accent, couldn't mistake it."

"Doesn't make him American, Eric. Half the English speakers in Europe have American accents, days of the Raj are over."

"He's Yank." Pottern was stubborn. "And he worked for Gaddafi's people. Correction. Works. Somebody had to be paying him for taking a crack at the President."

Archer headed for the sunlight. It was going to be hard when he took over from the Knight, stuck indoors most days, half the nights too, not counting all the high-level socialising. "Okay." He was good-humoured. "He's a Yank if you want him to be a Yank. And he's taken up an American national sport – get the President. Only he didn't."

Pottern tagged on behind, waving away a cloud of tiny insects. Londoner born, he wasn't so keen on the country as his boss. Archer stopped at the edge of the terrace, sucking in air and scenery. He could see a glint of light on the stream in the valley bottom. "A hush-up, Eric. A nice, neat hush-up in Washington. Why? one wonders."

"Face, sir? Loss of, I mean."

"Oh, that, certainly. Speaks pretty poorly for presidential security, especially after all that fuss. But there has to be more to it."

"Do we drop it?" Pottern, waiting anxiously, eyed a dove. White pigeon, really, what was so special? Crapped all over the place just like pigeons, too.

"Drop it?" The Director-General designate, knight-to-be, was crisp. "Like hell! They buried a body. Let's see if we can dig it up. Time we reasserted ourselves in Washington, Eric, now the Knight's off. Back into Uncle Sam's arms, one up on Epworth and the Friends, top dogs on the Joint Intelligence Committee. Knowledge is power, Eric. So is a little friendly blackmail.

*　　　*　　　*

Morpurgo's visits to his mother were circular tours of Wandsworth and his conscience. There was no great regularity, though he tried for it. This time he went by himself. Sylvie was out with *Time-Life* people from New York, a business thing.

"I think it's disgusting." His mother had attached herself, leech-like, to her favourite topic. "This one chap, more than six foot he must have been, black as the inside of my cellar. Had the cheek to ring my bell and ask me how much I'd take for the house."

"'It's not for sale,' I tell him, 'not so long as I have breath to run it.' What do you think he did? cheeky beggar!" A neaptide of indignation. "Laughed, then put his arms round me, big black hands, hugged me like a kid. I'm a fine old lady, if you please, and I shall stay as long as I like, but he wants to buy me out when I don't like it any longer. Cheeky devil!"

She took his plate with an angry rattle of cutlery. "I think it's disgusting. This used to be a decent neighbourhood."

Morpurgo was making his usual series of small, neutral noises, sympathy without commitment. "Times change, mum. Long time since it was all-white."

She looked at her distant yesterdays as if over a low, still scaleable wall, her fallen, pudgy face set in trench warfare lines of intractability. "Good middle-class area, this was. Look at it now. And the shop, proper shop it was when we had it, nice customers, decent English stuff. Now! Gumbo, chow-chows, whatever they call them, nasty muck. Why, our customers would have thrown it at us." She was talking of fifty years ago.

"Times were different, mum." It was all he ever seemed to say; culpable inadequacy. "It's getting on forty years since granddad sold out."

"Thirty-seven last November."

Inside his head a voice began: *He cried when he locked up* . . .

"He cried when he locked up for the last time." Even she said it as if by rote. "Had to take the keys to the estate agent and he cried all the way, your dad said." She would have liked to blame the blacks for that too, only they hadn't arrived then.

"He'd cry a damn sight more if he could see it now. And your dad, what would he say? Taught decent English lads, poor but

61

decent. Why, do you know? when they come out of school now, you have to look twice to find a white face."

He could hardly remember his father; self-effacing, ineffectual, a ghost before he died. The landscape of his past was over-shadowed by his mother, endlessly and inexplicably making him aware that he was different. Better, cleaner, no bad language or roughness, books of his own and a mapped-out future. The race was not to the swift but those who sounded their aitches.

What happened after he left university she saw as betrayal. Research assistant with the TUC; a sell-out to the shiftless working-class. Recruitment by Security Directorate on the strength of his anti-Trot activities, worse; a common policeman.

He had not troubled to explain his recent move, just a casual mention that he now worked south rather than north of the river. She had shown no interest.

"You know you don't have to stay here, mum."

She loved this one. "Come and live with you and Sylvie, is it? Oh, I know she says it, and I dare say she thinks she means it. I know different. It wouldn't work. You're never there, either of you. Spain! Would Sylvie give up taking snaps and stay at home? Would you get a decent job, nine to five like most folks?" Decent, for his mum, was the way things would be in Heaven.

"And would you move house? Only space you've got spare there is right at the top, I can just see me managing all those stairs. Doctor says the ones I've got here are too much, though he didn't say what I was supposed to do about it."

"When did you see the doctor, mum?" Sylvie, prescient as always, had given him a hint, he remembered.

"I forget. Last week sometime." The vagueness was deliberate. "Mind, not even then if it hadn't been for Mrs Wagner at Number 27. 'I'm not going to that surgery,' I said. 'Sitting there an hour or more with a roomful of blacks.' I think it's disgusting, pay no taxes, don't even work, breed like rabbits, and free medical treatment."

It *was* disgusting! He bloody well shouldn't let her get away with it. "But you went."

"I didn't. He came here, thanks to Mrs Wagner." A certain relish. She knew she had him in a moral stranglehold.

"What did he say?"

"A lot of rubbish, I dare say."

"There must have been something."

"Shan't know, shall we? Not until after the X-ray."

"When's the X-ray?" She had him on the rack.

"Next week, that and some other thing." He saw her hand descend unconsciously to spread itself across her lower abdomen. "Whatever they call it, couldn't be bothered to remember." Illness was weakness, lack of will.

"What sort of thing? What's it for?"

"They look inside you, some sort of tube."

"I'll take you."

"They'll fetch me. And bring me back."

"I'll come and see you straight after." Oh, guilt, you monster! And concomitant with it, a growing urge to look at his watch.

She was psychic in things like that. "You'll be wanting to be off. Well, at least you've had a decent meal. It isn't right, Sylvie being out so much." She knew nothing about the present relationship between him and Sylvie, nothing about its cause.

He bent to kiss her drooping cheek. As usual, she made no response. "Sylvie's talking about moving. Don't worry. We'll fix something up for you."

"You've yourselves to think about. I'll manage, don't you fret."

Through the narrowing gap of the door as he closed it, he had a last glimpse of her face, vacant as the shop that had made granddad cry as he walked away.

*　　　*　　　*

Two cars out of the millions, one from the east, one the west, the same destination. And the same purpose, the meet Barzelian had proposed to settle the hash of Hank Timothy. Neither of them knew for certain of the other. Everything was through third parties, an assumption headed toward an assumption.

The driver from the west had taken the road to Villaba, minor routes, traversing the smile of Basque Navarra, sun stinging the vivid browns and greens of fields and pastures. The gateway to the great valley was a thumbprint of darker green, halfway to the horizon.

At last, at Lumbier, the driver swung north, crossing the racketing tumble of the River Irati toward Navascués. The fewer who saw him, this side of the meet, the better. Chasing the endlessly winding tarmac toward the mountains, he stopped only when the Rio Salazar, grappling with its non-stop assault course, was little more than a cataract bisecting the slow explosion of the Pyrenean spring.

A track dropped steeply and invisibly to the water. He pulled off, relieved himself, picked his way down to drink from the icy tumble, splashing his face to refresh himself after the all-night drive. The intense sunlight dried his skin almost instantly.

Back at the car, hidden from the road, he peeled back the carpeting, adhesive yielding reluctantly. The soft bundle came like an egg from the nest. He unwrapped it. The sun conjured the delicate exhalation of oil from the parts of the dismantled sniper's rifle and its silencer, like fragrance from a blossom. He assembled, checked, nodded his satisfaction, stripped it down and re-wrapped it. Minutes later, the hired car gunned up the steep, unsurfaced slope on a comet's-tail of dust and small pebbles.

The descent on Ochagavía was unexpected; a small sawmill on a corner, a bridge to cross and he was back on the river as it churned, straight and managed, through a village no more than two or three houses wide up the steep slopes. The houses were sturdy; cut stone, steep-pitched slate roofs, a tiny bar dark and empty, no life in the noonday lull other than a dog sunning itself against a wall.

Just as he was congratulating himself on being through and away, a dusty green Land Rover emerged from a narrow alley by the church and paused waiting his approach. His left hand left the wheel to pat his hidden pistol, though a shoot-out would be unthinkable. Soldiers, four of them in their green uniforms and pecked caps, three with machine pistols resting, butt down, on their thighs, the ubiquitous anti-Basque terrorist patrol. None of them showed the smallest curiosity. Through his rear mirror he saw the Land Rover turn away from him, heading back the way he had come. This was terrorist country. You could be stopped, searched, shot.

That was the last place of habitation. He was up among the high peaks now, snow-capped crests and pinnacles topping upper slopes that contrasted their tawny flanks with the intense green of shrubs and woodland. He came to a junction, one road

back to Uztarróz, the other on to the pass. A notice said PUERTO
ABIERTO. The pass could not long have been open, or the snows
long gone. He shook his head at this extreme choice in seclusion.
Langley!

The huge, bare reaches began to swell, annexing and then
becoming the landscape. The sheep pastures had hardly begun to
green, the road a grey, serpentine ribbon in a majesty of solitude.

He checked his watch. Timing perfect.

The stillness struck as deeply as intense cold, permeating the
being through the open driving window. The sun was laser-
bright, the sky drawing the eyes to a blue, unfocussable infinity.
Tiny clouds were being born from the tip of Monte Gastarría,
drifting lazily away in puffs of milky smoke. High to the east he
picked out a pair of dots in the azure; golden eagles.

The birds swung in his direction, coming to inspect, but the
time was no longer theirs to use. The border post, a sturdy brick
building designed to stand the rigours of the snows for seven
months of the year, came into sight over the huge shoulder. A
guard sauntered out. The driver geared down to walking pace,
received a wave, gave a passing nod, and drove on. It would be at
the point of entry that he would be stopped.

Roughly twenty-five kilometres, they had said at the briefing,
nearly fifteen miles, between the Spanish post and the French.
Now he understood. The land belonged to the eagles, a tawny,
abandoned world. High to the west, snow-draped, the Pic d'Orny
signalled the approach to the col. The frontier actually ran across
its crest, but the last few meters of the summit were on the French
side. Who, he wondered, had made that decision, and for what
imagined advantage? Crazy continent! Crazy world!

He steered into the first descending hairpin, hauling against
gravity and centrifugal force and, in spite of his foreknowledge,
was taken by surprise, the two men emerging as if by partheno-
genesis from the great roadside boulders. Each had a knitted
helmet of white wool, only a slit for the eyes. Each slung an Uzi
machine pistol. They were Basque outlaws, terrorists, dangerous.
The CIA was cooperating with killers; so what was new?

One stood back, watching the upper and lower reaches of the
road. The other indicated a stopping place. The land dropped all
but vertically, three or four hundred metres. Far below, he saw

the other car, a speck of blue, a winking diamond where the sun caught glass or brightwork.

Another peeling back of the carpet, another extraction of the hard-centred bundle. The two men watched dispassionately as he assembled the gun, chose his spot, lowered himself to the ground, straddled his legs. He would be expected to put on a good show.

He did. Far below, the man he had come to kill, cigarette still between his lips, went down like a Langley training dummy, knees bending forward, trunk back, to slither, sitting, against the car. Nobody spoke. His two scouts joined him in his car. They drove down. He knew where he would find the film, the safest place, in the camera.

His target still breathed, bubbling blood, ivory-complexioned under scarlet warpaint. The man who had come to the rendezvous from the west snapped free his pistol, fired once, carefully. A small, fine sleet of brain and bone fragments Jackson Pollocked the door panel. He leaned into the car to take the camera.

He slipped the brake. The three of them, replacing the dead man in his seat, heaved to start the car moving, one of the Basques steering for a few seconds through the open window. The car developed its own vitality, lurched suddenly, took off. They watched it go, wheeled at first, then an unguided missile, three or four wild bounds and a short free flight before it struck rock. The sound of its end took a measurable fraction of time to reach them.

The man from the west handed over the rifle and a box of ammunition to his ETA accomplices, pulled a package of banknotes from an inside pocket, proffered it. One of the masked pair took it, dropped it inside his blouse equally negligently, the wool of his helmet stretching a little as he smiled. Seconds later, the two of them were devoured by the boulders. No one had spoken from start to finish. Operation Rumpus, as Dick Goss had christened it in the White House Situation Room, might be said to be over.

The driver, gulping chilled *Moët et Chandon* air, opened the door of his matching blue car, switched documents with those taped behind its sunshield, changed the plates. He drove toward France, far down the multiple twists of the road, the camera jouncing casually on the front passenger seat. At the Larrau frontier post, the French would pass him through and await, if the Spanish border guards had bothered to telephone this early in the season, the arrival of the second car.

He wondered how Barzelian and DCI would break the news, when it reached them, to the President.

*   *   *

"Don't get in a state over your mother." Sylvie was checking her cameras, one after the other. She set and triggered the Hasselblad repeatedly, listening with concentration to the shutter action. Finally satisfied, she laid it aside. "I know you, Johnny. Guilt is no substitute for understanding, so just try to understand."

She transferred her attention to the little Olympus. All three cameras had just been serviced, but this was her unvarying routine, not sterile, obsessive perfectionism, just nothing left to chance.

"She's old. She made you what you are, good and bad, all with the best of intentions. Now she's lost you, lost everything, really." She flipped open the back of the camera, triggered, squinting through the lens system on time exposure.

"You outgrew her, long ago. She knows you're far cleverer, far more experienced and capable, it's what she wanted for you. All the same, it brings a kind of resentment, you know, even if it's unreasonable. You don't appreciate what she did for you. You consider yourself superior. You find her irritating, rather pathetic, and . . ."

She saw him about to protest. "I know! I know! I'm just putting her point of view, not agreeing with her. You can get me another drink, not so heavy with the gin this time."

He got them both another drink. The setting, superficially, was domestic, Mozart limpid on the hi-fi, Sylvie squatting yoga-style on a heap of cushions, surrounded by her professional gear. Morpurgo himself found his mind split between the music, his mother and the continuing mess of his personal circumstances.

"She's sick. I could tell. I should have seen it before."

"She wants your attention, Johnny. Give her that much. The

67

rest is being taken care of, a specialist, hospital care, a proper investigation. Wait until she has the result before you start working yourself into a state."

He put her drink beside her, looking down on the soft crown of her head and feeling a crude, basic need to enfold her, to press his lips against that pale, silky hair, that would be at least as much for his own comfort as hers.

But first, months on from Helga, they must find their solution, and it was inextricably entangled in his own change of circumstances.

She found a brush, whisked it skilfully over whatever part of the camera needed the attention. He knew as little of her professional skills as she of his.

She was nothing if not shrewd. "Poor old boy, it's not just that, is it?"

Time to be candid. "It's everything."

"I know. And you think I'm hard. Trying to drive a hard bargain."

He tried, unsuccessfully, to look the opposite. She laughed.

"Two difficult women. Poor old Johnnie."

"Not so funny. Not really." He was walking on glass.

She knew it. "No. That's why we have to deal with it, once and for all. I'm glad I'm going away."

"Time to think."

"Time to think." Very carefully, she said, "And there will be, won't there? For you, I mean."

No use denying it any longer. "I'm off liaison. Epworth didn't say it in so many words, but now Steve's taking over I'm going to be persona even less grata with Curzon Street."

"Well, there you are." She nibbled her lip, unusual for Sylvie in this particular situation. She did care. It was just that her processes and his were different. Something of her suppressed feelings surfaced. "All right, I'm a bitch, a cold bitch won't settle it one way or the other. It isn't" – Oh God! She sensed a watery glitter in her eyes – "that I don't care enough. I care too much. I have to be sure, Johnny. This time I have, absolutely, positively, beyond the smallest shadow of doubt, to be sure. Because I couldn't go through this again.

"I know!" She said it quickly, anticipating his response. "It won't happen again." She knew it would have been as much reflex as truth. She set everything aside, careful but quick, the camera, the paraphernalia, the battered old camera bag he had tried to replace with something smart and sturdy until she had pointed out that it had to look shabby to avoid the attention of thieves and snatchers, had to be padded to protect its contents, had, above all, to fit under her seat when she flew, since it was out of the question that it should go in the baggage hold.

She was going to say, he realised, that Steve, like the rest of this bloody shambles, was his fault, no one but himself to blame.

She said, "Steve won't be as good in the job as you if he lives to be a hundred, but Steve doesn't matter now, does he? Not if you don't let him." She smiled, everything under control now. "What do you do, Johnny? Tell me, honestly. What do you really do?"

"Read files. Hundreds of files. Apart from going to meetings where I don't understand more than five per cent of what's going on. Don't understand more than five per cent of what I read, either." It was almost a relief to admit it. And it put him at her mercy.

She sank her drink at a gulp, suddenly tossed the glass at him. He caught it by reflex, diamonds arcing about it. "There!" She looked mischievous. "Took you by surprise, something unsuspected from cool, calculating Sylvie. There's plenty more where that came from."

She got up. She still moved like a young girl. She sank in her favourite chair, kicking off her shoes, curling up with her feet beneath her like a cat. "Do you understand what I'm saying, Johnny? Uncalculated. Unsuspected. Words that haven't been in your book for the past twenty years. With your kind of people, everything's calculation, suspicion, mistrust. Professional mistrust. What" – She said it lightly, and he blessed her for it – "a way to make a living!"

The Mozart came to an end. He got up to lift the stylus. Steve in the ascendant. Epworth, shawm, crumhorn and songs of Crusader treason, all set, behind his girlish giggle, to make sure that Steve, Curzon Street, anyone at Century House who didn't know which side his bread was buttered, would find the dark stairways of their joint business equally but more dangerously buttered, the smyler with the knyf under the cloke.

69

And the rest? They didn't even smile.

"I'll put through my resignation tomorrow, no idea how long it will take."

"No." The second time she had used the word, but, this time, no vehemence. She shook her head and her honey hair danced silkily. "Not like that, Johnny, down in the dumps, everything against you. If you do do it, I want it to be out of conviction, not from a sense of defeat. I'm off to bed."

Without troubling to replace her shoes, she padded lightly over, placed her carefully clinical kiss on his cheek, departed.

FIVE

"Bar, come on in." DCI waved Barzelian to a seat. DCI was a relatively modest man, particularly for Washington. His large, bright office in the "A" zone, a better class of hush, was relatively modestly furnished, good but not showy; pictures of his family, his dogs, the cabin in the woods on the shore of Lake Little Eagle, also a framed certificate in Finnish proclaiming him a Knight of the Sauna-Seura of Waskiniemi. Otherwise, the only ornament was his brass orrery, English, 1773 and authenticated, a model of the solar system that could be cranked by hand. Barzelian insisted that it represented DCI's sublimated power complex.

Wheezing gently, Barzelian dropped something on the desk, a spool of undeveloped film that, by a circuitous route, had travelled all the way from the high Pyrenees to Langley.

"We cleaned off the blood first." Barzelian, dumping himself in his chair, was a load of stripped bedding.

"Shot like a dog, right?" DCI flipped the spool. In spite of his bulk, Barzelian caught it.

"With Hank Timothy, nothing is by halves. Anyway, it had to look real, like those people weren't playing pattycake. Hank got away by the skin of his teeth, we got the plans of the fort. We made sure the story hit the Spanish press. Well," Barzelian conceded, "some sort of a story, Basque terrorists strike again. The meat's in the Pamplona morgue. You want me to have these shots developed?"

"Make sure whoever does it can't read French."

71

"They spell nuke pretty well the way we do. Still and all" –
Barzelian, with much heavy breathing, inserted the spool in a
pocket – "I take the point. So much as a sniff of that French
warhead technology and those guys in weapons research will be
swarming all over us hollering, "Gimme! Gimme!""

"The only thing that stopped the President going through the
roof at another screwed-up hit was the news that we stopped
Gaddafi getting warhead technology for his missiles. The Libs
couldn't put that stuff together, French knowhow or not, in a
month of Sundays, but it might have helped them do a deal with
Iraq or the Pakistanis."

"But Hank is still on the hook."

DCI wagged his head ruefully. "Hank is still on the hook, and
so are we. We come up with something fast, or the man in the
White House is going to hand Langley over to the Feds."

Barzelian settled his head more comfortably on his chins. "So
we just got a break, thanks to Dick Goss."

"The stuff from Mark Folger about Cochran's oil from shale
process? Well, maybe. Is Folger right to worry that much?"

"I just talked it over with the people on the third floor,"
Barzelian said. "Scholes knows oil the way you know stud poker,
and those Mid-East destabilisation studies Black and Kulish
made went dollar by dollar into the effects of falling oil prices on
Western and Third World economies. Folger's right to be worried,
it all comes down to greed."

DCI produced a bark of grim laughter. "No kidding! Go
on."

Barzelian was sinking into his chair like a collapsing soufflé.
"Imagine, if you will, a posted price for crude of a giveaway two
dollars a barrel. Some guy develops a process to make it at one
dollar ninety-five, a queue of other guys is going to line up
behind him hoping to get rich. They'll worry about the world
economy the way a lush worries about cirrhosis of the liver."

"But Cochran's process flopped."

"It flopped this time round. And it was illegal, so for a while he
dances to our tune. But there's always a next time. Brew Cochran
will get back at Big Oil and the Libyans if it takes his own blood."

"Getting back at the Libyans the President would buy. We
have to look like we're getting back at Hank Timothy too, or he's

going to find other people for the job, people we wouldn't want to have nosing around anything to do with Hank, the Libs, that whole scene."

DCI left his desk to come and stoop, his mouth an inch from Barzelian's pink and chubby ear. "Or do you want the President to get to hear all about that screwed-up hit at Gatwick, too? You want them to find out Hank was our boy on that job?"

Barzelian quivered to make himself more comfortable. "Can we have Pierre up now?"

DCI, straightening up, stood over him for several seconds with the air of a man contemplating how to get the toothpaste back into the tube. He sighed. Sticking his head into the outer office, he said, "Get Pierre Weber up here, will you?" He came back to take a dark blue folder from his desk, the scarlet TOP SECRET logo a silent shout. He used it to catch fragments of tobacco while he filled the pipe he would not smoke until this thing was settled. "I was just asking Bar," he said when Weber had pulled up a chair, "if you see all the Bombing Encyclopedia stuff?"

"Only our own Significant Summary Statements." Mention of the Bombing Encyclopedia, with its fifty thousand prime and eighty thousand secondary targets, always made Weber unhappy. One particular thing he was never able to forget was that it had a fat and even more secret supplement known as the Contingency Annex. It listed thousands of additional targets in allied and neutral countries that might be taken out in nuclear strikes if some future war saw them overrun or threatened by enemy forces.

DCI opened the blue folder. "This is the extract of Libyan entries. You can get through it in a couple of minutes, even including the non-nukes."

Weber went very uptight. "It's got that far?"

"Just making a point." DCI ran a finger down a page. "Three oil terminals, Ras Sidar, Ras Lanuf, Marsa el Brega. Two refineries, one at Marsa el Brega, the other, Benghazi, all on the Gulf of Sidra. Third strike category. Refineries Baker Tango 2, terminals Baker Echo 3 and 4, with a marine overrun upgrade if the Sovs ever took over. Class, Strat/Tact optional."

He turned a page. "A bunch of Echo Dog 3s here, out on the

oilfields. Pumping stations, that kind of stuff. And another pipe-
line, Jao-Tobruk. All low-grade options, short of a land threat.

"Take out one in two of those options" – He closed the file –
"bye-bye Libya."

"This," Weber said dryly, "has to be a real dipsy-doodle."
Barzelian chuckled.

"Suppose" – DCI laid a tentative hand on the solar system –
"There was another way of knocking Libya out of the oil
business."

"Suppose," Barzelian said, hamming it up a little, "hogs shat
flapjacks and syrup."

Weber waited.

"Suppose," DCI went on, "Hank Timothy came to hear of it."

"That's just the kind of threat the Libyans pay Hank to head
off." Barzelian rotated his head to look at Weber. "Isn't it?"

Weber studied each of them in turn. "Some fancy thing that
knocks out a whole oil industry. Non-nuclear."

Barzelian corrected him. "Some fancy stuff that takes out crude
oil. That turns crude into crud, just the way you turn milk into
yoghurt."

"What is this stuff?" Weber had never looked more politely
disbelieving. "Stardust?"

DCI nodded. "Kind of." As if that answered everything, he
turned to Barzelian. "Just one snag." He opened the Bombing
Encyclopedia extract again. "Only one field on the coast. One
small field, about twenty kilometres from Benghazi. Rest are in
deep desert, anything up to four hundred kilometres in."

"Four hundred klicks?" Barzelian managed a convincing imi-
tation of the President in one of his cold rages. "What are you
wild men trying to talk me into? Choppers, airborne troops,
offshore carrier support in the Gulf of Sidra? Jesus, Mr Director!
What we could end up with here is something worse than Carter's
Iran fiasco! Abandoned choppers, good men dead, the whole
world in an uproar? Not to mention Congress!"

Weber, retreating farther and farther into some subterranean
redoubt, reached his final conclusion. "Or we could enlist Hank."

They stared at him like a pair of basilisks waiting for petri-
faction to set in.

"For a price," Weber said gravely, "my bet is that he'd stuff

74

the wells with stardust. Cash, big money. An amnesty. Then he settles in Dominica, Anguilla, St Lucia, just like we did with Lebenson and Morello. At that kind of price he's buyable."

"Another snag," Barzelian discovered. "Hank wouldn't trust us. Even the President would think of that." He looked sorrowful.

"That's right," Weber said. "Another meet on a mountain to discuss the deal, and he takes out our boy."

"Hm." Barzelian's sloe-eyed, heavy face burrowed into its chins. "Intermediary? Talks about talks, tokens of good faith, that kind of crap?"

Weber, pushing the train of his thoughts through underground tunnels, headed for the gleam of daylight, having had the advantage all along of knowing what Barzelian had in mind. "The British."

"Epworth?" DCI looked contemptuous at the very mention of the name.

"He wouldn't expect it to be Epworth." Barzelian was wilfully obtuse. "And Hank's not the type to deal with the average British fieldman. He wasn't exactly the average Langley fieldman himself."

He pretended to think. "Come to that, SIS do have someone who's not the average British fieldman. Kind of person Hank might get quite a kick out of dealing with."

DCI, fiddling with his orrery, abandoned worlds to their fate. "What's his desk? Oh, wait, is that the guy who . . . ?"

Barzelian, who had had it all worked out from the start, sat back. "Sure, that's the guy who. Morpurgo."

Weber, resignedly, said, "And I'm the guy who, right?"

"How soon can you leave?" DCI asked him, longing for his pipe.

*   *   *

Heading into the tunnel that took the road under the main runway, Morpurgo thought one of his perennially reusable thoughts, that if there was one thing worse than air travel, it was the befores and afters of air travel, particularly when, as now, you were late.

Sylvie read his mind. "Not the best of incentives, is it?"

"For what?" He knew what.

75

"My offer you're supposed to be unable to refuse." The fluorescents flashed hypnotically by above them, yellow light locking them into a sterile and inhuman unreality. Parking, he thought, miserably; I'll never find anywhere to park.

"I accepted."

"You agreed. Not the same thing." They emerged from the tunnel to be faced with the mad welter of a Heathrow welcome, as if the entire British construction industry was using the place as a dumping ground prior to more important operations elsewhere.

"I'll put you down and find you after I've parked."

"Iberia desk."

"Yes." Even conversation disintegrated in these mentally dismembering surroundings. "I might be some time. And you haven't got much."

"I'll wait. You'll find somewhere." He listened to her with one portion of his riven mind while another gauged airport coaches, other cars, trucks, delivery vans and a variety of two-legged hazards.

Per me si va nella citta dolente. The words emerged from a newly exposed sub-layer of mind. When they were both little more than children and had been idiotically in love, Sylvie learning Italian, they had had a shared passion for Dante.

Per me si va nell' eterno dolore. Per me si va tra la perduta gente . . . the sorrowful city . . . eternal suffering . . . lost people. Dante had known all about airports. *Abandon all hope, you who enter*!

He squeezed in behind a departing taxi, scurried frenetically to extract her baggage. She conjured a porter where none had been.

She smiled. "I did say, not just to carry my baggage. I can always find people to do that."

She took her camera case herself, although she could watch dispassionately as the system devoured her expensive baggage with the probability that it would appear freshly scuffed, the possibility that it would not reappear at all.

She called. "Iberia desk. Then we've just time for a drink." Another taxi, sensing his imminent departure as sharks scent blood, was leaving him just enough room to get out.

He queued to enter the multistorey carpark, fretted while a car in front turned the wrong way, squeezed past it to reach the first ramp. No point in looking on the lower levels; he took four with a nonstop squeal of stressed rubber before beginning the agonising crawl. This need not be happening. He could be flying Iberia too.

Others, too, were crawling. It was a jungle in which, between massed rows of metal, he caught an occasional glimpse of lurking threat, ready to scorch at a deadly ten or fifteen miles an hour at the merest glimpse of sanctuary, the pattern of his life in not-so-slow motion. This floor, nothing. He went on up.

Was her flight ten or twenty minutes past the hour? Where was the Iberia desk? How long before they started summoning victims to the inner reaches of hell? This floor, nothing either. He roared up the ramp suicidally.

Nothing. Nothing. Nothing! Round again. Somebody *must* be about to leave. All these bloody cars must be over their time. Half of them, he was bloody certain, should probably be in the long-term parks. Nothing. Nothing. The pattern of his life, always seeking, never finding what was seldom worth looking for to begin with.

If he had any sense, the voice whispered, *he* would be in a long-term carpark; not he; they; the car. He would be with Sylvie, sitting in comfort – he had more than a suspicion she travelled first-class – having a drink in the first-class passengers' lounge where limbo was at least equipped with plush seats.

Nothing!

The flight was at ten past. It was five to, now, this minute. He had been scouring this . . . this concrete *pisshouse* for at least ten minutes. It was his fault they had been late.

He stopped at a corner of the level – what the hell number floor was he on anyway? – reversed on to the yellow diagonal stripes of a no-parking area. Let them find him. Let them fine him. It was their responsibility to provide adequate parking.

In the midst of his anguish, a sardonic gleam of humour. *They*! He, too, was they – faceless authority, unloved, unsung, a state-provided cat's-paw that could take the heat satisfyingly and – from their point of view – painlessly when things went wrong.

Locking the car, he thought, let them bloody well find him, leave him a ticket. He would take their ticket and shred it small.

And if they tracked him down, he would produce his own credentials, show them he was a they too, bigger than them, so that they too must creep away muttering a savage "*They*". God! he told himself, his was a loathsome job.

He was on the seventh level, for Christ's sake! The lifts were elsewhere. The lifts were always elsewhere. He barged through a scuffed and scratched door, ran through echoing flights, endless aerosol graffiti, mindless as snail-trails.

She was still there in the tumult, serene as a new moon on a blue April evening.

"You don't need me to manage you. I need you." He fought for breath. He was getting old, hair thinning, skin drying out.

She laughed. "It would be mutually beneficial. We should have started earlier. There isn't even time for a drink, I'm afraid."

"You ought to go soon." The door was open to a possible new world, the vista not just inviting but infinitely desirable. What had Doc Vickers, medical officer and resident drunk at Security Directorate's country rest-home, called him and all of them in his kind of work? Parasites on the body politic, sahib. Crabs infesting the national pudenda, the shameful parts.

He said, "I mean it, Sylvie. I've made up my mind."

"Good." She was smiling at him the whole time, a small, intimately understanding smile that X-rayed whatever he had in place of a soul. "Now you'll have plenty of time to find out whether you want to unmake it." Her hand rested, butterfly-light, on his sleeve. "And so will I."

The only thing he could say was, "You'd better go." He knew she liked to keep ahead of the clock in her professional affairs, time her slave rather than master. He, in his job, in himself, was the opposite.

He bent to pick up her camera case, bloody heavy really; extra lenses, hoods, filters, enough film to photograph a regiment of soldiers one by one.

There was still a little time. They both knew it, but there are occasions when it is better to conspire against the tick of the clock. She took the bag. "If you don't mind, then. Start off in the right frame of mind, stay in the right frame of mind, surprising how often it's true." They stood, two intimate strangers in all this Boschian hell of the transient.

"Have a good trip. And take care. And give my love to your parents." The Costa Dorada villa had been Sylvie's father's particular self-indulgence. Her mother's style was much glossier; Cannes, Cap Ferrat, the most expensive mountains in winter. Sylvie was flying to Barcelona, where she would collect her hire car and visit them before heading south and west.

"I will." She knew what he thought of her parents, and they of him, all well-meaning and mutually alien extra-terrestrials. "And you take care of yourself. I'll ring when I can, promise."

Unexpectedly, she was pressed close, her scent seducing his senses, her soft hair against his face, lips light but warm on his cheek. "Be certain, please, Johnny. One way or the other, you must be certain."

She stepped away, smiling her small but totally comprehending smile. "Bye, my darling."

He watched her walk away, the scruffy camera bag contrasting absurdly with her bandbox elegance.

Nel mezzo del camin di nostra via. The Divine Comedy! His memory had returned to the same corner of the ragbag. They were indeed *nel mezzo del camin*, in the middle of their life's road, but were they going in the same direction?

*   *   *

Warren Claas knew nothing of Weber's presence in London until Weber showed up at the embassy. "Oh-oh! When did you get in?"

Claas's square, bas-relief face, still Huckleberry Finnishly freckled in middle age, suggested slow wits, which was false and useful. Weber knew him well. They were both third-generation German-Americans. Weber's family had settled in St Louis, where the French connection still lingers. Weber's grandfather had been an Alsatian cross-breed, also called Pierre. Claas's family, Thuringians, had gone to Kansas City. Although Claas was a double graduate, he shared many of his educated country-men's habit of mauling the language, leading Weber to call him a cowtown hick.

"What kind of a welcome is that, junior?" Weber took his favourite chair, the red leather one with a button missing.

"*Ciao!* Welcome. When did you get in? Why wasn't I told?"

79

"I'm not here yet, that's why."

"Oh-oh!"

"You just said that. I'm here because Langley has a job for you and you need to have your hand held."

"The hell I do!"

"On this one, the hell you do." Weber went into details on the job. Di Pasolino, sticking his head in without knocking, wondered, as he mumbled apologies and departed, if his chief had had some kind of bad news.

Claas recovered his powers of speech. "I'm glad you're here, boss. You can hold my hand. Whose crazy idea is this?"

"Barzelian's."

"Barzelian! Hey, about early retirement . . ."

"Negative."

Claas sighed. "What I thought. You know what I think about Hank Timothy? Why don't we just nuke him?"

Weber let his eyes wander about the room, which was nothing very special in the way of an office, not even a decent view. "How's Ella? And the kids?"

Claas blinked. "Fine. Just fine." He couldn't say they had been having too many rows lately. "You're changing the subject."

"Waiting for you to adjust. You're just a rubber stamp, junior. Barzelian doesn't have to have your okay."

"This is supposed to be a friendly country. Anyway, since when did I work for a rubber stamp outfit? How's Pierre junior? You two making good vibes these days?" Weber was a widower with one son, a freshman at George Washington University.

"According to the Dean of Men, Pierre junior is an asshole."

"The Dean of Men said *that*?" Claas was temporarily diverted.

Weber's smile appeared as a pothook, laughing or crying, depending on which side you looked. "Used longer words, but that's the way they translate."

"Did the kid do anything bad?"

"Have me for a father, maybe." Weber looked like an intellectual priest with doubts. "Don't worry. We don't intend to let Hank win any downs. Give him some room, maybe, but in the end, a shutout. Anyway" – Weber moved to finality – "Barzelian calls the plays."

"You're a whole fresh kick, know that? You just made my

80

day." Claas used his intercom to have Cindy-Lou get Di Pasolino back again. Claas called Weber boss, which he was. Weber called Claas junior, which he was not, except in rank, but they liked each other.

"Okay, so I lay on stage one. Who did you get for stage two? Hank isn't going to talk to anyone from Langley, and I have no one on strength I'm prepared to see iced."

"We already have a nomination. Morpurgo." Watching with his deceptive languor that was almost anti-American, Weber saw reactions whisk across Claas's face like sun and cloud; surprise, speculation and, last, a wary interest.

"Morpurgo. You know he fell from grace? He's just nickels and dimes over there in Lambeth."

"I know it."

"He's a sucker if he agrees to play tag with Hank Timothy."

"That's something he doesn't know."

Claas pulled down the corners of his mouth. "You heard me say this is supposed to be a friendly country?"

"I heard you. And Virginia grew up and had kids of her own and *they* wrote letters to Santa Claus. I brought some candy for Ella and the kids."

Claas looked at him with mingled mistrust and affection. "You think of everything, boss."

"I like to think so, junior. I certainly like to think so."

And some of the things you think, Claas thought in turn, must be pretty damn sad.

* * *

Brewster Cochran wakened instantly, one hand on the phone while the other found the light switch. He listened only briefly. "Do you know what time it is? . . . I mean American time . . . You do? Then what in . . . ?"

He sat up abruptly.

"When? . . . No, wait! Don't call the police, man! . . ." He pressed the bellpush. "You already did? Tell them it was a mist . . . Jesus Christ! . . . No, you listen to me, Goldy, just get rid of them. Tell them . . . What do you mean, you can't? . . . Okay! Okay!"

Dobrovsky appeared, immaculate in his nightwear.

81

"Hold it!" Cochran waved his free hand at Dobrovsky. "Flight to London, first available reservation. Take my hurry bag, then bring the car round." Dobrovsky slid open a wardrobe door, extracted a ready-packed valise, vanished.

Back on the phone, Cochran said, "I'm on my way . . . London, where else? I'll see you at the plant. I want everyone, hear me? *everyone* to keep their goddam mouth shut until we see what we have here. Tell 'em any damn thing you like that'll cool it. And get those damn cops out."

He kicked the sheets back, a striped package of raw energy. "What do you mean, once they're in they're in? . . . Then tell 'em nothing. *I'll* get them out."

He sat on the edge of his rumpled bed, punching out the ciphers of a new call with vicious concentration.

"Mark? This is Brew . . . Brewster Cochran, damn it! . . . Sure I know what time it is . . . You bet it's an emergency! . . . Well now, let me tell it, will you? . . . Okay, okay, tell her I said sorry, but hear me first. I just had a call from England, from Billingshurst, you were there not all that time ago. Listen, someone just broke in there and took the culture stock . . . Let me *finish*, will you? All the freeze-dried bugs . . . No, there's worse! Golding called in the cops.

"What do you mean, you don't see it? . . . Okay, we have a temporary glitch, but that's not the way it'll go if the news gets out, did you never see what rumour can do? . . . Now you're talking sense. You bet! The mere idea will bring everybody out in goose-pimples, Brewster Cochran doesn't throw away money on turkeys. Big Oil! Wall Street! The Arabs! Imagine what State, Defense, Energy are going to say if this breaks before they have time to haul up their zip. It could drop on them like a load of wet manure."

The bludgeon of his personality told at last. "Right! Now you're beginning to tick over . . . You're goddam right there's something you can do. Use your connections, that's what . . . Okay, so you have to lift the wraps a little, it's rumour we're scared about. A process that fell on its ass, won't produce enough oil to light a lamp, but other people *might* see it as a threat . . .

"How do I know? You're the guy with the horsepower. Just get those British cops out is all, then leave the rest to me . . . Me? I'm taking the first flight out, what else? . . . Right! You got it! Give my regards to Edie, tell her I'm sorry I spoiled her sleep."

Slamming down the receiver, he went across the room like a Gulf hurricane zeroing in on Miami. "Dob! Hey, Dobrovsky! What's keeping you? Move your butt! Let's get this show on the road!"

*   *   *

In his luxury duplex over on Fifth, Mark Folger headed for his study and a private telephone. All right, he was the guy with the horsepower, as Cochran had put it, one of the movers and shakers.

He had shaken Dick Goss more than a little with his outline of what effect Cochran's process, or even an informed leak on the process, could have on the world oil market. The political consequences would be far worse, but that was Goss's province, not Mark Folger's.

And so, even at four in the morning, he was not going to believe there was no connection between his meeting with Goss and the fact that someone over there in England had decided to take a closer look at what was going on in a little place called Billingshurst. He was just going to make sure that Dick Goss knew too, if he didn't know already. Maybe Dick wouldn't want the British police in, either, especially if Langley had been there first.

*   *   *

The English weather had turned sulky, a bullying wind that hurled handfuls of rain in coin-sized blobs. Brewster Cochran's mood was not dissimilar. Out of the car before its chauffeur could open the door for him, he collided with Golding at the entrance to the office block.

"It's all right, Mr Cochran." Golding was philosophically calm. "I don't know how you did it, but it worked like magic."

Cochran put on the brakes. "What worked like magic?"

"The police. One minute they were here, the next, not, just like magic."

Good old Markus! There was a guy who could deliver. "Well, that's just fine and dandy, Goldy, but what about the rest? Did we get the bugs back? Do we know who took 'em?"

If Golding thought this less than reasonable, he kept it to himself. "Would you like to come up to the office?"

The place was deserted. Upstairs in Golding's small office, kamikaze raindrops immolated themselves on the windows, the song of a thrush urgent through the splattered glass.

"Nobody knows anything," Golding said. "Only me. Have you eaten, Mr Cochran? We could talk and eat."

"What do you mean, nobody knows?" Cochran wasn't interested in food.

"I was first in. I always am. I saw straight away there'd been a break-in. At first I thought it was probably just petty thieving, lads from the village. Then I realised the security system must have been bypassed." Outside, the thrush took its talents elsewhere, disturbed by a red Jaguar that cruised slowly past to park outside the extruded plastics plant.

"So you checked everything out?"

"A quick look in the office, then I went into the plant. I saw straight away what they'd been after, too late to stop the police, though." He was quiet, rueful, a man whose brains had been pillaged, overborne by a man whose ambitions had been thwarted.

"They cleaned us out?"

"Except for stock in process. They'd been through the files. Probably photographing, nothing taken."

"What's so goddam surprising?"

"As if they thought it would stop us altogether. It won't, will it?"

"Damn right it won't! So what happened with the cops? Did they want to know our line of business?"

"And what business, I wonder, might that be?" The voice was English, cultured, compact with pleasantly restrained authority.

Cochran spun round. "Who the hell are you? Who told you you could come in here?"

"My name is Archer. This is your property?" Archer, elegant in black tie and dinner jacket, made it a confrontation of ice and fire.

"You better believe it!" Cochran was on his feet. Between them, they made the room seem very small. "This is private property. And a private conversation. The sooner you get the hell out of here, the better I'll like it."

Archer smiled. "I quite understand your feelings, Mr Cochran. You are Mr Cochran? Yes, of course. To have strangers on your premises twice in twenty-four hours, a bit much, isn't it? Four times, counting my people and the local constabulary." His gaze switched to Golding. "And you, I imagine, must be Mr Golding. You're in charge here."

"I think," Golding said, "this gentleman may be behind the magic, Mr Cochran."

"Magic!" Cochran glared. "What in hell are you talking about?"

"The case of the vanishing policemen." Cochran had never had time to discover that Golding had a sense of humour.

Archer laughed, an attractive sound.

"Vanishing . . . !" Cochran deflated. "You some kind of cop?"

"Maybe." Archer's voice, never rising above conversational level, still managed to dominate.

"When I get a call" – No one had invited Archer in, yet now he was standing by the window – "from a very high source in Washington, asking me to persuade the Sussex police to lose interest in a minor case of breaking and entering, asking it" – He produced, once more, the easy smile that emphasised cleft chin, white teeth, relaxed charm – "as a personal favour, I naturally do what I can. I gather it was effective."

Cochran was making a hasty reassessment. "I guess it was at that." He thrust out a hand. "T. Brewster Cochran. Mighty obliged, Mr Archer. Maybe I was a little hasty."

Archer took the hand, and the shake, without flinching. Cochran was impressed. "M'friends call me Brew. I guess you could say you just became a friend."

"I'd like to think so. Please." Archer waved a hand. "Do sit. I didn't mean to intrude." T. Brewster Cochran meekly took a seat.

"Only one way to get the police out once they've been called in." Archer pulled out a chair, twirled it, sat on it back to front. "Pull rank."

Cochran guffawed. "Hey, listen, forget all that stuff I said." He eyed Archer's attire. "Cops in tuxedos at six p.m., it's a different world! Who'd Markus have call you?"

"Marcus?"

85

"Mark Folger. From Washington. May be those guys are worth our taxes at that."

"And maybe it's best I don't tell you, Mr Cochran. We have our little secrets, just like you."

Cochran's mouth, beginning to laugh, tightened. "Who said we have secrets?"

"Oh, come, I don't play this sort of game as a hobby, and Special Branch has other things to do."

"Special Branch." Golding looked thoughtful.

Archer nodded. "As I said, pull rank. Local police yield to the Branch, if the groundwork has been laid. I laid it." His dark gaze, blandly speculative, returned to Cochran. "I only hope these good friends of yours in Washington would be as quick to return the favour. In the meantime it would be friendly, don't you think? to give me an inkling of what was so important."

Cochran was less sure of his ground. "What's Special Branch?"

"Sort of FBI." Golding was quietly uneasy, the more so in that Archer sensed it.

"The Feds!" Cochran whistled.

Archer shook his head smilingly. "I'm not Branch personally. Let's say they dance to my tune. I was coming to this part of the world, social engagement, thought I'd drop by and see what it was all about. Not knowing, of course, that you'd be here."

"This is a research unit," Golding began. "Oil industry research. Mr Cochran's . . ."

"Promethean Oil." Archer was still looking at Cochran. "Never let it be said that we don't do our homework. Sixty-two, unmarried. Correction, married to the oil industry."

Cochran liked that. "Damn right! Only one girl in my life, black as the inside of a preacher's hat."

"And friends in Washington," Archer finished, "with secrets to protect." He sat waiting, the smiling essence of politeness.

"All right." Cochran reached a decision. "I'll give it to you straight, Mr Archer. Government work, strategic importance. That's why Washington played ball."

He jumped up, stuck out a hand. "I'm going to put in a good word when I get back, you can count on it."

"Very kind." Archer reversed his chair. "I didn't want to be difficult, Mr Cochran, but it has to be better than that." He crossed his legs, very much *chez lui*. "I have superiors too. They like to be kept informed."

Cochran and Golding spoke simultaneously. Cochran blustered. "Look, we brought work to this goddam country." Golding said, "We're not really breaking any rules. Everything's perfectly under control."

Like kids caught stealing candy, Archer thought. "A very fancy security system. The police notice these things, you know, they're not entirely stupid. So the people who got past it must have been fairly fancy, too." He glanced at his watch. "Hm, must be off soon. Don't like to keep hosts waiting."

He made no move to go. He had done his homework, just as he had said, with the very thorough help of Eric Pottern. There was something he was saving, perhaps because, as yet, it was, must be, surely? peripheral. Yet it circled slowly in his thoughts like a fish in dark waters.

Cochran glanced helplessly at Golding. Golding, as always, thought only in terms of his research. "Biological, Mr Archer. A biological method of releasing oil from shale. A development of the Chakrabarty technique."

Archer raised his hands. "Chakra what? Don't blind me with science, Mr Golding."

"The Chakrabarty technique's environmentally delicate. Of course, we follow the laid-down procedure in every respect. We . . ."

"Chakrabarty." Archer decided to be satisfied. Pottern would dig out the rest. Mustn't press too hard, just a lead to follow up. At last he stood. "I've already spoken to Washington, just to let them know we did our stuff. Though of course" – He grinned invitingly – "if you want to pursue the question of who dunnit . . . ?"

"No." Cochran was quick. "No harm done, nothing missing. We wouldn't want to take the publicity." He proffered his hand again. "Now we don't have to, thanks to you."

Archer shook hands with Golding too, imprinting the face on his memory. "If you change your minds" – He took a card from his wallet, gave it to Cochran – "let me know. The West Sussex police have closed the book. It'd take someone like me to reopen it."

Cochran, feeling better, laughed his booming laugh. "No chance! I guess those guys have enough to handle. No harm done, let's leave it that way."

Archer waited until the last moment before yielding to the circling temptation so long suppressed. "Promethean Oil. Dealings with Libya, I believe. Still go there?"

For a moment Cochran was baffled. Then his face suffused. "Those bastards! Nearly ruined me, back in '70. Still do business, have to, but the only way I'd go back would be to stomp on their graves."

"Really?" Archer's interest had apparently evaporated. "Well, not much to see there but sand, I suppose."

On his way to his social engagement, for which he was in fact very early, he called in a pub to use the pay phone. "Eric? Dig out everything you can find on Promethean and Cochran, will you? Also on Chakrabarty – I'll spell that for you – and a method of clearing up oil slicks. Then, first thing tomorrow, chase your pals in the Hazardous Substances Group, see what they have on this place at Billingshurst. Oh, and while you're at it, run one Charles Golding through the computer, see if anything's known . . . No, not a thing, old son, just a grubby-fingered test-tube merchant, but you never know, one thing leads to another."

The name of the game, he told himself as he slid back into his red Jaguar, was suspicion.

*   *   *

More or less at the same time, in the seclusion of his corner of the White House Situation Room, Dick Goss was talking to Barzelian on a secure conference line.

"You can consider yourself damn lucky I didn't break into your beauty sleep, the way Folger broke into mine. Anyway, it's all set up now, right?"

Barzelian, with DCI listening, said, "All sewn up, which is better. This guy Archer . . . Sure, he's the one who's going to go top of the heap at MI5 . . . anyway, he handled it in person. The lid is on, the screws have been driven home."

"And there's no way anything will pass from there to Epworth's people? The President has bought the ploy. Now it's up to you people to deliver. You won't get another chance."

Barzelian churned out his concrete-mixer chuckle. "Archer and Epworth are both new at the top, both competing for favour with their brass on the British Joint Intelligence Committee. They'll give each other the time of day if the order's in writing."

Goss laughed a lawyer's laugh; let's talk fees later. "I'll swear you could work up a rift between David and Jonathan and then exploit it."

"I'm not," Barzelian agreed, "a man you should buy a second-hand carpet from."

DCI, toying with his orrery and listening to the conversation on the speaker, waited until the connection had been cut.

"No chance of cross-fertilisation over there in London, you're sure?"

"Sure I'm sure. But better yet" – Barzelian watched the earth wobble under DCI's ministrations – "if Archer smells rodent."

"Because of the rivalry with Epworth."

Barzelian wobbled his jowls. "We're using Morpurgo. Archer wouldn't help Morpurgo if it made him a billion bucks." He watched Mercury and Venus inch around, as DCI manipulated the solar system. "Morpurgo is smarter, maybe. Archer is smoother. And meaner. And Morpurgo laid his wife."

DCI gave the solar system a whirl. Barzelian winced. "That thing needs some oil."

DCI, with his literal mind, had something to clear up. "You mean Archer's wife laid Morpurgo, outcome of the way she'd been treated by Archer. Makes it harder still for Archer to take, right?"

SIX

Lawrence Epworth had none of the sprawled heaps of files, print-outs, prosy minutes and esoteric bric-à-brac that reared like minor fortifications about the six regional coordinators. Nor were his walls a patchwork of maps, press clippings and photographs; the general impression was of disengagement raised to the level of art.

"When I want to see anything like that, Johnny, I – mmmm – go walkabout. Always visit them, don't let them visit you, that's the trick. You can walk away when you've got what you want. They won't."

There was nevertheless an occasional incongruity, as out of place as a beer keg on an altar, but more likely to be, as now, a case of sherry or wine. By this time Morpurgo was used to such things. Epworth thrust a glass at him. "Join me. I'd value your opinion."

"I'd something else in mind. I know nothing about wine."

"What you have in mind will keep." He poured a generous measure of red wine.

Sylvie, long ago, had taught Morpurgo the basic rules; look, smell, taste, consider. Her father kept a fat-cat cellar.

"Beaujolais?" He would be wrong.

"Wrong, actually, but not bad. Quite a few characteristics of the Beaujolais, especially when it's good, which this is. Roannais – mmmm – not easily found over here. I had Finniston hunt some down when he was in Clermont on the Rooster thing. A teeny bit earthy, would you say? Perhaps robust would be kinder. Still, for a modest little country wine, it earns some applause."

Thurber, pure Thurber! Except that it was impossible to tell when Epworth was being serious, about wine, about anything.

"Rooster would be a good place to start." This time he was not going to leave without something settled.

Epworth held his own glass to the light. "Good colour. Why Rooster? if one may ask."

"Ask away. Operation Rooster's been on the Gower Street agenda for the past nine weeks."

"Mmmm." Epworth sipped judiciously. Mrs Rattigan tiptoed in, stood, head on one side, looking at the desk, where the file trays were virgin, the desk clear save for the case of wine and a scatter of minor Epworthiana. She said, "Tsk!" tiptoeing out again. "Yes." Epworth ignored her. "Delicate creature, Rooster. Gallic species, of course, absurdly sensitive."

"Really."

"Really. One of the reasons de Gaulle kicked NATO out was his objection to all the CIA and SIS people who were spying on him instead of the Russians. Much harder for them to do it from Brussels, do you see?"

"No." This time he would refuse to trail after Epworth as he piped his beguiling way down utterly irrelevant paths, only to discover, in due course, that they led nowhere save back to Morpurgo's own office and the dead-end job that was his excuse for being there.

"Of course," Epworth said, "Fish was in the thick of that."

A typical Epworth ploy, the glint of gold at the very moment in which the seam appeared to have been worked out. Fish, following Epworth's infinitely subtle exploitation of the Sattin spy case to topple the top echelon of SIS – and, guilt by association, a Secretary of State for Foreign Affairs – had killed himself. The hushing up had been masterly, even by British standards.

He could, Morpurgo thought bitterly, say nothing, in which case the proffered bait would be withdrawn. Or he could say something and in due course discover that he had once again followed stinking red herring.

"Still." Epworth shook his baby-bald head. "Nothing gained in the end. Sad."

Hang on, Morpurgo told himself grimly, even though you've no idea where you're going. He presumed they were skirting Fish's suicide.

Epworth finished his wine. "Soon even the most minor French wines will be *appellation contrôlé* and no one will be able to afford them."

"There'll always be sherry." Don't just hang on. Dig in.

"Ah." Epworth looked pleased, a man who could go into raptures over some pale astringent liquid that, so far as Morpurgo's ignorant palate was concerned, might serve as an up-market aftershave. "Of course" – Epworth's tone was so reasonable that Morpurgo's hackles rose – "Fish's suicide had nothing to do with the – mmmm – change of management. Nothing at all." He himself was the change of management.

"No?"

"Nothing. You know" – At last, the heralding trumpet-note of revelation? Morpurgo figuratively held his breath – " the resemblance to the Beaujolais must be due to the subsoil of the Monts de la Madeleine, do you know that part of the world? Granite in both cases, and, of course, the Gamay grape. No, Fish was suffering from a bad conscience. And wife trouble."

Inside Morpurgo an entire infra-structure of muscle and nerve tautened. He himself had wife trouble. Steve Archer had had wife trouble. Now it turned out that Fish, who had blushed a deadly pink in his garage, had also had wife trouble. Was it a professional hazard, an industrial disease? Had Epworth married his plump Amaryllis only after her parents had produced a certificate of immunity?

The hell with it! "Do you know that's the first personal thing I've learned about Fish?"

"Really?" Epworth recorked his bottle.

"People don't talk to me."

Epworth had wandered windowards to the view of his toy train set and the cheap end of the Monopoly board. "I suppose we are inclined to be a bit – mmmm – unforthcoming." He giggled, the absurd sound Morpurgo had never heard anyone mock. "Not so much a community as a village clique. How long were you with Security Directorate exactly?"

"All right, I can't expect to know everything in SIS in five minutes. I know nothing. At the present rate I shall still know nothing when I retire. If I last long enough to retire."

"Ah." Epworth raised a coy finger. "But you park in the street, Fish *would* have a house with a double garage." If there was a joke, even a sick joke, it was well concealed, along with remorse, regret, compassion. He knew now why Sylvie's mistrust of Epworth bordered on fear.

He launched an attack. "Operation High Sierra. Operation Purple World. The Boat People project, the Igloo project! I sit at the bottom of that bloody table in Gower Street while your fellow villagers swap their bloody gossip and reach their bloody meaningless decisions, and I come away as wise as when I went in."

"Discretion is sometimes worth more than wisdom." Again the turtle-dove giggle. "The need to know. And of course, the need *not* to know. What you don't know, my dear Johnny, can't hurt you, as my mother, a trifle innocently, used to say. Though the need not to know is really the politicians' ploy. Shakespeare, Antony and Cleopatra, what I call the Pompeian syndrome. 'Ah, this thou shoulds't have done and not have spoken on't! In me 'tis villainy: In thee't had been good service.'"

"Are you telling me I don't need to know anything?"

"What you *need* to know has only just begun. Before that, things you very much needed *not* to know."

"Am I meant to infer that the rainy day you were saving me for . . ."

". . . has come? Not quite. But Weber has. You do remember Pierre Weber?"

The one that Sylvie liked. "I saw nothing in the Cousins' diary."

"Let's put it this way. We shall shortly hear that Weber has arrived. Even, perhaps, that he wants to see us. That's when you come off liaison."

He left the window to remove the case of wine from his desk. "I'll have a case of this dropped off for you and Sylvie, drinking, not keeping. Make sure your next house has a decent cellar."

Mrs Rattigan returned in the moment that he lifted the case.

"Mr Epworth!" She pointed accusingly. Where it had stood lay a CC file, the three red bars across its dog-eared corner indicating its top secrecy. "Registry's quite hysterical because that file disappeared from Mr Wriothsley's office without passing through them. I'll get them to send a transfer clerk immediately."

At the door she said severely, "You really *must* tell them when you do that sort of thing, Mr Epworth. After all, they *need* to know."

Epworth giggled, winked at Morpurgo and went through the motions of putting up an umbrella, leaving his precise meaning undefined. It was considerably later when Morpurgo realised that he was clearly not meant to know about Operation Rooster.

*   *   *

"Obliged," Cochran said for the fourth or fifth time. "Mighty obliged, Mr Archer. You don't have to tell me you're a busy man. Me too, but I figured maybe we should talk some more."

Did he, Archer wondered, know how much Archer himself, not to mention Eric Pottern, had shared the feeling? Probably not.

Cochran swallowed a mouthful of Mazos Chambertin as if it were something his doctor had prescribed to be taken with food, following it with a giant forkful of *boeuf braisé*. Neither prevented him from continuing the conversation. "One word made me come around to that idea. Guess I don't have to tell you what it was."

"Libya." Archer felt a small but fierce surge of triumph.

"Damn right. Libya. How much do you know about me, Mr Archer?"

"I told you" – Archer smiled disarmingly – "I looked you up. A quick glance at *International Who's Who*, that's all." That was before Pottern had combed the records.

"You check me out, you'll find I like Arabs the way I like taxes."

Archer waited politely.

"I'm in the oil business. Arabs have oil, I deal with Arabs. The Devil had more oil than the Arabs, I'd deal with him, not them. But that's not the half of it."

Lighting a cigarette, Archer raised one eyebrow. He was here to listen.

"Was a time," Cochran said, "when I took all my oil from

94

Libya. No Libya, no Promeco. Well, sir, if you know the history of Big Oil, you'll know that the OPEC squeeze play – I'm talking early '70s now – started with one man and one country. Libya. Muammar Gaddafi. In those days more than twenty companies, including Esso, Shell, BP, most of the majors, were pumping up Libyan oil like there was no tomorrow. Most of 'em didn't even need it, but it was there and it was cheap.

"Muammar and his Revolutionary Council decided to put a stop to it, also decided they were going to hoist the price and then some. Went a couple of rounds with the big boys, ended up with a stand-off, switched plays, looked for a fall guy."

He sloshed more wine. "This stuff okay with you? I say bring me good stuff, they bring it. I don't know from whichway about wine." His eyes, boring into Archer, were not interested in wine.

"Who was the fall guy? That you don't need to answer. Lil ol' Brew Cochran. No Libyan oil, no Promeco. The Seven Sisters didn't need Libya. Promeco did." He held a crooked forefinger as an extension of his nose, directed minatorily at Archer. "What do I do? I see the future, that's what. Domino effect, one down, all down, would have taken a dummy to miss it. I go to the Sisters – the majors, get it? – see if they'll supply me so I won't have to knuckle under to Muammar. Those sons of bitches! Muammar all set to snip off their balls, all they can think of is snipping off mine. Didn't turn me down flat, just asked a price so far over the odds it amounted to the same thing."

Archer went quietly on with his meal. He had learned the gist of the story before coming to meet Cochran. What had not been apparent from the summary was the cold venom those distant events had engendered in the man on the far side of the table, venom not only for the Libyans but the Seven Sisters; what he called Big Oil. Up to now it had all seemed a far cry from a suspected attempt to assassinate an American president, this almost coincidental connection with Libya, but then, so had a minor break-in at a minor industrial estate in a minor town in Sussex.

Cochran pushed away his plate. "What could I do? Shape up or ship out. I fell in line, paid Muammar what he wanted, with more to come. You could call it the breach in the dam. Before you could say OPEC, he's knocking off every company operating in Libya, every last one.

"But that was only the start. When the other producers, Iran, the Gulf States, Venezuela, you name 'em, when they saw what was happening, up went their prices too. I guess you know the rest."

He gave an unexpected shout of angry laughter, so that heads turned in their direction. "Didn't make me the most popular guy in the oil business, but I'm still around, and, one day soon, won't they just know it, the Libs, Big Oil, the whole goddam shoot!"

He slopped the last of the wine into Archer's glass. "So now you know why I get a mite itchy when I hear that word Libya." His fierce eyes scorched, demanding the answer to an unspoken question.

"And how do you feel" – Archer returned his own lazy smile – "when you hear the name Timothy? Hank Timothy."

He saw at once that he had got something wrong.

"Timothy? Should I have heard of the guy?"

A waiter came to clear. Way off target, Archer thought ruefully. "You want something from that thing?" Cochran, his hospitality impatient now, indicated the dessert trolley. Archer shook his head, thinking hard. Cochran ordered coffee.

"You must have something quite important going on over there in Billingshurst." This is where Morpurgo would have shone, commercial stuff, technical, boring but sometimes important.

Through a veil of cigarette smoke, he watched Cochran make the wrong choice of answer. "I thought we took care of that last time we met."

"Well, yes and no." Let him dangle and twist; Archer had an ace up his sleeve, thanks to Pottern and his ministry contacts.

"What's that supposed to mean, yes and no?"

"Perhaps your Mr Golding shouldn't have mentioned Chakrabarty."

Cochran was a cornered bull. "You telling me you did some digging?"

"A little." Archer, too, could produce a steady look.

"Goldy told you. A way of getting oil from rock, nothing so

96

very special." He could tell this fancy-pants cop knew nothing about oil.

"Maybe not. Environmentally delicate, wasn't that the way he put it?"

Cochran was still for bluffing. "A P1 process, harmless as mother's milk."

"But illegal without registration." Yes, this was where Morpurgo would have been in his element.

"So we stopped the process straight off. We're applying for authorisation. We have a patentable situation coming up out there."

"Would this" – Time to risk a second long shot – "be what you meant when you said it wouldn't be long before the Libyans and Big Oil knew you were still around?"

Bull's-eye; time, therefore, to press. "I'm not very well up in these things but I gather that the restrictions on using recombinant DNA in this country are even tougher than in the States."

Cochran abandoned an overrun position. "We have a process that turned bad on us. Whole thing fell apart and I just lost two million."

"But you have a patentable situation coming up. And you're applying for authorisation. And someone thought you were important enough to take a closer look at." Cochran might be big in oil. Any halfway competent Curzon Street graduate could run rings around him in interrogation.

A lifelong master of infighting, Cochran switched to attack.

"Now before we get to raising the temperature any higher, you just tell me why you mentioned that word I don't too much care for, Mr Archer."

Directness, Archer decided; that was what Johnny would have gone for at this stage. "Hank Timothy works for the Libyans. If what you're doing could affect the Libyans in any way, Timothy might have been your intruder."

Cochran tried to ride it, but he was jolted.

"What do you mean, works for the Libyans?" The more he thought, the less he liked it.

"Could what you're doing affect their national security?"

"Maybe."

97

Archer displayed his pleasant smile. "I'm not in the habit of saying such things, but I'm quite high-powered. Tell me a little more."

"Hank Timothy." Cochran was wriggling. "Sounds kind of American."

"It does, doesn't it?"

"So how come the Libyan angle?"

"So how come you don't want to tell me more?"

Cochran wasn't used to being talked to like that, but he was over a barrel. "I told you. A new source of oil." He looked rueful. "Only the process turns out to be a turkey. The oil changes to goo."

"But next time?"

"Told you that too. Ain't going to be no next time."

Archer was bored by technology, also impatient. "Mr Cochran, by rights I should report this whole business to at least three government departments. I don't suppose you'd like that."

He had his answer in Cochran's silence. "And I doubt you'd call in such high-powered help over a process that failed."

Cochran saw his chance. "That's where you're wrong. Rumour's all it takes to shake OPEC and Big Oil. Shake them, you shake the world." A flash of inspiration. "How'd you like to see the British pound fall through the floor because rumour knocks five bucks off the price of North Sea crude?"

Unlike Morpurgo, Archer's knowledge of finance and industry was sketchy, his attitude to money and the people who grubbed for it one of disdain. He sat back, once more relaxed, among the civilised appointments of a great hotel. On the other side of the big windows, the chauffeurs of one Rolls, one Mercedes and a couple of Bentleys, privilege protecting them from no-waiting regulations, attended their owners in Davies Street. All about him was the clink and careful clatter, the subdued but confident murmur, of wealth and eminence.

Opposite him was a hard-eyed, rough-mannered, no-holds-barred American who thought only in terms of profit, advantage and revenge. It was time to put the boot in. "Who did you get to ask favours in Whitehall, favours at a very high level?" It must be, it had to be someone in the White House itself. The White House was in combat with the Libyans.

"Some things you don't ask."

"Oh, but I do. And I use whatever it takes to get an answer."

So this cooky-cutter stamp-out of an upper-crust Englishman knew, after all, how to shoot dirty pool. "A guy with big muscle in Washington."

"I have muscle here in London. I'd like his name."

"Folger, Mark Folger. He has connections, you better believe."

"With whom, in this case?" The name meant nothing to Archer, though Morpurgo would have known it.

"Langley. I guess you know that's the CIA."

"It wasn't Langley that contacted me."

"So, wheels within wheels. It worked, right? You made those cops haul ass."

Steve Archer, no flight-of-fancy man, nevertheless had a vision. That it was blurred at this stage made small difference. At Gatwick, Hank Timothy, a man employed by the Libyans, had attempted the assassination of the President of the United States, whom the Libyans considered hostile to their national interests. At Billingshurst, someone had stolen details of a process the Libyans might see as a threat to their national interests. Hank Timothy had entered and left the UK once and been detected only with luck. Luck didn't work every time.

The wraps had been put on over the Gatwick affair. The wraps had been put on over the affair at Billingshurst. There had to be a connection, even if it were not yet clear. Langley had been given a two-fold task, a saving of national face, a settling of scores, the rest of the world to be none the wiser. Timothy was still active but Langley was closing in.

Knowledge was power. Archer looked at Cochran almost genially. "Look, Mr Cochran, I'm not out to make trouble. I don't condone commercial law-breaking, but it's not my field, so suppose we forget that bit."

Cochran headed, phototropic, for the gleam of light. "But if I read you right, this guy Timothy means something to the British."

"You aren't the only one with an aversion to the Libyans, let's put it that way. We wouldn't say no to a chat with him."

Cochran, giving Archer less a grin than a baring of teeth, looked about him with exaggerated caution. "Ain't nobody but us two knows we're here, Mr Archer. Ain't nobody going to, so far as Brew Cochran's concerned. And so far as things don't leak out . . ."

By no means unpleased with himself, Archer smiled.

"You oil people aren't the only ones with techniques for dealing with leaks. And on the whole ours work better."

* * *

Conveniently, Cochran left first, enabling Archer to make his appointment with his Home Office opposite number from the hotel, after which, back to the steadily increasing pressures of his new, if not yet official responsibilities. He stepped out jauntily, the walk from Claridges to Curzon Street a welcome leg-stretcher, the prospects of political one-upmanship adding spring to his stride.

* * *

"Hey, John, *ciao*!" Claas always greeted Morpurgo over-heartily. It said something about their relationship. "Where's brother Lawrence? Oh, you remember this guy? Product of St Louis, along with beer, shoes and chemicals. The shoes have gone to Taiwan, maybe the beer and chemicals too, but Pierre here won't get the message."

Weber produced his rare, illuminant smile. "St Louis has culture. Kansas City has cows, hence the bullshit. Good to see you, John. No Epworth?"

So Epworth, as usual, had been right; not just passing the time of day. "Sends his apologies, hopes to see you later, hopes I'll do for now."

"Culture," Claas was saying darkly, "goes where the need is greatest." He summoned coffee and cookies.

Weber, draped in his chair once more, studied Morpurgo. "So you crossed over the river. Did all the trumpets sound for you on the other side?"

"If they did, they must have been using mutes."

"A muted trumpet" – Claas was clearly going to put on his brash colonial act – "can sound pretty damn close to a raspberry."

"How's Sylvie?" Weber came in quickly.

"Fine. She's just gone to Spain, a commission for *Time-Life*."

100

Weber pulled a sad little face. "Damn, I was planning on asking her out. You could have come too. Listen, how would you like a trip yourself? Langley's looking for a favour."

"Glad to know Langley still thinks we can do them."

"Oh, the special relationship's as natural as bourbon and branch water."

Beware the Yanks when they come bearing folksy similes; especially Weber, basically as folksy as a Boston Brahmin.

Claas's secretary's hair was more purple than ever, and her new glasses had lenses like portholes. "Hi, Mr Morpurgo, nice to see you again." She brought everything in on a tray, including as well as the refreshments, a stoppered glass jar the size of a beer can, another no bigger than his thumb. The large one held a liquid; ebon, viscous. In the other were small granules, pale buff, looking like bleached instant coffee. She poured their coffee and left. Claas pounced on the cookies.

Weber, as if tired of inaction, came to sit on the corner of the desk. Claas beckoned Morpurgo, pointing at the larger container. "Go ahead, open it. Be careful, that stuff is messy."

Morpurgo opened it gingerly. Claas grinned. "Take a sniff. Sylvie wouldn't wear it but it has a certain *je ne sais quoi*."

Weber winced. "Your accent gets worse, junior."

Morpurgo sniffed. "Oil."

"Hey!" Claas stuck up a mocking thumb. "Not just a skullful of dull! Right, John old man. Crude. Libyan crude." Taking the jar, he waggled it cautiously, leaving slowly vanishing brown curtains.

"It's warm."

"Temperature of emergence," Weber murmured, offering Morpurgo a cookie.

"Want to take a look at the other stuff?" Claas, too, took a cookie, his third.

Morpurgo wiggled the stopper from the small jar, sniffed tentatively. "No smell, not to notice. Some kind of petroleum product?" He was baffled.

Claas, jarringly, commented to Weber, "Epworth sent no hired hand. This cat is cool." It was one of Morpurgo's permanent facts of life; Claas, six years in London, a wife and two kids in an expensive flat just north of Hyde Park, jarred.

101

Weber had closed his eyes wearily. "Cut it out, will you, Warren? Let's get on."

There was a newspaper on Claas's desk. He stood the two jars on it, pretended to push back his sleeves, rotated his hands back and front like a conjurer. "No strings, aces, rabbits." It was all, in one way, relaxed and rather childish, yet to the two Americans, Morpurgo sensed, basically serious.

Claas unstoppered the small bottle. "Never mind what this is, just for now. Tap a little in the crude, just a smidgeon, okay?"

Morpurgo complied, feeling foolish and therefore irritated. His irritation tended to focus on Epworth, who had given him this in place of liaison.

Claas, watching, poised a hand over the cooky dish. "You going to eat that one?" Morpurgo shook his head.

"Pity to waste it." Claas posted the last cookie whole. His mouth very full, he flipped his intercom. "Cindy-Lou, you forgot the box and all."

She came in with a box made from foam plastic, light but sturdy.

"Thanks, hon." Claas removed its lid, revealing a cylindrical cavity the size of the larger jar. "Screw the cap back, John, will you?" Morpurgo complied.

"Fine. Now shove it in there." Morpurgo slid the jar into the box.

Weber, yet more wearily, said, "You forgot the tape, junior."

Claas snapped his fingers, annoyed. "Not me. Her." He raised his voice, scorning the intercom. "Hey, four-eyes, what's going on out there? You didn't bring the tape. Maybe I won't miss you at that."

"End of tour," Weber explained. "Cindy-Lou's going home to beautiful downtown Langley."

Cindy-Lou came in. "What was that?"

"The tape, dummy!" Claas thrust the jar toward her. "How do we seal without tape?" Automatically, she took the jar. "A whole spool of tape, bubblehead." Claas commanded. "We aim to seal it good."

She rolled her eyes at Morpurgo, a middle-aged woman acting coy. "*He* won't miss *me*! Hmph! Boy, am *I* glad my tour is up!"

Claas shooed her away. She was back almost instantly with a

spool of white vinyl tape. "Here, do your own work, you snippy sexist. I voted for the Equal Rights amendment." She winked at Morpurgo on her way out.

"Equal rights!" Claas sighed histrionically. "Be typing my own letters before you know it." He motioned to Morpurgo. "You do it. Who won at Yorktown anyway?"

Weber chuckled softly. "Okay, you think we flipped, but play it along, right? Seal the thing, as much tape as you like."

Morpurgo, feeling his face tautening by the minute, particularly as the two Americans watched as if expecting to find him incapable of the task, swathed the jar in tape. Claas thrust a ballpoint at him. "Sign here and there. You *can* write?"

"They were going to post a notice for him back home," Weber said, "'Unwanted, dead or alive'. Then somebody said, 'How could you tell the difference?' and they had the CIA take him away."

Claas watched Morpurgo press his signature over the joins of tape for the last time. "You want to make the presentation, mastermind?"

Weber, his voice soft and placatory, gave Morpurgo the jar, indicating that he should put it in the protective box and seal it further. "This is the way we want it, John, the less fancy footwork, the better. You have a jar of Libyan crude. You added a pinch of that powder. You sealed it. In twenty-four hours . . ."

"Give or take," Claas interrupted, lounging insultingly.

". . . give or take, we'd like Lawrence Epworth to open it. Then we talk."

Morpurgo remembered something. "You said something about a trip."

"That's right."

"Where to?"

"Oh." Weber looked vague. "Not just a day by the ocean. Over the hills and far away. Let's leave it until we talk."

When Morpurgo had had time to reach street level, Weber opened his eyes. "Not the Morpurgo I knew." He looked sad.

"He's a closet wimp."

"You're lucky he didn't punch you in the nose. You ride him."

"I don't ride him. I goad him. Nothing comes out but sawdust."

103

Weber just looked.

"Okay. Okay." Claas was defensive. "He had something, once. Against my training to see a good operative go belly up."

Weber went on looking.

"Plus he has wife trouble."

"And he thinks he's through."

"Is he?"

Weber thought about it for a long time, then closed his eyes again. "This way, we find out."

*   *   *

Morpurgo crossed the wide gangplank between the Victorian Embankment and the deck of the *Tattershall Castle*, gulls wheeling appropriately overhead. She was an old sidewheeler converted into a pub and restaurant. She was also the kind of place Epworth liked to collect.

He crossed the deck with its view across the sparkle of the river to County Hall, went down two flights past the busy bar, found Epworth installed at a table for two, back against mahogany panelling. He took his place on the bench seat, placed the package on the table between them.

Epworth launched into a discourse on thirteenth-century isorhythmic motets. He illustrated in his carrying soprano. Eventually obliged to stop while they ordered, he regarded the package without touching it.

"Been – mmmm – shopping?"

"I bought into oil. It was cheaper than Westminster Bridge."

"Oil?"

"Libyan crude."

"Ah." Epworth hummed a little to himself while they were served with their first course, then delicately attacked his *paté maison*.

"Libya. Interesting."

"You think it's interesting?"

"Isn't it? Interesting?"

"Why?"

"Why?"

"Why is it interesting."

"Why is it interesting?" Epworth giggled. "Sorry. Echolalia."

"Echolalia is mechanical repetition. This is sheer, deliberate bloody provocation. Why is Libyan crude interesting?"

"My dear Johnny! You come aboard a converted paddle steamer in the heart of London – do you know where the *Tattershall Castle* used to run, by the way? – bearing a package which you nonchalantly announce as containing Libyan crude, meaning, presumably, crude oil from Libya, and you don't find it interesting?" Epworth, serene, munched a leaf of lettuce with the rapt concentration of an epicurean hamster.

"Must you always ask two questions at a time?" Determined not to be drawn, he ignored one of them. "All right. I find it interesting, particularly as they expected you to be there."

"Good. Absence makes the mind grow careless. Tell me what took place."

Morpurgo told him. Epworth asked no questions, but there was no doubt of his attention. They came to coffee. Epworth, thin as an Embankment lamppost, dropped a saccharin tablet in his. He did it, he explained, to keep his plump Amaryllis company and had gained the habit.

They sat in what, for Morpurgo, was an uncompanionable silence. Epworth broke it by asking, "Anyone mention – mmmm – anything about temperature?"

"It was warm. Weber, I think, it was Weber, said something about temperature of emergence."

"Nothing about down-hole temperature?"

"No." He could only guess what down-hole temperature was. Dismally, he accepted that Epworth had no need to guess.

"More coffee?"

"No thanks. Oh, they talked about a trip."

"Did they say where?"

"No. Well, not just to the seaside."

"And how" – Was Epworth actually serious for an instant? – "*do* you feel about trips?"

With Sylvie? More enthusiastic by the minute. "Anything," Morpurgo said with what he thought was admirably weighty ambiguity, "is better than nothing. And anywhere than nowhere."

"I wonder." Epworth signalled for the bill.

They parted on the Embankment, Epworth bearing the

package. He disappeared into the maw of the Embankment station, possibly the only senior member of SIS who ever actually arrived at Century House by the grimy Lambeth North Underground Station.

Morpurgo went back to investigate the antecedents of the *Tattershall Castle*. It had sailed the Humber estuary, a watery link between Grimsby and Hull via New Holland. His activities in the Sattin spy case had taken him, most significantly, to that part of the world, providing him with a triumph that had turned to ashes and brought him to his present nadir. Epworth had not chosen their meeting place casually after all.

*   *   *

Epworth's first act on arrival was to send for Hannay, a phlegmatic, bespectacled South London troll, addicted, interestingly, to dominoes and spotted bow ties, whom the inexorable laws of the Whitehall Medes and Persians would soon drive into retirement.

"What have we got this time, sir? Won the mystery prize again, have we? May I take it that there's nothing in this little chap that's likely to do us a mischief, sir?"

"The worst to be feared is a dry-cleaning bill and – mmmm – a rocket from Mrs Hannay."

"Is that so, sir? Just have to be extra careful then, shan't we?" Springing the catches of his battered case, Hannay began to set out his instruments with the methodical calmness of a GP attending his thousandth home delivery.

Some thirty minutes later he gave a little grunt, not so much satisfaction as the period to a task more finicky than difficult. He watched while Epworth performed his own much briefer operation.

"That's it, sir? Wish they were all as easy, still, beggars can't be choosers. Boredom'd be the problem, wouldn't it, Mr Epworth? Now, sir, everything back to square one? if you take my meaning."

Epworth interrupted the humming of some obscure refrain. "Back to square one it is, thank you, Mr Hannay."

SEVEN

Eric Pottern knew he would never be a member of Archer's social circle. Like a meter reader or the TV repair man, he came to Archer's Bayswater flat when duty called.

"Drink?" Archer held him at a precise level, a little beyond the TV man, who would enter the living room on sufferance, and the meter reader, forever restricted to the hall.

"Thank you. A beer." While his master went through to the kitchen, Pottern took his usual look around the large, elegant room, its balcony windows offering a distant segment of Kensington Gardens; grass, trees, a silvery wink of water. It remained just as it had been at the end of whatever sway Helga Archer had been permitted to hold, Archer's views on a woman's place varying only in degree from Hitler's *Kinde, küche, kirche*.

Except for the flowers. He knew another woman – not just the daily who came to vac and dust – had moved in to fill the vacuum created by Helga Archer's expulsion; there were little signs. Archer's separation, divorce proceedings, his split family – son siding with mother, daughter theoretically father-orientated but currently off on some wild, rebellious jag – were something that seldom came up as a topic of conversation in Curzon Street, though there were some who insisted that it was by no means all Morpurgo's fault.

Archer returned; one beer, one gin and tonic. He dropped into his oyster velvet armchair. "Strictly off the record, right?" The growing pressure of his new responsibilities was not the only reason for the increase in what Pottern privately described as his home calls.

Pottern nodded. "Of course." Suits me, he thought, if it suits you.

Archer toyed with his drink. "Because" – This was going to be a prepared statement, Pottern guessed – "we're walking close to the edge of our official remit. I mean what the powers-that-be see as our remit."

Pottern said nothing, his beer untouched. The boss had something going with the Home Office mandarins, maybe even higher, but the American connection touched dangerously closely upon interministerial rivalry. There were other powers-that-were, a little farther down Whitehall at the Foreign Office, still smug over their and SIS's victory in the battle between their respective secretaries of state at the time of the Sattin affair. Should they get wind of the Gatwick conspiracy, history might well repeat itself. Pottern, imprinted early in life with the essence of the old Chinese saying that in a struggle between elephants, it is the grass that suffers, was in no mind to be trampled.

"Point is, most of these Home Office jokers don't see far beyond their noses on this kind of thing, Eric. But in our game, it's not always enough to wait for things to happen. Sometimes it pays to run with the hare."

Pottern toyed with his beer. Archer the risk-taker was a new phenomenon, to be viewed with caution and preferably from a distance, the more so since, though his boss would swear that the quarry referred to was Timothy, he, Eric Pottern, knew very well it was Morpurgo.

"And since our kind of hare" – Archer drank some of his gin and tonic; Pottern, a careful second or so later, sipped his beer – "makes a regular habit of jogging into no-man's-land, well, to hell with Home Office jokers who say we wait until he comes out again."

Pottern kept a careful silence.

"Now." Archer was ready to come to his point. "Where does it stop? And what's the lie of the land either side? Are you with me?"

"More than one no-man's-land. Leastways" – Play it his way,

as far as you can. He's your future – "a lot of no-man's-land, not all in one piece."

"Gatwick. Billingshurst. Washington . . ."

". . . Libya."

"And a running feud between the Yanks and the Libyans. Well, what's the common factor?"

Wants me to say Hank Timothy, Pottern saw. He said, "How about Richard Goss? The President's National Security Adviser."

Archer checked what he had been about to say. "Goss?"

"Big pal of this man Folger. All roads lead to Rome, wouldn't you say?" He watched his remark ring a bell here, flash a light there before finally notching up a score. Not stupid, he thought, just slow.

"Any attempt on the President's life is a matter of national security." Archer frowned. "I see that." He thought it through. "And when Cochran calls for help because the Sussex cops are crawling all over an operation with major international implications . . ."

"Affecting Libya." Pottern could show all the outward emotion of an incubating King Penguin.

". . . someone has to coordinate. Goss kicks out Church. Goss calls in Langley. Goss . . ." Archer frowned again, more deeply. "If Langley is in from the start, why are we in at all? I mean, when they wanted a bit of swift, confidential help in getting the police out at Billingshurst, why not go through SIS? Cousins and Friends, that's the usual drill. If they need us or the Branch, Lambeth lays it on, both ministries in the picture through the appropriate civil servants, right?"

Pottern, more overtly confident, tossed off his beer. "Two reasons for going out into no-man's-land, wouldn't you say? Find out what the other bloke's up to. Or because you're up to a bit of monkey business yourself."

He saw he would have to give a nudge. "Cover-up over Gatwick, we happen to know why. What are they trying to cover up at Billingshurst that they don't want SIS to know about?"

"But they must know that we and the Friends work hand in glove on most things, most things in the UK, anyway."

109

"That's right. Maybe . . ." Pottern hesitated carefully.

"Go on, man. Maybe what?"

"Well," – Pottern radiated frankness – "Mr Epworth's new, and you're new, neither of you completely settled in yet, so to speak. Maybe they're hoping you, the two of you, haven't got your act together yet, hand in glove, but not always the right glove and the right hand." He smiled the apologetic smile of the man who knows he may have gone too far.

"Of course" – He watched beneath his stubby lashes as Archer took the bait – "over there in Lambeth they know nothing at all about Timothy. About what happened at Gatwick, I mean. So I suppose we haven't got the act together, not really."

"No." Archer was thoughtful. "But we've got the edge, Eric. And we're making all the running."

"Bit of ground to make up, Mr Archer." He made a joke, an unusual thing for Eric Pottern. "Wouldn't want to lose another Home Secretary or something."

"Eric." A hesitant, speculative ring to the name; try this one on for size.

"Sir?" A good time to throw in an oblique reminder of forth-coming honours.

"I'm supposed to pay a sort of courtesy call at Century House in the near future, unofficial, nothing fixed."

"Good idea, I'd have thought, at this stage."

"Yes." Archer looked at what was left of his gin and tonic. "Maybe this isn't quite the time to say anything about – well, what we've been chewing over."

"A bit premature?"

"Yes."

"It'd give me time to put pictures of Timothy around," Pottern said helpfully. "See if anyone remembers noticing him at any port of entry around the time of the Billingshurst break-in."

"And I could take the opportunity of asking Epworth what's new in Libya these days. I mean we do have a legitimate interest, now we've a positive identification of Timothy as a focus of terrorist activities out there."

"Good idea, Mr Archer."

Archer looked, as often, for a glimpse of Pottern's soul and, as always, failed to find it. Still, a small price to pay for industry and reliability. Oh, and loyalty, of course, especially loyalty. He tossed back his drink. "Another beer before you go, old son."

*　　　*　　　*

"Johnny? It's me, Sylvie. Can you hear me all right?"

"Perfectly. Where are you? Is everything okay?"

"Everything's fine. I'm in a little place called San Esteban de la Fuente, about sixty miles from Toledo." French, Italian, Spanish; listening to her rattle it off he thought, enviously, that Sylvie picked up languages by a kind of osmosis.

"See your folks?"

"They sent you their love."

"You didn't stay long." He knew how Sylvie's parents loved him. Her father, childish sense of humour, childish delight in making money, one of nature's Tories, thought him amusing rather than dangerous in his political views. Her mother, initially treating him as something that might go away if one took no notice, had never really become reconciled to her error of judgement.

"Just overnight. Work to be done. How are you?"

My mother may be going to die. I'm being used by people who see me as a sort of superior glove-puppet. Steve will shortly be in a position to dead-end me for the rest of my career, even get me kicked out as a security risk. "Oh, I'm all right. What's it like where you are?"

The street, through her window, ran straight, an unbroken double row of whitewashed, single-storey houses like a natural rock formation with windows, the only sign of life a somnolence of cows winding into a dark courtyard.

"I see a windmill. The one that Don Quixote charged on Rosinante." It posed on the near horizon, dominating pink roofs. The cross of its sails pinned streaks of sulphur yellow to a sky supercharged with radiance. Unexpectedly, she felt desolate.

"The very same windmill?"

"Well, a direct descendant."

"Sylvie?"

"Still here." She understood. Silence was absence.

111

"I saw Pierre Weber today, small world. He asked after you."

"Say hello if you see him again." She dabbed at her eyes with her fingertips. What we feel hides behind what we don't say.

"I might be going on a trip. Would you mind?" This was less a conversation than a situation report.

"Oh. Really? Where?" She knew she sounded unnatural.

"I don't know, not yet."

"Don't know or can't tell?"

"Don't know. Truly. Anyway, it may not come off." Without warning a word came into his head: Libya.

"Do you know when, then?"

"No idea."

"Well I hope it happens. Something definite." Liar! A trip was competition. A trip might cause him to unmake his mind. Between the street and the sky lay a patchwork of cultivation; the green of cereals, the pointillism of fruit and vines, a river that was already little more than a beadwork of muddy pools noisy with frogs. His trip might offer something better.

She found herself saying, "The trouble is, Johnny, I'm good at just this one thing. And only then so long as I put my whole mind to it. I could give it up but . . ." She stopped before her voice broke. She had had no intention of saying it.

"Sylvie, it's all right." He was shocked, all that distance away. "I told you. I've made up my mind."

She found a handkerchief, dabbed angrily. "I must go, my darling. Things to do. Too many. There always are." Damn, damn, damn! As good as saying: If you were here, if you worked for me . . .

She rushed on. "I'll try to call again tomorrow. I'll be in Badajoz. Then Mérida, the Emperatriz."

"Sylvie, you must understand, I've never loved anyone else but you, not even . . ."

She hadn't heard. "Johnny, if they've given you a job, do it well, the way you can, the way you used to. Stop feeling sorry for yourself. Call you again soon. Goodbye."

Left holding the dead receiver, he was overwhelmed by a sense of . . . uselessness. "If they've given you a job, do it well!" Not hopelessness, uselessness; a man who, not so long ago, had

112

been near the top in spite of having to work with people who only half-trusted him, some of them not at all. He had held to the middle path, worked for whichever party was in power, kept his prejudices in a separate compartment from his duty. It was the naked prejudice of others that had felled him.

He really believed it.

He went out to see his mother, glad to leave the empty house. It was typical of her not to have let him know in advance that she was going into hospital.

The atmosphere in the hospital was close, psychologically as well. Lavish and well-meaning use of colour in premises that had been old when he was a boy had achieved the effect of rouge on withered cheeks.

His mother was drowsy, the after-effects of an anaesthetic preceding the first of several tests. She seemed, he thought, to have yielded less to it than the circumstances, as if a long-drawn-out battle needed no longer to be fought.

"You should have told me. I'd have come sooner."

"Why? I'm not going anywhere."

"What do they say?"

"What do they ever say?" She smiled, a fleeting impression that fate had at last softened her, but then, in an embarrassingly loud whisper, complained that the Health Service had been taken over by the coloureds.

"I'll have you moved to a private room."

"What would I do in a private room? Anyway, the nurses are still black. Here I am, here I'll stay till they've finished with me."

"I may have to go away, mum. For a bit. On a trip."

A spark of old mischief. "Well then, if you have to go, you'll go, won't you?"

He asked to see the doctor on his way out. Like the ward sister – had his mother infected him? – she was dark-skinned, a plump Indian woman with a Welsh-sounding accent and a worried, gold-toothed smile. The tests? Just tests, too soon to go into details. She is an old lady who is living by herself – an Asiatically veiled reproach? – not able to stand tests if she must be in and out like a parcel.

A private room? Two other people were waiting to talk to the doctor. "Not here, not any more. And she is an old lady, Mr Morpurgo. She is making fusses sometimes, but no trouble and she really welcomes company."

Out into a golden evening, his mood edging it with black like a tastelessly ostentatious funeral card.

* * *

For the coordinators and their satraps, every day at Century House began with what was universally known as morning prayers, a meeting which, since Epworth had become king of the castle, was through in a thirty-minute gallop. Morpurgo attended, foot of the table, naturally. It was held in one of the modular conference rooms which had the older hands talking nostalgically of Queen Anne's Gate, where at least the walls were solid, even if you did get lost in the corridors. Here, the only compensation was that the coordinators' washroom was close at hand, urinals dribbling nonstop, roller towels invariably jammed or trailing damp and grubby banners.

Today had all the current imperatives; another reshuffle of courier lines, a second-grade analysis, from dying Hong Kong, of Peking's oil prospects in the East China Sea, a no-money bleat from the Navy over a proposal to replot Swedish underwater defences in the Kalmarsund and the Aland Channel. Any Other Business arrived after an angry spat over a reference to Cat grasses in the West Belfast Intelligence District, Elsenham being himself a Catholic and retorting with icily pointed references to Prod prejudice.

Epworth, who could sometimes be anything but vague, repeated, "Any other business?"

Kennet, Inter-Operational Relations, a ferrety schoolmaster-type who played in chess tournaments and rolled his own cigarettes with black Balkan tobacco, had been waiting. "Rat-King, Chief Coordinator. New from Mrs Rattigan this morning, your initiation."

"Yes." Epworth could make mildness wildly provocative.

"Category, Chief Coordinator, please?' Kennet was entitled to ask.

"Mmmm – PE."

There was a small stir of interest among the scatter of files,

114

empty coffee cups and untidily full ashtrays. "Ministry authority, Chief Coordinator?"

"Not yet." Epworth initialled something he might or might not have been reading. "May or may not – mmmm – gel."

"Topic? Or is that not to be recorded at this stage?"

"Oil." Epworth made it sound vague, even uncertain. Morpurgo looked up.

Wriothsley, thick mane glowing like bullion, tended to regard oil, regardless of source, as his private domain; his region was Middle East. Rumour whispered that he had been promised a highly-paid advisory post with British Petroleum after retirement. "Region, Chief Coordinator?"

Epworth appeared not to hear the question. "Any other business, gentlemen?"

Kennet had a last shot. "Referees? Apart from yourself?"

"John Morpurgo. Any other business?"

Did they realise, Morpurgo wondered, aware of the impression Epworth's answer had created, that he was as ignorant as they?

Epworth was standing. "Thank you, gentlemen. Johnny, my office in about thirty minutes. Mrs Rattigan will give you a buzz."

When he went up, Epworth was standing by his bookshelves – an amazingly heterogeneous collection ranging from the *ABC Shipping Guide* through such storehouses as *Hansard* and the *International Year Book and Statesman's Who's Who* to the *World Bibliography of Bibliographies* and numerous bound volumes of *Early Music, The Freethinker* and *International Affairs* – staring thoughtfully at the sealed package he had taken from Morpurgo aboard the *Tattershall Castle* the previous day.

Morpurgo, too, stared at it. "Operation Rat-King?"

Epworth, smiling vaguely, picked up the Cousins' package, considered it vaguely, put it down again.

Morpurgo tried again. "What's a PE operation?"

"Private enterprise. Unofficial classification for something that may or may not – mmmm – take off." He responded to the buzz of his intercom, using the phone, not the loudspeaker. "Have them bring him up, Mrs Rattigan."

Morpurgo heard someone delivered to the outer office. No

one, no matter how exalted, was permitted to wander about Century House unescorted. Epworth, correctly interpreting his unspoken question, said, "Stay." Steve Archer walked in.

There is a rare moment, late on a winter afternoon, the temperature hovering on zero, the sky clear, the sun just vanished, when one may witness the turning of surface moisture on a road or pavement to ice. It brings a sudden, subtle glazing, a tiny but audible snap.

It happened, there and then.

In the same moment, Epworth said, "Steve, welcome. Just got to slip away for an instant. Johnny will look after you." It was the first time Morpurgo and Archer had met since Morpurgo's departure from Curzon Street.

Archer's gaze followed Epworth from the room, then returned to Morpurgo. He delivered an almost imperceptible nod, saw a copy of *The Economist* on Epworth's desk and took it to the window.

It was Morpurgo, driven by what he decided was chutzpah, who broke the silence. "I hear you're to be congratulated. You have mine, most sincerely."

Archer stopped flicking through the pages of the magazine. I am a gentleman, his manner said, but oh! how I wish I were not. "Good of you. Thank you."

Next? Morpurgo asked himself; next? for Christ's sake!

"You always said you didn't see your role in life as being a permanent 2 i/c."

"Did I? Yes, I suppose I did." Still looking toward the window, Archer closed the magazine.

The silence, making one aware that there was life in other places.

Archer turned. "Settling in?"

"I suppose so. Yes, I must be, mustn't I?" A hideous, impossible urge to ask after Helga.

Steve turned back to the window, contemplating Epworth's distant train-set. "Don't sound too sure."

"Probably because I'm not." Where the hell was bloody Epworth?

Staring fixedly through the window, Steve said, "Don't know that I'm fully settled in myself."

"And now the Knight's off, you have to start all over again."

Steve turned. His face, patrician as ever, was graven. "Wasn't my doing. His leaving."

"I'm sure. No need to have it on your conscience."

"It isn't." A flash of the old near-arrogance. "Only hope I'll be able to do his job half as well." A faint trace of self-annoyance, realising that he was inviting a compliment. "Bit out of my depth, I dare say."

Morpurgo, wryly, said, "Snap." It was their first directly personal exchange. "On the other hand" – Where *was* Epworth, for God's sake? – "it's a job."

"They haven't given you a territory?"

That was dangerously close to a taboo. Twin services, maybe, but each largely secret from the other. Need to know – remembering Epworth's little joke – was the supposed yardstick, but a yard, in the security community, was highly elastic.

"No, not yet."

"Any preference?" Making conversation, no hint of thaw.

Morpurgo shrugged. "You know me, Steve." The first name, slipping out, was instantly, like spilled quicksilver, highly conspicuous, virtually irrecoverable. He went on quickly. "Everything I know is UK-related. Take . . . well, take Libya, for example. In Curzon Street it meant terrorism, murder squads. Here it's oil, Soviet infiltration, US stick-waving."

Looking back much later, he was to realise that the mention of Libya had been natural enough, since the odd business of the Libyan crude. He even registered the fact that Steve looked at him strangely, and put it down to the mention of a country that would be by no means the first to come to most people's minds.

Steve turned looking at his watch into something gracefully elaborate. "What's brother Epworth up to, anyway?"

"God knows!"

Steve decided to sit, still keeping his distance. "Odd you should mention Libya. Does the name of Hank Timothy say anything to you? Any echoes from the past?"

"No. Should there be?"

"Just happened to come up recently, that's all. One of that bunch of odds and sods the Libyans hired to run the training centre outside Tripoli."

Morpurgo shook his head. "Don't remember him. Two or three Americans there, aren't there? Two Dutchmen, a Belgian and the ex-Rhodesian."

"English ex-Rhodesian. He's small fry. Timothy isn't. We've only just managed to put a name to him, actually. Still, no great importance."

A moment later, Epworth was back. "Terribly sorry. Most – mmmm – rude. Still, I've no doubt you two found plenty to talk about." You bastard! Morpurgo thought. You shameless bloody bastard!

"Thank you very much for standing in, Johnny," Epworth was saying. "Steve and I are going to have a *tour d'horizon* now, so I'm afraid our – mmmm – little chat will have to wait until later." Looking at his blandly amiable face, Morpurgo, definitely *not* echolalia, heard him saying once more: *Libya. Interesting.*

*   *   *

"Why don't I," Claas said, settling himself comfortably in Epworth's best guest chair, "get straight to the point? which is a guy called Hank Timothy." On Epworth's desk stood the jar of Libyan crude, to which, so Epworth and Morpurgo had discovered on opening the package, something strange had happened.

"Full name" – Weber, having taken a lesser chair without resentment, slouched almost at full length – "Henry Bush Timothy, aka Hank Bush, Tim Bush, Henry Timms, permute ad infinitum."

"Take a look." Claas passed a photograph. What struck Morpurgo most was the man's obvious arrogance.

"Tell you anything?" Claas was looking at Epworth.

"Mmmm – tough customer. Probably clever, too. Or thinks so."

"One very smart cookie, numero uno on my list."

"Of what?"

"Of smart cookies. As opposed to intelligent."

"As contrasted with," Weber corrected. "Meaning that Hank is smart *and* intelligent, but mostly smart."

Claas jeered. "Metaphysics yet!"

Weber ignored him. "And a luster after gold." The words had a curiously Old Testament ring.

Claas nodded. "Money is what Hank is all about. But good," he added reluctantly. "It has to be said that the schmuck is good."

"Ex-Langley," Weber said sadly. Morpurgo was wondering about the connection between Steve Archer, Hank Timothy and Libyan crude.

"But not everybody" – Claas looked at Morpurgo almost accusingly – "got the news." Epworth was listening with a faint smile, fixed and polite.

"You mean he's crooked?" Morpurgo had given Epworth the first chance to ask questions.

"One day," Claas said, "Hank will walk round a corner and straight up his own ass."

"Anal fixation," Weber explained apologetically. "Sometimes known as the Kansas City syndrome. Comes from a lifetime of walking behind cows." His melancholy deepened. "Hank specialises in wrong turnings, but so far he's kept ahead of the opposition."

Morpurgo pushed. "Meaning Langley?"

"Langley. Also Mossad, SDECE. BND. For starters."

An ex-CIA man wanted by the Israelis, Paris and Bonn as well as his former employers, must have made big waves. "What did he do?"

"Let me tell you." Weber seemed to be leaving most of the talking to Claas. "Recruited in '61, went through his training summa cum laude."

"Latin yet!" Weber murmured.

Claas ticked off stubby fingers. "Cuba, after the Bay of Pigs. Dirty tricks, speaks good Spanish."

"Give Hank a clean trick" – Weber's gloom was driving him lower and lower in his chair – "he just naturally dirties it."

"Guatemala," Claas's next finger told him. "Counter-intelligence on behalf of the regime. You could call it putting down the opposition."

Morpurgo grinned. "I did."

"Yeah." Claas gave him a cold stare. "I never forget, colour you pink." He addressed himself to Epworth. "Ever heard of Operation Phoenix?"

"Vietnam. Putting down the opposition." Epworth produced his giggle. "Or perhaps pushing's a better verb."

"Check. Hank's customers mostly fell out of choppers." Claas's forefinger sketched a brief descending spiral. "When Uncle Sam pulled out, Hank and his outfit kind of lost a lot of cryptos who'd been waiting to help the Cong take over Saigon."

"Of course" – Weber, eyes closed, voice exhausted, reminded Morpurgo of the Dormouse at the Mad Hatter's tea-party – "they were only gooks, so what the hell?" His gloom was the product of a devastating shame.

"Well," Claas continued unabashed, "the great retreat . . ."

"Defeat." Weber's voice came from the depths of the teapot.

"Retreat, defeat, I should still be wearing black or something? Hank had to find his fun someplace else, Thailand, Angola, you name it. Then, come '73, Chile."

"'Society offenders'", Weber quoted, "'who might well be underground and who never would be missed.' General Pinochet had a little list, Hank had another. We don't think it was actually Hank who killed President Allende."

Unexpectedly, he sat up straight. "This guy is *bad*!"

"Then," Claas said unemotionally, "we had '76."

"The Bicentennial," Epworth said brightly.

"Also Get the CIA Year." Claas whistled. "The CIA was gone over, but good. The CIA got theirs."

"And Hank Timothy" – Weber cheered up a little – "got his. Not that you'd have noticed. Early retirement, full pension rights, everything but a razzmatazz presentation on the White House lawn."

"Plus the kind of character references," Claas said, "that could get you a bank presidency."

"Didn't make bank president. Set himself up running a security business in Dade County – that's Miami – his own money plus some backing from a bunch of pals he made in Cuba before Castro kicked them out."

"They" – Claas took over again – "*had* made bank president, or anyway that kind of dough. Hank rounded up two or three of his old Nam buddies to work with him."

"All class of '76." Weber waved them goodbye.

Claas scratched his crotch cosily. "His Cuban amigos ran a

nice clean show, import-export. Arms, drugs, paying passengers. Good money, but Hank got bored again."

"No chopper," Weber explained. "Not so much fun pushing people out of boats. Also one or two uncouth individuals with Mafia connections were beginning to wonder about that ex in ex-CIA."

"So," Epworth said, "he went to Libya." Morpurgo all but jumped.

Claas, about to continue, screwed up his eyes as if Epworth had just begun to burn with a very bright light. Epworth, looking amiably apologetic, extended a finger towards the metamorphosed Libyan crude.

Weber, respectful, said, "Libya is where Hank is alive and well and living in, yes. Kind of quartermaster general, procurement of lots of specialised weapons and equipment those people are not supposed to have."

"Almost everything" – Epworth had become something more than a passive audience – "except nuclear warheads."

Weber's respect visibly increased. "So far. He also runs a very efficient intelligence service out there, as well as supervising the training of what they like to call their revolutionary commandos."

Claas made a vulgar noise. "Hit squads. Taught them all his dirty tricks, them and visiting firemen from a whole bunch of terrorist organisations, all the way from Japan to Northern Ireland." He looked toward Morpurgo. "I guess we don't have to tell *you* that."

Without that jar of gummed-up crude, Morpurgo thought, it might sufficiently have explained Steve Archer's interest.

"Terrorists," Weber said, "are what Hank has plenty of. You could call them his personal version of the CIA."

Epworth giggled. "Or SIS. Would anyone care for a glass of sherry? A rather special parcel – mmmm – just in from my personal *almacenista*, Amontillado Viejo from the Balbaina district." His full smile was as brilliant as Weber's fitful dazzler.

Claas had long since decided that Epworth was mad, but Weber's own smile peeped out. "A little late in the day, wouldn't you say? Or maybe early? You see why so many people would like to get their hands on Hank?"

"Near miss quite recently," Claas told them. "All set to pick the guy off . . ."

"Where?" Epworth's interruption showed eager interest. His invitation to sherry was as if it had never been made.

"Someplace in Spain," Claas said. "Up in the mountains." He shook his head ruefully. "'Thrice is he armed that hath his quarrel just, But four times he that gets his blow in fust'. Which Hank did, with the help of some ETA terrorists. Probably alumni of Hank's Tripoli hit school."

"What happens" – Epworth's interest switched – "if you add a little – mmmm – something to a Libyan oil-well instead of to a jar of Libyan crude?"

Everybody laughed, even Claas. It was all as natural as canned studio applause.

"Mmmm – bait?" Epworth's face shone with enthusiasm.

"We'll come to that." Weber saw Morpurgo's doubt. "What happened to that jar of crude is a bacterial thing. Seems there's always bugs in oil. At certain temperatures and pressures they get out of hand, start multiplying until the oil's choked with waste products. Some corrode the wellhead gear. Some produce sulphur products that make the oil unsaleable. Some thicken it up so that it's hard to pump. In bad cases the whole well seizes up, takes years to clear.

"In practice they take precautions, everything sterile, especially the drilling mud. Even if things go wrong it's a slow thing, time to take steps before it gets out of hand."

"But this . . ." Epworth, at last, picked up the jar of semi-coagulated crude.

"That," Claas said, "is something else."

Why, Morpurgo wondered, should the prior meeting with Steve Archer introduce a doubt? "A threat, is that it? And Timothy's paid by the Libyans to handle threats, but when he tries to fix this one, you'll handle him." He had one doubt, all the same. "And he's not going to smell a CIA trick? One man, against everything Langley could line up? Anyway, what could he do? Steal it? You'd simply make more."

"We don't want him to steal it," Weber said. "We want him to use it."

"Shut down the Libyan oilfields." Epworth said it as if they were discussing the closing of a neighbourhood porn shop. "What would he get in return? Money? Immunity? Hardly an offer – mmmm – of reemployment."

Morpurgo was watching Weber. *This guy is bad!* Translation: He works for the opposition.

"We could make a deal all right," Claas said, and Morpurgo, surprised, heard a note of regret.

"Just one small snag." It was Weber who was soft and persuasive. "Timothy would sooner cosy up to a rattlesnake than anyone from Langley. We need a third party, in and out fast, no follow-up, no track record to upset Hank, but plenty of experience."

"Like looking for a virgin in a cathouse," Claas said. "Though Hank does have this weird sense of humour, kind of likes people who buck the system. Well, you can understand that, I suppose. I mean, he certainly bucks it himself." His eyes settled on Morpurgo.

"We got as far as naming the operation." Weber was concentrating on Epworth. "We call it Operation Rumpus."

"Mmmmmmm." Epworth contemplated infinity for an appropriate length of time while Morpurgo felt his anger and mistrust become increasingly difficult to contain.

Epworth brought his gaze back, focusing it on Morpurgo. "Johnny?"

*   *   *

When Claas and Weber had gone, Morpurgo, whose chief problem was knowing where to start, found it quickly resolved. Epworth started for him.

"So Steve Archer asked you about Hank Timothy?"

"He told you, did he? Yes, well don't just say 'Interesting'."

"Isn't it?"

"I suppose you're going to tell me Steve knows all about *that*." Morpurgo jerked his thumb at the jar of crude. "And about Claas and Weber."

"Oh, indeed no. I suppose you're going to tell me it's all coincidence."

"Isn't it?"

Epworth picked up the jar of crude, unscrewed the cap, sniffed as delicately as a cat. He made a *moue* of distaste. "A big offer. Put Libya out of the oil business. An impossible offer, but the man Timothy is doubtless too arrogant, too full of hate to see the impossibility."

He replaced the cap and, seeing Morpurgo's bafflement, smiled his apologetic smile. "Yesterday afternoon, after you'd given this to me, I came straight back here and sent for Hannay."

One of the things Morpurgo had managed to learn since coming to Century House was that Hannay's particular skills could extract the kernel from a nut while leaving the shell intact. After a while, his voice rough with self-disgust, he said, "The tape. Claas's secretary brought the box. He pretended to bawl her out for forgetting the tape. She went to get it, only a moment, but she had the jar in her hand."

Epworth nodded. "When Hannay opened it, the – mmmm – goo was already there. They switched jars under your nose. Thimble-rigged you, Johnny."

Morpurgo sighed, half sorry, half relieved. "That's why you agreed I should act as go-between for Langley with Timothy. I thought you'd gone out of your mind."

Epworth mimed a sprinkling motion with thumb and fore-finger. "A few pinches of powder here and there and we could say with Pitt, 'Roll up that map, it will not be wanted this ten years.' Only for ten we would be obliged to say – mmmm – a hundred? The Middle East. Mexico. Alaska. And of course, the Caucasus, the Urals, Siberia. No need for the nuclear threat, the balance of terror. A little bacterial sabotage in the Caucasus, the Urals and Siberia, and the USSR falls apart, industry crippled, economy in ruins. If they really had such a potent substance they'd hardly be using it to play games with a thug like Timothy or a statelet like Libya."

Morpurgo, deflated, could have kicked himself. And yet – how perverse the human mind! – for a while he had almost had a purpose. Now it was gone.

"It doesn't work. It couldn't work. I should have seen it." He saw something else. "A hit. Has to be, doesn't it? Bait, after all. Bait for Timothy."

"The idea works, that's all that's necessary. That's all our dear Cousins need, just an idea. But how very curious that they had it

124

just as . . ." Epworth's mild eyes clouded. "Poetism. Pure poetism."

Morpurgo was belatedly jerked from his own thoughts. "What? What on earth is poetism?"

Epworth looked surprised. "Oh, you haven't come across the word?" His surprise was so naked that Morpurgo instantly suspected him of having made the word up. "Poetism is the art of making the false sound true because it's so aesthetically satisfying. Like the earth being the centre of the universe. Like God being made in the likeness of man, or have I got it the wrong way round? Like the human embryo passing through all the stages of evolution during its nine months in the womb, or . . ."

"I get it." Morpurgo was impatient. "So where's the poetism in oil that turns into gunge? Or doesn't. And where's . . ."

But Epworth's serpentine mind had already moved on. "Tell me, did Libyan terrorism cause you any sleepless nights during your latter days in Curzon Street?"

"No. Once upon a time they gave us problems, but it simmered down." Morpurgo was wrestling with temptation and his conscience. "I suppose there'd be better people than me for the job. Trained in that kind of work." He grudged every word.

Epworth's smile became fixed, the mad, determined rictus of the vicar not quite getting the point of a risqué joke.

"Look." Morpurgo became quietly desperate. "They asked if we'd play ball in setting up a meet with Timothy. To make him a proposition. We said yes."

"*You* said yes."

"And you agreed."

Epworth sat musing for a moment. "Operation Rumpus. Well, that's their name, not ours."

Morpurgo wondered if he would ever understand the man. "Rat-King. You're telling me this is the beginning of Operation Rat-King. Private enterprise. Oil. But how, in God's name, could you have known?" He found himself, figuratively speaking, back at the bottom end of the table. "I can't be told?"

"Best not."

"Is it something worthwhile?" He was going to have to go back on his word to Sylvie. It would have to be worthwhile.

"The Foreign Office appears to think so."

"The Foreign Office!"

"My dear chap, you really don't think we could afford to fly solo on a trip like this? Besides" – That giggle, which could, in certain circumstances, sound quite sinister – "Archer's already got the backing of the Home Office. We can't afford to be out-gunned." He giggled again, and this time it was amusement. "Rat-King and Rumpus, sounds just like a shady firm of lawyers. By the way, I see no reason for you not to tell Archer that the man Timothy has swum into our ken. It would be a neighbourly gesture, don't you think?"

Morpurgo was taken even farther aback. "I can't tell him anything without telling him everything."

"Oh, absolutely. Tell him everything. After all, you two are – mmmm – friends again, aren't you?"

*　　　*　　　*

"About Morpurgo." Weber watched Claas check his Omega as the taxi swung around Parliament Square. "You play rough, really rough, junior."

"Shake him up, get his mind off himself." Claas was un-troubled.

"We are what we are," Weber said sententiously. "A bad patch since Curzon Street, but he's good when he gets it all together."

"Guys in his position should know better than to sleep around. Okay, so he has a chill chick for a wife, but he could have picked someone outside the firm. What's eating you? Afraid he might get himself cleaned off the slate?"

"I certainly hope not."

"Look, Pierre, the guy's demoralised. With Hank, that could get him killed."

"He'll pull it off *because* he's demoralised. Because he needs to remoralise himself. Anyway, Langley will be riding shotgun."

"If you want to know, Epworth worries me more. We took a chance over that switch. I mean if that had gone wrong, every-thing would have gone wrong. I mean Epworth is no dope, whatever Barzelian thinks. Crazy, but no dope. What if he'd peeked or something?"

Weber regarded Claas pityingly. "What *do* you mean? *If* he'd peeked? You bet he peeked. Barzelian knew he would peek. You really thought he bought all that stuff about putting the Libs out of the oil business? Junior, you're cowtown clear through."

Claas turned sideways to stare at Weber, too shocked to be resentful. "But if Epworth *knew* it was a switch . . ."

". . . he'd have to guess it was really a hit. The Friends are tied to the Foreign Office apron-strings, you know that. Those Foreign Office people are mostly Arabists. You think they're going to risk stirring up the whole Middle East by getting themselves mixed up in something that can take out oilfields?"

Claas had gone into overdrive. "Pierre, are you telling me that stuff really *can* take out oilfields? Are you telling me that what we just laid on for Epworth was a sting?"

Weber was patient. "What we just laid on for Epworth will let the British Foreign Office look the other way while the Friends help us take out Timothy. Now do you get it?"

"Whoooo!" Claas wagged his head in exaggerated relief. "That Barzelian! He can sting you and you think it's butterfly kisses!"

Claas, Weber thought, was in a position to know, since he had just been on the receiving end of Barzelian's second sting.

*   *   *

The attentive but stupefying earnest young man – the hot-blooded Spanish have exoskeletons of *formalidad* – from the Archaeological Museum, introducing himself as Juan Felipe Roberto Carillo, had insisted on speaking English, execrable, while disdaining Sylvie's Spanish, fair. As well as a guided tour of Mérida, he had inflicted an interminable account of the Roman theatre; "my leading ardour". He had, she discovered, learned his English at a minor German university while studying archaeology.

Leaving her after the usual mid-afternoon lunch, he presented her with a pass to take her wherever she pleased in Extremadura, compliments of the Ministry of Tourism in Badajoz, and left her with much of her first day in ruins. Now, still among ruins, she sat high above the auditorium of Mérida's Roman theatre, waiting to begin a salvage job. For a photographer, as she had often told Johnny, an opportunity missed was usually lost forever.

While she waited, relaxing in the late afternoon sun, watching swallows and martins wheeling and screaming in the updraught between the amphitheatre and the crest of the hill, she enjoyed a rare sense of timelessness that rapid-fire bursts of working-class Spanish from the stonemasons did nothing to diminish, since it was originally by stonemasons, two thousand years earlier, that it had been brought into being.

The light, spilling down the cascade of seating in rouches of fawn and violet, giving the paved orchestra a checkerboard effect, striking purple bars of shadow from the double arcade of columns, finally matched itself with the waiting images in her mind. Walking slowly and diagonally down, she went through a spool and a half of colour, switched to wide angle for her panoramics, used the second camera to capture the workmen, little more than slow-moving silhouettes, in black and white, then returned to the highest tier where, as Juan Felipe Roberto had phrased it, 'the nether classes' of Hispano-Roman society had been allowed to watch the spectacles. The drop between one row and the next was so great that their long dead occupants must have dangled dusty, sweaty feet about the faces of those beneath.

Now she was left with the boring bit, but none the less important. She wrote out the coloured self-adhesive labels for her exposed rolls, completed her exposure record, cleaned cameras and lenses with the puffer and brush, packed everything away in the holdall and lit the most enjoyable cigarette of all, the one at the end of a session . . .

Propping her back against cool stone she half-closed her eyes, trying to picture the motley, semi-barbarous peoples – Iberian indigenes, Celts, legionaires from a score of lands – who must have packed these terraces. Even Juan Felipe Roberto, in some respects more Teutonic than Spanish with his pedantic talk of *scaena*, *postscaenium* and *ima cava*, had been unable to wring that remote past totally dry.

But instead she was once more thinking of Johnny, who should have been here at her side, work well done, pleasure to come, ready to share a leisured evening, with tomorrow, all the tomorrows, to look forward to. And she must go back alone to the hotel, complete her records, get film packed ready for airmailing, check the street map ready for morning, together with all the pre-trip notes she had made, call Cáceres to confirm later bookings . . .

She sighed, hoisted her bag and went down the tiers, through the brief coolness of an archway, back to where the car waited. It was still in shade; one of the things you learned to anticipate. Sharing the shade, relaxed on a roadside bench near the office of the *conserje*, was a young man, sun lenses and bleached denims. She prepared herself for sexual harassment, but he simply watched with discreet interest while she unlocked, laid her bag on the rear seat, slid behind the wheel. The car refused to start.

She got out, released the bonnet, made a quick check of basics. Oh Johnny! Meet me halfway and we'll make a go of it.

"*Se puede ayudar, señora?*" The young man asked diffidently, without leaving the seat.

She slipped into Spanish. "Do you understand cars?"

"Quite well. If the señora will permit." He bent over the engine. He looked for some time in silence, gently touching leads, connections. "If the señora will return to the driving seat."

She went back. He continued to probe.

"If the señora will try once more."

The car started instantly. He smiled.

She leaned out. "I'm really most grateful."

"*De nada.* Happy to be of service." He stood back. At the last moment, markedly hesitant, "The señora is going back to the town?"

"Oh, would you like a lift?"

"If the señora is quite sure." His voice, though the accent was somehow not good Castilian, had some culture. "I would not wish to impose."

By the time they reached the river they were chatting amicably. He was fascinated by her commission. Before they parted in the Plaza de España – not the least suggestion that they should not – he was expressing gentle envy of her itinerary and her job.

With a last, "*Encantado. Adiós, señora. Buon viaje y que no te marees!*" he stepped back, waving as she drove off.

EIGHT

There had been a perceptible pause before Steve's voice, lazy over the telephone, said, "Timothy! Well, well, talk of the devil! Yes, by all means. Come on over."

After that, everything had been a little easier than Morpurgo had feared, though it was the first time he had been back to Curzon Street. He saw it as he had never seen it before, a squat, ugly, somehow seedy building, wearing its blast canopy like a pulled-down hat-brim, not worth even a first glance from the passer-by. Yet it wormed its way into the lives of tens of thousands as undetectably as a virus.

Every day its occupants went to and fro between it and the Euston Tower and the Yard and Gower Street and Horseferry Road, as well as smaller and quite unknown premises, plotting against plotters real and imaginary, functioning as part of the grey, subterranean organisation of vigilance and control, yet, at base, conspiring for themselves and their jobs and their families, with cause and country only the means to their private ends.

How dangerous, he thought bitterly, to be concerned for the cause when everyone else was primarily concerned for himself.

Entering the building to a respectful greeting from the duty uniform policeman, he found himself waiting for the lift with Kennedy of Political Research, and they chatted as if nothing had happened since their last meeting. He even – a pang there – met his onetime protégé, young Sibley, in the corridor to Steve's room, and Sibley was clearly pleased to see him.

Steve's room! Steve sat at Morpurgo's old desk. Morpurgo sitting where Steve had always sat in the old days, the scruffy green leather chair with the burn mark where the glowing tip of Steve's cigarette had once dropped off unobserved. He got a brief, familiar glimpse of Curzon Street. Every vehicle in sight, he knew, was 'staff' or 'known' or, once spotted by the closed circuit snooper cameras, had its registration fed into the Hendon police computer for vetting.

How the tables were turned, he thought. Steve, pride riding roughshod over cuckoldry and a broken marriage, had been carried clear by poise and rising professional fortune. Morpurgo, consigned to transriverine darkness, had sunk almost without a trace.

He told Steve about Langley and Hank Timothy, in an edited version agreed between himself and Epworth. Finished, he watched Steve put out one cigarette after using it to light the next, then throw himself back in his chair to smoke in silence, while Pottern, silent throughout, occupied his corner as unobtrusively as a house spider.

"Ex-Cousin." Archer glanced at Pottern. "Didn't know that, did we, Eric?"

"Weren't told puts it better."

Archer laughed. "Cousin Claas holding out on us. Understandable, now."

Morpurgo was surprised. "You discussed this with Warren Claas?"

"Not recently." Why was Steve guarded? "Not specifically, either. Quite some time back, checking on Gaddafi's mercenaries. Claas said Langley couldn't help."

Morpurgo twitched his lips. "Not surprising, is it?"

"Esprit de corps?" Steve's voice sharpened. "So what's changed? First they know nothing about him. Now, they need him so badly they swallow their pride and come to SIS for help." Something more than curiosity, Morpurgo thought, lay behind that overreactive tone.

"What do they want him for? Did they say?" Oh yes, far too casual, and Pottern, in his corner, had the absolute stillness of a suddenly wary cat.

Morpurgo followed instructions resented because Epworth, king of cats, had not explained them. "They have some scheme for damaging the Libyan economy. You know how paranoid the

White House has always been about Libya. Something that has to be done from the inside. They'll offer Timothy a pardon, big money, something like that."

Steve pounced. "A pardon! For what?"

The strength of his reaction lifted Morpurgo's eyebrows. Steve saw, and changed his tone. "I mean, governments don't like the idea of their nationals as mercenaries, but ordinarily speaking, it isn't a crime."

"No. I shouldn't have used the word. Cash, I think that's the main thing."

Pottern's drab voice almost startled after its long retreat. "A man like that's going to take some convincing. He must know how Langley feels about him."

"That's why they want to use me." Epworth, you subtle sod! What do you know that I don't? He had known Steve a long time, strengths and weaknesses, foibles and bedrock beliefs. Something at the back of all this had struck deep – Pottern too – but what? Something to do with Claas's – Langley's – unwillingness to be frank with Security Directorate and then go openly to SIS for cooperation? That, certainly, would rankle. The suspicion – they were all good at suspicion – that the Cousins were planning to snuff Timothy when Security Directorate – any anti-terrorist organisation – would much sooner have him as a subject for interrogation? The latter was more likely; Morpurgo, still only months from his old job, even felt a certain sympathy.

"Where's the meet to be? Can you tell us?"

"Don't know, not yet. We don't even know how they're putting the proposition to him, but it obviously takes time."

Archer, urbanity recovered, took up a legitimate line of speculation. "Wonder what they have in mind. Something to damage the Libyan economy. What economy? They only have oil."

It wasn't, Morpurgo decided, simply that he knew Steve as well as any man. Or that Pottern, in his corner, had become stiller than ever. It was the virus; the deadly virus; those whose profession it is to be suspicious are themselves infected by deceit. The word "oil", now more than just a word to him, was more than a word to them, too.

Steve, an unlit cigarette between his fingers, reached a decision. "What would you say, Johnny, if I told you that comrade Timothy was in this country only . . ." – He veered smoothly – "not so very long ago?"

Morpurgo made no attempt to hide his natural surprise, but he saw something else. Pottern, too, was surprised; no, not surprised, alarmed, though it came and went as quickly as the flicker of a serpent's tongue.

"Here? In the UK?" That much was expected of him. He had, in fact, seen two things; Pottern's unhappiness, and the fact that his supposedly new relationship with Steve Archer was as false as the kiss of Judas. These two were out for plunder, and it would not be plunder shared.

"Do you," Steve was asking, "know a place in Sussex called Billingshurst?" That question was not what had alarmed Eric Pottern in prospect. There was, therefore, another, deeper secret. All three of us, Morpurgo thought, tainted.

"About two-thirds of the way to the coast, turn right for Midhurst and the polo, dare say you know that." Steady, Morpurgo, your class prejudice is showing. So is Pottern's relief, though he'd rather this one hadn't come out either.

Steve went to the window, just as Morpurgo used to do in days quite gone. Instinctively, Morpurgo joined him, just as Steve had done in those lost days. The roof of the Mirabelle was partly open; it was the right sort of day. Steve's fingers fluttered once on the dusty window ledge. He told Morpurgo the story of T. Brewster Cochran and the theft of a secret.

"What's your theory?" Translation: How are you going to twist the truth?

"Theory?" Archer turned to lean on the window ledge, regarding Morpurgo with the faint, synthetic amusement Morpurgo had described to Sylvie as cheek with a private education. "Isn't it obvious? Timothy came over and nicked something that Langley wants back."

He went back to his desk. "Libya's an SIS affair, no question. Terrorism's ours. So happens they coincide this time."

He cocked his head at Morpurgo. "Epworth sent you. Why?" His face was tough.

"Don't ask me to explain Epworth." Morpurgo said it with feeling, but he, too, had had his training in deceit. "We – you – were talking Timothy, then up he pops, jack-in-the-box. Only civil to share and share alike." He smiled, pretending puzzlement. "I mean, we are on the same side, aren't we?"

Steve stayed tough, not returning the smile. He could be very tough, Morpurgo knew that; nobody tougher than your civil English gentleman when he senses himself challenged by inferiors. "Give us half a chance and we'd pick comrade Timothy off and to hell with the Cousins. To hell with your mob too, come to that, but there's no reason why it should, tell Epworth that, Johnny."

He produced the smile that was supposed to expunge thinly disguised thuggishness, crossing his feet on his desk top. "Of course, I could go to my minister and tell him a tale, probably should have done already. He'd have a word with Epworth's minister. What then? The usual boys' school jostling, all good fun until somebody falls over. Or over to the head pen-pushers, ending up in committee, carving each other's face with exquisitely sharp memoranda weighted with Latin tags. God save us! Is that what we want?"

Answer, no. Except that, according to Epworth, both parties had already called in their highly placed seconds, whether the ministers themselves or, for Epworth, that slipperiest of Assistant Under Secretaries, Hugo Pendleton, the androgynous android.

Steve gushed smoke through his confident nose. "Room for a deal, wouldn't you say?"

"That would be up to Epworth." A valve had opened, reinforcing real smoke with murky outpourings of distrust. They wanted a deal, Steve and his silent lieutenant, but they were holding something back – why should he be so certain? Experience, he reminded himself; experience – more important than anything revealed.

An instant later, he was reminding himself that he, too, had withheld vital information. A moment later still, he remembered – had never really forgotten – that Epworth was holding back on all of them, Cousins *compris*.

"No need to spell it out, right, Johnny?" Steve was saying with his old familiarity that bordered on offensiveness. "Give us the chance of a chat with friend Timothy or we just might queer your pitch. So off you push and talk to brother Lawrence."

*   *   *

134

"A straight," Claas asked, "or a mug?" They were in a pub, ordinary, crowded, uncomfortable, that he liked to use when he was on duty off duty.

Weber, who had spent some time talking to Barzelian through CINCSAT in the small hours and had more to worry about than lack of sleep, stared. "What was that?"

Claas wiggled himself into a minimal space at the bar, next to a bare arm on which was tattooed a crest and, in curlicued capitals: THEY WILL ONLY PRISE MY GUN FROM MY COLD FINGERS, followed by FALKLANDS 1982. "You want a straight glass or a mug? People over here are particúlar." He caught the young soldier's eye, nodded at the tattoo. "Pretty neat." It was not what he was really thinking, so he added, "Have a drink?"

"Fanks, mate. Pinta special."

"Particular?" Weber repeated. "Not me. I'm with you."

"And me mate?"

"Okay, smartass, you still didn't answer the question." Switching to the soldier boy, Claas said, "Sure, your mate too."

Weber said, "Does it matter?"

"These are things you only learn" – Claas took the opportunity of sneering at Weber – "when you really know a country. I mean, *know*."

"So tell me."

"Wait a minute." Claas returned to his soldier. "Straight or mug?"

"Straight, mate, ta. 'Ere, you, miss!"

"You can have your pint" – Claas preened – "in a straight-sided, thin glass – well, it has a bulge near the top, but they call it a straight."

"A glass-shaped glass, that what you mean, junior?"

"Or" – Claas was not to be diverted – "you can have it in a mug. Thick glass, dimpled. With a handle."

"Same beer?"

The young soldier said, "'Ere, you, miss! We been 'ere ten minutes."

"Same beer, sure."

"Then what the hell?"

"Anthropology. Want me to spell it? Four pints of special, miss. Straights."

" 'Ave to shout," the young soldier advised. "Cloff-ears, thas what, 'ere."

"Thin straight glasses," Claas explained, "are preferred by the lower classes. More upper-class and refined."

"All be the same in Spain," Weber told him.

"Mugs are preferred by the upper classes because the lower class won't drink from them. That makes them upper-class. The upper-class won't drink from straights because they're lower class."

"Four pints 'ere, miss, straights."

"Now just a minute." Weber began to frown.

"Social nuances." Claas was complacent. "Meat and drink to a top class operative. Tell Langley. And if you have a mug, it has a handle, but your upper-class Englishman won't use it, slips his fingers through and holds it like it was a straight."

"But you just said . . ." Weber sighed. "In Spain it's wine."

"I know what I said. Now, what do you say? Mug or straight? It's a class decision."

"I say the hell with it!" Weber caught the girl's attention. "Large scotch, two pints of special for the soldier and a coke for my friend." He spilled money, raked up change, said, "Cheers!" to the soldier, pulled Claas to a vacant corner. "Goddammit, junior, did you hear? Spain. Madrid."

"Spain? You mean Hank?" Claas, taking the point at last, decided to be irritable. He and Ella had had another row over the kids the previous evening. It still rankled. "I don't have these fancy lines of communication. Why Spain, for Chrissake? Why *Madrid*, for Chrissake?" He noticed his coke. "Jesus!"

"Because Hank says Madrid, I don't know why. And where, exactly, he'll fix when Morpurgo is there."

"We have to know how he comes in."

"Sure we do, but this isn't the hit, remember. We can't take the guy out in the middle of Madrid."

"Needn't necessarily be Madrid airport," Claas decided. "Going to take some covering."

"Leave that to Madrid station. They'll trace backwards, not forwards, after the meet."

"Where's Morpurgo staying? Hank specified, right?"

"The Eurobuilding Hotel. Know it?"

136

"He won't like it. Big, big, modern building, Plaza de Cuzco, right downtown. Oh, it has everything, so long as your idea of old-world Spanish charm is what goes down big with the Peoria jet-set."

"Remind me. How long were you in Spain?"

"Two years. No, twenty months. Boy!" Claas shook his head in recollection. "Did Ella ever like it! 'How long do we have to stay here? Why can't you put in for a transfer? When do we get to go home?'"

"You speak Spanish. How a Kansas City Kraut comes to speak Spanish I never will understand. Still, Langley likes to use the whole man."

"Yeah." Claas was morose. "And what Langley wants, Langley gets." He drank some coke resignedly, then choked. "Oh *no!*"

"What's up, junior? Bubbles get up your nose?"

"*You* just got up my nose! You can't do this to me! Go with that pinko bleeding heart? Listen, that wimp doesn't even like me."

"You spilled your coke," Weber said pleasantly.

"You wouldn't, would you?" Claas dabbed ineffectually. He became serious. "You know Hank's just as likely to blow him away as talk to him."

"I said we'd ride shotgun, remember? You speak Spanish. You know Madrid. I don't trust Madrid station when it comes to a blocking play."

"I haven't spoken Spanish in damn near ten years. Ramirez, right here in London station . . ."

"Ramirez is twenty-seven. I need more of a mature type. I need you."

"That's why you were smirking when I said about the Euro-building. Hey, Pierre, seriously, I'm old. No kidding, last time I toted a piece was at Warren Junior's birthday party."

"Pretty recent, that's good. Just hoist the idea aboard, junior, and start practising your *olés.*"

* * *

"For a moment," Pottern said when they had finished their revew, "I thought you were going to tell Morpurgo that Timothy was at Gatwick."

"I wouldn't" – Archer was nursing a secret rage – "give anyone in SIS, anyone, Eric, so much as a sniff at this one."

"You've given them Billingshurst. Cochran."

"Spoiling tactics. Something they won't mention to the Cousins, you can be sure of that. Not much they *will* give to the Cousins, now."

"Trust," Pottern said with apparent seriousness, "is worth more than a gold watch, but it's apt to be less reliable." He considered something, then looked directly at Archer. "Of course, we could cover him. Morpurgo."

"SV? Mount surveillance on someone in SIS? Eric!"

"Been done before, hasn't it? Drop him at the airport when we knew where he was going, better than nothing."

Archer laughed, not troubling to deny it. "You realise my time for this kind of thing is running out? More meetings every day, particularly since the Knight departed. Won't be long before this particular potato is too hot for my tender hands. Of course" – He looked mockingly at his henchman through a drifting haze of smoke – "if anyone should come up with a wheeze for delivering the ungodly into our hands rather than those of the Cousins . . ."

He took his feet off the desk. "I mean, we do know now, don't we? who stole those bloody bugs. And why?"

"Langley? To catch Timothy? Pretty fancy bait." Pottern permitted himself to sound dubious.

"Pretty fancy prey! An ex-CIA man who took a crack at the President. If he's capable of doing that, he's capable of checking back on the story they're setting Morpurgo up to feed him, so they've gone to the trouble of making it look authentic."

He laughed silently. "I don't pretend to understand these things, Eric, but I raise my hat to the Cousins for spotting a way of turning Cochran's misfortune to their advantage. His failed process for squeezing oil out of rock becomes their phony gimmick for turning oil into shit. Now if only *we* could squeeze something out of it . . ."

"As for the whereabouts of the meet, good God, Eric! you're an ex-SIS man, like me. I'll wager you I know the whereabouts of the meet almost as soon as comrade Morpurgo knows it himself."

*   *   *

'Mmmmmmmmm." It was just about the longest that Morpurgo had ever heard Epworth emit. "Interesting."

"Plausible?"

"Plausible? Mmmmmm."

"You don't think so?" Keep pressing, something would have to give.

"Timothy broke in and stole – mmmm – the inoculum. And Langley wants to do a deal."

"When I say plausible, you know what I mean. Is it really what Steve thinks?"

"Who is the man Timothy more important to? Steve or the Cousins? And if Steve, since it isn't a question of terrorism, why?"

"That's two questions, no answers."

"Three. And the third is also an answer."

Morpurgo muttered an obscenity.

"If the answer is Steve" – Epworth's mildness was incitement to murder – "then the bug that kills oil is a hoax, and Timothy didn't steal it."

"He didn't. We know he didn't. The bloody Cousins stole it."

"There you are then. In which case, is it a hoax after all?"

"We know it's a hoax!"

"What if they want us to *think* it's a hoax?"

"*What*?"

"They've told us nothing about Cochran. About Billingshurst. If they had done, it would have given artistic verisimilitude to what could otherwise seem a bald and unconvincing narrative." Epworth watched Morpurgo anxiously. "Whereas if they'd taken it for granted that we would take a peek . . ."

"*You* would take a peek." Morpurgo began to see it.

". . . at their little demonstration twenty-four hours before we were supposed to, the effect would be to disguise the truth as bald and unconvincing verisimilitude."

Morpurgo, closing his eyes, sighed. Epworth, showing no sympathy, said, "Tell me again what Steve said about Timothy."

"He claimed proof positive that Timothy was over here."

"At Billingshurst time?"

"He didn't say that. Not in so many words. 'Not so very long ago', that's what he said."

139

"Ah. Not the same. But that, presumably, is what gave them their lead on identification."

"A name to a face, yes."

"Timothy was positively over here. To steal something we positively know was stolen by the Cousins." Epworth recited it like a lesson well learned. "Something we positively know is a hoax."

He produced his slow, peeping smile at Morpurgo's expression. "Culture shock, that's your problem. Meaning here, after Curzon Street; me, after the Knight and Archer; and abroad rather than home. You haven't adjusted yet. You will. I didn't sign you up out of pity."

"Thank you."

He ignored the irony. "Just one thing we can be sure of. Timothy was over here. So, two more questions. When? And where?"

"Which Steve knows. What he's after is an explanation."

"Or he has the explanation already. And it's made him very anxious to get his hands on Timothy."

"Just like the Cousins. What's the man done that's so important?"

"Mmmm, only one way to find out."

"Play along."

"Exactly. Which reminds me." Epworth, pretending to remember, made no attempt to disguise the pretence. "The meet's to be in Madrid. Weber called. Funny thing" – He considered the minimal humour of it – "however badly Langley wants Timothy, their lines of communication appear to be swift and sure."

"Madrid!" Morpurgo realised that he must, all along, have expected Libya.

"Madrid. Spain." Epworth's smile established him as blood brother to the Mona Lisa. "Interesting."

*   *   *

The Hercules Tavern is roughly equidistant from Century House and the Central Office of Information at Hercules House, its ideological opposite. It is a pub little frequented by the intelligence community, being, perhaps, too plebeian. Morpurgo,

140

looking up, was surprised to find the unplebeian Steve Archer standing over him.

"Why not?" Steve said. "Brass never uses it, right? Only secretaries and filing clerks." He looked around at the cross-section; layabouts, van drivers on lunch-break, a group of regulars Morpurgo had decided were retired cabbies.

He looked back at Morpurgo as if he were a filing clerk. "I had business over there," jerking his head in the general direction of Century House. "Genuine. Wriothsley, ask him." He displayed a pack of cigarettes. "Came in here for these, ran out in Wriothsley's office. Ask him."

By the book; don't say this is what you did, do it, then you can prove it. Morpurgo waited, any idea that he and Steve were assisting in the slow recuperation of a friendship already faded.

"Madrid." Steve sat, stripping the wrapper from his cigarettes. "You're meeting Timothy in Madrid." "Wriothsley," Epworth had told Morpurgo, some time back, "is an old friend of Steve Archer." He saw it now as a warning.

Steve began to feed cigarettes into his case, slowly, method-ically. Steve Archer did little in haste, so what had brought him to the swift decision of this encounter?

Steve shut his case with a soft snap. "Nobody sneaked. Brother Lawrence apparently mentioned to Wriothsley that you were off on a little trip to Madrid."

Morpurgo duly took note. Someone came to the end of the horseshoe bar and shouted, accusingly, "Two toasted ham and cheese."

Steve tucked away his case. "Think they'll do it there?"

"What?"

"Snuff him, old boy. What else?"

"I thought your idea was a trade."

"Trade first, snuff later."

Morpurgo ate a corner of his own toasted ham and cheese sandwich. Steve had bought himself a whisky. Across a red vista of upholstery and carpet, a lad in blue overalls operated a gaming machine with the concentration of a grand master.

"I'd say not." Steve answered his own question, a trick with uncooperative interrogees. "Not in Madrid. Spain matters to Washington, those big air bases on the south-west flank of

NATO. Besides, they're not dealing with an amateur. Sorry, should have said you're not."

Morpurgo drank beer. The retired cabbies' club argued over the likely effects of hard going at Newmarket.

Steve leaned forward. "I want him, Johnny."

Morpurgo ate more cheese and ham.

"I can't ask Epworth, you do realise that?"

"Why?"

"He'd have to say no. SIS and Langley, he's committed."

"So am I."

"No. You're not. Engaged, old boy. Not committed." The boy at the machine had got it right, money gouting out in a metallic haemorrhage.

Steve tapped a cigarette on his case, purely mechanical, totally unnecessary. He must want something very badly. "You could come back, ever thought of that?"

It jolted Morpurgo. "Back? Where?" He knew where; it was below the belt.

"Home, old boy. Where you belong." He lit his cigarette, kept the lighter in the palm of his hand, fingers curling over it, symbolising . . . what? Protectiveness? Possession? Capture? "That dump" – Another jerk of the head for Century House – "isn't your style, and you know it."

His hand closed about the lighter.

"Going to be frank, Johnny. You're three people. One I could do without." The seducer, breaker of homes. "One I can take or leave, always could." Morpurgo the oik, the lefty, exerciser of powers and privileges in which he had never wholly believed.

"Plenty of time for the third, the pro, always had, even more now I'm in your old seat, and that's God's honest truth."

Steve believed in God, genuinely, his kind of God. The rich man in his castle, the poor man at his gate, God made them, high or lowly, and – yes indeed! – ordered their estate. Steve's people had their own pew in the village church.

Morpurgo's estate was that of talented thief-catcher, the property at risk being information. To people like Steve, governments of Steve's choosing, information – ideally, all information – was private property, his and theirs.

He found a suitable response. "What about Eric Pottern?"

"Good God, man! Not your old job! You know Westerman's going? Always was the Knight's man, doesn't take kindly to the idea of change."

"You're offering me Westerman's job?" Westerman was Deputy Director-General, a post the Knight had told Morpurgo to forget about.

"I think I could swing it." He probably did. More to the point, did he mean it?

Morpurgo was anxious to get this embarrassment out of the way. "Sorry. Century House may not be heaven on earth, but it's where I work."

On the surface, Steve Archer was a good loser, bred in the bone. He made a last bid. "We're both patriots, I fancy. You find less to dislike" – The old, arrogantly mocking Steve – "in this country than any other."

"I prefer it to Moscow."

"And to God's Own Country. The Land of the Free. Don't deny it. So do I. That's what we're talking about, Johnny. Not about selling out on brother Lawrence behind his back. About doing him a favour he'd like to do himself, only he can't, hands tied. Committed, there's the difference. *He's* committed, like it or not. You're only engaged."

"You mean Timothy's worth more to us than them?" Steve knew far more than he was revealing. His natural instincts would long since have said: Stuff it, you closet commie! It took something very big to make a rigidly proud man beg.

"That's it." Someone started the jukebox at the far end of the bar; heavy metal, making the air buzz. The retired taxi drivers' club didn't like it.

"Johnny, think. Not just a terrorist's quartermaster and arms buyer for the most nuisancial bloody country in the Eastern Med. Ex-CIA! A week or two in the country" – He meant Security Directorate's interrogation centre – "and we'd learn some useful things."

"They're our allies."

"Since when did they treat us like allies? Or want anything from us except to hear us say, 'You lead, we'll follow.'" No wonder they loved the Lady. Steve Archer, too, had loved the Lady, grieved when she went.

"Sorry, Steve."

"A telephone call to a number in Madrid, as soon as you know the place and the time. Then everything according to plan, except that the comrade wouldn't show up."

Christ! he really wanted Hank Timothy, hinting at an extra-territorial snatch. Of course, Steve was ex-SIS, Pottern too. They knew the ropes.

"Sorry."

Steve's hand opened to reveal the lighter. His gaze switched to it as if its presence baffled him. He put it away. The sun, reflected from somewhere outside, touched the crimson shades and brass fittings of the hanging light clusters, as if someone had just switched them on.

"That's it, then?"

"Afraid so."

"Back to tell Epworth about it?"

"No."

Steve produced his most insolent smile. "Honour among thieves?" He stood. "Well, good luck." He hesitated. "If he should happen to say anything about that trip to the UK, you might at least . . ." He shook his head briskly. "Watch your step."

Morpurgo watched him go, then finished his sandwich. Might at least . . . ? Pass it on? It was all too difficult. He was a displaced person, homeless, rootless, the puppet of forces outside not only his control but his understanding. Sylvie must ring, or he wouldn't be able to tell her – irony of ironies – he was going on a day trip to Spain.

He sat, lonely, with his beer and Steve's empty glass, every-thing about him crimson from carpet to light shades. Imperial crimson. No, emperors were purple. Crimson was for lesser mortals, presidents, for instance. The thought sank like a stone into his unconscious.

He must, after all, tell Epworth of Steve's final bid, though not about the proffered bribe. They were all tainted. Only loyalty was left.

*   *   *

The centre of Madrid had been packed with a million parakeets and set to music. "Wouldn't you know it?" Claas demanded.

"Didn't I tell you the guy is smart?" They were in the *plaza mayor*, outside the restaurant Timothy's message had specified, the high-pitched staccato of a city in fiesta producing the impact of massed riveters' hammers.

Claas sipped his scotch moodily, his humour unimproved by the gaiety that swirled about them in crackling currents of excitement. "On active service, at my age, goddammit!

"Los reyes católicos." He was talking of King Ferdinand, who scowled, sulky as Claas, at Queen Isabella, both of them ten feet tall. "The Catholic Monarchs. Stay in Spain five minutes and you get the idea they invented the goddam country." Among the brilliant, constantly changing coagulations of costumed paraders, their families, friends and half the population of the city, the *gigantes* towered grotesquely, their bearers emerged from the stifling robes to breathe an air that was spring-fresh in the sun's hard evening shadows.

"They did." Morpurgo was inclined by the scene to be tolerant.

"What?" Claas's response was mechanical. His eyes continually scanned the perimeters of the great square with its quadruple march of arches, triple balconies and ornately embellished stonework. Spired towers and an incongruous plantation of television antennae snipped at the edges of a blind blue sky.

"Invent Spain. Cut the nobles down to size. Turn a collection of private estates into a kingdom." Morpurgo poured himself a little more wine. Epworth had given him a brief parting discourse on which to drink.

"I thought you started off as an economist, not a historian." Picking at their *tapas*, Claas eyed a titbit mistrustfully. The head of a baby squid, it stared back no less coldly. He ate it out of bravado.

"Economics, political science, history, you know that. Haven't you checked my file lately?"

Claas hesitated elaborately over a pimiento-stuffed olive. "What file?"

"If you don't have a file on me, London station's getting sloppy."

Claas let it ride, his eyes promenading the arcades wherever the slowly moving throng left room. Eight entrances. Every one, according to Claas, was supposed to be covered. Timothy would

145

be tagged out, not in. Morpurgo couldn't really understand why. What he did wonder was whether there were other eyes out there, eyes that ought to be much, much nearer to Curzon Street. The thing that lodged in his mind was that Steve Archer, about to take over Security Directorate, about to receive a knighthood as the Buck House seal of approval, was willing to risk so much for so little.

Explanation – unsatisfactory – it wasn't so little.

A shoeshine boy had been working the crowd near their table. Now he arrived, grubby, poorly clad, street-smart eyes and a thousand watt smile. Claas, fluent in Spanish and English, said, "No." The boy veered toward Morpurgo.

Claas chuckled nastily. "From each according to his ability, to each according to his need. Isn't that your thing?"

Morpurgo let the boy tuck a slip of paper around the instep of one shoe to protect the sock. "This is venture capitalism, Warren. Be supportive." The boy, cloth flickering in a blur, worked on Morpurgo's shoes with the dexterity of a cardsharp.

"Damn right," Claas said. "This kid could probably buy you out."

The boy gave Morpurgo's shoes a final flick. Morpurgo produced a hundred peseta note. The flick extended to the note. "*Muchissimas gracias, señor.*" Boy and note vanished in the crowd.

Claas was delighted. "Welfare's a bottomless pit. Hell, he even left the paper in your shoe."

Morpurgo bent to remove it. As he did so, Claas, in a different voice, said, "Shit! Let me see that." He snatched the strip. There was writing on it. Claas's chair clattered across the cobbles. "Stay right there, I'll be back."

Morpurgo, happy to stay, wanted to laugh, though he had been obliged to leave London without hearing from Sylvie, and his mother was still undergoing tests. But Claas's haste said everything. The note was from Hank Timothy. The obvious explanation was that Timothy was aware of the net that had been spread for him. The meet had been changed, or was off.

A chair scraped on the cobbles at his back. "Don't turn around, Morpurgo. We can talk fine just like this." A deep voice, cocky and compelling.

He decided not to turn for the moment. "You got rid of Claas."

146

"You guessed."

Where was the surveillance? "He'll be back."

"Not yet, he won't. Relax, pally. We can talk. Wasn't that the idea?"

A waiter came, tired eyes, false teeth and smile, white jacket frayed but thick with starch. Timothy ordered a beer in loud, confident Spanish. "I heard a lot about you, Morpurgo."

Morpurgo wondered how long he would wait before turning.

"The resident pinko." Laughter, deep-chested and derisive. "They fixed you, pally, isn't that so." The laugh again, soft but stinging. "Don't care to talk about it? Well, neither would I, I guess, not if I'd been all kinds of a damn fool."

He had come to deal, Morpurgo told himself grimly.

"That's the truth, ain't it?" The semi-literate speech, he would bet, was less lack of education than contempt for accepted form, just like that peculiarly insulting 'pally.' "All kinds of a damn fool?"

The small snap of a lighter. Smoke drifted past Morpurgo; cheroot, cigar. "Pretty smart job you pulled, Sattin. Saved the government, the way I heard it, not that you've had a government worth a damn since the dame went. Still, what happens? A medal for John Morpurgo? Top slot in the next shuffle? Nope. He gets shafted. For shafting his number two's wife, that's their story, anyway. If there's one thing that gets up the nose of the brass worse than being stuck with a loner, it's being hauled out of the shit by one." His beer came. The tip was clearly extravagant.

Morpurgo, hearing the hiss of poured beer at his back, watched *los reyes católicos* lurch before swaying off, teetering above the multi-headed throng. Who among them had Hank Timothy in sight? The weak, divided British government that had followed the Lady's departure would have fallen if the Sattin spy scandal had broken in full. Even now, the full story would spew headlines. Timothy apparently had it.

"You want to say something? Or did they buy your tongue?"

Morpurgo swung round angrily. Timothy bellowed amusement, a harsh, macho sound that made heads turn. "Kept you quiet all of five minutes. That's your problem, you do what you're told."

A fawn lightweight suit, an expensive shirt of red and white check open on a thick, deeply tanned neck, the face more potent than the picture, beak-nosed, eyes fire-bright and unpouched, teeth strong, yellow, equine. Only the beginnings of a double chin suggested high living.

"Okay, Morpurgo, what's the sting?" The beer went down at a gulp.

"Claas could be back any time." Anyone could be here any time, triggering violence.

"So I'll shove up my hands and say, 'I quit'. Relax. You think I came all this way just to pick up and run when some Langley deadbeat puffs onstage? Claas could be back! Claas could crap honey, but he don't."

"There's no sting. No catch at all."

"Yeah? They give you that in writing?" Timothy snapped his fingers for the *camerero*. The Catholic monarchs, tumbrilled, rolled toward an exit. At the far end of the square, from a stage draped bright in yellow and orange, amplified music squalled.

"If you know so much about me, you know I play straight." What had made him say that? priggish, pompous. An awkward but instinctive response to a man for whom he had conceived an instant dislike.

Timothy bellowed amusement, tiny bubbles of spittle at the mouth corners. "Principles! You have principles the way a hound dog has fleas, so how come you want to scratch *my* back?"

Flexible principles, Morpurgo thought; what won't bend in this game snaps. Snapping principles can lacerate. "Nobody made you come."

"Hey! Feisty! I like that." Timothy held up two fingers to the waiter. "*Coñac. Dos. Y una cerveza mas.* Okay, you play straight. Ever do you any good?"

"Never mind. They need your help. No beer in Libya, no anything very much. They're making you an offer of something better, the same deal they gave Morello and Lebenson. They said you'd understand that."

The waiter was back. Timothy tossed several coins, waved him away. "There's a tale to talk a possum down a tree! But when that old possum hit bottom" – He joined thumb and two fingers, aimed them at Morpurgo's head – "boom!" He pushed one

148

cognac toward Morpurgo. "Hank Timothy don't take sucker bait and they know it. What's worth so much to them?"

The canned music was very Spanish, a hint of Moorish discord. Groups in the crowd sang noisily. Sylvie, his mind whispered, was offering stranger sights, wilder music. He told his well-rehearsed story. When he had finished, Timothy simply went on looking at the crowd, then lit another small, slim cheroot, using a lighter that had more gold than the treasury of an African bush state.

"That's quite a number." He downed his cognac with a quick tip of his head. What struck Morpurgo most was that he seemed perfectly relaxed, a tourist enjoying the fiesta. "Bugs clog the wellheads, huh? Know how far down? Know how long it takes?"

"How far, no. They say two or three days."

"They say. And to clear?"

"That would be for the Libyans to find out."

Timothy stared at the tip of his cheroot. "Yeah." He looked up at the vapid blue of the sky. "And the word is passed, quit the monkey shines or we fix your oil for keeps."

"That's it." It even sounded convincing.

"Could they?"

Morpurgo watched a family go by with a tot in flamenco dress. No kids. Where would he and Sylvie be if that were not so? "You think they'd give someone like you something like that?" Playing rough with this man could be dangerous. He wondered about the man Timothy had killed on the last meet; who he was, what he had wanted. No one had said. Neither he nor Epworth had asked.

If Timothy had taken offence, there was no sign, just the hard look, the steady gaze. "I'd need to know more than that, pally. You know?"

Morpurgo watched the tot.

Timothy guffawed. "Maybe you're not so dumb at that. Maybe you think I am. That would be bad thinking, okay? What makes the bug run out of steam?"

"It stops. They wouldn't hand over something that didn't." But it was a good question. Too many things, far too many, that were unanswered questions. He supposed he and Timothy were about the same age. Timothy could eat him.

149

Timothy prodded the gold lighter he had laid on the table, rotating it with a forefinger. The lighter was more ingot than artefact. It gradually edged toward Morpurgo. "How do I know that stuff works? I mean, I say yes, next time they blow me away like smoke."

"SIS didn't come in on that basis." No? What did John Morpurgo know about SIS?

"Yeah, well that would be a big comfort when they blew out the back of my head. They tell you about the last guy that came against me?"

"The mountain top."

"The mountain top." The lighter was nearer Morpurgo than Timothy now. "I have friends, Morpurgo. Okay, they cleaned up Baader-Meinhof, the *brigati rossi*, I still have friends. That scare you a little?"

Morpurgo, idly, nudged the lighter back toward Timothy.

Unexpectedly, Timothy grinned; sharp, triangular. "Okay, let's deal. I need a demonstration. Hank Timothy buys nothing on say-so." He signalled the waiter.

"*Si, señor?*"

"*Los servicios?*"

"*En el interior, señor, detras y derecha.*"

"I have to go to the john. Don't go away, we only just started." Timothy left behind his gold lighter and cheroots. Morpurgo moved both squarely in front of the vacated seat. It was approaching ten minutes before he realised that Timothy was not coming back; much longer before Claas did.

"That sonofabitch!" Claas threw himself down, his face as pink and shiny as a sucked lollypop. He saw the lighter. "Don't leave that goddam thing there, for Chrissake. This place is full of light fingers." He flicked it irritably toward Morpurgo.

He said, "You don't smoke. You . . ." His eyes bulged. "Oh *no!*"

He slammed the note on the chipped table-top. CHANGE OF MEET. SAUNA, YOUR PLACE, NOW. DON'T BRING YOUR POODLE.

"How do you like that? Forty minutes in the goddam sauna. I damn near died." He kept looking from side to side, as if hoping to spot Timothy. Why hadn't all those CIA men spotted him?

"He wants a demonstration."

150

Claas, about to bitch again, fell over his tongue. "A demonstration? *Jesus!*" Recovering, on the whole, admirably, he shrugged. "Well, that's reasonable, I guess. Where? When? Come on, what'd he say, you Limey poodle?"

"Wuff!" Morpurgo said. "Wuff-wuff!"

* * *

They lunched in a former wine vault; to be precise, one of a linked series of vaults. They had a table in the farthest corner, the lighting minimal. Above their heads, from wall to wall, ran a cast-iron pipe, perhaps a yard in diameter. The floor was paved, the walls bare brick on which time had laid heavy fingers. Their table was the upturned half of a wine cask on which their plates and glasses jostled uncomfortably. Epworth, as host, had chosen the venue.

Claas was still inclined to snarl. "Jesus Christ, you think it makes me proud? He sold me a dummy. That makes me a dummy."

Although this was farce, Morpurgo told himself, it must be well acted. "What about me, bourgeois enough to think he wouldn't walk off without his gold lighter."

"What's this bourgeois schlock? More Marx?" Claas's humiliation had left him with a need to lacerate.

"Perhaps," Weber said soothingly, "this is the time to tell you what Hank has in mind."

"Wants us to turn some North Sea oilfield into molasses?" The kowtowing to Langley, Morpurgo felt, was going too far, although Epworth, typically, had made and continued to make little or no comment. Only one thing, in fact, appeared to stir him to a mild interest, Morpurgo's suggestion that they might discover a little more about Timothy's supposed victim in the Pyrenees, an interest Morpurgo himself, on reflection, now saw as decidedly morbid.

Weber, all soft shine and shadows in the minimal lighting, though the place was packed and noisy with City lunchtimers, shook his head. "Not an oilfield. A tanker."

Morpurgo mentally tipped his hat to Hank Timothy, no half measures to call a Langley bluff. "A tanker! He must be joking."

151

Weber finished his wine. "No sense of humour. He just laughs a lot."

Epworth, in the darkest corner, visible only by glow from the distant bar, fired a dart. "Did he send his terms – mmmm – from Spain?"

"Hank's a man with a private army. Armies have channels."

Skirting the evasion, Epworth picked up the loose thread. "I presume we're talking about a ship."

"A small one."

"How small is small?"

"Around a hundred and twenty thousand tons. They tell me," Weber said, "that's pretty small for an oil tanker." Claas, still sulking, was studying the great pipe above their heads.

"It seems – I'm no expert – these things are divided crossways by bulkheads." Weber made boat shapes with his hands. "Tanks go in threes, one line down the middle, one line either side. Four tanks are for ballast or something. The crude is in the rest."

"What's in that thing?" Claas asked suddenly, and it took them all a second or two to understand that he was talking about the pipe.

"Mmmm," Epworth said. "Main sewer."

Claas's eyes bulged. "You've got to be kidding."

Epworth giggled. "It's quite safe, been there well over a hundred years." Claas seemed to shrink in his seat.

"One of those tanks holds around seven thousand tons of crude," Weber said patiently.

"Nothing to it." Claas wrenched his thoughts away from the sewer; if it really was a sewer, Morpurgo thought; with Epworth you could be sure of nothing. "They have these little doors in the top of each tank hatch, use 'em to draw off samples of crude. All you'll have to do is tip the bugs into a sampling can, lower it down, slosh it around some, and that's it." He made it sound like mixing packet soup.

"Been doing his homework," Weber explained. "Meaning picking the brains of some guy back in Langley. Hank thinks that's pretty modest."

"Seven thousands tons of crude to be turned into sludge." Epworth's high-domed head turned to give Morpurgo an unfathomable glance. "Can it be done?"

"Langley says yes. Don't ask me how they know." Weber gave them his lopsided smile. "We don't have too many hundred thousand ton tankers."

Morpurgo sat silent while his brain cells came out in mass protest.

"And the tanker is specified?" Epworth was a man with a few minor technical points to settle. "I assume his reasoning would be that if you can't do it on his terms, you can't do it at all."

Weber looked at Morpurgo. "The question is, will *you* do it? You're part of the specification too."

"Do what?" This was a dream. He would leave this ill-lit corner of unreality and walk through the Barbican, down London Wall to St Paul's, stark naked.

"Be put down," Weber said, "on a tanker off the coast of Spain, broad daylight, to shoot a charge of those bugs into a nominated cargo tank." He looked politely anxious.

"Put down?"

"Chopper."

"We'll lay it on," Claas said, as if that settled the whole thing.

Morpurgo took Epworth in from his eye corners. Epworth displayed nothing but bland interest. With a sense of total disbelief, Morpurgo smiled at Weber. "Why not?"

"Tarragona," Claas said. "Coast of the Med, south of Barcelona."

"He looked it up," Weber explained.

Morpurgo said, "I know it." To reach Sylvie's parents' villa south of Cambrils, you drove down the *autopista* from Barcelona. It passed within miles of Tarragona. The Markhams often went to Tarragona to shop.

Claas looked at him as if he had just confessed to treason. "So maybe you know what a tankerload of Libyan crude is doing off Tarragona?"

"It's the second largest oil terminal in Spain. And a sizeable refining and petrochemical complex just down the coast."

"Hey, heavy, man!" Claas decided to be jaunty. "Okay, a split cargo, half to be discharged there, half going on up the coast to France, a place called Lavéra, near Marseille."

"We play with the Tarragona half?"

"Because" – Weber took over – "he'll be able to observe the

153

whole thing without putting himself at risk. You know that coast, right? Langley's checked it out. High, not exactly cliffy, but good viewpoints north and south, also from the city itself. No problem keeping the tanker under observation, making sure there's no shenanigans."

"Like secretly replacing seven thousand tons of oil with gunge?" There had to be more, far more, to all this than they knew, he and Epworth, or these two Cousins were happily digging themselves a hole to be buried in.

"How long does the tanker – mmmm – have to sit off the coast?" Epworth, at any rate, was taking it seriously.

"Twenty-four hours. Those bugs work fast."

"May one know how there comes to be a tanker so conveniently available for this little – mmmm – *coup d'essai?*"

"It seems," Weber said, "that Spain gets a high percentage of its oil from Libya, sailings all the time, Ras Sidar and Ras Lanuf to Tarragona and some place way down in the south. I guess the Libs can call the shots on tanker sailings. And if a few thousand tons of the crude to be pumped ashore at Tarragona turns out to be gunge, there's no way it's going to stay a secret."

Emerging after lunch into the maze of small streets behind the Barbican, they agreed not to compete for taxis. Claas and Weber, guests of the country, had first pick. Watching their taxi turn the corner, Epworth, blinking in the bright sunlight, said, "Of course, we must keep Curzon Street informed."

Once again Morpurgo tried to read his mind and failed. "You think so?"

"Oh, of course. Common interest. Inter-service liaison." Epworth stuck two fingers in his mouth and produced a whistle that virtually stopped a taxi in its tracks. "After all, we're all on the same side, them, us and the Cousins."

"You don't really think this thing is going to work?" Morpurgo mimed Hank Timothy's action in the *plaza mayor*, turning two fingers and thumb into a gun. "A hit, a very palpable hit."

Epworth held open the door for him to get into the taxi. "Don't worry. We'll make sure you're suitably protected. Or perhaps you'd rather accept Steve's offer and go back to Curzon Street?" Morpurgo, abstracted, had not yet remembered to tell him about Steve's offer.

NINE

Eric Pottern mistrusted emotion, one reason why he was still a bachelor. Like Chief Superintendent Capstick, for whom, otherwise, he had a quiet contempt, he was capable of receiving patently untrue information with every muscle cataplectically controlled.

Fixing his eyes on Archer's elegant desk calendar as the most unemotional thing in sight, he delivered his reaction in a plain wrapper. "Things picking up between us and Century House. Not before time."

"We have to work together, Eric. When all's said and done, we have a legitimate interest in comrade Timothy, even if we've been elbowed out."

Pottern was picking his way with the legendarily light-footed skill of an Indian scout, not too fanciful a simile since he was an avid reader of Westerns. He had two reasons for caution; something to sell, and an instinctive certainty that he was himself in danger of being sold.

Archer's little rendezvous with Morpurgo had borne no fruit, but a well-tuned instinct for double-dealing, plus an ability to read his boss like a large-print edition of *Winnie-the-Pooh*, told Pottern that Morpurgo had received an offer. It could only have been the DD-G slot. The fact that Morpurgo had clearly declined merely pigeon-holed the threat. Archer's determination to make Security Directorate top dog in Whitehall put more jobs than Pottern's at risk.

"We could elbow our way back. Even now." He slid Archer a secret glance.

"You interest me, Eric, not to say amaze. Timothy's smart. This time the Cousins will be smarter. Now or never, that's the box they're in."

"Yes, sir." The same applied to Archer. His new responsibilities, with their siren song of power, were luring him, little by little, toward the abandonment of a long shot.

"All right, let's have it." Eric, too, could be smart, and Archer could still be tempted.

"Let's start with the tanker, sir." Sirs well to the fore; Pottern was not offering his own head on a platter.

"*Oklahoma Star*, registered in Panama, on charter." Pottern had had someone consult Lloyd's. "She's already taken up her oil at Ras Sidar. Normal sailing speed, eighteen knots, sailed just after 06.00 GMT today." Pottern watched his boss wavering between instinctive distrust of too much cleverness and the satisfaction that it was his to command.

"A thousand miles in round figures. That bloke Connery, Naval Intelligence, did the sums for me. He says call it something over two days barring foul weather, but the forecast's good. She'll be off Tarragona long before noon."

"Full daylight from early morning." Archer laughed wryly. "Got to hand it to the comrade." He meant Timothy.

"Yes, sir, but another twenty-four hours for the stuff to work, once it's added."

"Oh, with you, yes. Won't work, mind, doesn't matter though. Bait is bait."

"That's something Timothy can't be sure of. Suspects it, I'll bet, but still thinks there might be something in it for him."

"All right." Archer was interested. Eric was good at this sort of thing. "So Morpurgo's put aboard, does whatever it is he has to do, broad daylight. Friend Timothy, anywhere along five miles of coast, maybe no farther away than some seafront hotel bedroom, doesn't take his eyes away longer than he needs to go for a pee. The Cousins are looking for a needle in a haystack."

His imagination warmed up after a slow start, Archer took it out for a spin. "I mean, damn it, Eric, you were a fieldman, so was I, now we're poachers turned gamekeepers. Small hope of finding brother Timothy in circumstances like that, agreed?"

156

"Look at it from his point of view, sir. Timothy's. Thinks the thing just may be genuine, wouldn't take the risk otherwise. But twenty-four hours is twenty-four hours." He let Archer's cogs crawl round for a second or two. "Still over seven hours of darkness. What's Timothy going to do? Go to bed?"

"What are the Cousins going to do, for God's sake? Swap tankers?"

"If I were Timothy," the unimaginative Pottern said, "I wouldn't rule out even that possibility. This is big stuff, on both sides. And there's no moon."

Archer lit himself another cigarette, swung his chair ninety degrees, stared at distant rooftops.

"The Cousins will think of that."

"Sir?"

"I take it you're contemplating the idea that the comrade might want to take a closer look. Might, so to speak, have a sudden yen for a trip round the bay."

"Sort of."

"Might" – Archer's cigarette was well down before he spoke again – "also be a trifle worried at the prospect of roadblocks, hotel checks, all the little things we're rather good at ourselves."

"The Spanish cops have a lot of practice at that sort of thing. Langley could spin them a tale."

The chair swung back. "Harbour watch, boat checks, can't see the Cousins missing out on that one."

"Which one in particular?" Pottern's clone-stereotype face had less expression than a used dish-rag.

"Arrive by boat, observe by boat, leave by boat. Damn it, Eric, I'm not stupid."

"Which boat?"

"Which boat?" Archer's self-confidence wavered. "How on earth do I know, which boat? *A* boat! What do you want? Its name?"

"How about *Oklahoma Star*?"

Eventually, Archer's cigarette burnt his fingers.

Choosing his time, Pottern began a recitation.

"'The Security Directorate is part of the Defence Forces of the country. Its task is the Defence of the Realm as a whole, from internal and external'" – Was it uncertain memory that made

157

him falter and then repeat? – "'external dangers . . . etcetera, etcetera . . . which may be judged subversive to the State.'"

Archer was looking exactly what he was; knowing, ruthless under easy charm, occasionally less than supersonic on the uptake. He made an effort, recovered, continued the recitation of Security Directorate's Prime Ministerial brief. "'No enquiry is to be carried out on behalf of any Government Department'" – The statement was intended to be firm but those last two words said something to him *en passant* – "'unless you are satisfied that an important public interest bearing upon the Defence of the Realm' . . . blah-blah . . . 'is at stake'. No enquiry, Eric, none, without permission.

"Who do you suggest I ask for permission to go outside the territorial boundaries and knock off an American citizen, old son?"

Pottern wasn't finished. "'You and your staff will maintain the well-established convention whereby Ministers do not concern themselves with the detailed information that may be obtained by Security Directorate in particular cases, but are furnished with such information as may be necessary for the determination of any issue on which guidance is sought.'

"You've already put the Ministry in the picture. We're not acting for anybody but ourselves. Are we in need of guidance, sir?"

"The Cousins will get there first." Archer's tone had changed.

"They'll be looking. Whether they find anything is another matter. We agreed – if it was us – we wouldn't be anywhere they might look. Before, during or after."

"Eric," – Archer began to function properly – "Panamanian-registered. Even if Timothy gets aboard her – I presume you're thinking his Libyan bosses could fix that – after Morpurgo's been and gone, it would be, well, an act of piracy to try to take him on the high seas. As for Spanish coastal waters . . ."

"Exactly."

"Then where the hell's he going to be until then?"

"Some little boat, hired up or down the coast, maybe even as far away as Barcelona. Fishing, pottering about, always where he can watch what's going on, but always out to sea. Pound to a penny the Yanks won't look, hard to see how they could anyway."

"Neither could we. I just said, Spanish territorial waters. We've enough trouble with Gibraltar, God knows. Boarding a Spanish boat, the comrade probably armed, us out in Tom Tiddler's ground . . . ! What do you want me to do, Eric, get myself booted out of the Directorate just when I'm about to take over?" Archer was laughing, a pleasant sense of superiority, the feeling that the cunning little sod wasn't so smart after all.

"We're dealing with terrorism." Pottern wasn't laughing. "Antonio Rielo, Barcelona terrorist squad, he owes us. And he knows all about the Libyan link with ETA and GRAPO. Give him reasonable grounds for suspicion, he'll check all boat hirings in the province, pick up Timothy for us. After that, we do a deal and we're all in business."

You cunning little sod! Archer thought, impressed.

*   *   *

There are stretches of central Spain that are another planet. In this one the trees, squat, tortured, were an extension of the harsh soil, an alien but disciplined army occupying captured and demolished fortifications of rock.

The road, emerging from a chasm that could have been the entrance to Hades, stretched to a distant, semi-desert horizon. For the past two hours it had been a kind of time machine, its occasional cars ranging from air-conditioned giants, hell-bent from Antwerp to Andalusia, to antiques closer to Benz than Mercedes. Two wheels, less frequent, were rickety life-support systems; knife grinder, basket weaver, laundry-woman. Farther still into the past were the donkeys.

Sylvie pulled in near one of the occasional mounds of stripped and drying bark; strange that the flayings of these southern trolls of trees should be used to imprison the delicate essences of the grape. But then, it had been strange last year in Portugal, she remembered, to hear the funeral beat of the evening drum, to see pickers stiff and exhausted from a day on the hot slopes treading the fruit, arms linked, lips unsmiling, eyes dead, for another two hours to start the port on its way to great restaurants and club and college tables.

Automatically taking her camera bag from the rear seat, she found herself thinking how Johnny, unconsciously, had changed her vision over these past years, letting her see beyond the picture to the truth. People and landscapes were her speciality, but now she saw them interrelated, the one worked upon, influenced, moulded, even tyrannised, by the other.

Here where she had paused, it was the land that dominated. On the larger time-scale it would consume people as voraciously as a wild beast, little but bones to mark their passage. She looked about her. There was always the one shot that spoke for all the others. Far away, the road was no longer totally empty; a speck. In the other direction, the muted snarl of a car being driven at speed.

It came from the gulch in a swirl of dust, a big white Mercedes, moving aquatically in the dance of the heat ripples, swelling as if rapidly inflated until – *chuff* – it was past in a hard buffet of wind. She watched it dwindle toward that slow-moving dot that the quick gale of its passage might almost be expected to whisk off the road like dust. She could define the dot now; a figure, a burden, a donkey.

There was something that Johnny, particularly Johnny a little impassioned and a little drunk, used to recite:

> At the head of all is God, lord of heaven.
> Then comes Prince Torlonia, lord of earth.
> Then comes the armed guard of Prince Torlonia.
> Then come the hounds of the armed guards of Prince Torlonia.
> Then nobody else.
> And still nobody else.
> And still again nobody else.
> Then come the peasants.

Now nobody else was between her and the donkey.

Where she stood, one of the cork oaks straddled a hump, its roots combatting the earth, its limbs the sky. Its shadow was spilled ink. It was the general of all the troops deployed across this brassy battlefield. The sun, from one spot on the far side of the road, would pass, declining, behind its squat bole within the next ten minutes. The scene began to form in the theatre of her mind.

The dot on the road had grown unmistakable legs. It, too, would pass much at the same time as the sun was occulted. A fast wide-angle lens, a starburst filter; the occulted sun would blaze like a bombshell against the deepened blue, darkness giving birth to a star. She snapped the filter on the lens barrel, set focus and approximate speed, sat down to wait.

The donkey's burden was a woman nested on a tottering load of fodder. The woman was a bundle of black, a hole in reality. White feathers of cloud, gossamer-light, linked her to the tree. In a few minutes more she might, for a matter of seconds, form part of a technical perfection.

Except that there was never perfection. Perfection was always just round the bend, just over the brow, the day after tomorrow. She was asking Johnny to sacrifice himself for the day after tomorrow.

Helga, a neurotic and unhappy woman; Steve, a husband with paleolithic ideas of her place and function; Sylvie herself breaking up a dinner *à trois*, in Steve's absence abroad, in order to go abroad herself, on business. Dear God, she had practically tucked Johnny and Helga between the sheets.

Those of her things that had been monogrammed, he had once said, and only once, after her reincarnation as the successful Sylvie Markham, were still usable, but not her husband. She had come to Spain to learn how to despise herself.

Now the sun, entangled in the lower-hanging branches of the cork oak, had ignited it, the mythical burning bush. The woman on the donkey with its green, unstable burden – a Spanish Birnham, an Extremaduran Dunsinane – was riding a long-legged shadow that dissipated the slow clop of the hooves in its silence.

She got up, squinting to frame her shots, took a light reading to guide experience. Nine or ten shots if she were quick. One of them might be to perfection what the shadow was to the donkey.

The stillness had gone; another car, beginning as a murmur, swelling to a growl. Far down the road, a large car, Lord Torlonia closing the gap. It would be past before the sun was totally consumed by the tree.

Wrong. It slowed as it approached. It was the Mercedes, portly and sleek as a white-suited tycoon, that had swept past heading north. It came to a halt precisely between her and the burning tree, two occupants, clipped from black paper. A voice, "*Señora,*

161

buenas noces. I told my friend it was you." Behind them, tree, sun and donkey approached conjunction.

She waved imperiously. "Please! Move on! Quickly! Quickly!"

The car leaped, spitting grit and dust. The last of the sun's disc vanished, the sky turned electric, tree, beast and human two-dimensional and jetty-black against the solar flare. There was nothing in her mind but the repeated operation of the mechanism of which she was part.

The light began to dazzle west of the tree bole. The donkey ambled gently on. Small, incandescent beads burst from the rough bark, then there was new heat on her face as the disc began to emerge. Down the road she was vaguely aware of the slam of a car door.

"My deepest apologies, señora. It was unforgivably stupid. The first time, I didn't recognise you until too late. Then I began to wonder if you were once again in trouble, if your car had broken down again, and so we returned." It was the young man from Mérida.

Now she was ready to forgive. "I think I owe you an apology. I was very rude."

"I perfectly understand. But you have no other problems? The car behaves?"

"The car's fine. It was good of you to come back." She was looking past him at his car.

He understood. "Why the lift into town in Mérida?" He laughed. "The car is not mine. I am only its driver. My client wished to see the Roman theatre, but then remembered urgent business in town. He allowed me to stay, on the understanding that I would make my own way back. Thanks to you, señora, it was not too arduous."

His employer, window wound down, was taking pictures of them, zoom telephoto. Seeing it, the young man laughed again. "Oh yes, he too is a photographer, but only for his friends. Click, click, click" – He mimed – "always pictures, but I think they are probably not very good."

The man in the car, seeing them watching, put down his camera, sketched a mock salute to Sylvie, then tapped his watch and pointed along the road.

"Forward. Always forward." The young man sighed.

162

"Goodbye, señora. I am most happy that all is well. *Buon viaje*. Not too late to your hotel. This is wild country."

She watched them drive off, diminishing, soon to vanish. She began to pack away her equipment.

In the Mercedes, the big man, too, was dismantling his camera. "Let's get out of these badlands," he said in English. "I can use a drink, so put your foot down, pally."

*   *   *

An odd thing happened after their late night arrival at Barcelona airport. A car and driver – American; young, neat, respectful – was there to meet them, but so was someone else.

"Señor Claas?" A man wearing a light raincoat and a look that said police as plainly as the blazon on the side of a patrol car intercepted Claas. He displayed something in the palm of his hand.

Clearly taken by surprise, Claas spoke English. "Yes. What is it?"

The man launched into rapid Spanish, indicating a car that sat, lights extinguished, across the no-parking area outside the arrival hall.

Claas hesitated. To his driver, he said, "Take Mr Morpurgo to the car. Be with you in a minute." Morpurgo saw Claas accompany the man to the waiting car, bend to look through the passenger window, then, somehow reluctant, get in.

Whatever the business was, it was quickly dealt with. Claas came back. "Okay, let's go. Some country. Franco dead all this time and you still can't go to the john without somebody wants to know why."

"You came a long way to go to the john. Maybe that's what interested them."

"They know me. Did, I guess I should say. You don't go through on the nod at Spanish airports. They read the passenger lists like they were lottery results." Claas settled back and closed his eyes.

Brushoff, Morpurgo thought; so what was new! One of many hovering questions reached the head of the queue; how odd that the security police should be waiting – top man, too, was Morpurgo's guess – when they arrived from London, yet Hank

163

Timothy, in Madrid, had slipped twice through a supposedly impregnable cordon. And Warren Claas, more than twenty years with Langley, tricked, in retrospect, by a ploy that should not have fooled a pink-cheeked rooky.

They went less than ten miles, leaving the *autopista* almost at once. The hotel, small, secluded, lay at the foot of low hills, the night dark but an impression of orchards. Claas, in the next room, proved to be a talented snorer. Lying wakeful while Claas rumbled seismically, he contemplated the fact that he and Sylvie were now in the same country, that he could get up, dress, and be where she was in so many hours. Except that, since Mérida, he had received no calls, didn't know where she was.

He had managed a quick visit to his mother. At the hospital they were still professionally vague; old age, time, the benefit of supervised rest. They made him feel guilty, a role he had long since perfected.

She hadn't really been interested, his mother. "If you've got to go, well, that's that. What else do you want me to say?" But then she had surprised him. "Both in Spain, together but separate, that's a rum arrangement." It was the nearest she had ever come to mentioning the present state of affairs, but she had noticed, and there had been more.

"She's no fool, isn't Sylvie, so it has to be you. Doesn't like that job of yours, is that it? No more than me. Well, you'll do what you do, always have, but you want to be careful. A marriage needs working at, give and take. It's what me and your dad had, not that you ever noticed."

Then the nurse had come back. "Little and often, Mr Morpurgo, that's the way with visits, your mother in her present state."

So goodbye, mum, and be a good girl, and see you soon, and she had produced her biggest surprise, reaching briefly to pat his cheek. "You're a good lad, even if you always know best. Well, maybe Sylvie knows better, just you think about it."

Even if he always knew best! Well, Sylvie knew better than best.

It had been the first touch of affection he could recall since childhood, but the last thing she said was, "Take no notice of that nurse. These blackies don't know how to mind their own business."

Lying there in the deep of a foreign night, he knew two things. His mother was going to die. And Sylvie had put together a rescue package for their marriage. Get this present incomprehensible item of farce out of the way, then call it a day.

The next morning, the return to the airport took them to the military zone, far from the jumbos and Costa Brava charters. The helicopter was a little Bell-Agusta, nothing but civil markings and a weathered blue and white livery. The pilot, tall, laconic, wearing white coveralls, no markings there either, had greying hair, huge yellow sun lenses, a spectacular tan. No introductions; after a casual "Hi!" he went back to his mechanic. Claas and Morpurgo stood awkwardly under a sun that was stretching, yawning, and flexing its muscles.

Claas squinted in a reflected dazzle from the Plexiglass cockpit bubble. "You got a piece? A gun?"

"A bit late for that now, isn't it? Anyway, I don't like them."

Claas shook his head. "You Brits, too damned casual!" He thumped Morpurgo awkwardly with a balled fist. "Okay, but watch it."

It was time for a cliché before the thing became emotional. Morpurgo grinned. "I didn't know you cared."

Concluding his inspection with a kick at the nearer skid, the pilot came back. "All set?"

Claas decided to resent his unbuttoned attitude. "There's a whole lot hanging on this. I wouldn't want to see it screwed up."

The pilot flashed his teeth mockingly. "Ain't about to lift the hubcaps off your scene, Jackson."

"Just so you remember this is no coffee klatsch."

The pilot motioned Morpurgo elaborately. *"Señor, por favor."*

Claas stepped back, wary of the oil-stained concrete.

The hatches thumped to. The engine fired shatteringly. The pilot twisted the throttle, fed power, pulled on the collective. They were lurchingly airborne, a giddy half-circle spin then away in a nose-down sweep that temporarily separated Morpurgo from his stomach. Claas, dwindling to a dot, gave a tentative wave. Morpurgo thought: I didn't know he cared, and was not reassured.

Across the *autopista*, lightly sprinkled with traffic, trailing their small shadow over orchards, market gardens, vineyards. Morpurgo remembered another chopper trip, another time, not that many months ago, that had saved a government and lost him his job.

The sprawl of Barcelona faded beneath its khaki haze of pollution, a white cruise ship sleek as a swan where the Ramblas came down the port. The sea looked oil-smooth, no whitecaps. A course change brought them parallel with the steely glint of the railway that crept through tunnels and cuttings, hugging the shoreline.

To begin with, each small town was guesswork, but eventually, with a small shock of surprise, he began to pick out names on the living map. First the higgle of Torredembarra, beyond it the Roman aqueduct and the Bará arch. Tarragona itself, golden, rolling out of the haze, the highway under their nose, the buff sprawl of the city stretching ragged pseudopods inland to Rues, Constantí, Vilaseca. Crowning the hump of the old town, the cathedral, half church, half fortress in the hug of its ancient walls, spilled a scribble of narrow streets down to the ruler-straight ramblas where he and Sylvie had sat, shaded, over a midday drink while Sylvie's parents and he indulged in mutual patronisation. He saw in the town the colour of Sylvie's hair; her eyes in the colour of the sea.

Now they were following instructions – how *did* Langley talk to Hank Timothy? – circling the old town to turn and head directly down the Rambla Nueva, passing over the Balcón del Mediterráneo and, holding the course, out to sea. Timothy could be watching from any one of a hundred different places, even the Balcón itself or the steep straggle of the Parque del Milagro directly below it. No, Hank Timothy was far too smart for that.

To starboard, the maritime port and docks, the permanently berthed service tanker as a reminder of what they were looking for. Ahead, a scatter of small craft, some motionless as dropped sticks, some incising the mingled blues with cuneiform wedges of white. Beyond, the glowing carpet of water inverted itself to become the sky.

And there it was, unreal in the vaporous light, the *Oklahoma Star*, 110,000 tons deadweight, officered and crewed, according to Weber, by half the nationalities of the Mediterranean littoral, plus a sprinkling of Gulf Arabs and Pakistanis. She lay at the heart of a milky band of blue-green water, placed by Hank Timothy with the precision of a piece on a chess board.

"Okay" – The pilot was talking – "coming in for a look first." Morpurgo realised he must be in radio communication. The little Bell was losing height rapidly, coming in from an acute angle astern. The descent gave Morpurgo more unease and he heard Claas again: *On goddam active service, at my age!* Me too! he thought unhappily.

The tanker grew swiftly from toy to boat to giant, immaculacy gradually yielding to rust, patchy paintwork, the general decrepitude bestowed by sun, salt and weather. As tankers went these days, a baby, nevertheless the sheer bulk and length of her impressed.

He had thought, so far as he had thought at all, that they would put down on the metal wasteland that is nine-tenths of a tanker's length. He had thought vaguely that it was flat. But amidships reared two great derricks, in the bows a stubby mast, while from superstructure of fo'c'sle, like the backbone of a fish, ran a cluster of massive pipelines topped by a catwalk and bisected by loading and discharge lines. Dotting such space as remained were winches, a series of elongated oval hatches, several life rafts. Flat it was not.

They were passing the stern at close quarters, a miniature archipelago of floating refuse scurrying in their down draught. The rotating radar antenna gaped its black arc at them. The raked funnel, black with a green P, spewed a thin shimmer of hot air.

Intent, yet relaxed as a bird in a tree, his pilot said, "They tell me callers are usually winched aboard, Jackson, but this baby doesn't even run to a rope, so we have to set her down." The helicopter was edging forward, very low now, moving parallel to and to port of the great hull. They crept past the white cliff of the superstructure. He could see faces through the glass. They seemed much too close. The gap between the helicopter and the vast forward sweep of the tanker remained narrow but constant, the tip of the portside hose-handling derrick appearing to Morpurgo to threaten from above. Beyond it, halfway to the fo'c'sle, he finally spotted a yellow-painted circle blazoned with a bold H.

A ship's officer, white-clad, and a crewman waited at a respectful distance. Morpurgo found he was sweating more profusely than could be put down to the sun through the smeared bubble of the cockpit.

The little Bell-Agusta inched forward level with the landing circle, hovering to port and some feet above deck level, then, at the last moment, taking him by surprise, slipped neatly sideways to settle with a light bump at the centre of the circle. The pilot cut the engine, snapped off switches, the rotor blades spinning idly to a halt. "That's it, Jackson. Figure on being here long?"

"I'm not sure, but I don't think so."

"Okay with me, friend. Langley foots the bills." The pilot produced a paperback, science fiction of the old school, bare breasts and monsters, and prepared to vacate the rapidly heating cockpit bubble.

A junior officer watched Morpurgo emerge. The air, after the cockpit, was good. The sun bit. A seagull dropped a splatter of white on the cockpit bubble.

"Captain waiting you on bridge, sah."

Behind him, the pilot called, "Hold it, Jackson." The box holding the bloody bugs, he'd left it behind! He took it, feeling doubly foolish, the whole point of the mission overlooked, the mission itself impossible. He followed his guide along a couple of miles of catwalk above a hot deck that smelled of salt, giving way, as they entered the crew quarters, to diesel oil and the aroma of exotic cooking.

The bridgehouse, with its wings and long promenades, seemed vast, a purring new world only tenuously linked with the old. A seaman in dungarees cleaned metalwork. The captain, white-uniformed, hot-faced, bounced, hands clasped behind, on the balls of his feet, emitting jerky hostility. A civilian, back to Morpurgo, broad-shouldered in a pale blue suit, turned. "Hi, pally. Welcome aboard."

Hank Timothy bared his equine teeth. "That the stuff?" Taking advantage of Morpurgo's disconcertment, he slid the box free. "Let's take a peek."

The captain's fragile restraint crumpled. "Mr Morpurgo," stressing the first syllable instead of the second, "I must tell you, I don't like, understan'? This is my ship. I say what okay, what not okay, understan'? So, I have orders, but I am captain, understan'? This completely my ship. Completely!"

Morpurgo floundered. "I'm sorry, captain. I'm under orders too." Timothy was ripping tape from the sealed box.

"Okay." The captain fell back on dignity. "Okay, you too, but I am captain, understan'?"

"Let's cut the yack and do what we have to do, okay?" Timothy prised open the box. "Then we can all haul ass. This it?" He shook the container. It made a dry sound, like sifting salt.

"What this stuff anyway?" The captain was anguished. "Why nobody tells me nothin'? I insist to know."

"Baby food, *capitano*." Timothy clapped the tarnished gold braid of his shoulder. "Just baby food. You had your instructions, right?"

The captain spun on his heels, spraying angry plosives. "Twen'y-four hours I lose over this business. Is money, you know? Is money!" He stamped away to glare out at nothing.

"Don't flip off, *capitano*." Timothy grinned at Morpurgo. "Number six tank, starboard."

"That's what they told me."

"And you always do what you're told." Timothy's wet yellow grin taunted him. "Where's number six tank, *capitano*?"

The captain flung a finger in the direction of his first officer. "He tells, not me. Me, finish. *Finito!*"

The first officer's English was better. "Number six right below, nearest here." Morpurgo glanced through the raked glass of the bridge windows. The red-painted acreage of steel stretched immensely toward distant bows.

He had a huge urge to be done himself, *finito*. "I'll take that." He held out his hand for the container.

"Uh-uh." Timothy wagged his head. "*He'll* take it." He gave it to the uncomprehending first officer. "You could turn shit to shampoo between here and those tanks, and me none the wiser. You go too, pally, but strictly as sidewalk superintendent." He picked up a pair of marine binoculars. "And poppa's going to be watching real close."

"You're not coming?"

Again that maddeningly knowing grin. "How do I know who's out there? You think I was born yesterday?" There was a scatter of small boats all about them. Any one of them, theoretically, might carry a sharpshooter. Now, for the first time, Morpurgo had time to wonder how Timothy had come aboard, and when. If Langley had people looking for him, they were going to be disappointed.

A moment later, the supplementary question: How was Timothy proposing to get away?

"Okay, you ready to strut your stuff? You and him" – He nodded at the first officer – "are going down to the crude, since there's no way it can come up to you. The inert gas has been vented off, but the air down there ain't what you'd want to breathe." He laughed his great laugh. Morpurgo's fingers itched, but his unarmed combat training, like his pistol practice, was one with time.

Timothy slung the binoculars about his thick neck. "On your way, pally." He turned away from them toward the diminishing perspective of the long hull. "Just one thing. Not number six starboard. Number one, port."

Even in his suppressed anger, Morpurgo saw the point. If there were to be any trick on the part of Langley – though what it might be defied the imagination – a switch of tanks would put a stop to it. In sending Morpurgo to the tank farthest forward, Timothy was showing that he was less interested in watching the operation than in having it take place at the maximum distance from the previously agreed point. Morpurgo shrugged inwardly as he followed the first officer. That, like the rest of this crazy business, was Langley's problem.

Down on 'A' deck a seaman was waiting with two sets of breathing apparatus and coveralls. The first officer helped Morpurgo before donning his own, the masks, for the time being, left about their necks. They went out on the foredeck.

The sun reached down to smack them about the face. So did the smell, brine mingled with raw sewage. A silent scatter of gulls drifted hopefully overhead. Following them as they glided away, Morpurgo's eyes passed beyond the smokestack to where Tarragona lay distant to starboard, half real, half mirage. Down the coast, he could see the glint of the petrochemical complex.

They climbed the catwalk that piggybacked the long spine of steam and oil lines. Morpurgo turned to look back. From the bridge, Timothy waved mockingly. *Bastard*! The first officer's startled look told him that what he had thought, he had spoken aloud.

They descended, crossing to the portside hatch farthest forward. It had a vertical coaming, roughly knee-height, capped by the hatch itself. In the hatch was a small sealed port, perhaps six inches in diameter. Morpurgo was reminded of Claas's assurance that there would be no more to it than lowering the inoculum through such a port in a sampling vessel, without ever coming any nearer to the crude.

If Timothy knew that, and Morpurgo found it difficult to believe otherwise, he had ruled against it. Yet, surely? it would have been preferable, if Timothy, back there with his damned binoculars, really did wish to observe the operation from start to finish.

The seaman spun lugged handles to release heavy cleats while the first officer helped Morpurgo with his breathing apparatus, adjusting the demand value on the cylinder before attending to his own. The hatch swung back. The seaman handed over a large, rubber-encased inspection torch.

The first officer put a leg over the coaming, found a foothold on a grip bar and swung his weight over, transferring himself to the head of a steel ladder that dropped vertically into darkness. He indicated that Morpurgo should follow, and the pair of them went down the ladder. Some twelve to fifteen feet down, Morpurgo, helped by his guide, found himself on a narrow platform from which a further ladder descended. Somewhere below them, stygean and invisible under its lethal blanket of hydrocarbon vapour and residual inert gas, seven thousand tons of Libyan crude; only the platform between them and the vilest form of drowning, only the mask between them and almost instant asphyxiation.

It also occurred to him, paradoxically, that if he were not actually here, he would, now, think this whole thing preposterous.

The first officer looked a question. Morpurgo nodded. Off came the cap from the container, over it went. A pale buff, granular sleet drifted briefly through the beam of the torch and vanished into the depths.

Out on the deck once more, even the sewage smelled good after the close and fusty odour of the breathing apparatus. For the third time, Morpurgo looked up at the bridge. This time it was the captain who had the binoculars. The first officer dabbed at his face with a handkerchief of dazzling whiteness. Heat? Or nerves? They had been in the presence of something that, given one spark, could have turned the ship into an inferno.

As they climbed back up to the catwalk after the first officer had supervised the battening down of the hatch, there was a sudden racket. Nerves and association of ideas made Morpurgo jump. Then, sickeningly, he knew what it was. From its perch in the landing circle, where he had left his pilot, the Bell-Agusta lifted gently. Shifting neatly sideways to clear the hull of the tanker, it rose, black dragonfly against the hard blue emptiness, then shrank to port and astern, turning, though not too fast to prevent him from seeing that it carried a passenger. Still climbing, it tilted away toward the aetherial city.

Later, back on the bridge with an irate and uncooperative captain, waiting and not wanting to be put in touch with Claas by ship-to-shore telephone, he took the final punch to the stomach. A light breeze had got up. It stirred the flag at the stern, swirling it languidly to display, green on black, Prometheus with a flaming torch under the threat of a hovering eagle. The *Oklahoma Star* belonged to Brewster Cochran.

*   *   *

Claas, poking viciously at his *pollo con gambas* as they awaited their return flight to London in the airport restaurant, had had, Morpurgo decided on repeated reflection, a choice of two possible reactions, being Claas, a cool enough hand, but unimaginative and no kind of actor.

He could have played it straight: *So he switched tanks, so what? The bugs aren't choosy?*

Or he could have blown it: *Jesus!* followed by a hasty recovery.

He had done neither and a little of both. Replaying the scene over and again – he was replaying it now, as he closed his front door behind him and felt himself numb under the anaesthesia of a house without Sylvie – he reached the same conclusion every time.

Of course, there had been the intolerable preliminaries, Morpurgo himself finally getting in touch by ship-to-shore telephone, Claas incoherent with disbelief that Timothy – no, Morpurgo! – had done it again. After that – fatigue? forgetfulness? unconscious malice? who knew? – he had only mentioned the switch of tanks when both of them had sunk, exhausted, into the lethargy of the aftermath. "Warren, I don't know if it matters" – He was supposed to think it should not – "but he had me put the bugs into a different tank."

Well, Timothy had suspected trickery, that was natural. But, so Claas must have wondered, did Morpurgo? Did Epworth? How plain had Timothy made his suspicions during his time with Morpurgo? Had the encounter, in fact, been as brief as Morpurgo had told it? Or had Timothy said much and Morpurgo reported little? And so on.

The questions must have flooded in on Claas. All right: *What the hell? You accusing Langley of cheating with SIS as well as Timothy?* Sound and fury signifying much and more. Or *I don't get it. Who cares what he did? so long as the bugs met the crude.*

Instead of which, Claas, a forkful of chicken poised, stared much too long while his eyes, the one peephole in that blank Germanic face, gave a glimpse of total chaos. Then, belatedly, too belatedly and after being almost human just before the chopper flight, he produced *echt* Claas. "So what do you want me to say, man? He pissed all over you on the strength of a phony CIA identity pass, and all you can do is futz around wringing your hands over how much piss got into which tank!"

It was offensive. It had been meant to be offensive, because it was also defensive and the best defence is attack, so Morpurgo took no offence, nor made any comment when, too soon, Claas scrubbed his mouth with his napkin and got up too hurriedly. "I have to call Weber again. I just remembered something I forgot before."

He had had to tell Weber and, through Weber, Langley, that a gigantic bluff had been called by Hank Timothy.

And now all the sawdust had run out of John Morpurgo, ex-Security Directorate, recently-appointed nobody in Her Majesty's Secret Intelligence Service, cat's-paw and dupe of

Friends, Cousins and enemies alike. Not to mention failed husband. This house – Sylvie was right, they must leave it if only because it stank of violated trust – saluted him with a salvo of wet powder, a march-past of defeat.

He wanted nothing, not food, not even sleep. So he opened the refrigerator and closed it, went upstairs and came down, poured and tasted a drink before leaving it, sat at his piano and made so many mistakes in so few seconds that it was like setting his life story to music. Stricken with guilty recollection, he rang the hospital. Mrs Morpurgo? Well, it's very late, but put you through to the ward. Mrs Morpurgo? She's asleep, sister's not here this minute, could you call back tomorrow?

So she was still there, had he thought otherwise? and yes, he could call back, but how was she? Surely someone must know? As well as could be expected, only what, in Christ's name – only he didn't actually ask – did they expect?

He rang off, Morpurgo, also as well as could be expected, except that no one, any longer, did. Almost at once, in that empty house where even the street sounds had left the neighbourhood, only the Underground, as deeply buried as hope, rumbling beneath his feet like a series of events that were always about to happen but never did, the telephone rang.

He pounced, starveling tiger, starveling hope.

"Sylvie?"

It was Epworth. Epworth, they had told him from Century House, had gone, unexpectedly, to Berlin.

"Have – mmmm – an interesting trip?"

"How's Berlin?" A manic desire to dominate rather than serve yet again as target.

"*Ich bin nicht ein Berliner.*"

Very funny. And possibly the only true thing he had had from Epworth in days.

"The trip was full of surprises." That must be some kind of record for understatement.

"With a man like Timothy, what else? How did he arrive? Or was he there already?"

Shit!

"You'd do better to ask how he left. Except that the Cousins can hardly wait to tell you."

"Ah, he was there already. To be – mmmm – expected, the ship being Cochran's."

Morpurgo, dog-weary, diminished, depressed, raced through an excremental interior monologue.

"I wonder," Epworth was saying, "who leaned on whom? Langley on Cochran. Libyans on Cochran. Timothy on the Libyans. Not that it matters."

"You knew. Why didn't you tell me?"

"Mmmmmmm." Shuffling through lies like a man with a full deck of aces. "Just checked with Lloyd's, curiosity, not hunch. Archer's man Pottern checked too, but not about the details of the charter."

A woman's voice, interrupting. *"Sie sind am Telefon?"*

"Ich spreche, fräulein, danke."

"Ach, so! Pardon!" Something else learned, Epworth spoke – fluent? – German.

"I suppose you know about the switch, too? You knew about the first one."

"Found out about the first one. Oh." Epworth produced his soft giggle. "Guessing games. Not number six tank?"

"Number one. And port, not starboard. So it won't work, will it? At least" – Oh God! He was suddenly so tired – "it wouldn't have worked if the thing had been genuine." He knew what he meant. Epworth, God rot him, knew what he meant.

"I *think*" – He could visualise Epworth, somewhere in Berlin, pulling one of his judicious little faces – "one – mmmm – might have expected that, don't you?"

"Oh yes, if you're lucky enough to have twenty-twenty hindsight." But the bloody man was right. "Anyway." He checked the time. "About twelve hours from now, that ship will dock and they'll start pumping. The oil in number one will run normally. Fare thee well, brother Timothy." Why should he feel such a sense of personal failure?

"Mmmmmmm. Maybe."

Maybe, for Christ's sake! He bit back what was on his lips. One shot left in his locker. For the first time, he began to doubt that it would come as news.

"Claas was shaken to his foundations by that switch. He was

175

also shaken at being met at the airport by a high-up in the Spanish security police."

"Ah."

"Tell me you know."

"No. Please, tell me more."

Morpurgo told him.

"And Claas was surprised."

"Surprised. Embarrassed. At a guess, surprised at something he was told, embarrassed that I was there to see it."

"But not hear it."

"No." He gave up. It was trying to outwit God Almighty. "But it got me thinking. This great tie-up they're supposed to have. Madrid station – how big is Langley in Spain anyway? – the Spanish police and security people, all the likely points of entry staked out tighter than a frog's arse, yet Timothy pops in and out more or less as he pleases.

"They set up a meet – so they tell us and he confirmed it – in the mountains – he says the Pyrenees – and Timothy kills a man and gets away. They agree . . ."

"A Frenchman. Well, nationalised Franco-Algerian, has a key job at a French weapons-grade plutonium plant, took him to the morgue in Pamplona. We're still working on it, your most – mmmm – useful suggestion."

"Glad to be of help." Weapons-grade plutonium! Hadn't Weber said the French had Timothy on a list? "Okay, that meet in Madrid. All right, the square's full of people, fiesta time, but only so many entrances, perfectly possible to cover, it used to be my business, remember? And the whole place overlooked by windows, rooftops, as well as more police than you'd find in Trafalgar Square on New Year's Eve. Yet Timothy drifts in and out like smoke. After fooling Claas with a baby-trick.

"Now it's a tanker, Libya to Spain, not exactly a round the world trip, not exactly anything at all that presents insuperable difficulties to people who are supposed to be expert in surveillance . . ."

Epworth interrupted again, quite firm for once. "And the tanker is Brewster Cochran's."

"All the easier to check, so why didn't they?"

"*Augenblick, bitte.*" The operator was back again. "*Hallo! Ich*

176

kann Sie nicht verstehen, Köln. Sprechen Sie weiter . . ." The voice vanished abruptly.

"This," Epworth said unnecessarily, "is by no means a secure line. You were saying?"

"Was I? Well, bugger secure lines. You'd better think what you're going to tell your bloody Foreign Office pals."

"My dear man, exactly what they'd want to hear in the circumstances, which is nothing at all. The Pompey syndrome, have you forgotten? 'Don't tell us about it, because we'd rather not know.' They want us to fly solo, Johnny. Then, should we crash, they don't even have to send a wreath. Now, Claas was disturbed by the news of the switched tanks, but what about Weber?"

"I haven't seen Weber. When I do, he'll have had time to recover."

"Don't be so sure that he'll need to. Ask yourself why. Ask yourself, not why Timothy slips in and out so easily, but why they have such an elaborate set-up to give him cause. Ask yourself why Brewster Cochran has been keeping so remarkably quiet. And a great many more whys that may occur to you after a good night's sleep and a day or two off. Speculate, in brief, on the deceptive allure of poetism."

Morpurgo, tired, missed the vital point. "What day or two off?"

"I don't want you in after the weekend. I shan't be in myself."

"Still in Berlin?"

Ever the master, he sideslipped the question. "Make sure the Cousins know where to find you. Don't stray far from home. Have a good weekend." Berlin was off the line.

* * *

"Good of you to come, Eric." Someone else already in the flat, Pottern's sixth sense told him as Archer let him in. A woman, one of his other senses told him shortly afterwards; warm, scented air from the direction of the bathroom. And yes, it bloody well was good of him to come, Sunday evening and working practically all the weekend after that knackering trip to Spain and back.

All very well for the boss, claiming that his out-of-town weekend was all part of the getting-to-know-you socialising that was an essential preliminary to his forthcoming elevation. And all very well that someone like Eric Pottern was neither welcome on a flying duty visit to Hampshire or Wiltshire or wherever it was, nor able to deliver his full report over a telephone that was open to the world and his wife. The fact remained, essential business got held up, and Eric Pottern had his weekend well and truly buggered.

Definitely a woman, smells, as they passed the kitchen, that were definitely too exotic for the boss's skills, not that he was likely to do so much as put on a pinny and help with the washing up. In the corner of the sofa, as Pottern was graciously seated, a small, fancy-looking handkerchief peeked coyly, embroidered monogram. Too bad he couldn't read it.

Archer didn't beat about the bush. "Washout, then, your little jaunt to sunny Spain."

"'Fraid so. From that point of view."

Archer looked up from lighting his cigarette. Pottern wondered what the boss would say if he knew his lieutenant despised him for the smoking habit. Probably wouldn't give a damn.

"That point of view? Was there more than one?"

"Well, the one we went for, that was a washout. Tony Rielo, in Barcelona, was cooperative, swallowed the story, turned out the men, but nothing."

"Until too late."

Pottern showed his teeth, trying to smile it off. "Oh, they found the chopper went to some military airport at a place called Reus, if that's how you pronounce it. A few miles inland from Tarragona, used by charters and private civils as well. That's where Timothy was put down all right, but the chopper was charter, too, left Spain for France later, no chance of a trace without alerting the Cousins."

"And Timothy?"

Pottern snapped his fingers. "Vanished. Poof!" He contemplated that part with no visible emotion. "Morpurgo came ashore by boat. Class sent a car. They flew back well before us."

Archer had on his thinking frown, or was it his cigarette smoke? Someone closed a sliding door – wardrobe? – down the far end of the flat. There were fresh flowers in the room, expertly arranged if you liked that kind of artificial, hotel lobby look.

"You did the proper thing," Archer decided. "Looked for someone on reliable information, didn't find him, thank you very much and out."

"Rielo wasn't exactly nosy but . . ."

". . . more questions than answers. At least he didn't press them. You couldn't see anything aboard the tanker?"

"Damn near impossible. They're big, especially when you're in a small boat, like trying to see what's happening on the top of a cliff when you're half a mile out to sea. We had glasses, but hopeless, really. It was the shore search and the boat checks I was counting on, and so were they. Oh, we saw a couple of people, maybe three, going forward, coming back, then up and away went the chopper." Pottern showed his teeth again. "Not that we knew who was aboard, not then. Thought it was Morpurgo, job done and away."

Archer smoked in silence. "Rielo's people," Pottern said, "were getting quite keen to go aboard, but we talked them out of it. At least, Sibley did. His Spanish must be quite good." He shared the silence before adding, "Would have been a waste of time anyway, way things turned out."

"And the other thing? The non-washout."

"Oh, that." Pottern produced his most expressionless look. "If the Cousins *were* planning a snuff, they didn't exactly put themselves out. One man and a dog."

Archer's heavy eyebrows rose. "Claas and Morpurgo? Are you telling me that was it? Not even Weber?"

"Claas and Morpurgo. Rielo would have been quick enough to tell us if they'd been operating mob-handed. Tony Rielo and that bloke Figueroa, State Security or whatever they call it, are cat and dog." Just like you and Epworth, Pottern thought, only not such gents. "They didn't even stake out the airport, let alone Tarragona. No boat check, either, not even a hire. Rielo'd confirmed that before we left, and his people had already done a boat-hire sweep, full length of the coast." He waited to see if the boss could put that one together.

The boss was certainly trying, though the muffled sound of a radio, down the bedroom end, nipped grooves in the flesh above his lordly nose. He tapped a cigarette on his case but neither lit the one nor tucked away the other.

"If they're not trying to knock Timothy off, what the hell *are* they at?"

"Good question." You do the talking, brother. You're supposed to be in charge.

Archer laid cigarette and case on the small table with the ashtray and the pretty flowers. With a sudden spurt of inspiration, Pottern thought: she's trying to stop him smoking, whoever she is.

Archer said, "Recap, right?" Pottern projected earnestness.

'Comrade Timothy, on behalf of his nutty Libyan bosses, tried to blow up the President on his way home from Gatwick. Would have succeeded too, if the Yanks didn't organise those trips by numbers."

"Certainly looks that way, sir." Pottern himself had not actually been present to witness the business of the blood buggy. He was beginning to take nothing for granted.

"Was that way, Eric. Big hush-up afterwards, obvious reasons. Orders from on high, find him, fix him, fast. And brother Church gets the smooth heave-ho, he's gone, by the way."

"With you so far, sir."

"After that?" Archer's hand moved toward the cigarette, lost its nerve. "Gets a bit complicated, certainly does, but good luck, good judgement – what's this game all about, anyway? – and we found ourselves in the running."

The distant radio went off abruptly, but no sound of anyone emerging down the other end of the corridor. What did he do, keep her locked in the bedroom? Just his style, Pottern thought, little woman in her place, which was why the first one, German Helga, no longer was.

"All that business at Billingshurst, rum, very rum, Eric, Cousins overplaying their hand, wouldn't you say? Never mind. We had the breaks, no complaints. Cochran's failure is the Cousins' bait and Morpurgo is their stooge. Fair?"

"In the circs, fair enough." Archer still has a sneaking respect for Morpurgo, though, Pottern noted. Like to see him down, but not actually out. Offered him the DD-G slot, after all, or had that been bait too?

"Yes." Archer was faintly complacent in spite of disappointments. "I think so. Right, Morpurgo's meeting with Timothy in

Madrid was to bait the trap for Langley's hit, next time, that's what we thought."

"Next time being Tarragona."

"Tarragona. But now . . ." Archer's flight of fancy, stalled, started to go nose down. He looked to Pottern as co-pilot.

"Willing and able to keep the meet. But not to pull the trigger." Pottern was at his most helpful.

"What?" It was as if Archer, having been told to bail out, had obeyed only to discover, belatedly, the absence of an essential item of equipment.

"Only one person at the meet, sir."

"You're surely not suggesting . . . ? Morpurgo?"

"Nobody else there. Not even Claas. Either Morpurgo was going to do it or nobody ever intended to do it."

He had thrown the boss this time, and no mistake.

Archer struggled with conflicting feelings; a kind of animosity, a sort of loyalty, a problem of belief. "I don't think . . . no, Eric, I really *don't*! Johnny Morpurgo? It takes a different type. Hang it" – a tinge of ex-Guards disdain – "never fired a shot in his life off the practice range.

"No! Really! All right, so the Cousins didn't swamp the place. Outwitted, like as not. After all, so were we, the comrade's no bunny, got to give him that. But Johnny Morpurgo as a hitman?"

Shaking his head decisively, Pottern saw, but he wasn't, not absolutely, decided.

"Then what was it all about, sir?"

Glancing longingly at his cigarette, Archer caught the tail end of Pottern's look of superiority. Too smart, too cocky, too clever by half, that one; it was a crime in Archer's book. At the same time . . .

He laughed, annoyed to find it sound a bit forced. "That stuff, the stuff the Cousins nicked from Billingshurst. Maybe it actually did go wrong."

"Not sure I'm with you this time, sir."

"According to Cochran, second time we met, it was supposed to squeeze oil out of rock – the technical stuff bored me, to be frank – but it went wrong. At least, if I got it right, it worked at first but the oil went wrong, sort of went bad. No good to man or beast according to Cochran."

181

"Isn't that what he would say?"

"Yes, yes, but *if* it did. I mean, if those bugs could turn one lot of oil bad, really, not fake . . ."

Pottern – Archer was beginning to have second thoughts about Eric Pottern's future – was being deliberately slow in response, no doubt about that. Pretend to be dim, make the old man go through the hoops. Right, Eric my little friend, we'll see. But later, not now. Now is when I need you.

Perhaps Pottern, too, had done his thought-reading, don't push your luck with a man who just might take Morpurgo back. "If it wasn't a hit set-up, was it a deal after all? That what you mean, sir?" The woman, tippy-toe, had come down the corridor, gone into the kitchen.

In Archer's mind, dawn was breaking over a new world, different paths, different horizons. A deal? Between the Cousins and a man who had made an attempt on the life of the President of the United States of America? Only if it involved something big, bigger, even, than any attempt to spike Libyan oil wells.

He could see that Pottern knew it, too. Eric Pottern, perhaps, as things turned out, knew a bit too much, but even so, neither of them knew enough.

Yet they still knew more than anyone else, because they were the only ones who knew what had happened at Gatwick.

He had not needed Pottern to recite the rules on what Security Directorate was and was not supposed to do, nor had he needed Pottern to interpret or misinterpret them. Steve Archer had been brought up in a class of society that laid great store by rules, principally because it was the class that had made them. But it had not made them for itself, except the unwritten ones, and even those, like the rest, could be bent, sometimes broken. It all depended on who you were and how you did it. That was the point of rules.

He had put himself straight with his Minister, not directly, but according to the letter of the rules. And the Minister, given the scent of political advantage, one victory already notched up with the outcome of the Sattin spy case, had also been careful, equally indirectly, to adhere to the letter of the rules. The pursuit, fair means or foul so long as one wasn't found out, of a certain Henry Bush Timothy, resulting in his capture and interrogation, would redound to the credit of Her Majesty's Government in Washington, even if Washington, behind closed doors, called it blackmail.

It would also redound to the credit of the Minister, who had already shown himself more skilful than one Foreign Secretary in exploiting the no-man's-land between home and foreign affairs. International terrorism, Archer and his minister agreed, though never in so many words, and never face to face, was as good a no-man's-land as was currently on offer.

As to the spirit of the rules, well, they were both practical chaps, not much time for balls-aching sophistries. In any case, Steve Archer told himself, dying for a cigarette, he would only be trying to pull off what Morpurgo and Epworth were quite incapable of pulling off left to themselves, wet enough to let themselves be used but not smart enough to find out why.

He could make swift decisions when the need was clear. He became very crisp in his instructions to Eric Pottern, especially in stamping promptly on the suggestion that they should be put in writing, and sent him packing. And when Fiona finally put in an appearance, looking very much the daughter of a viscount, he said, "Shove off, Cloudesley. Not through yet," and sent her packing too, before, quietly, lighting up.

TEN

"Where the hell have you been all weekend?" Claas demanded when Weber finally showed up.

Weber, eyes a little red-rimmed, dark smears beneath, looked at him like a spaniel spurned. "Don't you start on me, junior. I've been gone over by experts." In spite of weariness, he seemed reluctant to settle, wandering over to the window.

"You didn't answer the question. And where were you this morning? I've been trying everywhere."

"You know something?" Weber was looking out of the window. "You must have the best view of the garage entrance in this whole building. You can even read the car registrations. Now I know what it's like to be a spy satellite."

He finally came back to the chair with the missing button.

Claas had not enjoyed his weekend. Ella Claas had an old friend from Morgantown staying Friday through Tuesday. The friend was what Claas, not to his advantage, had called a macho bachelor lady, who taught obscure aspects of sociology at the University of West Virginia. Claas had ploughed through the wreckage of the Tarragona fiasco being a refugee from lectures on women as slave labour, as well as having to take the kids to and from two successive parties at which there had been plenty of tea and buns, no hard liquor.

All the time he had been brooding on Tarragona and trying to track down Weber.

"How about some coffee?" Weber's eyes had closed for some kind of duration. "I would have asked, but Cindy-Lou wasn't around."

"Cindy-Lou's gone, you know that." In spite of all his anxieties, Claas looked momentarily smug. "And the replacement is fetching some coffee. For me."

Weber said, "I was in Langley. I just got back."

The smug look disappeared. "Langley! You mean you went to Langley and back since Friday?"

"Since Saturday morning."

Claas stopped pretending to go through his Monday morning mail. "That bad, huh?" He waited, but Weber stayed closed. Claas watched him a while, blinking a little faster than usual, tucking his lips in and out between disapproval and defensiveness.

"We didn't even have time to talk."

"We talked enough," Weber said in his sleep. "How about that coffee, junior?" He sounded plaintive.

Claas decided on attack. "Pierre, where the hell was everybody? Okay, the guy fooled us again – incidentally, that chopper pilot of yours must be a real airhead to swallow Timothy's Langley big shot spiel – but there wasn't enough backup to swat a small-size fly."

"There was. That guy, Rielo, from the Barcelona anti-terrorist squad. Rielo had enough back-up to take out the Libyan army."

"Rielo! Rielo's not on our side. Figueroa wasn't much on our side either, come to that." Claas finally went on to the offensive. "Two times he made monkeys of us. Two times he gave us the finger. What's with those jerks in Madrid station? What's with those jerks in Langley?"

He warmed to his grievance. "Come to that, what's with you? Or Barzelian? You've just seen Barzelian, right? He over the top or something? I tell you, I'm beginning to think there's something more than a little screwy about this whole thing."

Weber opened his eyes. "Sure there is. How about some coffee?"

The door opened and coffee came in. Tired though he was, Weber's toes curled. He was ashamed about his toes, also about the thoughts that curled them, but it didn't stop him enjoying it.

"This" – Claas was temporarily diverted – "is Miss Woloszynowski, Cindy-Lou's replacement." Even his smugness returned, partly because he had had plenty of time to practise his pronunciation.

"Hi!" Miss Woloszynowski was stunning, sinuous and, at least for the time being, red-headed. "You're Mr Weber, right? I guess you'd like some coffee." She gave him the coffee she had brought for Claas.

Claas, making the best of a battle lost, said, "Sure. Go ahead. I can wait."

Shaking hands with Weber, Miss Woloszynowski laid him waste with her eager smile. "Kind of a mouthful, I know. My first name's Barbara, Barbie for short, but everyone calls me Wol."

"As in Pooh." Claas took Weber's glassy stare for incomprehension. "A.A. Milne? Wol? Bird, smart but not too hot on spelling?" He circled his eyes with his hands and even managed to look like an owl. He gave up. "I guess you never had to read it to your kid."

Snapping out, Weber said, "My kid never was a kid, not really."

Miss Woloszynowski said, "I'll get you some coffee, Mr Claas. Is it all right if I do a little rearranging out there?"

"Sure." Claas, Weber saw, was going to find it hard to say no to his new secretary about anything. "You go right ahead, honey. Cindy-Lou was kind of muddly at that."

They watched her leave. "Wow!" Weber had woken up. "When does Ella get to meet her?" Claas knew a rhetorical question when he heard one.

He remembered where they had been. "Pierre, okay, you're tired, and I'm tired, and most of all I'm tired of futzing around on this one. We blew it, right? No, the hell with that! Langley blew it. I don't know how they aimed to kid Hank Timothy the oil in that tank had changed, but he outsmarted them by switching tanks. We aren't going to see him again this side of Judgement Day." He waited for Weber to say something.

Eventually, Weber did. "Look, Warren, there's more to this than you've been told so far."

"That," Claas said bitterly, "I might have guessed. Okay, let's hear it."

Miss Woloszynowski brought in his coffee. Weber's toes curled in spite of his preoccupation. They watched her go out. Weber cleared his throat. "Okay, it was a sting. You could say a double sting, two people, Hank and the other guy."

Claas stared. "And who in hell is the other guy?"

Weber produced his pothook smile, the down side predominant. "The President."

"The *President!*"

"You heard. Keep it down, will you? The President. He wasn't satisfied with the idea that we just fix Hank. He really believed we could fix the country too, Libya."

Claas worked hard at it. "The oil. You mean fix the oil."

"Right." Weber made a gesture of apology. "I know. It wouldn't work. We knew that. But DCI needed something at the time, something to take the heat off. You know how the President feels about Langley."

"Damn right! Tries to get his own boy in to run the place like it was the White House annex, gets his ears pinned back in the Senate, bear with a sore head ever since." Claas was still finding it all hard to digest.

"But hell, Pierre, it wouldn't have worked. What then?"

"We'd have tried. And we'd have settled Hank's hash. Dick Goss is on DCI's side. DCI figured the President would have settled for Hank's scalp, come the reckoning."

Claas left his desk to look at the entrance to the basement carpark, but his mind wasn't on registration plates. "And now we've struck out. No Hank. No oil wells gummed up. No nothing. What happens next?"

Weber sipped coffee. "Langley's working on it. Somehow we have to get Hank interested again. That's Barzelian's department."

Claas turned, incredulous. "You won't get Hank to come within a thousand miles of any more propositions. You want to remember, Pierre, I know that sonofabitch! One of the reasons Ella couldn't wait to get away from Madrid station, he spent half his time trying to get his hand up her skirt." He was really angry now. "If Ella had told me at the time, we wouldn't have been trying to find a way to fix that mother these past weeks. I'd have killed the bastard, way, way back."

"Which is why Ella didn't tell you, junior. The way she saw it, he'd have killed you. Anyway, he went to Central America and

Nam and then he was out, so forget it. What we're concerned with is now. Barzelian's expecting us to handle Epworth." Weber failed to add that Barzelian was also expecting him to handle Claas.

"Epworth's gone to Berlin."

"We know why?"

Claas shook his head. Weber was disapproving. "Those guys doing things in secret? I don't like that."

"The Secret Intelligence Service."

"That's what I mean, secret *and* intelligent. He should be here, wondering what happens next."

"He knows what happens next. The wrong tank, you think Morpurgo didn't tell him or something? So he'll be waiting to see what *we* do next."

"How about Archer and his people?"

"Everybody back where they should be by the weekend. Pottern took a night flight from Barcelona, spent all Saturday at his desk, went out to the SD place in Sussex in the afternoon, treated himself to a fast food meal at . . ."

"Okay, okay, that boy's a worker, we all know that. Gets home a stack of flights later than you, back at his desk while you're still in the sack."

"Knock it off, will you?" Claas was really annoyed. "All right, so I'm small potatoes in this whole thing, used to do boy's work and not even told why. How do you think I feel when I arrive at Barcelona airport and find Figueroa waiting to tell me Antonio Rielo's running a terrorist sweep with a couple of people from British Security Directorate? Jesus! I've got Morpurgo with me, who used to be big in Security Directorate. I want to get him out of the way before he hears anything. Or maybe sees something. How do I know Pottern and the other guy . . ."

"Sibley."

". . . Sibley aren't setting up to tail us with Rielo's people? I trust those Spanish anti-terrorist hoods the way I trust terrorists. So I don't have time to go off for a nice cosy-up with Figueroa, just tell him we're running a strictly private, all-American . . ."

"I know what you told him, Warren. I was in with Barzelian when Abbott came through from Madrid station to report what Figueroa passed on."

"All right! What I'm saying is, all unecessary, all a waste of time, and only now do you tell me . . ." Claas stopped. "Oh-oh!"

"Waste of time for Rielo and Pottern too. And Epworth took off for Berlin."

"Two stories." Claas smacked his forehead with the butt of his palm. "The break-in at Billingshurst. The bugs that Timothy's supposed to use to fix the Libs. And Archer has both. He's put two with two and come up with a fancy number."

"Does Epworth have both?"

"You tell me. What's the odds, now? We spent a lot of dough, a lot of time, all to have that sonofabitch Timothy kiss us off."

He hit the desk hard enough to rattle the crockery. "Shit! I don't go too much for the bang-bang stuff, you know that, Pierre, but there is one guy I would have liked to see something laid on."

Weber nodded sympathetically. "With you there, junior. Now we just have to wait on Barzelian." He could imagine Claas's face when Barzelian came through, but then, there was a lot that Warren Claas still didn't know.

Claas was still brooding. "Listen, how *do* we hear from that sonofabitch Timothy, anyway?"

Weber, trying, as light relief, to think of an excuse for having Miss Woloszynowski back, shrugged. "Now that you'd have to ask Barzelian."

*   *   *

Morpurgo's weekend had been, admit it, miserable. The house began to wear him down, his home that he had defended so strongly against Sylvie. His neighbours – why had he never noticed it before? – pounded upstairs, then pounded down, slammed inside doors, outside doors, car doors. They got up too early, went to bed too late and in between committed the unforgivable offence of living. He thought they would drive him mad and he had met them, over and over again, mild, inoffensive people.

Nothing from Sylvie since before Tarragona. He had been to Spain twice, and Sylvie was in Spain, and he couldn't even tell her. He rang her agent after poking guiltily through Sylvie's desk to find the number. The agent – Stephanie, Stella, Sally? It took him ten minutes of dither to remember her name – lived in Battersea with a distinctly suspicious husband. "No, Mr Markham – oh, terribly sorry, *such* an easy slip! – no, darling, just a business call – I haven't heard from her since, let's see – well, ages – Trujillo, Trujillo, Tru – no, Mérida, after Badajoz. So, Trujillo, Tru – ah, Zafra and Placencia, then Cáceres, do you speak Spanish, Mr Morpurgo? No, me neither, probably got these all wrong. No, it's Sylvie Markham's husband, darling. *Any*way, Cáceres this weekend if she's on schedule, would you like the number? Hold on a tick – *Bus*iness, darling, through in a jiff. Ah, yes, here we are. Mind, these Spanish phones are sometimes a teeny bit naughty, of course I'll say you rang if she comes through to me first, but she wouldn't, surely, would she, Mr Markham?"

And she hadn't, not to him, not, presumably, to Stella – he remembered now, tall, lanky, intense, with a sort of fringe – and he got a Spanish-only imbecile at the hotel – "*Si, Mark-am, certo, señor, reservado, reservado.*"

He ended up shouting, traditional way of dealing with idiot foreigners who hadn't the nous to speak English. "Morpurgo, ask her to telephone Morpurgo," and the other – "*Telefón, señor, si, si, pero de donde?*" – probably thought Morpurgo was some fancy Spanish word his vocabulary had never risen to.

And finally the thing did ring and he damn near broke an ankle leaping half a flight of stairs and it was a woman, but not Sylvie.

"John? Amaryllis. Amaryllis Epworth. Listen, don't interrupt, I've got to fly, not a second to waste. Lawrence told me to remind you you were going to pick up that case of wine, so would you like to come and collect now and stay to lunch? Super. Any time after twelve. 'Bye."

He was left wondering if he was mad or was it everybody else? He knew practically nothing of Epworth, even less of his private life, but part of the less was that Epworth's wife's name was Amaryllis.

Sylvie, who, before fatally taking up photography, had done practically every ILEA adult education class from art appreciation to Zen, including three years running on the English poets, had refrained from overt mockery, solemnly reciting:

Alas! what boots it with uncessant care
To tend the homely, slighted shepherd's trade,
And strictly meditate the thankless Muse?
Were it not better done, as others use,
To sport with Amaryllis in the shade?

which was apparently a bit of Milton.

So he wrestled his car away from the scrum of cars that more or less permanently cluttered this dead-end street and set off to sport with Amaryllis, who had called him John, referred to a case of wine he know nothing about and invited him to lunch without giving him time to say a word, which was just as well, since he had never, ever, met her.

Epworth's house looked remarkably like its picture, by Amaryllis, that hung in Epworth's office. Amaryllis, who was working in the garden, looked like her photograph on Epworth's desk, but much prettier. The house sat at the centre of vast lawns in the middle of a Surrey wood, and looked about a thousand years old. Amaryllis, pink-faced, ample and engagingly sweaty, was on her knees in the centre of a lawn and looked about twenty.

"Hello, you found us then? Jolly good! Bloody plantains!" She dropped the miscreant weed in a box, took off a stout leather gardening glove and stuck out a hand. The shake was the kind that pumped water from deep wells. "Lawrie said you'd twig. Come and have a drink, jolly well do with one myself."

He followed her into cool, low-ceilinged comfort – "Mind your head, those beams must have brained hundreds of folk over the centuries" – primal oak, chintz, good though worn carpets, with a wall – two feet thick as shown by small, leaded windows looking on to a regal herbaceous border – smothered in books and records.

"Of course" – Amaryllis doffed her green overall, revealing a summer print that made her kin to the plump, chintzy arm-chairs – "you guessed your house is bugged?"

"My house? Oh, yes." He hadn't. Wake up, Morpurgo!

"So Lawrie warned me. That's why I dealt with you pretty smartish, no giveaway interruptions. He's still in Germany, by the way. Say when."

He said when over a generous gin and tonic. Somewhere outside a very small child began to bawl healthily. She vanished, swift and lightfooted in spite of her generous build. Cooing sounds, a pram being repositioned, and she was back to flop in the chair facing his. "Cheers. Mmmm. Jolly well earned that, I have. Lawrie doesn't know a lupin from a lettuce, suits him to say so, anyway."

Lawrie! After months with an enigma, it was a little like hearing God referred to as Dad.

Amaryllis Epworth, bonny and brisk, was also shrewd. "Keeps you in the dark, I'll bet. You should call his bluff, you know, tell him to come off it. There's the wine, by the way, shouldn't you open it until you get home if I were you."

An unopened case of . . . he leaned to look. Chateau Haut-Battailley. Pauillac. 1970.

John Morpurgo, he reminded himself, used to be a man who could think. "I don't know much about wines. Is it any good?"

"Neither do I, really, but I shouldn't think so. Bottled and packed by a little man called Hannay." She knocked back an impressive gulp of gin, watching him over the rim.

"Hannay! Oh!" Hannay was the man who at Epworth's request had opened the package containing the original crude and Morpurgo hadn't been able to tell.

"Hannay could filch the bubbles from a bottle of champagne without disturbing the foil."

She giggled; it was in the family. "So I've heard. On the other hand, cat's on the tiles, mousies' fun time. I've pinched a rather super Meursault. You do like asparagus? And sole bonne femme? Bet you're not exactly doing the Cordon Bleu while your wife's away."

Out in the hall, which smelled of lavender, the phone began to ring. She sent the rest of her gin after the vanguard. "His grace, right on the dot." She was back in a moment to beckon.

No time wasted. "You'll know now to be careful. Rilla will have said." This was a different Epworth, crisp as fresh lettuce.

"Thanks for the wine."

"Handle it with care. It's worth the trouble. Oh, and it might come to your attention that you have company out and about."

"Tail?"

"You should know. Your line of country. Could you – mmmm – manage to play the innocent nevertheless?"

"You mean not notice?"

"Harder yet, act as if the thought had never occurred to you."

He saw the point, not so easy after all those years in Curzon Street. "Do my best. Do we know who?"

The old Epworth, a neat sidestep and away on a fresh course. "The – mmmm – bugging's a problem, can't ignore, mustn't take any notice. You do follow?"

"Watch what I say but behave naturally."

"That, yes, but more. *Think* what you say. Then say it. Is Rilla giving you a decent lunch?"

The abrupt switch caught him out. "If it's as good as it sounds."

"It will be. Has she been at my cellar?"

This time he was ready. "I really couldn't say."

The giggle, nothing at all foolish about it. "You'll wine as well as you dine. Heard from Sylvie?"

A momentary pang, but this was the new – correction, the old – Morpurgo. "No. Somewhere betwixt and between, I think."

"Betwixt and between where?"

"Cáceres. It's right over toward . . ."

"I know where it is. If she rings, don't let the phone tap inhibit."

Shrewd; a shrewd pair, the Epworths. "I'll try."

"You're on leave, by the way, all squared up with Admin. You'll find a sum of money, quite – mmmm – substantial, has been paid into your bank. Accountable, of course. Expenses."

"Do I know how long I'm on leave? Or why?" Especially why, things being what they were.

"Oh" – Vaguely – "open-ended. Is Rilla giving you fish?"

"Yes, so I'm told."

"Mmmmm. She'll have pinched a bottle of the Meursault, thinks I can't count. Still, she knows enough not to overchill. Don't have too many G and Ts, numbs the palate. Good hunting." He was gone.

"Have another palate paralyser. Bet he warned you." Amaryllis poured them both more gin. "Put on his old omniscient-mysterious act, did he? He can't help it, you know, terrified anyone should find out he's nothing in particular. Comes of being the only child of a bishop, piffling little colonial bishop at that. Cheers! Lunch in ten minutes."

Morpurgo dutifully cheered, happy in his company, happy that God was taking on substance, possibly a slightly more piffling god at that.

His drive back was thoughtful; a sensation of cold and disused circuits re-energised, a powerhouse returning to life after a months-long shutdown.

From the powerhouse came light, and it shone into dusty corners. The corners, not unusually, proved to be stacked with junk. He poked about among it all the way home.

One item of junk was the rationale he had put together for his attitude to Sylvie Markham. He found that he had never really attempted, as it were, to look at life through her viewfinder.

He did so now, and found himself a victim of juvenile brain-washing; the pressures his mother had brought to bear with such effect. Life was to the sloggers, those who passed examin-ations and received their alphabetical reward, exchangeable anywhere in respectable society for salary, security, status. Nor was that the end of the barter. Those three Ss, potent symbols to the aspiring working-class, had their own trade-in value; bed, board and general solicitude provided by a good – and grateful – woman.

Not that he believed that shit any more, but its iron idol was the work ethic, and to that he had been dedicated at birth. And so it was not the idea of woman working, woman independent, woman equal but different that had poisoned him like slow doses of arsenic. It was the idea that a whim, a passing fad that had stayed, had turned Sylvie Morpurgo into Sylvie Markham, turned his wife into a celebrity, turned what his mother still called snaps – not really work, just pressing a button – into a life richer and more meaningful than his own.

Morpurgo, you brainwashed bastard!

He made promises, resolutions, plans, all the things a man does when he sees himself to have been in the wrong and is determined to make a virtue out of the discovery. He swore at traffic in Croydon and dreamed of castles in Spain. He came back in mind to his mother, whose fault it all really was, and made a guilty loop to pass through Balham.

She was asleep, Mr Morpurgo, but he could sit by the bed until she woke up, they were helping her sleep since the rest would do her good. And Doctor Sahoo was at the weekly meeting and they hardly ever finished this side of four, so he went down the shiny corridors and out round well-remembered corners to a vegetable shop that sold flowers, and bought bunches and a box of her favourite toffees from the shop next door and went back and left them with a message that he would call again, and felt everyone's eyes in his back like fingernails as he left.

The house was still there, and the bright scarlet door that Sylvie herself had painted looked fine, a good first impression for would-be buyers. The air inside was still comatose but he soon got the molecules doing push-ups to Brendel playing the thirty-three apotheoses of Mr Diabelli's little tune.

The neighbours had died or shoved off for the evening. The stillness was balm. He found a knife and ripped open Mr Hannay's chateau-bottled claret.

Twelve bottles of good Bordeaux wine there were not. Instead a good deal of foam plastic packing and a gunmetal grey case, complete with strap, that he took out with care. He placed it on the piano to do the calibration, plugged in the wand, let Brendel finish, then went walkabout.

The first sortie brought him straight back to the piano. He peered beneath and checked a grunt of satisfaction. Morons! He would see they got an earful of something mercilessly loud before the evening was out, but just how thorough had they been?

Answering that question took rather longer, bringing the tally to three; kitchen and dining room apart from that idiot spot just below middle C. But had they covered their bets? He dug out a heavy tommy-bar from his toolkit and dialled Amaryllis, just to say thank you.

"Oh, I enjoyed it too, we'll do it again next time Lawrie's away." She giggled. "Shouldn't say things like that on the phone, you never know who's listening." Oh yes, very shrewd, these Epworths. Instead of replacing the receiver, he substituted the tommy-bar and unscrewed the mouthpiece.

The phone in the bedroom, too, calling to check a cinema programme; the house was bugged from breakfast to bedtime.

Who? Well, that was something to think about. He poured himself a drink and thought about it.

The Cousins? Curzon Street? He would, he realised, have added Epworth, except that Epworth had gone to no little trouble to warn him.

Why the Cousins? Because they must know, now, that he suspected. So elaborate a scheme, to be turned upside down in moments by Hank Timothy. Who would not suspect? And if Morpurgo, Epworth, in which case, knowledge of Morpurgo's contacts, Morpurgo's movements, might now be of major importance to Langley. Keep the Cousins on the active list.

But what about Steve? His mind went back to the Hercules Tavern, a man not with a longing but a lust. Why so sudden? Why so eager? Such buried intensity for such a frigid man. Why?

He took his drink to the piano, ripped off a jangling tumult for the benefit of unlawful ears, then attempted, from memory, the first movement of Schubert's G major sonata. He got the deceptively simple opening more or less right, then predictably, went to pieces.

Steve in the Hercules, all that crimson background, imperial for imperiousness until he had remembered that emperors wore purple, that crimson would be more in keeping with the imperial presidency.

What if I told you Timothy . . . ?

But that hadn't been in the Hercules. That had been his office – Steve's office! – sly Eric Pottern looking as momentarily startled as if Steve had been about to say, not without some justification, "I forgive you for Helga, Johnny. It was all my fault."

What would you say if I told you that comrade Timothy was in this country only . . . was in this country not so very long ago?

Well, if he'd been in the country at the time of the Billingshurst thing, he'd still had nothing to do with it, so when else, or what for? Something that could stir up Langley and Curzon Street like a couple of hornets' nests?

He brought both hands crashing down on the piano keys. The imperial presidency!

It was something to do with the President's state visit.

After that, just like the sonata, opening bars fine, then . . . hopeless.

Why aren't you here when I need you? he demanded of the absent Epworth. But was Epworth already in another place beside Berlin, patiently waiting?

The phone rang. This time he took care not to break his neck, partly because the telephone had changed, no longer simply an instrument of communication, good news or bad, but also a spy in his home. He must not give the smallest intimation of awareness, not even, if it were Sylvie, steer her away from whatever intimacies she might broach. He found the thought of that, as something for others to listen to, infinitely repellent. He picked the thing up with something like aversion. His was a lousy kind of work.

A well-known, much-disliked voice. "Hi, pally. Well, it looks like we have a deal."

Telephone bugged. and an impossible deal. For an endless moment, Morpurgo found himself unable to think anything at all. Someone rang the bell of the street door.

How had Epworth put it? "Think what you're going to say. Then say it." He said, "I have an unexpected visitor." Just how good was Hank Timothy?

Answer; very good. "Okay let's just say they took number one to Lavéra but things got a little sticky. So what you do is get yourself back where we started, okay? Bring the package and hole up with the two Ricardos, they're in the frogs' little red book but don't expect them to grubstake you. I'll be in touch. *Hasta la vista.*"

That was it, and it meant nothing, but its very meaninglessness lodged it in his memory. He went to see who was at his scarlet door and found young Sibley from Curzon Street, finger to his lips like the sleepytime fairy. Sibley put something in his hand, said, "Mr Aveling?" and was re-directed to the Avelings, three doors up the street, whom, certainly, he neither knew nor wished to see. Dark, fresh-faced, not yet marred beyond redemption by the slow abrasion of flying dirt, young Sibley had been Morpurgo's joy and pride in his last days at Curzon Street; willing, hard-working, honest. A perpetual source of guilt, too, in the knowledge that the work would transmute everything to a resentful doggedness, virtue plastered over with layer after layer of callousness and expediency.

He closed the door before looking at what he had been given.
A piece of paper. A label, torn top to bottom. Reading vertically,
it said: GRAND CRU CL, half a gold crest and then *CHAT
HAUT-BAT* . . PAUL . . I.

It was Curzon Street that was bugging the house. And Sibley,
flower of the forest, who, temporarily succumbing to the universal taint, had briefly suspected his own admired master of being
a potential traitor, was making amends, helped – or bought? – by
Lawrence Epworth.

*   *   *

Pottern listened in silence. "Play it again." Sergeant Vaisey
went on to REWIND. Pottern listened with self-punishing intensity.

"Rum stuff, sir, apart from the name."

"Shut up, will you?"

"Sir." Close bastard! Up yours! Pottern wasn't popular with
the Branch.

"The two Ricardos."

"Had them run through aliens on the computer, sir. Nothing
known."

"Wouldn't be. He's talking Madrid."

"Sir." On your own, mate, not biting my head off again.

"The one at the door, did you check?"

"Yes, sir. Wrong address. Aveling's number 16, just up the
street."

Quiller, listening out, one earphone pushed back so as to miss
nothing here as well as there, caught Vaisey's eye, face immobile.
"Red book, sir, that used to be Mao." Try that one for size, you
jumped-up little git.

Pottern's eyes searched him for contraband humour, found
nothing. He got up. "Just keep listening. Call me if there's anything the least out of the ordinary."

"Sir." Vaisey watched Pottern leave. So did Quiller. When the
door closed, Quiller made the time-honoured gesture.

*   *   *

Claas handed it to Morpurgo. "Here, since you have to have it in black and white." All the time his flint-grey eyes kept flickering toward Weber. He had something of the air of a man in shock. Barzelian had delivered.

CONFIRM it said after all the cipher jargon PROMECO TANKER OKLAHOMA STAR BERTHED NUMBER FOUR JETTY LAVERA DISCHARGE FIFTY THOUSAND TONS CRUDE STOP DISCHARGING TEMPORARILY HALTED 1947 HOURS GMT AFTER FAILURE PUMP NUMBER ONE REPEAT ONE TANK PORTSIDE DUE QUOTE HEAVY SLUDGE CONTAMINATION UNQUOTE.

Morpurgo had given up trying to think how it could have happened.

Weber produced his most effulgent smile for Morpurgo. "Looks as if you're becoming pretty central to this whole operation, direct line to our man in Tripoli. Can you go? To Madrid, I mean. Today?" They knew Epworth was out of town.

"I don't have to get written permission." Why, in his mind should he hear Epworth say "Spain. Again. Interesting." Why should he think of poetism?

Weber looked again at the notepad provided by Miss Woloszynowski, by whom Morpurgo had been grudgingly impressed. "But you can't provide a translation, written or not. You don't know the two Ricardos. Or the red book. And why the cute bit about grubstaking?"

"Ricardo." Claas was the old Madrid hand, though his general attitude toward Morpurgo was distinctly more respectful. "One Spaniard in fifty is probably called Ricardo. He looked at Morpurgo. "You sure it says nothing? Never mentioned aboard the tanker?"

Morpurgo shook his head. Nothing about the ownership of that tanker. Nothing to suggest why Claas had been temporarily stunned by the switch of tanks. Nothing at all, naturally, to explain why a fake had suddenly turned into fact. Smoke, thick black smoke, all for the benefit of the Brits.

Miss Woloszynowski came in, briefly distracting them. "Mr Claas, you're going to have to do better than this" – She tapped a scrawl in Claas's handwriting – "if you want Langley to okay your expenses."

Claas switched on ingratiation. "What did I do?"

She treated him like teacher with a child delinquent, much, much smarter, Morpurgo decided, than Cindy-Lou. "Details,

Mr Claas. Langley doesn't just want to know you ate and slept. Langley wants to know where."

"I told you. I lost the check." He appealed to Morpurgo. "You remember the name of that place outside Barcelona? Or the name of the hotel?"

Morpurgo thought: Smoke for smoke. "You told me nothing. I remember nothing."

"Cindy-Lou made that booking. There's got to be a record of it someplace. Hey!" Claas remembered something. "She used a guidebook. There's a whole bunch of them on that middle shelf."

"There's a whole bunch of things on every flat surface," Miss Woloszynowski told him. "I think I said, I'm planning on doing a little sorting out, but not yet."

"Look." Claas had his mind on other things, such as the fact that something aboard that tanker which couldn't possibly work, had. "That hotel was picked because it was quiet, small but quiet. Those guides list that kind of place with a rocking chair. A little rocking chair."

He saw their expressions. "A symbol, goddammit! Listen, there was even a special map of Spain showing all the little rocking chairs."

Weber, about to humiliate Claas, was enlightened. "French! The Michelin guides. Peg and I used them the year we did the Grand Tour."

"Michelin." Miss Woloszynowski's intelligent face lit up. "Gotcha! Little red books."

*　　　*　　　*

From where she sat she could count twenty-one, no, twenty-two stork's nests, complete with storks. They stood or sat almost motionless, as content as she to enjoy the warmth of the afternoon. On her list of subjects was the Casa de las Cigüeñas, but how could they tell? Everything in sight was a stork house.

Two men walked by, gazing openly. One of them said, "*Guapa*." She smiled a little, accepting the compliment so long as it stopped there, but though they went on, someone else, from the opposite direction, halted at her table. She prepared to repel Spanish machismo.

200

"*Señora, buenas tardes*. You will think I am following you."

"I'm beginning to think you must be."

"I assure you, señora." His soft voice had an attractive burr, though the accent still puzzled.

"You're still sightseeing? Still driving around in your fancy car?"

"Yes, señora. We were on our way here to Cáceres when we passed you on the road, but we have seen many things since then."

"Would you like to sit down for a moment?"

"You're very kind, señora, but my *cliente* will be waiting." A hesitation. "If you would give me the pleasure of introducing my *cliente* to you, we could have an *aperitivo* together. He is a most interesting man." He smiled. His smile, as she had noted before, was charming. "It does appear, *verdad*? that fate wishes a closer acquaintance?"

She laughed. "Since you put it that way, why not?"

He took a polite step backward while she left money on the table.

"This way, señora. It's not far."

*   *   *

Archer studied the street map of Madrid as suspiciously as if he suspected it of being fake. "A long way from the centre. Suppose that's why comrade Timothy chose it."

Pottern gave his little cough. "Sort of hotel we would put a bloke into, good as a safe house. I could have a word with Rielo, get him to pull some strings."

Archer chose not to answer at once, a trick that Pottern was getting used to. "Bit clever-clever, the red book, the two Ricardos and such. Not everyone would have got it."

Like a lot of people, Pottern thought contemptuously, finds it hard to think there are people with more brains than he has. "Inspiration in my case, just a bit of luck." Like hell it was! He might not have Archer's advantages, or Morpurgo's education, but he could think a blue streak when it was a question of reading the mind of someone like Hank Timothy. Birds of a feather? Could be, thought Pottern the realist.

It wasn't going to work this time, he could see that. The trouble was, Archer was a gent, dirty word in Pottern's vocabulary. Gents had too much to lose.

Archer arrived at the point predicted. "We stuck our necks out once, daren't run the risk again. Rielo would talk."

"That's it then? Leave it to SIS and the Cousins?"

"Drop it?" Archer leaned far back, put his hands behind his head so that the cuffs of his discreetly striped shirt displayed themselves in full immaculacy. Him and his Jermyn Street specials, thought Pottern, who favoured Burtons and Marks and Sparks. "No, Eric. I don't think we'll drop it, not really, not with what we know, just box a bit clever."

He lounged back, looking at his second-in-command with cool indulgence. Sylvie would have recognised him, Prince Torlonia, lord of earth. "Gone as far as I dare with direct action at this stage, Eric, got to think of my position, but unless I'm mistaken, there's someone else who'd be willing and able to go all the way."

Christ! Pottern thought, he's had an Idea. He waited, ready to disdain.

Archer gave him a grin that told him his future wasn't necessarily founded on rock. "Be a good chap and do whatever's necessary to track down Master T. Brewster Cochran."

*   *   *

One dark doorway, no larger than to a private dwelling, less inviting than some of those. One small plate: *Hotel Dos Ricardos*. One dark hallway leading to darker stairs.

It was well south of the city centre. Minimal Spanish – he hadn't Sylvie's gift – a difficulty in reading the street map the car-hire firm had provided and driving at the same time, he had been taken in charge by a plump and jolly man with several gold teeth, and pince-nez on a flowing silk ribbon, who, dumping a bundle of music scores on the back seat, had moved in to guide him, with a nonstop monologue of voluble incomprehensibilities and large gestures, all the way to the Avenida Antonio García on the strength of nothing more than the address and the forlorn appearance of an *extranjero*.

Avenida Antonio García was long, wide and lined with a mixture of shops, business premises and apartment blocks, and formed part of a ringroad system for southbound traffic. The area was distinctly working class.

At the top of the stairs was a small lobby, not quite so dark, and a small, fierce lady with swinging jet earrings. She processed him briskly, his Spanish, thanks to his visits to the Markham villa, at least adequate for a discussion on *habitaciones* and *camas*. The *habitacion* was clean, as was the brass-railed *cama*, but simple in the extreme, with an uninterrupted eighth floor view of an airshaft. There was no restaurant: *Don't expect them to grubstake you.*

The fact of his car established, it was down to the street once more. There was no sign of a garage, but double doors rumbled open some little distance from the hotel entrance and a wispy old man in shirt-sleeves, clearly warned that he was dealing with the foreign equivalent of a deaf mute, indicated that he was to drive in. The doors were only a little wider than the car, the space only a little longer, just sufficient room for the old man to avoid being crushed. The only remaining problem, Morpurgo couldn't open the car door far enough to get out.

The mystery resolved itself. At the touch of a button and with the sustained whine of a grizzling child, the entire space descended to a cavernous cellar, the only other vehicle an old Citroën van stacked with empty laundry baskets, suggesting that it belonged to the hotel. Comfortable in the front seat, and halfway through a cheroot, was Hank Timothy.

Predictably, watching Morpurgo emerge, he said, "Hi, pally." The old man had vanished.

"Are you going to disappear before or after we finish?"

Timothy laughed his booming laugh. "Getting to you, huh? Listen, friend, in my business you can't be too careful." He stretched vastly. The garage smelled of petrol, rubber and mysteriously, cheese. "You bring the stuff?"

"Maybe." Had those bugs really – *really* – changed seven thousand tons of crude?

Again the laugh. This was a very self-confident man. "Hey, come on! You didn't make this trip for nothing." He dragged out one of the baskets, set it against the side of the van, settled on it creakingly. "What's the word from Langley?"

"You know the deal." Only there was more to it now.

"Yeah, same as for Morello and Lebenson. How do you know they aren't dead?"

"I don't." He didn't want to sit with Timothy. He walked a little away.

"You don't know much, do you, Morpurgo?"

He snapped, "Shall we stop? I don't have to do this."

"Turn around." Warned by the tone, he turned. It was a small gun as guns go, but the stubby barrel seemed as wide as a howitzer. It could blow his spine through his back.

"Back up." Timothy motioned with the gun. "C'm'on. Against the wall, spread those feet and hands." He kicked at Morpurgo's feet, hard. There was no option. Worse, Morpurgo's anger was shot through with the high voltage of fear, outside his control. You were trained, but not for this. The only thing for this was to experience it and live to learn.

Timothy's left hand went over him with ungentle thoroughness. He laughed almost indulgently. "Okay." He thumped Morpurgo's shoulder. "Relax. Breathe. Loosen up."

He stepped back, the gun vanishing. "No piece! How do you like that? Come over here. Sit down."

He even turned his back, going to haul over another basket. He motioned impatiently. "Sit. We have to talk, so sit, damn it." The only sound was the rumble of heavy traffic, high above.

"The Secret Intelligence Service. Oh boy! How are the mighty fallen! You know, there was a time Langley gospel was the Brits invented the game. All that cool! A Langley guy just naturally took off his hat when the Brits walked in. Well, let me tell you, that was then, this is now."

He grinned his yellow grin. "You're just another fall guy, wrong shape, don't fit round holes, don't fit square. I could use a guy like you."

Morpurgo just sat, feeling his heart dropping toward its normal beat.

"Not for sale? Never believe it, there's always a price, but I don't have time. Okay, who's calling it, back there in London?"

"You know. Claas."

"You're full of shit, you know that? Claas couldn't call turns at a hoedown. Who else? Weber?"

"So you know that too."

"The doe-eyed faggot." Timothy looked pleased. "Must make him sick to the stomach, having to deal with Hank Timothy. How about Barzelian?"

"Never heard of him."

"He's there, take it from me. Now your end. The high-hat SIS." Timothy saw Morpurgo's instinctive reluctance. "Look, I want names. Names are insurance."

"Epworth. Lawrence Epworth."

"Never heard of *him*. Yeah, well, I heard things had changed and ain't you the living proof! Okay, where's the paper?"

With a numbing feeling of unreality, like buying the Ritz for real and not just on the Monopoly board, Morpurgo handed over the envelope from Weber. Timothy ripped it apart, extracted the receipt documents.

"Hentsch, Bär, Seligman-Schürch, Pictet. Four of the top names, friend, nothing but the best for Hank Timothy." He put them carefully away, and now it was no longer Monopoly. Real money, credits of one and a half million dollars in Swiss francs, four top Swiss banks, all into Timothy's private accounts; Geneva, Zurich, Basle, Lugano, risks nicely spread. The hoax had become fact. The bugs changed the crude into sludge. The sludge had changed into gold, with more to come when Timothy had completed the deal. There was no longer any reason to doubt, Morpurgo told himself, that the Americans had found a way to take Libya out of the oil business.

"Okay, so tell me the Libyan end."

"You have the list of wellhead installations and pumping stations. They tell me you head up the security checks. What you have to do . . ." Morpurgo went through the whole business, pretty well word for word as it had come through to London from Langley, with Timothy asking plenty of questions.

Finally, he seemed satisfied. "Now you should maybe see my other receipt." Another baring of equine teeth as Timothy unfastened his jacket. He was wired, mike and small recorder, the full story, complete with names.

And the whole thing was wide open again, with every worthwhile card in the hands of Hank Timothy. Not forgetting the gun. And – no question – the fact that Timothy, in a roughhouse, would leave Morpurgo a suitable case for treatment.

So where in God's name, did it all leave room for the President of the United States? There was only one explanation. He, John Morpurgo – dogsbody, cat's-paw, decoy duck, a zoo choice – had got it wrong.

Timothy said, "How is Claas anyway? Still badmouthing me?"

"Still?" Timothy wasn't just sitting here talking for nothing. Nor was Morpurgo. He was waiting for the signs that Timothy was about to attempt his third vanishing trick.

"He didn't tell you? We were both in Madrid one time."

"That's where you got your Spanish."

The bellow of amusement – "No sense of humour," Weber had said. "He just laughs a lot." – "I got my Spanish in Havana, time of Batista and Papa Hemingway, polished it up in Guatemala, Chile and a few banana republics. Madrid, well, that was just a place where that Kraut and me didn't hit it off."

Why hadn't Claas mentioned that?

"Made a play for his wife, one thing. Some chick, little Ella, could have done a whole lot better for herself than that thick-skulled Heinie. Plus" – He lit a cheroot, taking his time – "I knew a couple of things about that klutz he wouldn't care to be re-minded of." He grinned again. "Your phone *was* bugged, right?"

He was middle-aged John Morpurgo, longtime desk driver and do-this-go-there man, and he would love to plant his fist right on that knowing, confident grin.

"Yes, it was bugged."

"Know who?"

"Yes." He forced his fists to unclench.

Timothy gave him a few seconds, then leaned forward. "Listen you ain't got much going for you. Don't add to your problems. I'd eat you alive. C'mon. Who?"

"Security Directorate." Morpurgo's lips were stiff with rage, knowing Timothy was right. "MI5, if you like." At least he might sow a seed of anxiety.

Timothy's head went back; strong, tanned throat. His laughter, and the insult it conveyed, echoed in their ill-lit rendezvous. "Can't be bought. A guy with principles, mighty particular about the company he keeps. Friends! Cousins! So what do you call them over there in Curzon Street? Brothers? Or bastards? Oh, I almost forgot. You used to be one."

He tossed away his half-smoked cheroot. "Let's go get the bugs."

Morpurgo took a deep breath. "After you."

Another shout of laughter. "Think I'm going to smoke off again? Forget it. For a mill and a half, with more to come, Hank Timothy delivers. And to deliver, he has to collect, okay?"

There were wooden steps, narrow, dark. Somewhere just below ground level, Morpurgo took a kick in the chest that sent him back half a flight. When, raging, he scrambled back up, a very solid door had been fastened against him. Minutes later, knuckles barked, bruised, his voice raw from shouting, a bewildered chambermaid, gipsy-looking, dull-eyed, little more than a child, stared dumbly as he stormed past.

There was no sign of Timothy out on the street. The door of his room was still locked. The case holding twelve small plastic containers of freeze-dried inoculum – inoculum Epworth had assured him couldn't possibly work – was exactly where he had left it.

ELEVEN

Less than two hundred miles to Cáceres, a car in that dungeon of a garage, and he, to all intents and purposes, a prisoner. She was not in Cáceres. Or was she? He had no choice, before finding out, but to wait on Timothy, although, just a short distance away, the ring road past the Hotel Dos Ricardos ran into a junction where, among sparse grass verges littered with the petty detritus of civilisation, were the road-signs: TOLEDO, GRANADA, CÁCERES.

Timothy, knowing that the hotel had no restaurant, must know, too, that there was a café-bar literally next door. Morpurgo managed to convey to the hotel receptionist that he was expecting a telephone call. That it could equally well be a shoeshine boy was beyond his crude Spanish.

He must, vaguely, have registered the arrival of the car, too big, too expensive to look at home in these parts, that pulled into the kerb outside. He finished his tough veal and blood-thick *vino tinto de casa* before going back to prison.

They were waiting for him, two men, one thin, dark, sparse-haired and somehow saurian, the other chunky and squat. They closed in. The car was American, a vast Mercury; ridiculous!

Mentally cursing Epworth for sending him on an operation without accreditation, and stuck with little more than his English, he said, "How about some identification?" though he knew security police when he saw them.

He got his answer in American; oh-oh! not security police. "Just play along, Mr Morpurgo. Someone wants to see you." That was the lizard, a man for a knife in the night.

They took him across town to the Ritz, for God's sake!

Nobody explained, nobody even talked, Morpurgo didn't ask; a whole new kick as Claas liked to say. He was swept through the cathedral-calm lobby, into a private lift and up, up, to a silent Prado-style hallway that said penthouse.

The penthouse was light and coolly sumptuous, tall rouche-curtained windows loftily condescending on trees, grass and hushed corteges of traffic. Amidst the casual luxury a man glowered.

"Siddown, Morpurgo. Give him a drink, Dob."

The saurian, Jeeves with built-in refrigeration, moved to an array. Morpurgo, still standing, said, "No thanks." His unwished-for host had a face like one of those cartoons you recognise the instant you've been told who it is.

"He'll take scotch. So will I. Ice, no water. Then beat it." The bull in the thousand-dollar suit, tie loosened at the knot and an inch from the vertical, held out a hand like a dockyard grab. "Name's . . ."

"Cochran. T. Brewster Cochran." Morpurgo kept his hand to himself.

"Hey, come on! Nobody muscled you. Nobody pulled lead." Cochran commandeered Morpurgo's hand, imprisoned it between both of his. "M'friends call me Brew. Ain't one durn reason why we shouldn't be friends." He was, Morpurgo thought, fundamentally as friendly as fusion power; elemental fury unwillingly restricted.

He impelled Morpurgo toward a four-legged length of silk and walnut elegance before which the drinks had been placed, his cropped, steely hair stuff for rubbing down rust.

"Who's that?" Morpurgo, yielding to main force, nodded at the top of a head visible above a chair near a window.

"Name's Golding. He doesn't come into this."

"Let's have him where I can see him anyway." After Hank Timothy, Morpurgo was in no mood for further intimidation.

Golding came, silent, withdrawn, ill-dressed for this high life, a man, Morpurgo decided, with his mind elsewhere and a wish that his body could follow. He nodded, murmured, sat as far away as could reasonably pass for near.

Cochran sank half of his scotch as if it were an irritating but

necessary preliminary. "Let's save some time. You know who
I am. I know who you are. I'm through talking with Langley.
Archer talked to me. Now I aim to talk to you."

"Does Langley know that?" The fact that some questions were
instinctive made them no less germane.

Cochran's flush, incipient, came to stay. He finished his drink
at a gulp, slammed down the glass, took off. "Brewster Cochran
talks with who he goddam likes, you better believe it. A man
who set out with nothing, never took a government handout in
his whole life, took on some of the world's biggest, meanest
outfits and made 'em move over, you think he has to ask who he
can talk to?" The elemental force had escaped.

Morpurgo glanced at Golding. Golding was in another world,
but he had shrunk in his chair.

Cochran had only just begun. "Those that's got, they work for
it. Those that don't, don't want to work. You take your goddam
Arab. You think he ever in his whole goddam history lifted one
finger? No *sir*! Just sat on his duff, waiting for the white man to
come along and find oil so he could figure out how to get it away
from him."

It took away Morpurgo's breath and at the same time, ludi-
crously, reminded him of his mother.

"Now politicians," – Cochran was in full passion, rumpled,
glitter-eyed – "who are another bunch of parasite sons-of-bitches,
don't need to be told about haves and have-nots. Ain't a man
with sense that would go into politics if he could make his
million some other way."

He loomed over Morpurgo, two hundred pounds of rabid
private enterprise and not much fat. "You want to know where
this gets us, right?"

"It would help."

Cochran mimicked. "It would help. You another like Archer,
keep your balls tucked in silk Jockeys?"

He must not, Morpurgo cautioned himself, let himself be
provoked. There were things to learn.

Cochran nodded grudgingly. "Know how to keep your cool.
Drink your goddam drink. We were talking politicians. Rich
guy's dough to get elected, rich guy's dough to stay elected, kiss
the poor man's ass. Handouts! Easteners, negroes, white trash!

Plus all the raggedy-ass countries that think Uncle Sam is a soft touch with the help of a little blackmail."

He stomped another circle on a carpet made for kings. "Drink your drink, goddammit! Fifteen-year-old scotch isn't good enough? I'm going to tell you what happens. All those sonofabitch raggedy-asses, they think they ain't getting enough, they're coming after it."

It was getting wilder and wilder, but then, Morpurgo reflected, men like Cochran were born wild. He sipped his scotch as a gesture. "Is this getting us anywhere?"

"You bet it is! You know what happened to me back there in England? Sure you do! That guy Archer told me you do. You know what's kept me quiet? Lies!"

He punched the air with the full strength of his heavy body. Golding sat like a man in a dream. "Lies, lies, lies! But where everybody lies, my friend, things start to cancel out. Things start to make a little sense, the way you can tell what kids are up to from what they put into telling you it just ain't so."

He bent over Morpurgo, put an index finger over Morpurgo's heart and leaned on it. "You know how much I put into that process? Near on one million and a half, American. Know how much it costs to hold up a charter shipment of crude just twenty-four hours? Thirty thousand, give or take. You know what Langley says? They'll fix a tax adjustment to cover the loss."

He stood glaring at Morpurgo as if expecting him to react. "Those dumbos think I employ accountants, pay Mark Folger consultancy fees, and still pay taxes?" In the still classicism of this room where even the sunlight walked on tiptoe, his fury was a towering thing.

Langley, not Hank Timothy, not the Libyans, had delayed the *Oklahoma Star.*

Morpurgo cut in. "I take it the thirty thousand doesn't include the loss of the crude?"

It was as if Cochran, poised to throw a knockout punch, had tripped. "The loss of what crude?"

"The crude you couldn't pump ashore at Lavéra. The crude that went bad." He saw Golding look round, suddenly heedful.

"Couldn't pump . . . What the hell are you talking about, mister? Bad enough being a day late. Who says we didn't deliver?" He was dangerous, violent, megalomaniac. He was also an oilman.

"You did deliver?"

Cochran was looking at him as if he had lapsed into gibberish. "What the hell *is* this? Sure we delivered, fifty thousand tons of Libyan crude, check with Lavéra, goddammit!"

Very quietly, Golding said, "It couldn't work." But, to Morpurgo's ears, he sounded thoughtful, a man considering and by no means rejecting an interesting possibility.

Cochran spun round. "Have you two gone crazy? *What* couldn't work? Listen, I have this guy Barzelian, voice like a whole chorus of swamp frogs, he's speaking for the Director, Central Intelligence and if I want that guy Timothy fixed, the bugs kept out of the hands of those sonofabitch Libyan hoodlums, the British government off my back, I better play ball. One whole day sitting out there off Tarragona, telex machines getting red-hot, goddam phones ringing like crazy, running out of excuses while the French and the Spanish go through the roof, and you tell me it's all for nothing?"

It was a lot to take in, but it fitted together like a Rubik cube. Now all he had to do, Morpurgo thought, was solve the Rubik cube.

Thinking of Sylvie, of himself, he said, involuntarily, "It could be."

For a moment he thought Cochran had been deflated. He had seen the look before, at the end of a really tough interrogation, a spark of instinctive resistance but no coordination, no firm ground, nowhere left to go.

He was wrong. Cochran, arms hanging loose, head thrust forward on his thick neck, eyes smouldering under his beetled brows with the ferocious watchfulness of a wild thing baited, said, "If it's all for nothing, then what in hell are you doing in this town, mister?"

Steve Archer had talked to Cochran, recently. Cochran had known Morpurgo was in Madrid, had know where to have him picked up. Epworth had warned him he would be tailed. This time, if he found that Archer – Pottern would be the means – was operating outside his legal territory, geographical, political, especially political, the gloves would be off. They would say, afterwards – the 'they' of the privately communing security

212

community – that it was Morpurgo's cheap revenge, the typical response of his kind to a better man's success. Let them say! With no Epworth to check him, he would blow a whistle that would be heard all the way to Whitehall.

"Didn't Archer tell you what I was doing in this town?"

He thought for a while that Cochran would not answer, but it was simply the time it took for suspicion to yield place to speculation.

"He told me. Left it to me to find you, that wasn't too hard. A buck buys as much help here as anyplace else. How many bucks does it take to buy *you*?"

The camel's spine broke with a snap, but that was the camel, a beast that might complain but could not buck the burden. Morpurgo was no longer any kin to the camel. He had reached the door before Cochran had time to react. He supposed, indifferently, that Cochran's iron-souled Jeeves was not far away. So much the worse for Jeeves.

Cochran said, "Now wait a minute." He shouted, but anger was mingled with a note of alarm. "I know you're meeting up with Timothy." Morpurgo's hand was on the richly moulded knob of the door. "I know you're fixing to do a deal." Morpurgo turned the knob. "I don't trust any deal you make for those crooks in Langley or that crazy bunch in Washington."

Morpurgo opened the door. There was no sign of Jeeves or his granite-block sidekick. Golding sat upright in his chair like a playgoer riveted by the plot. Someone in the distant street had the effrontery to sound his horn.

Cochran took a step toward him, one hand outstretched. "They're set to fix me, them and those guys in Big Oil." His eyes were wide, wild, unblinking. "Been aiming to fix me this many a year, but this time for real. Think I don't know Folger sold me out?"

Morpurgo stood in the gap of the door.

"Don't get me wrong." Cochran took another step. "If I offended you I surely do withdraw. But you do business with Timothy for me, not Langley, and you'll find I can be a mighty generous man. Just fix for me and Timothy to meet up before he makes any deals. I'll make him a deal will fix him up for life."

Morpurgo went out into the lobby. Dobrovski, Jeevesian-smooth, was coming through the door leading from the penthouse to the real world. He saw Morpurgo's face and stepped aside. Behind them, Cochran emerged. As Morpurgo entered the lift and reached for the button, he heard Cochran's voice, harsh, strained, shouting. "You're making a big mistake, Morpurgo. Brewster Cochran always gets what he wants. You don't shake me off that easy. You'll see."

He had no choice but to return to the hotel. He was not followed. That was certain. It took him a little longer to see that Cochran, or whoever else, Archer's people included, had no need to follow him. They already knew where he was. Perhaps even knew that he had no choice but to wait. It was something else to worry about. Steve's passing his whereabouts to Cochran was an old, old trick, part of the standard issue dirt. You weren't ready to move in, or couldn't move in, so, sand in the works, slow the quarry down by forcing him continually to look over his shoulder.

Much later, at the price of much thinking and a headache, he saw something else. Cochran said the bugs hadn't turned the oil, but Cochran was, however unwillingly, in Langley's pocket. Golding had said the bugs couldn't have worked, but with less than total conviction. But Hank Timothy knew they had worked, or he would not be risking his neck. And Langley knew they had worked, or Hank Timothy would not have been paid all that money.

It was just before six the next morning when he was called to the phone. The windowless reception area had the ill-lit unreality of a stage set after the curtain comes down.

"Johnny? Is that you?"

He was awake at once, amazed. "Sylvie! Where are you? How did you know I was here?"

"Johnny," – Something wrong with her voice – "I don't know where you are. And I don't know where I am." A small, unconvincing laugh. "I'm quite all right, you mustn't worry, but . . ."

Bumping sounds as the phone changed hands. "Hi, pally."

Something squeezed his bowels, tautened his larynx so that it was hard to speak. "What have you done with my wife, you bastard? If you so much as . . ."

"Shut up, will you? You want to hear what it's all about, you better listen."

Heart pounding, mouth dry, high voltage electricity running amok in his nervous system, he listened.

"That's better. Your wife's okay, hear? No, don't interrupt. Use your head, you won't sort this one out by interrupting. Okay, I want those bugs, but my way, not yours, not anyone else's. Listen hard. This is what you do."

He listened with a concentration that grew pain in his head, locked in a nullity that was generated by hate and the voice in his ear.

Timothy finished. "Got it?"

"Yes."

"Then get moving. And just keep thinking, she's okay, but all it takes to change that is one damn fool thing from you. One itty-bitty foolish thing, that's all it takes."

The first thing he did, back in his bare room and preparing to leave, was to check the gun Claas had insisted on getting to him at Barafas airport. He fed in five fat shells, lowered the hammer on the empty chamber, stowed it carefully. Never in his life had he fired a shot in anger. Now he had the anger.

*　　　*　　　*

The previous day, seeing the road signs, he had longed to drive until he reached Sylvie. Now he was driving, south, always south, no idea whether it was toward Sylvie, no idea where Sylvie was. Far behind, Madrid was no more than a stain of tainted air on the skyline. Ahead, rolling, empty-looking countryside, mountains on a distant horizon, a sign to Toledo at every major intersection. He had done what Sylvie had wanted, severed all links with Epworth, SIS, the Cousins. This was not the way she had meant it.

His mind crossed and recrossed its tracks, always in tight circles, like a beast in a cage. Epworth had said the Cochran inoculum was a fake. Timothy had called the bluff. Langley said the fake had worked. Cochran said it had not, Golding that it could not. Timothy had accepted that it had. Langley had paid Timothy one and a half million dollars – no fake there! – to employ the fake to do what it could not do.

Could the fact of the fake be a fake in itself? Whose truth was a falsehood?

He went over and through it until he could no longer bear to think about it, and then went over it again. The land became wilder, more arid. The mountains swelled, approaching. In due

215

course he became aware that the rocky thrust crawling to meet him was pinnacle-crowned, Toledo the golden.

The crown and its jewels barely came into his thoughts. He was not a tourist. He followed the road in a great curve about the feet of the city, came to the gorge of the Tagus, crossed, skirting a granite cliff and went on. Aranjuez, the Mancha; every town and village a meaningless congregation of letters. Only one word mattered. Sylvie.

Vast plains, an ocean of growth, periodically swelling in frozen breakers of rock, treeless, grassless, crested with Quixotean clusters of windmills, the occasional bony remains of a castle. He would have raced across the implacable scorch, shadows, as the sun climbed, dwindling like drying puddles, but his instructions precluded hurry.

He found himself thinking of Warren Claas, who knew Spain, spoke Spanish, had been, for an unknown period, on the staff of CIA's Madrid station. And had, while there, known Hank Timothy. Why had it never been mentioned? So much time in Claas's company, Madrid and back, Barcelona and back, and it had never been mentioned.

Timothy had made a play for Ella Claas, vividly attractive in the loose-knit American style, that was something in itself, but what else? *I know a thing or two about that klutz he wouldn't like to be reminded of.* Minor indiscretions, or more?

He found himself thinking that things could hardly have been easier for Hank Timothy if Claas had never been around. In and out the *plaza mayor* in Madrid while Claas was away on a wild goose chase. He had not seen Timothy's note until Claas showed it to him. Not even any evidence that it had actually come from Timothy. And should Claas – he had thought it before – have fallen for an old trick so instantly, unhesitatingly?

Suspicion, he told himself dutifully, was a thing that fed on itself, never more so than when consciousness had been reduced to a tight nucleus of obsession. Things could not have been easier for Hank Timothy if Claas had never been there. Or had been there but turned a blind eye because he was a klutz Timothy knew things about.

He was passing through vineyards on the Brobdingnagian scale, a figurative ocean of wine, though hardly a wine for

216

Epworth's discriminatory palate. *Spain. Interesting. Heard from Sylvie?* 'She's in Cáceres.' *I know where it is.*

What was the saying? 'Suspicion always haunts the guilty mind.'

Valdepeñas. He had neither eaten nor drunk since the voice on the phone. He stopped at a roadside cafe, pinewood, the smell of hot resin, cascades of crimson blossom above a crumbling terrace marinating in hot, herb-scented shade. Lorry drivers stared at him openly, yet without inquisitiveness, while he ate and drank mechanically, no awareness of taste. Pay up, drive off, the road little populated, his immediate past and imminent future always visible in terms of shimmering tarmac.

He had not been followed, of that one thing he was sure.

But why this journey? Why the continued spinning out? Timothy could, surely? have accompanied Morpurgo to his bare, clean room, received the inoculum, vanished among the anonymous streets. Or arranged another rendezvous, all his experience at work, maximum protection, minimum risk. Instead, the beginnings of another special performance, on and off the stage like an acrobat through a trapdoor. Only this time, things would be different.

Things *were* different, what was he saying? Timothy and Sylvie.

Far ahead, darting through the sun-glare, a helicopter, heading north and east, a reminder of the *Oklahoma Star*; a fresh parade of the old, insane contradictions. It made a lazy turn west, passing low and close. It was not a Bell-Agusta, not blue and white. It was something to watch, all the same.

It disappeared beyond yet another surge of low, eroded hills. In these wide tracts of cultivated emptiness it could land and take off almost at will, no need for any airport.

If Steve Archer had proof positive that Hank Timothy had recently been in the United Kingdom, it would, ten to one, have come from Special Branch or immigration control at one or other of the major airports. Steve had said they had been able to put a name to a picture. This was the stuff Morpurgo had lived with from day to day at Curzon Street. You had a picture, you showed it around. Ports of entry; a generic description embracing sky as well as water. Men whose daily routine was the scanning of faces, names, pictures; seen this bloke recently?

He was passing through La Carolina, tawny huddle of houses,

tall church, bells roosting like crows in its open-topped tower; getting close to his destination, but his inner journey had brought him back to the sudden general interest in Hank Timothy, to his own isolated and consequently unpursuable thought that it was linked with the state visit of the President.

I hear their top man is being eased out. The echo of a voice from the wastebin of his memory. Weeks back; a casually dropped remark, incidental. When someone said 'Incidentally,' you always listened twice as hard. 'If you meet Death on a stroll, you'll know your time's up when he says: Incidentally . . .'

The speaker had been Epworth, the top man Doug Church, head of the US secret service.

The mind, like a trained tracker dog, is sometimes best let loose to forage. It had been the day Epworth had told him of the Security Directorate knight's compulsory retirement, the consequence of alleged security failures. For what kind of security failure might the head of the President's bodyguard have been eased out?

Superficially, easy to answer; a terminal failure; but nothing had happened. The President was still around.

The helicopter had not disappeared for good. It was returning, parallel with the road, coming toward him. As it passed he could hear its racket through the wound-down window of the car. It had projections either side of the fuselage; crop spraying, Lord Torlonia widening the gap between him and the peasant. He wondered if Sylvie, among the peasants, ever remembered. He wondered if Lord Torlonia, these days, was into oil.

Nothing had happened to the President, either at Heathrow on arrival, or Gatwick on departure. A frustrated threat was not a happening. But had Hank Timothy happened? And had Steve Archer, responsible for the British side of airport security, somewhat brusquely handled by the agents of a foreign power, happened on the non-happening?

He liked that, the US Secret Service as the agent of a foreign power. It was the way they saw the British. Perhaps things would go better if the British thought it more often of them.

He came unexpectedly, crossing a hill range, on a sharp left-hand bend, had to haul on the wheel and accelerate hard to keep to the centre of the road. A classy-looking castle where he might have dropped in uninvited had his tyres lost their grip; fancy cars in a wide sweep of orange-gravelled forecourt. Mr Morpurgo presents his compliments to Lord Torlonia and apologises for his inability to give notice of his arrival. Incidentally . . . does Lord Torlonia happen to have a helicopter?

Then he was overlooking a small town and a destination. Bailén. He slowed, aware of the heat of noon like red-hot iron inches above his head. Knowing that the motel specified by Timothy was on his side of the town and therefore not far ahead, he pulled in under a shade tree, the air pungent with the hot scent of thyme. Through his offside window the sun laid one slender finger on the seat. He touched it. It scorched. To his left, below, lay a great plain, collaged with crops. A threat to the President's security was never less than a threat to the President's life. The crop-spraying helicopter buzzed waspishly toward him across the plain, to vanish over his head. You don't shake me off that easy. You'll see. He wondered. Brewster Cochran could afford to hire a fleet of helicopters; Steve Archer, barely one.

The taking of a man, American citizen, ex-CIA, who had attempted the President's life, by a British security service would be a master-stroke. No publicity. Simply the achievement and the shared knowledge. The benefit to the British government would be incalculable. Steve Archer, riding to knighthood on the steed of power, bearing a great gift.

It was aesthetically pleasing. It was also what Epworth had called poetism; a theory whose only claim to be considered was that it was aesthetically pleasing. Because, far from hunting down and killing Hank Timothy, Langley had just made him a present of a million and a half dollars, with more to come.

He started up, drove into the motel forecourt, and, before long, was installed in a more than adequate little suite; lobby, well-furnished sitting-cum-bedroom, bathroom and a shady veranda looking out on pines, oleander and a scatter of cactus. Half a dozen bottles of San Miguel in the refrigerator, a pleasant enough dining room, a shower; few problems in getting through the rest of the day and the evening, beyond the fact that he must wait, with nothing to do but think. He tried not to think of Sylvie.

*   *   *

Weber came in, for him, at speed. Claas, unable to concentrate, had been making finicky adjustments to the stacked paperwork on his desk. "Well?"

"Nothing. Vanished, early a.m." Weber knew Claas's reaction to Morpurgo's disappearance in advance.

"Just like that?" Claas abandoned his pointless distractions. "Timothy got to him, right?"

"Looks like it."

"So how come those guys over there in Madrid missed it?"

"Let's just say" – Weber had no better answer for Claas – "they screwed up."

"Pierre, we could have had that guy iced six times over, only it's never the right time. How come it's never the right time?"

It was getting harder by the minute, as Weber had pointed out to Barzelian, to stall Claas. "Next time will be the right time. This is no banana republic we're fooling around in, Warren. This is Spain, tricky, proud, very, very independent. Washington has a hard time keeping these people from withdrawing our military facilities. One clumsy move, the way the President feels about Langley, and we'll all be on the breadline."

"I know how the President feels about Langley. I know how I feel about this. Next time will be the right time, only we happen to have lost him."

"Morpurgo will find Timothy."

"So we have to wait on Morpurgo, that's good? That guy has tied Morpurgo in more knots than a piece of macramé. Morpurgo is slaphappy. Punch-drunk."

Miss Woloszynowski opened the door a little. "Mr Claas, I don't want to interrupt, but do we have to keep this? Looks to me like something went bad."

Claas curbed his anger, looking at the glass jar in her hand. "I thought we threw that out way back. Mind you don't spill it on that pretty dress."

Holding the jar fastidiously, she withdrew, leaving Claas staring after her. He called, and Weber looked round at the sound of his voice. "Hey, Wol, honey, bring that stuff back here."

She brought it back, giving Weber, who had just had a letter from his son asking for money and needed a break, a little time to admire her. Claas unscrewed the cap of the jar, sniffed, and hastily withdrew his nose. He tilted the jar. For a moment or so, nothing happened. Then it oozed thickly.

Weber frowned. "Why'd you make up two, junior?"

Claas looked, distraught, from him to Miss Woloszynowski. "Good girl, good question, we'll keep this one, glad you asked."

She laughed, puzzled but pleased. "What did I do?"

"You did right, honey. Now go tidy up some more." He all but shooed her out. The door closed, he said, "Nobody made up two. This is the switch. Cindy-Lou must have forgotten to get rid of it."

"Good God!" Weber stared at it, clearly shocked. "It's changed! No switch! It really has changed!" He took the jar, sniffed and was repelled like Claas. "Warren, you're sure? This couldn't be some kind of mistake?"

Claas just stood looking. Several times his lips moved a little before he said, "Sure I'm sure. That's the one Morpurgo tipped those damned bugs in, way back, right here in this room." He looked up from the jar. "Jesus Christ, Pierre, that stuff could be dynamite."

Weber no longer looked tired. "And Morpurgo's out there somewhere, all set to hand it over to Timothy." His pothook smile plucked at his mouth corners tentatively, as if he were unable to make up his mind whether to laugh or cry. Even in their shared shock, the impact spreading and deepening by the minute, it struck Claas as a strange way to act.

The rictus vanished. Weber said, "Going up to Communications. I have to talk to Barzelian," moving, for once, with the speed of a snapping spring. Claas looked at his watch. "Barzelian! It's only a little after six over there in Cleveland Park."

"So I'll wake him up," Weber said over his shoulder. "It's later than he thinks."

He came back a long time after, just when Claas had extracted the last scrap of diversion from watching cars go in and out the underground garage.

"Hold the fort, junior. My turn to go to Spain." He had just delivered Barzelian's third sting.

*   *   *

At eight he dined, early, in mock-timbered isolation. Then he did the one thing he would still claim to be good at, sat on the hardest, most upright chair, in the corner nearest to where the veranda door opened into the room but not on the side to which it opened, and began to wait.

Eventually, when night finally came, he went out into its hot blackness where stars burned with an unwinking brilliance, the air charged with foreign smells and alive with the chime of cicadas. Two more cars had arrived, both late. One was an old, battered Seat, back seat half-buried in kiddy clutter. Spanish, he had heard them arrive, heard a child grizzle after the high heat of the road. The other, a shiny, pale blue Peugeot, had French plates, a Guide Michelin on the driver's seat, a straw hat and silk scarf on the other. A silent arrival, apart from the slam of doors, the crunch of gravel.

His own feet crunched softly. Miniature stars winked briefly in the gravel, reflecting the harsh glare of the floodlit parking area. Dogs passed an endless word back and forth over an invisible plain with rare sparks of illumination. The lights of Bailén, on down the road with its steady traffic, mostly great trucks headed north, fruit and vegetables for the cities, were sparse, white, raw-looking.

There was a question he must ask, only one person of whom he could ask it.

In the dining room, two tables occupied, close in the emptiness for the convenience of the solitary waiter. One, the Spanish family, two small, huge-eyed, flush-faced children who should have been in bed. Across the other table, one empty wine bottle, one on its way down, temper flowed in quietly furious bursts of French contempt. The waiter, by the long, bottle-laden server, pared his nails.

He obtained change from reception, returned to the pay phone in the far corner of the lobby, where a potted palm stood in a white speckle of cigarette ends. The receptionist had had a limited supply of coins.

It took no time to set the phone ringing at the other end. He fought, for the thousandth time, to keep Sylvie out of his thoughts, aware that she must not be allowed to intrude if he were to have the smallest chance of finding her.

The ringing stopped. A woman's voice, upper crust, languid. "Yes?" He fed more money into the box.

"Is Steve there?" A hard enough task face to face, and this was across nearly a thousand miles.

"Who's calling?" Coolly possessive, the right to know that normally went with a gold band, yet Steve's divorce still had a long way to go.

"John Morpurgo."

"I see." Never had two syllables carried more comment. "Wait, please." He looked at his waiting time, stacked neatly in the coin box.

It took two hundred pesetas. He hadn't said where he was calling from. Steve, guessing the distance, might have decided that it was one way of dealing with the undesirable.

"Johnny." Another frigid speech in miniature. He waited, but that was it. Cold as the light of those distant, unwinking stars.

Incredibly, until that moment, he hadn't considered what he was going to say. A brief, almost panicky hesitation. He could see Steve across the night, chill, calm, but – He *must* be, damn it! He was only too human – curious.

"Steve, he's got Sylvie."

He had delivered himself into the hands of his enemy, an eye for an eye, a wife for a wife. The last coin in the meter slid through.

"Steve, will you call me back? It's a pay phone. The last coin's just gone." He gave the number, the termination signal cut him off. There was a burst of laughter from the Spanish family in the dining room, the voice of a child in shrill protest.

Now he was alone. He could go into the town to get more coins, call again. No; he could not. Timothy had Sylvie. Steve Archer, whose private life Morpurgo had unintentionally wrecked, had simply to say that he'd missed the number, or got it wrong, or tried and couldn't get through . . . or nothing. That was it; simply not to call back.

He waited while centuries and the frequent heavy trucks ground by. The mass chorus of cicadas, audible even indoors. Another car arriving outside. The silence, absolute, of the telephone. Steve belonged to a class whose moral code had Old Testament antecedents.

The telephone rang.

"Where are you, Johnny?" Still no warmth at all, only a clinical crispness.

"About two hundred miles south of Madrid, on the road."

Another silence; tell me everything or tell me nothing; goodbye.

"What do you want?"

"Epworth's in Berlin. Will you track him down, tell him to stay out? Same with the Cousins?"

"Do you know where Timothy is?"

"No. Only that he's got Sylvie. He'll make contact with me when he's ready."

"You can't go this one alone." Steve the professional, dispassionately assessing the odds.

"I can. I shall." Time for Steve to strike his bargain; no information, no cooperation.

"You're going to sell out?" That, of course, was how Steve would see it. They were enemies, duellists, standing back to back, pistols at the ready.

"I'm going to do whatever's necessary to get Sylvie back."

"The man's a traitor. And a killer. As much regard for human life as a bloody shark."

"As much regard as I have for his."

This time the silence was broken by the Spanish family retiring, one of the children being carried, asleep. The father nodded. In the distance, the receptionist yawned loudly. He could visualise Steve, face expressionless, torn between personal and professional codes.

"Johnny, he's a trained killer. A killing machine."

"He's got Sylvie."

Seconds dribbled away.

"What else do you want?"

"Something I have to know. Something that matters."

"Then ask it, for Christ's sake!" He was putting an enemy under intolerable stress.

"At Gatwick, when the President was on his way home. Did Timothy have some plan to kill him?"

He had taken Steve's wife. Now he was asking for his professional life. They were both in a business where information was power. If they were duellists, it was as if, without waiting

224

for the drop of the handkerchief, the ritual punctilio, he had turned and shot Steve Archer through the head.

The silence, like an inimical virus, paralysed his breathing.

He heard the quick intake of Steve's breath, its slow release, and knew he had his answer.

Steve took another deep breath. "Will you give me your word that you need to know? That it might help Sylvie?"

"I need to know." Morpurgo considered, almost unconsciously, how much he should give Steve in return. He was, perhaps, vaguely aware of seeking to benefit from that breeding he had so often mocked. It was his own special grace to decide that he should hold nothing back.

"Timothy" – Morpurgo had the impression that Steve had sent his woman away during that prolonged silence – "had a crack at blowing up the President's plane at Gatwick. Managed to worm his way through security that should have been absolutely impregnable, clever, but the luck of the devil, too. All that stopped him succeeding was a bureaucrat with more zeal than humour."

Think! Think! Think! "And all this business with the bugs the Cousins stole from Billingshurst . . ."

"Just manoeuvring him into the right position for a hit. Langley I mean. I'd have thought that was obvious." That was the real Steve, angry, patience running out. "Damn it, Johnny, he knows it himself. That's why he's taken Sylvie. As insurance. He'll have you too, if you go on behaving like a bloody fool."

"I shall do my best not to." Two and two, Morpurgo's mind was telling him, don't make four. They make a million and a half, with more to come.

Steve – Morpurgo could sympathise – was finding self-control hard to maintain. "You realise what you'll be doing? You'll be trying to bargain with a fake. Those bugs won't work. But of course, you're still going to try."

"I'm going to kill him if I have to. Does that make you feel any better?"

"No, it does not! Because I think that means he'll kill you, not to mention Sylvie. Strange though you may find it, I don't particularly wish you dead." Reluctant but roughly urgent, not the usual suave Steve.

"Thank you." It seemed an asinine thing to say, yet necessary.

"Don't thank me, you bloody fool! You're crazy, you do know that? Johnny, listen to me!" Good God! Morpurgo thought, he really minds. "You can't go it alone. You've got to have help. The Cousins . . ."

"The Cousins have just paid Timothy one and a half million dollars."

Steve wasn't listening. "Just tell me where you are and how we can keep in touch, and leave the rest to me. And don't do anything silly. We're both too old for this sort of game."

"There's no doubt about the Gatwick thing? About the assassination attempt?"

Steve's response, he realised afterwards, was a very human thing. "Doubt? Of course there's no doubt! Let's get this settled, damn it! This is my bloody phone!"

Hank Timothy could hardly have sailed more smoothly through all the supposed precautions, the highly professional precautions, of recent times if not just Warren Claas but Weber, Langley, a man called Barzelian, had shepherded him every inch of the way.

The luck of the devil, as Steve had put it, might enable Hank Timothy to penetrate impregnable security. But what if, instead of luck, he had been relying on all but impregnably concealed cooperation?

You could pay a man a million and a half dollars to do something that all the evidence said was impossible. Or you could pay it for something he had already done. Something that had almost succeeded. Something so big, so fraught with giant implications, that the cover must be as deep and elaborate as the plot itself.

Something worth all of and more than a carefully laundered million and a half to keep under wraps, particularly if it had been the intention to lay it at the door of a country that was a running sore on the American body politic.

Revelation often leads on to revelation. With Cochran insisting that the crude had arrived at Lavéra unchanged, Golding casting doubt on the very idea of the inoculum's being able to change it, he might have guessed, sooner or later, that the cable Weber and Claas had shown him had been a fake. What had stopped him was that someone as pathologically mistrustful as Hank Timothy had rung to say the bugs had worked, that they had a deal.

But if Timothy was Langley's creature, he would have known

in advance that his unexpected deal would be later backed by Langley's faked cable. Langley would have known in advance that the faked cable would act as justification for Timothy's fake deal.

Now it was time for Morpurgo, in return for Steve's behaving, after all, like the English gentleman he had always derided, to present his quid pro quo.

"Don't go to the Cousins, Steve. Don't go to anyone until you've spoken to Epworth. Hank Timothy may be ex but I think he's already done his main job for Langley. The bugs won't work. That's all a fake. There was nothing fake about the money. I think it was Langley that was behind that attempt to kill the President. Epworth will fill you in on the gaps."

He rang off, belatedly conscious of the fact that although a car had arrived some little time back, no one had come into reception.

*   *   *

In Madrid, on the fourth floor of the embassy on mid-town Serrano, Weber, talking yet again by satellite to Barzelian, was learning that Langley had temporarily lost touch with Hank Timothy. It was one of a number of disturbing items of information that had come in over the last several hours. Another was that Brewster Cochran, breaking free from his Promethean shackles, had defied the eagle and taken a scheduled flight to Madrid the previous day. He had booked in at the Ritz, where the penthouse was still in his name but currently occupied by Charles Herbert Golding, now cooperating with Madrid station.

Cochran himself had left town after hiring two helicopters, one of them, for God's sake! a rickety crop-sprayer. And sure, the Spanish air traffic control authorities would know where they were, but as they worked closely with the military air traffic controllers and Jorge Manuel Enríquez de Figueroa, professionally suspicious ever since the Anglo-American descent on Barcelona, had undoubtedly tipped off his superiors in CSE that odd things were afoot, it would be distinctly unwise to press enquiries.

*   *   *

Morpurgo, as he replaced the phone, had never felt so alone or so vulnerable. Steve had been right. He was too old for this kind of game. There was also the fact that he didn't know what to do next. He had only arrived at the last twist of that imaginary Rubik cube in the instant of persuading Steve to part with his own jealously guarded, inestimably valuable item of information. It went a long way toward explaining and justifying Steve's behaviour over the past few weeks. That he had yielded it up went an equally long way toward making Morpurgo reexamine his fixed attitude toward Steve Archer.

He crossed the foyer toward the night. There was a new car under the woven bamboo roofing that shielded the parking area from the daytime scorch of the sun. He studied it, as best he could, from a curtained corner of the glass-fronted entrance to reception. The interior lighting was far stronger than that outside, but it appeared to him that the car, travel-soiled, anonymous, was unoccupied.

He faced his quandary. To close the last gap in Langley's dizzyingly complex cover-up – the President was hostile to the CIA, had tried and failed to take control, was still a threat and there were those who still said the CIA had killed Kennedy – Timothy must have the inoculum. Whether he took it to his Libyan masters, where it would prove to be impotent but nonetheless reinforce his standing as an ex-CIA renegade, or, with Langley's under-cover aid, solved the problem in some other way, was immaterial.

Morpurgo had the inoculum. Timothy had Sylvie. In his present mood, Morpurgo would have settled for a straight swap, but there were currently three things between him and that.

One; he didn't trust Timothy. Two; Timothy didn't trust him. Three; who and where was the driver of the newly-arrived car?

He went back inside. The men's room was at the back, and had a window opening on the darkness to the rear of the motel rooms. The window was small, Morpurgo was not. Nor was Morpurgo – he might as well face up to other facts beside his age – any longer particularly agile. He had not fired a gun since . . . when? that was the answer. His reflexes were those of *Homo sedentarius*, coming up fifty. Whether he killed Timothy or Timothy killed him, it would do nothing for Sylvie.

He left his gun holstered, and got through the window by a combination of skinning his shins and falling on his face.

Someone waiting for him said, "Don't do anything rash until you've taken a look at this, Mr Morpurgo."

'This' was a piece of paper, a vertically torn label that, reading from top to bottom, said: . . . ASSÉ EN 1855, followed by half a gilt crest and then: *TAILLEY* . . LAC . . 970. The gilt shone wanly in the light from the men's room. The other half of the label had been given to him by Sibley. The label was as near as he'd got to sharing Epworth's connoisseur's taste in claret.

He didn't even resent it when the late arrival, following closely as they went the dark way round to his room, said, "Don't put the light on." The most reassuring thing about him, oddly, was his voice, English with a chirpy colonial accent.

He was young, that much was plain in reflected light from the parking area. He took a chair in the darkest corner, a shadow with highlights and an easy grace of movement.

"Names don't matter. Dangerous, too." *Daingerous*; Aussie, New Zealander, what used to be Rhodesia before it became Zimbabwe. "First thing, your wife's okay, don't let it bother you too much."

"Do you know where she is?"

The other, doing an Epworth – and hadn't he brought Epworth's visiting card? – sidestepped. "Tomorrow, nice and early, let's say seven, shall we? you hit the road again." Something arced across the intervening space to land on the bed beside Morpurgo, a soft chink. Car keys.

"I'll have yours, if you don't mind, don't worry about the rental company."

It was the calm, almost cheery tone, near whisper though it was, that made Morpurgo part with the keys, which the other, in spite of the twilight, caught dexterously.

"Got a change of clothes in that bag? Great. Catch." Something else, pale like a night-owl, plumped gently on the bed, a cotton beach hat, shapeless bucket variety and, by its feel, well-worn. "Just so you look a little different, okay? Left anything in your car?"

"No." It was amazing what confidence that accent and the matching half of a wine label could bring.

"You'll find a road map in mine, all the other papers you need. Your route's been marked. Just follow it. You'll be tailed a while, grey BMW, not for long, just till the chopper picks you up. Don't let that worry you either."

"You mean I'm being watched? Now?"

"Two men and a woman, blue Peugeot." The other was preparing to leave.

"The French? One man, one woman, more than a bit tight."

"Three, not tight, not French." His unknown visitor was amused, a gleam of teeth in the half-light. "Other one's off on a wild goose chase, he comes back, I'll be gone." He stood.

"One thing more. The Libs have a commando group running the road, white Mercedes, big one, they never learn. Just act natural. They'll be looking for you, but you'll be me. I'll be you, don't let it bother you too much. That label" – *Libel*, Aussie, En Zedder, what? – "shred it and flush it down the bog, make sure it's all gone." He waited. "I mean now."

Morpurgo hesitated. "Sylvie. You're sure?"

"I'm sure."

"Timothy. He's . . ."

"Don't you worry about Hank. Me and Hank have been mates. She's all right. How about that label?"

He shredded the label in that warm gloaming, a moth fluttering at the window, a faint odour of perfume – soap? shampoo? air freshener? – from the bathroom, and went to flush it away. The noise of gushing water was alarmingly loud. He knew what he would find when he came back, and he was right. Hank's one-time mate had learned at least one of Hank Timothy's tricks.

* * *

The map was the Michelin 1/1000 000, not new, but unmarked save for an inked-in route running due west from Bailén to Córdoba, then south toward Malaga and the Costa del Sol. But at Antequera – no more than a name to Morpurgo – it cut across what suggested itself as wildish country to Ronda and then coastward once more, reaching the Mediterranean near Gibraltar and Algeciras. From Antequera the inking was much more tentative, as if whoever had done it was himself uncertain.

He was, as forecast, followed. The French-speaking couple, joined by another man, were stowing baggage away when he came from reception to his new car. The fact that the car was different produced an unmistakeable effect; mainly, he thought, relief succeeded by elaborately disguised puzzlement. They had thought they'd lost him.

He nodded politely and drove off. The grey BMW appeared in his rear mirror before he had traversed the outskirts of Bailén. He came down to the River Guadalquivir at Andújar, crossed it in the town centre and was soon aware that the following BMW had not crossed it with him, nor did any other car appear to take its place. On the open, gently hilly road between Andújar to Córdoba, aerial crop-spraying – the same helicopter – on a somewhat haphazard basis, was in progress.

There was something for conjecture. Who was doing the tailing? Curzon Street, unlikely candidate from the moment he left Madrid, was out. That left the Cousins and Brewster Cochran. He was not going to make the mistake of underestimating Cochran, the man himself was such as to turn his reputation into something of an understatement. What ol' Brew Cochran wanted, so far as Morpurgo was concerned, was something he would undoubtedly do everything that power, money and the total unscrupulousness of paranoid megalomania could help him to get.

The Cousins were something else, and it required a major mental somersault to adjust.

The supposedly French trio must be linked with the helicopter. They had seen him leave Bailén in different car, different clothes, the floppy hat his night-time visitor had left. The crop-spraying helicopter had picked him up as the BMW dropped him. So the helicopter knew what it was tracking.

The Cousins knew he was still following Timothy's instructions, although the connection between his unknown visitor and Timothy was impossible to explain. The man with the colonial accent had been a 'mate' of Hank Timothy, but as well as Timothy's orders he had carried impeccable credentials from Epworth. And, through Timothy, he must be connected with the Cousins.

He decided that the Peugeot-BMW-chopper team was acting as pathfinder for Brewster Cochran, who might not have Langley's facilities but, between vast resources of money and relentless will, was more than capable of staying in the running.

Oddly enough, Cochran worried him least. He took another look about him for the helicopter and was in time to see it replaced.

The newcomer was larger; he guessed a capacity for as many as six passengers. It had come from the north, no point in speculating where, and his imagination could almost sense Cochran's presence; fierce, implacable and not a little unbalanced. Brewster Cochran was a man with a mammoth grudge; against what he called Big Oil, against the Libyans on whom he was still so much dependent, against anyone at all who stood between him and his plans to shoulder his way into a position of dominance in the oil industry. A confrontation between Cochran and Hank Timothy would, from a safe seat in the stands, be something to see.

The big chopper had settled behind him, flying at perhaps two thousand feet and maybe half a mile to the rear. He had no idea of its range before refuelling, but imagined it was at least that of the car. The distance between his present position and the coast, if he was meant to go all the way, was less than two hundred miles. He could be kept in sight without difficulty and guessed that the cropsprayer might well be on call in reserve.

He was still postponing his final consideration of the Cousins. The road stayed within sight of the Guadalquivir, the country rolling, a mixture of arable, orchards and vines. The sun was already savage and there was a heaviness of humidity in the air. The route on the map, so plainly hesitant over the final fifty or sixty miles, ended in Algeciras. It began to make a hazy sense.

From Algeciras the distance across the straits of Gibraltar to Africa was no more than twelve miles. The twelve miles crossed, you were among Arabs, with a land route all the way to Libya and Tripoli.

So what? And yet there were regular sailings to Ceuta and Tangier, and Algeciras would be low on any official list of exit routes from Spain to what Timothy or his masters might call neutral territory. From his memory, Weber, somewhere back near the beginning, said: *Flies his own plane.* Yes, Algeciras had to mean something. But where was Sylvie?

He didn't want to think about that, so he thought about the Cousins, occasionally checking on his aerial escort, knowing that Cochran wouldn't give a damn whether he did or not.

Timothy, after all, was a Langley hireling. Dismissed in private disgrace but with public honour, he had not been so befouled that Langley, like the KGB, the SIS, any competently self-corrupted espionage service, was unwilling to overlook his viciousness if it matched the viciousness of the job in hand.

Weber again: *This guy is bad*! No wonder he had looked ashamed. Bad, a cold, braggart killer, and back on the payroll. But Weber was in on the game. What did that make Weber? He liked Weber. Sylvie liked Weber.

Oh, the dirt! he thought; the stinking, sticking, ineradicable dirt! The oil – crude, well-named – and the black, noisome muck into which, theoretically, it had changed, source of power, source of corruption, was an apt enough symbol.

But could Weber go along – was he, too, so besmirched? – with something that brought harm to Sylvie? Or was the presence of Weber in the affair some kind of guarantee of her ultimate safety? If only her photo-tour had been somewhere else, France, Italy, Germany; the worst part of this miasmic odyssey would never have taken place.

Timothy, based in Tripoli, had come to the Pyrenees for a meet in which an unknown nuclear engineer had ended up in the Pamplona morgue. Based in Tripoli, he had arranged his first meet with Morpurgo in Madrid; Spain, Claas would have added. His second meet in Tarragona, the third back in Madrid, the fourth . . .? He was in Andalusia, approaching Córdoba, following a route that would end in Algeciras. Epworth, that Cheshire smile, that donnish baby-face, said: *Spain. Interesting*.

Spain. Always Spain, always a little farther to the south in the end. And if this were fiction, an elaborately synthesised but, in the end, predictable plot, what would be the final stroke? The kidnapping, by a ruthless killer, of the hero's woman, lover, wife.

He wasn't a hero. He was middle-aged, *Homo sedentarius*, unfit in mind and body, far from home, lost in the dark, pushed and tugged around with as little real awareness of what controlled his destiny as a puppet of its strings. And a victim of poetism.

Poetism; a neat plot with a neat solution; everything in Spain because Sylvie was in Spain but he was on the side of the good guys, the Cousins. He would find Sylvie, they would walk, hand in hand, away from the years of vocational mistrust, into the sunrise and the land of happy ever after.

He saw that a much neater ending, from the point of view of the poetists, might be one in which both he and Sylvie, each of them knowing too much and able, reunited, to fill in more gaps in each other's knowledge, were written out of the story.

He was coming into Córdoba, touring Spain and seeing nothing. He stopped for petrol on the outskirts. The big chopper sat up in the offing like a hovering hawk. He sought shade – the sun was torrid – and thought, witlessly, how he might lose the chopper. He watched it lose itself, something coming adrift from the tail propeller, a straw in the wind, while the big craft itself spun like a top, tilted, rolled over and dropped almost vertically, rotors still spinning. It went below the rooftops. Smoke soared and then gushed, a black, billowing tree of flame-shot darkness. The sound was a few seconds later.

*　　　*　　　*

And now he was frightened. Not edgy, nervous or a little afraid, but worms rending his guts with a thousand needle-teeth. Frightened to drive on, frightened not to drive on, frightened in a mind-crippling, demoralising, rat-in-a-trap fashion that he had never experienced before.

He drove on, Córdoba no more than a blur of wide, weed-scribbled river, dotted with sandbanks, a distant glimpse of ancient streets topped by a tiered tower, and then the road out, broad, passing alternately through closely built-up suburbs and wide, empty lots, strewn with debris, stalking-ground for the voracity of the developers.

Then the wide sweep of the countryside; the lush infancy of grain, the dusty green polka-dotting of endless olive groves, the infinitely multiplied ideograms of the vines. He was no longer followed, not by road, not from the air, but his fear alternatively rode in the car and snapped at his heels. Brewster Cochran had been plucked from the board; by Timothy for the Libyans if Timothy still owed service to the Libyans; by Timothy for the Cousins since Timothy was dark brother to the Cousins; by the Cousins for themselves.

Or by any person or persons, representing any organisation or conspiracy of organisations, public or private, determined to avert what Morpurgo, by education and early training could

234

clearly foresee and had, for the same two reasons, been wholly insignificant to Steve Archer. The threat that could turn crude oil into sludge was imaginary. The prospect, once various teething troubles were resolved, of a technology that might, cheaply, release unimaginable quantities of crude from rock, was one that could strike at the economic foundations of the world; the rise and fall of OPEC on the scale of the Apocalypse.

Yet still there was nothing but to drive on, through Antequera, an upthrusting of castle, belfries and white walls like crumbed chalk on a green and yellow patchwork, and steadily south and west, with the land becoming wilder, the roads more tortuous, the hills higher and the sun a blowtorch melting the roof of the car, filling its interior with an endless blast of numbingly hot air.

Temporary relief, nerve-wracking, unwelcome, came when least expected.

A white Mercedes, horn blaring, hogging the uneven, repeatedly patched road whose fragmented edges mingled almost undetectably with the broken rock of its underlying terrain, buffeted past him so swiftly as to change from blur in his rear mirror to blur in a trailing dust cloud within seconds. His tension was such that he overreacted to its recklessness and nearly went off the road, but even in making the hasty correction of unpractised reflexes taken by surprise, he was able to register basics. The occupants, four, all men of around thirty, were black-haired, skin a different brown from that of an Andalusian peasant. The rear registration plate, glimpsed with the fleetingness of hallucination; Arabic lettering and numerals.

There had been so much to think of that he had forgotten this, the real reason for a different car, a change of clothes and a floppy hat. *The Libs have a commando group running the road . . . white Mercedes, big one . . . they'll be looking for you . . . don't let it bother you.*

Well, there was one thing that John Morpurgo, reject, washout, puppet, clown, did know about. What the Jahamiriyah graced with the title of revolutionary commando, Security Directorate, in Curzon Street, described in plain, blunt English; murder squad.

So he drove on. A series of manmade lakes, startlingly peacock-blue among the arid hills. Alora, a dead town on a dry-bed stream; Pizarra, same stream, death at a different stage, what could live in this heat? Fork right for the mountains; I will lift up mine eyes and see death tumble from the sky in a wild whirl of blades and a pillar of smoke by day.

There was, he thought, when you came down to it, a time when choices became simpler by degrees, a reversion to prehistory. Alliance crumbled to nation, nation to city, city to tribe and in the end there was the nucleus common to every sentient creature; you and yours. He had descended the ladder of history in a matter of hours. There were himself and Sylvie. Everything else was sacrificeable. Whatever his lack, he would not lack the will for that.

He pulled off the road, sandwiched between the bake of the sky and the bake of the rock, unpacked to find the pistol, loaded the one empty chamber, then clipped the angled spring holster to his belt, tugging out his shirt so that it hung stickily free about his waist. He looked at the sweep of the sky and it was empty. So was the road. So, as far as could be judged, were the great slopes of the hills, redolent with herbs, reeking with sweaty heat.

He saw everything, now, as a contest of which, in the minds of others, the result had already been decided. If the result were one, and it might yet be, that favoured him and Sylvie with freedom from harm to either, he would accept and walk away without thought to any other consequences. Sometimes the world was that small. Sometimes it was no more important.

If things were otherwise, and 'otherwise' was something he chose to leave as shapeless as the threat it implied, he would do his best to show that *Homo sedentarius* and the rabbit, cornered, had at least one thing in common.

He got back into his four-wheeled oven and drove on.

*   *   *

Weber had had the report within the hour; a hired, French-built six-seater Ecureuil helicopter, pilot and three passengers, no survivors. Studying the scene of the crash on the big wall map of Spain with Ramirez, Costa, and Robb Escher, who ran Madrid station, he caught a questioning look from Ramirez, first time on an operation since leaving Langley for London. "No," he said, pure reflex, "I damn well did not, not me!" He wished he could

236

be sure he was speaking on behalf of everybody at Langley, and, particularly, on behalf of Barzelian.

Nick Pentz came downstairs from Satcom. "Just in. The Lib hit car went as far as Antequera, put in a call to Córdoba, then set off the hell back."

Weber, the priest with doubts, put them aside. "After what happened over Córdoba my ambitions stretch no farther than pedal power, two wheels, better yet, three, but I think we have to board our own bird now and make like the Lone Ranger."

He took another questioning look from Ramirez, patted him with absent-minded gentleness. "I forget how young everybody's getting to be in this job. The password is 'Up, up, and away!'"

*　　*　　*

Ronda was an eagle's nest, cleft through the centre by a river gorge. He came in through the new town, facing the old, with its citadel and a church whose belfry seemed to have begun as a minaret and changed its mind on its way through the centuries. Now, on his map, he was about to run out of decisions. The gorge, as he veered west, following the road, was not visible to its foot, only the raw sides below the old town giving an indication of its sheerness and depth. It appeared to him, as he drove on, that there must be a bridge to cross if he were to continue where the route on the map showed the mark of an uncertain pen.

Perhaps it was the hesitancy of his unknown guide that prepared him for what happened next. He came out by the bullring, was led toward the gorge, and entered the *plaza mayor*. There was bridge indeed, and all traffic continuing toward Algeciras was obliged to cross it. It was somehow no surprise, as he swung past a tourist information centre, to see, sitting under a white and yellow sun umbrella advertising *Aguila Imperial*, at a white-topped table by the kerbside, the omnipresent Hank Timothy. Timothy flipped off a mock salute, then pointed. There was parking. Morpurgo, a man with an unwished-for mission narrowed down to a single objective, parked.

As they met, Timothy said, "Hi, pally."

TWELVE

The shadow of the big Sikorsky helicopter chased it across the wild country with no hope of catching it, since the route was south-west and the sun had got there first. Weber, watching the other three nursing their weapons, shook his head, melancholy tugging at all the thin, tired lines of his face.

"If it comes to a gun fight, and I hope it won't, we have a choice of getting shot by the Libs ourselves or, if things go wrong, the Spanish. Don't decide in advance."

Ramirez, who, as Weber had acknowledged, was young and saw bullets as things that hit other people, grinned. "Just so we hit Hank first, right?" Weber watched the land crawl by beneath them through a silence so long that Ramirez felt himself somehow rebuked, but Weber had only been bringing himself to the sticking point.

"Okay, this is where it has to come out. You don't pop off at all if we can manage without. It's the bugs we're after. If there has to be shooting, and that's for me to decide, you lay it on the Libs, and since this particular bunch are crazy people, you make sure to put it where it counts. But Timothy you don't shoot, even if it means he gets away."

He shook his head again, visibly embarrassed. "Hank Timothy isn't something we stumbled across on the garbage tip. He's hand-picked."

Ramirez, after a general hush, said, "You've got to be kidding."

Weber looked sadder than ever. "No kidding, junior."

*   *   *

Timothy was soldierly-looking in a casual, weekend furlough sort of way; open-necked khaki shirt with military pockets and shoulder tags, pouched khaki slacks tucked into dusty but expensively tooled cowboy boots. Watching Morpurgo, sweat still glistening on his face, put back the beer, he laughed silently.

"Pardon me for being personal, but your piece is showing." He tapped Morpurgo's pistol through his sweat-soaked shirt. "You want to see the inside of a Spanish jail instead of your wife, you're going the right way about it."

Morpurgo wiped his mouth with the back of a hand. "Is she here?"

Timothy looked ostentatiously about him. "I don't see her."

"How do I know you're going to keep your side of the bargain?" Poetism demanded this exchange. Poetism was a kind of aesthetics of cliché.

"You don't. You don't have too many options, either."

What just might puncture him, Morpurgo thought, just might get behind that macho confidence and prick something vulnerable, was: *What went wrong at Gatwick?* or *Did the CIA really kill Kennedy, or was this Langley's first try for the biggest man in town*?

Even through his fatigue and his tightly focussed concentration on the only thing that mattered, he recognised that it would get him killed.

"You planning on drinking any more of that stuff?"

He came back with a start. "What?"

Timothy tapped Morpurgo's glass with the back of a fingernail. "You figuring on tying one on, or did momma say no?" There was a blizzard of swallows over the *plaza*, and above the minaret that had aspired, something larger than a swallow – high, high – swung in slow circles.

"All right, where now? And how?"

Timothy indicated Morpurgo's car. "Your transportation." His hand shifted to point across the gorge.

They crossed the bridge, getting a dizzying, eagle's-eye view of the remote river-bed and a corkscrew road to nowhere, before worming a devious way through the old town with its deep alleys, secret white houses and spying ironwork balconies. Then Ronda was behind them. All about was a rough crumpling of mountain, gouged with crevices, ravaged with a litter of raw rock scattered with stands of emaciated pine that stretched out blue shadows to the east.

Timothy eventually pointed. "There." A minor road broke away, once surfaced, now so crumbled as to be almost indistinguishable from the rock. It deteriorated into a track that climbed the side of a ridge and vanished. Morpurgo told himself that he would kill Timothy if Sylvie wasn't there. But if she wasn't there, he wouldn't dare.

What was there, when they arrived, was a clearing; in it, a single-storey dwelling, rough stone, ancient timbers, bleached and sere, buried in one of the rifts with which these mountains were riddled. Shaded by a blue depth of ancient pine, it was almost invisible until they were upon it.

He stopped the car and they were at the bottom of an ocean deep of silence. Timothy waited until they were both out of the car, "You still going to carry that?" He meant Morpurgo's pistol.

Morpurgo had reached the stage of finding it difficult even to speak to this man. His voice cracked as he answered. "Yes."

Timothy straddled, raising his arms sideways. "You want to go over me? You won't find anything. I already took out my insurance, back there in Madrid. That's good enough for me." Morpurgo knew at once that Sylvie was not there, for he could have claimed her and shot an unarmed Timothy. He told himself he well might have.

There was no sign of life from the house, lodge, whatever it once had been. It was semi-derelict, heavy wooden door part-open and atilt on its hinges, the glass of its small windows shattered behind broken or missing shutters. The stillness was a potent thing, a growing compression of senses and spirits. No birds here, no movement, not even of the air.

Timothy clearly enjoyed his uncertainty. "Got you to wondering, right? You tried a sting. Now you're asking yourself the same thing I asked, what's the bottom line?" The archetype of all-male assurance, around Morpurgo's age, Morpurgo's build, but super-charged with refined and tested violence.

"Okay, Morpurgo, where's the stuff?"

"Where's my wife?"

"You give me the stuff, you get told."

"You tell me, or you don't get the stuff."

Timothy laughed aloud, that unrestrained, arrogant bull-bellow. In these high hills, it was the sound of sacrilege. "In the car, right? I could get it myself. I want you to get it."

Without even hurrying, Morpurgo slipped out his pistol. It felt unreal in his hand, a hunk of smooth metal that hefted well but had nothing to do with him. Timothy watched with the grin still on his face.

Morpurgo levelled it at Timothy's feet. "One foot. Then the other. And so on. Where's my wife?"

Timothy's arms, hanging loose, moved slowly out from his body. He shifted, settling his stance. They were two, three yards apart.

"The kick that thing has, you'd surely miss my foot. That's if I stay still. I don't aim to stay still." He bounced gently on the balls of his feet. "I move at the first twitch of your finger. Okay, so maybe you nick me, though I don't think so. Then I'm on you, friend, and I don't play tag."

He did a small standing jump, arms coming lazily level with his shoulders, dropping loosely back, physical jerks. The ground under his feet, gritty, strewn with pine needles, crunched softly. A small, irridescent insect scurried for cover.

Morpurgo's gun had come up. He felt his heart hammering imperiously. Timothy laughed again, gently, through closed lips.

"Or maybe you don't miss. Maybe you hit. You picked quite a cannon, Magnum, .357, one of those slugs can kill a man, big, solid, kick of a mule, that's what they're meant to do. Maybe you hit where it does big damage. That's going to help?"

He turned, insolently indifferent, to look toward the car. "Fetch the stuff, Morpurgo. We don't want to be here all night."

Poetism, Morpurgo thought; the final, ritual humiliation.

"What happens then?" His own voice was hard to recognise.

"I take your car. Jake's car, remember Jake, last night, my errand boy? When I've gone, you walk back to Ronda, maybe an hour, maybe ninety minutes, you ain't that fit. Oh" – Timothy held out his hand – "and you give me the gun." Standing there, hand outstretched, he said, "As I leave, I tell you where she is. Safe. Well. Jake's taking care of that. When you get there, he'll be gone, she'll be waiting." He wiggled his fingers. "C'm'on, pally, the gun. You got no options."

*   *   *

The pilot, jabbing downward, portside, shouted, "Ronda. That blur is Gibraltar way over to the sea."

Nodding acknowledgement, Weber, pulling against his seat belt as he turned to look at the others, repeated the question just asked by Ramirez. "Do the bugs matter? Listen, forget oil-fields. Just take the US strategic oil reserve. Five sites. Just five. Bryan Mound, West Hackberry, Bayou Choctaw and Sulphur Mines – you should all know these things – plus the salt mine at Weeks Island. Planned to enable us to go on fighting a war for six months with all outside supplies cut off. Just five little shots of those bugs and what we'd have would be so much goo. You don't think that matters?" It was necessary that they, like Claas, should believe the bugs worked.

To himself he posed another, unanswerable question: What kind of madmen did they have in the Pentagon who could think of fighting that kind of war for six months? Six weeks? Six days!

*   *   *

Morpurgo, going to fetch the small case holding the inoculum, saw that one thing must have been wrong with all his fancy theorising. The bugs – fake, not fake, fake, not fake – had been switched, switched and switched again. All this – from Gatwick through to this present baking, acrid, stony wilderness – was not for nothing. The bugs that could kill oil really could. Nothing else made sense.

Behind him, Timothy, Morpurgo's gun hanging by the trigger guard from a negligent finger – Morpurgo tried to shut out of his mind the possibility that he himself could be shot dead at any instant – stood waiting. The sun, still a shimmering furnace, was dropping toward the high ridge beyond the pine stand. There would be light for perhaps two more hours south toward the sea. Here, twilight would come in an hour. He knew where Hank Timothy would be taking the car; to Algeciras, where a waiting boat could land him on the Moroccan coast. Or a waiting plane, there was an airport down there. Timothy would be on the

242

Barbary Coast, or farther, before Morpurgo got himself away from Ronda.

Timothy called. "Take out your baggage. Hank Timothy's no small-time thief." It made him laugh again.

Morpurgo lifted out his bag, then the case holding the inoculum. If the bugs really worked, he was holding in his hands a threat that could destroy nations. He carried it back to Timothy. Sylvie was worth nations.

Timothy accepted it one-handed, shook it gently, nodded. "I don't even need to look, right? You wouldn't dare. Here." He gave Morpurgo back his gun, fished briefly in a pocket to display its six shells before dropping them back.

"Keys?"

"In the car."

Timothy tucked the box with its twelve containers of inoculum under his left arm, the thumb of his right hand tucked in his belt. He stood looking at Morpurgo for a long moment, his expression untranslatable. He nodded. "Nice knowing you. Don't take any wooden nickels." He laughed all the way to the car, Morpurgo following in a corrosive mist of hate. Once in the car, Timothy leaned through the open window. "Sylvie, huh? Nice name. Nice dame, classy. Know what I told her? I told her Hank Timothy never gives a sucker a break. So long, sucker." He took off in low gear, foot down, stones flying like shrapnel.

Eventually, Morpurgo went back to where he had left his bag. Eventually, he sat on it, head in hands.

He had no idea how long it was before he heard the car coming back.

But it was not his car, now Timothy's. It was a white Mercedes, dusty, roaring, bucking toward him to brake in a pother of dust. Armed men scrambled out, four, olive-skinned, hot-eyed; revolutionary commandos.

They backed him toward the deserted lodge, faced him to the wall, spread-eagled, the muzzle of a gun thrust viciously against his back while he was searched. They took his gun without troubling to discover that it was not loaded.

They hauled him round; young men, fit men, radiating hostility of race and religion. One of them, difficult to understand, snapped, "Where *al-qua' īd*?"

Another translated. "The commander. Where is the commander Timothy?"

Morpurgo gestured wearily. "Gone."

"Gone? Where gone? How long gone?"

He shook his head, not caring. One of them still covering him, they clustered, arguing among themselves in loud, angry-sounding voices. From somewhere to the right of the lodge, in the growing darkness of the pine stand, came the roar of a heavy-calibre rifle, shockingly loud. The man covering Morpurgo was flung backward, shot through the head. Blood spattered Morpurgo's face.

The others, like Morpurgo, were briefly paralysed. Then they broke, clumsy, shouting, no discipline. The gun roared again, and again. Two more of them fell, untidily, in running dives, raising dust, one of them kicking spasmodically with his left leg. The last, gasping hysterically, raced, arms pumping, toward the car. The hidden marksman dropped him halfway, his arms continuing to flail while his legs buckled abruptly. Hank Timothy stepped out of the shadowy wood, cradling a hunting rifle.

"Swell, pally. You made great sucker bait."

He strolled around, examining each Libyan in turn. The one who had kicked was still now. Nevertheless, Timothy, casually, put a bullet through his head.

He came back toward Morpurgo, rifle lowered but still covering him. "You don't look so good, friend. Long way from London?"

No more poetism, Morpurgo told himself idiotically; this was realism *in extremis*.

Timothy grinned his equine grin. "Going to look good in Tripoli, wouldn't you say? Old Hank turns up with the bugs, sole survivor of a CIA-SIS stakeout, all his bodyguard cold meat." There was something very much at variance between the grin and the way his eyes scanned Morpurgo's face. "Devotion above and beyond the call of duty, ain't that the kind of garbage they use?"

Thoughts as nebulous as the beginnings of creation swirled in Morpurgo's brain.

"By the skin of his teeth," Timothy repeated. "But then, I guess a sensitive guy like you would say old Hank is as thick-skinned as an Iowa hog, ain't that so?"

The tip of the rifle, a round, dark, lethal eye, described a small, peremptory arc. "Take a seat, pally. You look like you could use one."

There was a scatter of pine logs. Morpurgo sat, reluctant, at the behest of the gun.

The murderous farce of which he had been the butt was over. Timothy had driven away in the knowledge that the Libyans – yet he had called them his bodyguard – were on their way here, leaving Morpurgo as live bait. Parking the car out of hearing, he had circled back to the previously stashed rifle and calmly waited for the kill. But what was the point?

"Is my wife still alive?"

Timothy stiffened at the question, then raised the rifle, one-handed, levelling it, an extension of his tanned, heavily muscled arm, directly at Morpurgo's head. His finger curled through the trigger guard.

The rifle was clearly heavy, but its muzzle pointed unwaveringly. "I don't kill women." Aware that the stillness of one finger stood between him and extinction, Morpurgo said nothing. He had, grotesquely, touched Hank Timothy's vanity, which – that, if nothing else, had long since been made clear – was colossal.

"You got standards, right?" Timothy was further angered by Morpurgo's silence. "You think you're the only one with standards, smart guy, you think wrong." After a historical age, the tip of the rifle lowered. Still staring coldly, Timothy seated himself on a boulder. With his free hand, he produced one of his small cheroots, stuck it between his fleshy lips, felt again to light it with a red, throwaway lighter, intent upon Morpurgo as a stalking predator.

"So look where your standards got you." He streamed smoke contemptuously, but something still irked him. Morpurgo, willing his muscles to relax, his heart to relent its hammering, said nothing. All about them, the trees, the rocky slopes, the derelict lodge with its tipsily tilted door, stood still and mute. Flies were already investigating the four sprawled bodies. The nearest to them had drawn a funeral procession of ants, big ones, glistening like blood in the angled sunlight.

"Okay, what do you say, Morpurgo?" Timothy's lips were stiff and protruding about the cheroot whose smoke contributed only partly to the narrowing of his eyes.

For himself, Morpurgo sensed this black comedy was all but over, only one last, obvious climax impending. But instead of writing an end, Timothy wanted to talk. Why?

The answer came from what had just taken place. Vanity; driving, unsatiated vanity. What Morpurgo found stunningly final, Timothy, in the aftermath, saw as a letdown.

Whatever its purpose, he had put on a sustained, bravura showpiece, not just this brief, pitiless and shocking *coup de main*, but something that stretched all the way back to their first meeting in Madrid during the festival of Saint Isidore. Perhaps farther back than that; perhaps even to a death in the Pyrenees.

Most performers expect to earn their applause. Timothy, virtuoso of violence and towering hubris, clearly demanded it, but because Morpurgo, his sole audience, was uncomprehending, there could be none. He plucked out his cheroot, flicked it impatiently aside. "Don't tell me you haven't doped out a thing or two. C'm'on, bright boy, how'd I do?"

Morpurgo, moistening his lips, chose his words like darts. "Don't ask me. Ask the people who gave you the part."

Every muscle in Timothy's face died simultaneously. "What the fuck's that mean?"

Aware, in every cell of his body, of the danger, Morpurgo shrugged. Timothy's right hand was flexing rhythmically about the action of the rifle.

"Jesus!" Timothy couldn't bring himself to take it seriously. "I knew you were out of your league, but I didn't take you for a jerk." He stamped a heel impatiently. "Are you telling me you still don't know what this is all about?"

Morpurgo wrinkled his brow apologetically.

Suddenly, unpredictably, Timothy laughed, that booming, insensitive bray that made Morpurgo's hackles rise. "You Brits are really something! You had a gun. You could have used it, chances were that wife of yours was still alive, you'd have found her with the help of your Langley friends, but no, you have as much red blood as a leech on slim pickings. You lost your guts, you people, the way the kind of people that get to Washington these days are losing theirs. One day, some president of the

United States is going to wake up in his silk pajamas and find the Russians running the White House."

He could, Morpurgo realised, if he had yielded to Brewster Cochran's imperious demand, have brought the two of them together, Cochran and Timothy, and there would have been a clash of Titans.

"Like I just told you," Timothy said, "I never yet killed a woman. But if she knew too much . . ." Any pretence at humour had packed its bags and left. "Right now" – He looked casually, too casually, around the clearing before his eyes came back to Morpurgo – "she knows nothing."

It was, Morpurgo saw, the death warrant, with a blank space for him to fill in names.

But Timothy was not yet through. "What would you say," he asked, "if I told you that you and me have all along been on the same side?" There was a hunger in his eyes, the hunger of a man with only one direction in which to look for praise.

Morpurgo smiled wryly in spite of himself. "You could have fooled me."

"I did, pally!" That hateful word, that hateful laugh. "I sure as hell did! You figured me out for a black hat, and all along I was wearing white."

"I'm afraid I don't understand."

"You're afraid" – Timothy mimicked a prissy British accent – "you don't understand. You never watched Westerns? Old Westerns? The good guy always wore a white hat. The bad guys always wore black." He fought back irritation that verged on anger. "Okay, let me lay it out for you. You were big in British Security Directorate, MI5, whatever you want to call it, right? I mean, until you screwed up."

Morpurgo risked another shrug.

"Don't give me that British false modesty shit. There's too many of your kind over there in Langley, maybe you Brits did have some influence at that. Okay, there was a time when the Lib hit squads were giving you people in Curzon Street problems, ain't that so?"

"For a time."

"For a time! Listen, just for a time, people like these" – Another scornful jerk of the rifle toward the dead Libyans – "were scaring

247

the Jesus out of governments pretty well everywhere, even got a couple of presidents of the United States to jumping whenever somebody popped a champagne cork. Gaddafi, the boy from the desert they figured as some kind of Koran-punching hillbilly, more dough than brains, did they ever get *him* wrong! Shook up half the countries in the Middle East, then Africa – Egypt, Sudan, Chad, Volta – guns here, tanks and planes there, mischief every whichway, not to mention arms for any bunch of trigger-happy goons with a grudge against the people in power. I *know*! I've been in the middle, trained 'em all, equipped 'em all, had 'em'' – His free hand lifted above his head – "right up to here."

"And been paid uncommonly well for it, from what I gathered."

"From what you gathered! You know nothing, nothing at all, hear me?"

Legs apart, both hands palm down on his big thighs, the right encompassing the operative part of the rifle, he leaned toward Morpurgo like some bush king on his throne, big shoulders braced back to emphasise his barrel chest, head thrust forward on that thick, muscled neck as if to project the force of his personality almost physically. His voice, never far from a boom, had acquired the resonance of the mentally deaf. He had, Morpurgo thought, all the hallmarks of the Nazified Nietzscheian *Übermensch*.

"Three tries at dusting him off." Timothy said it with a reluctant wonder. "I guess the guy stands in well with Allah, or he had the luck of the devil." There was something personal, almost resentful, about the way in which he said it.

He leaned a little farther toward Morpurgo. "Want to guess who was the mastermind in back of all those hits?" Seeming to swell a little, he jabbed his chest with a big thumb. "Hank Timothy, Gaddafi's CIA-trained security adviser, who else?"

He sat back. "That surprise you, smart guy? I'll bet! Two coups, three hits, planned by yours truly, backed by Langley, and that sonofabitch camel trader's water-boy walked away from all of them. The luck of the devil!"

He was psychologically unable, Morpurgo saw, to accept anything but luck as an explanation for failure on the part of Hank Timothy. Morpurgo was also, as through the glass, darkly, beginning to distinguish the rough outlines of something more immediately relevant.

"And Hank Timothy" – It was as if Timothy, reading Morpurgo's thoughts, were already strengthening those outlines – "who's head man in security in that asshole country, is suddenly beginning to feel he's getting suspicious looks. Like – you know? – if he's so goddam smart, how come he never knew about any of those hits until after? Or did he maybe, this Yank infidel, this supposed renegade, did he maybe know before?"

Timothy bared his yellow teeth. "Something had to be done, get me? Something to restore confidence in good old Hank among the people who were fattening up his bank account. Something to steer them away from any idea that all those attempted wipe-outs were inside jobs and who better to set them up than an ex-Langley man who is maybe not so goddam ex after all."

The picture in Morpurgo's brain snapped into focus like a colour transparency adjusting to the heat of the projector.

"So-o-o-o." Timothy was enjoying playing the lead in a one-man show, a pseudo-genial tyrant whose poorest joke is guaranteed a laugh. "Comes the shooting down of those two Lib fighters by the US Navy in the Gulf of Sidra. Gaddafi is hopping mad. He wants blood, and what do we have? A chance to make Hank Timothy look one hundred per cent kosher again." The humourless bellow, shattering the ambient stillness with the effect of blasphemy in a graveyard. "Only I guess that's the wrong expression to use with a bunch of Jew-haters."

He had arrived at some kind of crux. It was plain from his look, part guarded, part – the greater part? – a suppressed but avid hunger for – what? Admiration? Respect? No, Morpurgo decided; something bigger, something like – the word came unprompted – awe.

"Well, let me tell you, pally, Hank Timothy is not a guy who misses out on chances, especially big ones. And was this one ever big? Let's just say it was bigger than anybody could imagine, even a zoomy college boy like you, Morpurgo." The tone was mocking now, but beneath the mockery was something as desperate for release as a fox in a cage.

Morpurgo said, "It must have been very big." Simultaneously, he had an incongruous recollection of Mrs. Rattigan's face, all that time past, when the file for which she and Registry had been searching proved to have been there all the while, hidden by Epworth's case of Roannais wine. The image translated itself and he knew the exact nature of the big, big thing that had rehabilitated Timothy with Gaddafi, had known it for some little time.

Fraction by fraction the sun had been burning westward, shadows extending across the clearing. High over their heads, a bird similar to that which had floated far above them as they sat in the square in Ronda, displayed a patient, circling interest in the carrion that, so recently, had laughed and dreamed.

"Now wouldn't you just" – Timothy, reluctantly accepting the demands of secrecy, lit another cheroot and found consolation in taunting Morpurgo – "love to know how old Hank, after taking some heat that might have burned him bad, fixed it so he could be Muammar's blue-eyed boy all over again."

He looked at his watch, simulating regret. "Too bad, no time. What do you say if I tell you that faggot friend of yours, Weber, is due to drop from the sky any time now to put on a show of stopping bad guy Hank Timothy from stealing those goddam bugs and handing them over to his bosses in Libya?"

He puffed smoke luxuriously, his sense of superiority resurgent, restoring his good humour. "Should've been here this while back, only that pissant, Jake, just what you'd expect of a kind of second-rate Brit, right? he had to get his times wrong when he briefed you back at that motel last night. Started you off an hour early. Near as hell screwed up the whole goddam act. Just time to let me know I have to be back in Ronda but fast from another little job, the hell with Weber, if it was going to be played like it was written."

Morpurgo decided the time had come to test the most pressing of his own several theories. He stood up, ignoring the instant movement of the rifle-tip, and bent to lift his bag.

As he had expected, Timothy, with cold good humour, said, "Sit down, friend. You know you ain't going anyplace."

Morpurgo sat. Jake, the boy with the Antipodean accent and Epworth's visiting card, had the care of Sylvie, who knew nothing and was therefore safe. Jake, for whatever reason, had also changed an original plan. It was a minor comfort to know that it could hardly be to Timothy's advantage. Now, all that remained for Morpurgo himself was to play the rest of the game to its no-longer-surprise ending.

Timothy watched him, cat and mouse. "Hey, we didn't even finish the story. You don't want to know how it all turned out?"

Morpurgo shrugged.

"Do I have to tell you" – Timothy's tone signalled a question requiring no answer – "that troubles never come singly? Old Hank's big, big play gets him back in the Libs' good books all right, but his reward is just another hot potato. Would it be news to you to know those crazy men from the desert have been trying to get some kind of nuclear capability this past fifteen years?"

Morpurgo shook his head. The Pyrenean hit was about to make sense.

"Wow!" Timothy said mockingly. "The SIS is right in there! Okay, so they've finally done a deal with some Frenchified Arab technician who's working on weapons-grade plutonium separation up there near Orange in France. They want data. He wants gelt. He fixes to sell them photographs of a bunch of data. A meet is set in the Pyrenees, twenty kilometres of mountain that's neither France nor Spain, how do you like that? And who is the only guy the Libs are prepared to trust to collect and pay off? This'll kill you!" Again the thumb to the chest. "Old Hank."

He took his cheroot from his lips, blew a long plume of smoke An incipient breeze carried it partway to Morpurgo, a luminous, dissipating wraith. "Now do you get it?"

Morpurgo, suddenly anxious to get the whole thing over, felt like a man who, after years in the sewers, finds his first venture into a cesspit making him nostalgic.

"Langley had to stop those photographs getting into Libyan hands. You were the only way they could do it. You signed up some ETA terrorists, old students of yours, I expect, kept the meet, killed the man, passed the pictures to Langley, went back to tell the Libyans how the CIA had laid a trap and you'd been lucky to get away alive. By the skin of your teeth."

Timothy nodded, all cocksure complacency. "Right. By the skin of my teeth." He extended a finger that traversed the sprawl of Libyan corpses. "This time, they gave me a bodyguard." He jabbed his sternum. "*Al-qu'aīd*, that's me. The commander Timothy." He laughed. "Sent them on a wild goose chase. Jake switched cars with you, sent them back here for poppa to deal with once you and me had met up."

Morpurgo took a deep breath, sick that it should all end like this, yet finding some satisfaction in the fact that he would not make his exit without deflating Timothy's monstrous ego at last.

"You've been Langley's man all along. I made the mistake of believing Claas and Pierre Weber when they said you'd been kicked out back in '76."

"Claas didn't know different, still doesn't. He's been thinking, all along, this crazy business with the bugs was just to set me up for a wasting. That dumb Kraut can't understand at all why Hank Timothy is still treading the hens and crowing."

"And Weber?" Morpurgo hadn't forgotten his primary purpose, but he felt sick and sad about Weber, the man Sylvie liked.

"Weber?" Timothy scowled. "That sidewalk cruiser? Sure, he knows what it's all about." One of his quick switches of mood produced his foghorn laugh. "He's on his way here to play cowboys and Injuns, round up my goddam useless bodyguard, maybe shoot 'em up a little if the noise don't make him pass out, while Hank gets away with the goddam useless bugs."

He saw Morpurgo's expression. "That's what I said, useless, no harm you knowing that now. I know they're useless. Barzelian knows they're useless. DCI knows it too." Another shout of laughter. "Weber thought so as well, only Barzelian got cold feet about letting me handle the payoff on my own. He had the idea of sending one of his personal troubleshooters, a chick called Woloszynowski, would you believe? to pull a switch so that soft-centre faggot can kid Claas that Uncle Sam's accidentally giving a genuine oil-killer to those wild men in Tripoli. That gives Barzelian the chance to tell Weber to get off his butt, raise a posse and come storming down here. Strict orders not to touch old Hank, mind, just get the bugs and the bodyguard, rescue this guy Morpurgo."

He checked his watch. "Well, Jake put paid to that when he screwed up on the timing, that's something Barzelian doesn't know yet. But Weber's in touch with Langley all the way down. Barzelian would've told him to let go me and the bugs both, once the bodyguard was cleaned up. Makes a better story for me to tell those guys in Tripoli; and too bad when they find the bugs don't work after all."

His face hardened. "Only maybe Jake did better than he knew. The job is yet to come that Hank Timothy can't handle without the help of fags and fresh-trained college boys, and he don't leave loose-mouth bodyguards to maybe guess what they're not supposed to know."

He gave Morpurgo a look that would have dropped the mercury in a thermometer. "You got anything to say, pally?"

"Not really. Madrid, Tarragona, Madrid again, all these miles and weeks – getting the bugs first time would have looked too easy – so that you show up in Tripoli a hero, only one to escape another CIA trap. Cleared of suspicion beyond all doubt, ready for the next coup or whatever Langley has in mind. Barzelian could hardly use the same trick twice, even I can see that."

"That's right." Timothy flicked away the cheroot that had gone out in his mouth. A moment later, he spotted the deliberate mistake. Very softly, he said, "And just what trick would that be?"

Morpurgo made an apologetic gesture. "Isn't it obvious? I mean it was a bit too soon for you to prove your trustworthiness to your paymasters in Tripoli by having a second crack at the President. A tricky one for Langley, too, Presidential security stepped up, the President himself shouting for blood. I mean, just firing Doug Church wasn't going to satisfy him, was it? He wanted the head of the man who'd tried to kill him. He wanted *your* head. I imagine Claas wasn't the only one who thought this whole business was just a way of setting you up for the chop. I expect that's more or less how they sold it to the President, too."

He stood up for the second time, neither haste nor undue caution. "Are you sure Weber's been told to let you get away? Are you sure Barzelian hasn't decided you're not just another loose-mouth who's served his purpose so far as Langley's concerned? Who might even be dangerous if he decides to sell out again?"

Timothy sat quite still. Morpurgo stood quite still, his hands loose at his sides, his heart and breathing, miraculously, just about manageable.

"I had it wrong for a time. I thought you really had tried to kill the President. I even thought Langley had helped you. I'm afraid there are quite a few people, by now, who still think that, all Brits; but not so soft-centred they won't see you on trial or dead before you touch any of those Swiss bank accounts."

He half-turned, paused. "I don't mean *they'd* kill you, not necessarily. I think your Langley friends would do that, rather than have the story get out." Just as they might kill this guy Morpurgo.

He watched Timothy get up slowly, his left hand reaching to join the right on the rifle, then he turned and set out toward the road back to Ronda. Somewhere in the distance, he could hear a helicopter. Clearly, unlike Brewster Cochran's, he thought, it had not received the Langley-directed attentions of Hank Timothy, who'd had to get back to Ronda, but fast, from another little job.

In the silence of the middle evening, not even a cicada as yet tuning up, the earlier breeze stillborn, the first shot sounded thunderous. He found himself face down on the ground, conscious that he had bloodied an elbow, probably a knee too. Only as the second shot crashed through the echoes of the first did it occur to him, stupidly, that if he could feel pain he was still alive.

On hands and knees, he shuffled around. Outside the gaping door of the lodge, Epworth crouched in the classic stance, one hand supporting the heel and wrist of the other, an exclamation mark of vapour from his gun emphasising the double period. Behind him, men, three, four, all armed, whom Morpurgo had never seen before.

Timothy, rifle raised one-handedly and pointing erratically skyward, had turned to face them. Halfway down the back of his creaseless khaki shirt was a ragged double blossom, dark, that flowered while Morpurgo watched. With slow care he turned back toward Morpurgo. In a loud, complaining voice, all confidence gone, he said, "Who . . . who the hell . . .?" before folding forward in an act of obeisance to Epworth. The clatter of the helicopter was much nearer.

Picking himself up, immensely weary, Morpurgo started back.

"Mmmm." Epworth absent-mindedly blew into the muzzle of his pocket cannon before handing it to an instinctively accepting

Morpurgo. "Leave this mess for the Cousins to clear up, I think, after all, it's their show. They'll say we shouldn't have shot him, Johnny, but Weber will be secretly glad that we did. Did you know you've got blood on your face?" Morpurgo found himself resenting that 'we'.

A big helicopter, not Brewster Cochran's, quite different, passed low over the clearing, barely moving, to settle, an ugly bird looking for its lost nest, not far away down the slope.

Epworth's hand, small, feminine in the fineness of its bones, wrapped itself about Morpurgo's and the gun, forcing it gently but firmly downward. "Shocking noise those things make. Better put it away. Well, come on, you want to see Sylvie, don't you? Get there before dark if we get our skates on and Weber doesn't hold us up too long."

The invisible helicopter cut its engine. Silence enveloped the clearing, leaving Morpurgo to listen, foolish, to the buzzing in his head.

THIRTEEN

Weber and his small group entered the clearing like men come too late to a battle, yet even the nightmarish unreality did not prevent Morpurgo from noting Weber's relative lack of surprise. "Well," he said. "The St Valentine's Day massacre." His look snapped up the gun in Morpurgo's hand.

"Myself," Epworth said, "I was thinking – mmmm – of *The Duchess of Malfi*. 'Cover her face. Mine eyes dazzle. She died young.'" He linked arms with Weber, drawing him aside. "I speak, of course, of Truth."

Remarkably soon after, driven by an unknown and silent member of Epworth's party, they were bumping out of the clearing, cars, as Epworth remarked happily, having sprouted like mushrooms in the forest glade.

Thoughts, meteors from outer space, sped through Morpurgo's darkened consciousness with a brilliance too fleeting to illuminate.

"Weber didn't seem to ask many questions."

"Questions demand answers."

"What did you tell him?"

"All he wanted to know."

"Which was?"

"Virtually nothing." Epworth was maddeningly patient. "That's what he wanted to know. It's what *they'll* want to know, Langley."

"Are you telling me they don't want to know?"

"They very much" – Epworth rephrased with donnish pedantry – "want *not* to know. One does, rather, don't you think? when

256

one has been rather spectacularly caught out." They turned along the road from Ronda to the coast, sunlight flashing a gibberish of Morse between trees and jagged rock. A distant racket drew their attention. The Sikorsky was rising from its hidden nest with all the grace of an airborne bedstead, five corpses as cargo.

"How did you know?" Morpurgo fought against the rising pressure of the intolerable. "To be there? To be anywhere?"

Epworth registered reproving surprise. "I told you you were being followed. After all, we are the *Secret* Service."

"This man Jake. He's yours?"

"Mmmm. Timothy's right-hand man, was. Parents killed by the Patriotic Front in Zimbabwe, Rhodesia as it was then. Army intelligence, got out just ahead of Mugabe's avenging angels. A spell in Angola, another in Chad, then allowed himself to be recruited by Timothy."

"With some encouragement from you."

Epworth made a deprecatory gesture. "The Libyans will give him Timothy's job when he makes his triumphant return with the inoculum.".

"With the . . . !" Morpurgo's mind spun like a top. He had last seen the bugs under Timothy's arm, but that was in another version of truth. "Which don't work. They *don't* work, do they?"

"They do not! Directly after you saw Claas and Weber that first time, we paid our own visit to Billingshurst, not so clumsy as Claas's people, either. Enough inoculum left for us to run our own tests, *most* exhaustive. The bacteria didn't last five minutes in Libyan crude, aerogen couldn't release oxygen, anaerobe couldn't live without it."

Epworth had had Claas and Weber under surveillance. Epworth had known for certain, all along, that the bugs were harmless!

"I could have been killed back there."

"You weren't." Epworth produced his small leitmotif of amusement. "After all, you and Timothy were on the same side. We all are, aren't we?" There was no amusement, not really.

"All a question of viewpoint, Johnny. There never was Langley *and* Timothy. Timothy *was* Langley, it alters the whole perspective, Gatwick, Madrid, Tarragona and so on. Take the

Oklahoma Star. Cochran was in Langley's pocket from the moment that Folger blew the whistle on him to Dick Goss, had to do just what he was told once Barzelian decided he wanted that tanker. The helicopter pilot? Well, he was Air America, acting under instructions, take you out to the ship, bring Timothy off . . .''

He caught Morpurgo's baffled frown. "Air America is the name Langley uses for its own private airline. You've a lot to learn, of course. You travelled first class. Air America's economy class passengers don't all make the return trip." Morpurgo remembered Operation Phoenix.

"There are things I'd rather not learn."

"Oh." Epworth was indulgent, vicar with a rebellious choirboy. "Unwise, don't you think? When you've done so well this far." The car was gradually leaving the wild country behind, breasting the full golden flood of the westering sun.

"Perhaps you don't quite understand." Epworth was the gossiping dowager out for an evening spin. "A matter of some national significance, considerable, oh yes. The Americans simply don't understand Libya, any more than they understand Cuba or a dozen other places. Now, we *do* understand Libya, and from now on, if they want to know what's really happening there, they'll have to deal through us. We shall have Jake, and they've lost Timothy."

Morpurgo finally glimpsed it, a power play beneath a power play. In the murky waters the American had patrolled with their tame shark there had lurked a subtler fish. Epworth, throughout, had had one eye on Washington, the other on Whitehall. With this final masterstroke and Jake, whose *nom de famille* was clearly not on offer, as his own deep cover man in Tripoli, his standing would receive a potent boost.

"I suppose it was you who had Jake get me away an hour earlier this morning?"

Epworth, like the figurative shark, swam briefly closer to the surface. "Timothy's time, Weber's time, Barzelian's time; you've heard of Barzelian, yes? To use that dreadful space jargon, there was only a very small window, an hour or so, to place ourselves, between your arrival from Ronda and Weber's descending in his – mmmm – chariot of fire."

258

He looked at Morpurgo with opaque but unmistakable speculation. "Steve Archer came through, by the way. After your – mmmm – remarkable phone call. All the warmth of a melting iceberg, but Steve, as the Cousins might perhaps put it, delivered." Epworth smiled, the Mona Lisa version, as if hiding bad teeth. "Steve still thinks Langley really was gunning for the President. I rather think we may be regrettably dilatory in putting him right."

Allow Steve Archer, Morpurgo translated, time to put his own and his minister's neck on the Joint Intelligence Committee block before unveiling a triumphant upswing in SIS influence in Langley and the White House. Epworth could have taught the infant Machiavelli how to steal candy from grownups.

"And of course," he said, "there's Sibley. Is there anyone you haven't suborned?"

"Nice boy." Epworth was shiningly enthusiastic. "Strong sense of guilt over his temporary disloyalty at the time they winkled you out of Curzon Street, not too difficult to turn him round. You know the sort of line; all on the same side really, Queen and country, greatest good of the greatest number, all the runes that fill a young man's head with noble ideals and hopes of gain. You choose your protégés well."

"People who talk about the greatest good of the greatest number usually can't count much above one. My protégé?"

"Oh, I wouldn't dream of poaching."

"I suppose he stays at Curzon Street."

"Where else, if he's to be of use?"

"Not my protégé. I'm quitting." The first thing he was going to tell Sylvie; he was leaving the sewers to carry her bags. If she could stand his stench. He dropped Epworth's gun in Epworth's lap.

The country was less wild. They had entered a long, straight stretch of road. The car fled furiously, howling with joy.

"What will you tell Sylvie?" Every time he reached a vital crossroads, Epworth was there, waiting.

"The truth."

"What is the truth? A riddle inside a mystery, wrapped – mmmm – in the Official Secrets Act." Epworth had turned to face Morpurgo, forcing upon his unwilling head an implied burden of complicity as painful in its pressure as a crown of thorns.

Sylvie, Morpurgo saw, had summed the man up accurately at first meeting. His stock in trade, like a range of treacherous toys, came in a hundred gaily coloured shapes and sizes, but all with hidden edges of sharp steel.

"Besides, Sylvie thinks otherwise." A sudden sharp bend threw them together. Epworth's arm, fending Morpurgo off, was as steely as his will.

"You've actually seen Sylvie!" He was trying to keep all his intimate thoughts about Sylvie packaged away, not to be opened until . . . ?

"But of course. Didn't I tell you she's fine? And in good hands. Jake has been keeping an eye on her, though the man Langley sent Timothy also stood between her and anything really threatening. The man who helped kidnap her, though, of course, it was just to make sure you arrived down here in time for the last act. Sylvie thought he was Spanish but he's actually Puerto Rican American. She did say his accent puzzled her a little."

"If you squinny," Epworth said seriously, "you can make out the Rock over there. Of course, we're looking at the tradesmen's entrance, so to speak." The backstage view of Gibraltar, so unlikely in its wan bulk, could have been a cloud, a mirage.

"Yes," Morpurgo said savagely. "Algeciras soon. I did work out that's where Sylvie was."

"You see, Johnny" – Epworth performed his habitually adroit sidestep – "if you'd known too much, too soon, you might not have gone the course. See over there? Africa. That patch of light's just about on Tangier." Beyond the cloud that had become Gibraltar, across a streak of evening-hued sea, was a paler cloud, purple, with a garish smudge of orange light.

"The course!" Morpurgo wrestled with his bitterness. "Don't you mean the show? Rat King and Rumpus. Well, the Rat King's dead. John Murpurgo? Open to offers, his well-known bit part as buffoon? No thank you!"

"Rat King?" Epworth simulated puzzlement. "Ah. Yes. I see. No, not Timothy, you haven't got it quite right. Rat-King – there's a hyphen – is – mmmm – a sort of natural phenomenon, rare, but well-documented."

He had reassumed his own favourite role; Oxbridge tutor,

cosy in his pale study by his pale stone fireplace with his pale, chill sherry, very dry. And, Morpurgo reminded himself, the stink of death and cordite on his pale chill hands.

"Rat-King. Mmmm – one of Mother Nature's minor mysteries, records spanning the centuries." Leaning back, relishing their pantherish pace as they bore down toward Algeciras, Epworth interlaced his slim fingers to twiddle his thumbs sensuously.

"A group of rats, sociable, snug, tails in a cosy tangle. Then, a Gordian knot. Why? Nobody really knows. Panic sets in, every rat for itself, knot tightens, end result slow starvation, hopelessness, death. Forty-two is the record, all in a single 'king'."

Morpurgo contemplated the stark image. "How many this time?" But Epworth had apparently gone into a revery.

A great silence later they came down to the edge of the town, a hypermarket, a Spanish *olla podrida* of houses, minor industry, scrap metal dumps and smallholdings. Epworth leaned forward to touch their driver's shoulder. "Hard right at the end, or we'll end up in that ghastly municipal housing estate. One theory" – His tone barely changed – " is that it only takes place in circumstances of extreme threat. They huddle together for mutual protection and their – mmmm – intertwinings are cemented by excreta. What one might term excrementally exacerbated extinction." He giggled. They were skirting the port, a skyline of funnels and masts tangled with white buildings and a ragged deference of cranes. Morpurgo, puzzled, saw that they were continuing on.

The road climbed. Gibraltar reared once more, drenched with the lifeblood of the expiring sun, Morocco peering myopically over its right shoulder. A last hotel, a last bar, then rocky, scrub-stubbled hills with ruined towers, and a taut ribbon of tawny beach, the breeze bringing a salty breath of Atlantic from its lace-edging of surf.

Eventually forced to it, Morpurgo said, "I thought Sylvie . . ."

Epworth patted his knee absently. "Patience. Oh, by the way, I told Weber *you* shot the man Timothy. The image, you see, mine, not yours. Except yours too, you owe it to Weber to keep him happy since he seems to like you. He loathed Timothy, but he had to run him, all the way from Madrid to Ronda." He shook his down-topped head. "Barzelian! Mostly Armenian, not a man to buy a carpet from."

He looked mildly anxious. "You can live with the myth, surely? Oh, and the legend? I can't. Wouldn't do. Besides" – That douce, disarming giggle – "I don't really look the part."

"I bloody well told you," Morpurgo began, the fly explaining to the spider that this particular web is, sorry, just not its style, but they topped a last hill, made a vast sweep, and came to another, smaller town. The car swung off the highway, spurned the outskirts, came to a halt under a procession of tall palms in a white, squat jumble of architecture that seemed to have a greater affinity for Africa, eight miles across the straits, than anything Morpurgo had seen in Spain.

Epworth got out. "Tarifa. Southernmost town in Europe, nearest to Africa, useful little sea passage to Tangier for those who like exclusivity. Spanish forget it's here, half the time. Hardly anyone else even knows."

They went down wide steps to a long *plaza* paved with decorative tiles, the patchouli assault of blossom laced with sweaty wafts of cooking and trapped tidal waters. Epworth, walking stooped and very fast through a tangle of alleyways where shop and street lights pressed the darkness into the interstices between the evening throngs, came to another square, smaller, trapped in a jostle of white, tall houses with balconies that spouted cataracts of flowers. He knocked at the door of one of them, its time-blackened oak panels studded with diamond-headed nails. "Safe house, courtesy of Langley. Timothy was supposed to give you directions."

Morpurgo knew that Timothy would have shot him out of hand.

He could hear footsteps in a paved interior hallway. The door opened. A man in his thirties, bearded, faded khaki shorts and a tee-shirt proclaiming NOTRE DAME, though whether cathedral, university or football team was a mystery, stood grinning, hand outstretched.

"Good to see you, mate. Glad you made it."

Mite. Mide. Taking the hand, Morpurgo, back in the land of waking dreams, had his own pumped enthusiastically. He said, "Hello, Jake," and, pushing past, "Where's Sylvie?" The dusk of the long hallway led to an inner courtyard where butter-soft light from a hidden source showed blossom like brilliant butterflies held in mid-flight.

"Johnny? Johnny!" A voice that plucked ice splinters from his heart. She came running to throw herself, flustered, un-Sylvielike yet infinitely Sylvielike, into his own rough grasp. His face buried in her honey-silk hair, the scent of her body blissfully exorcising the real and imaginary stench of his own, her arms so tight about him that he struggled for breath, he thought, could only think: *Never. Never again*, seeking to wipe from his senses every trace of that sour, dark other world in which life, ratlike in its desperate, destructive energy, fought itself for survival.

Only gradually did it penetrate his mind that she, over and again, was saying, "I knew. I knew you'd come. Oh, Johnny, dearest Johnny, I had no right. You must live your own life, my darling. You have the right. You have the right." He would tell her later, he thought.

They went through to the courtyard, the house seemingly empty all about them though he had seen no one leave. An age afterwards, he heard Pierre Weber, newly arrived, say, "Hey, anybody home here? Oh, pardon me, you two."

The house and his thoughts came back to life. Somewhere in a past existence was a recollection of Weber's shame that Langley had ever used men like Hank Timothy. *This guy is bad!* Somewhere, separate but parallel, was a world temptingly strewn with Epworth's bright but sharp-edged toys. Somewhere, in all that mental wilderness of mirrors, was a stark scrap of madness suggesting, insisting, that only some kind of temporary, unspoken and wholly private understanding between Weber and Epworth could have brought Epworth to the right place at the right time for a *just* and strictly necessary purpose.

Jake, a familiar package under his arm, reappeared, passing softly through the moth-dotted radiance from the courtyard. "So long, you two. Time and tide wait for no man."

Weber, wearily dutiful, said, "Hey, now just a minute there," to stop abruptly, even theatrically, at the sight of the gun in Epworth's hand. Jake and the inoculum vanished with a last wave.

Epworth pushed the gun a little farther toward Weber. "Souvenir. Sorry we couldn't give you a head to hang on your wall. Still, you've got Golding to give to Langley, haven't you?"

Weber, eyes swivelling comically to Morpurgo, shrugged. He took the gun.

Epworth looked at Morpurgo and Sylvie. "Mmmm, haven't you two got a silver wedding quite soon? Ridiculous, you don't look old enough, but I hope Amaryllis and I are invited to the feasting. After all, your mother will be expecting something special, Johnny."

"How do you know my mother will even still be . . ." Like Weber, Morpurgo checked himself. "Yes. Of course. You're all invited," and, to Sylvie, "Aren't they?"

Top Fiction from Methuen Paperbacks

While every effort is made to keep prices low, it is sometimes necessary to increase prices at short notice. Methuen Paperbacks reserves the right to show new retail prices on covers which may differ from those previously advertised in the text or elsewhere.

The prices shown below were correct at the time of going to press.

☐ 413 55810 X	**Lords of the Earth**	Patrick Anderson	£2.95
☐ 417 02530 0	**Little Big Man**	Thomas Berger	£2.50
☐ 417 04830 0	**Life at the Top**	John Braine	£1.95
☐ 413 57370 2	**The Two of Us**	John Braine	£1.95
☐ 417 05360 6	**The Good Earth**	Pearl S Buck	£1.95
☐ 413 57930 1	**Here Today**	Zoë Fairbairns	£1.95
☐ 413 57620 5	**Oxford Blood**	Antonia Fraser	£2.50
☐ 413 58680 4	**Dominator**	James Follett	£2.50
☐ 417 03890 9	**The Rich and the Beautiful**	Ruth Harris	£1.75
☐ 413 60420 9	**Metro**	Alexander Kaletski	£2.50
☐ 417 04590 5	**Sometimes a Great Notion**	Ken Kesey	£2.95
☐ 413 55620 4	**Second from Last in the Sack Race**	David Nobbs	£2.50
☐ 413 52370 5	**Titus Groan**	Mervyn Peake	£2.50
☐ 413 52350 0	**Gormenghast**	Mervyn Peake	£2.50
☐ 413 52360 8	**Titus Alone**	Mervyn Peake	£1.95
☐ 417 05390 8	**Lust for Life**	Irving Stone	£1.95
☐ 413 60350 4	**Depths of Glory**	Irving Stone	£2.95
☐ 413 41910 X	**The Agony and the Ecstasy**	Irving Stone	£2.95
☐ 413 53790 0	**The Secret Diary of Adrian Mole Aged 13¾**	Sue Townsend	£1.95
☐ 413 58810 6	**The Growing Pains of Adrian Mole**	Sue Townsend	£1.95

All these books are available at your bookshop or newsagent, or can be ordered direct from the publisher. Just tick the titles you want and fill in the form below.

Methuen Paperbacks, Cash Sales Department,
PO Box 11, Falmouth,
Cornwall TR10 109EN.

Please send cheque or postal order, no currency, for purchase price quoted and allow the following for postage and packing:

UK	60p for the first book, 25p for the second book and 15p for each additional book ordered to a maximum charge of £1.90.
BFPO and Eire	60p for the first book, 25p for the second book and 15p for each next seven books, thereafter 9p per book.
Overseas Customers	£1.25 for the first book, 75p for the second book and 28p for each subsequent title ordered.

NAME (Block Letters) ....

ADDRESS..

....